I0698937

AFFIRMING IMOGENE

AFFIRMING IMOGENE

Copyright © 2025 by Desiree Moore

All rights reserved.

No part of this book may be reproduced in any form or by any electronic or mechanical means, including information storage and retrieval systems, without written permission from the author, except for the use of brief quotations in a book review.

A Desiree Moore Books publication

ISBN 979-8-9880206-3-9

To the souls who shared their stories
and to the experiences that shaped my own,
thank you for giving me the courage and inspiration
to transform our lived truths into something meaningful.

Because of you, I have hope that life might surprise me.

CONTENT WARNINGS

This book addresses the following topics: transphobia, physical assault, discrimination, loss of a parent, cancer, gun violence, and anxiety.

AFFIRMING IMOGENE

DESIREE MOORE

CHAPTER 1

WHEN PUSH COMES TO SHOVE

Stacy

My favorite thing about being a nurse is the routine. I love the predictability of vital signs and chart notes—the methodical nature of rounds. I thrive in the stillness of order, the comfort of the known. I appreciate the early hours in the hospital, when shadows blend into the corners before the morning rush of penciled-in C-sections and spontaneous labors.

Some would argue that nothing about labor and delivery is predictable. However, there is an undercurrent of sureness to the process of birth. Regardless of the journey and outcome, it has an underlying rhythm that carries through.

I wish everything in my life felt as steady as my work, but most days, it feels like I'm constantly flailing—a clumsy lurch as I struggle to keep my world from falling apart. My worry rests with my daughter, Imogene, today as she is in the next town over on a field trip. I'm never more than a 15-minute drive from her, and now that I am, I'm uneasy.

"Stacy, did you hear me?"

I flinch, shaking myself out of my thoughts. "What?"

"We are short-staffed, so it's one nurse to every two patients today. You're assigned to rooms twelve and thirteen."

"Got it," I say. A sigh escapes my lips, betraying my frustration with myself for letting my mind wander. Despite my attempts to stay focused, my thoughts keep drifting back to Imogene, and the nagging feeling that something is off today refuses to leave me alone. I stand with a group of nurses in our morning huddle, and despite my best efforts, my attention is divided. Half of me is worried about Imogene, and the other half dreads working with Jackie, my charge nurse.

"You sure?" Jackie says, raising an eyebrow.

"I said, I got it," I repeat, a sharper edge to my tone this time.

After I receive my assignment, I go to the nurses' station to get updates from the night crew. My sneakers squeak against the speckled beige floor, and I'm relieved when I finally reach the desk, eager for a break from the noise.

"Can you brief me?" I ask.

"Sure," Lucas starts. "Patient, Alison White, in room twelve is a multip—multiple vaginal births." I know what a multiparous is, but I smile at his need to define it. Lucas is fresh out of nursing school, and although he's new to the staff, I got to know him a bit during his clinicals here at Sarasota Memorial Hospital. It's one of the largest hospitals in this region of Florida, and in a town like Sarasota, where retirees outnumber kids, his youthful enthusiasm is welcome.

"She just came in an hour ago. At last check, about ten minutes ago, she was dilated two centimeters. The one in room thirteen, June Vega, is a first-time mom, making steady progress. She was six centimeters dilated at my last check. We administered an epidural several hours ago, but it seems to have stalled her labor. Oh, and just a heads-up—" His lips twist to the side. "Her boyfriend is a dick."

I exhale through my nose. "Thanks for the heads-up." There's nothing worse than watching my patients go through one of the most wonderful and difficult days of their life with a shitty partner.

Lucas provides the remaining details, and I head off, mentally creating a checklist of things to do. My sneakers still squeak as I walk. They need to be broken in. I couldn't afford these shoes, but when the seam on my last pair ripped, I had no choice but to get a new pair.

I decide to confront the tricky situation head-on and go to the new mom's room. When I walk in, June perks up, a small movement amidst the blue and white fabric of her labor bed. Meanwhile, her boyfriend slouches on the sofa, crouched over his phone, swiping. A quick glance confirms he's scrolling through a dating app. As disheartening as it is, it's not the first time I've seen this. Unfortunately, the middle of labor isn't exactly the right moment to break the news that her partner is cheating. As much as my husband, Garrett, gets on my last nerve, at least he's not a cheater.

With a warm smile, I introduce myself. "Hello, June. I'm Stacy, and I'll be taking over for Lucas today. How are you feeling?"

"I'm okay. Just really hungry. I didn't know I couldn't eat, and I haven't eaten since yesterday at lunch." Our hospital requires women to fast during labor to prevent the risk of aspiration in case general anesthesia is needed, but the evidence supporting this is flimsy. How can we expect women to push for hours without any sustenance?

"I'm sure you're starved." I place my hand on my stomach to show that I empathize.

"I was too nauseous to eat last night, but now I'm hungry and nauseous."

I nod. "Have you been consistently nauseous, or has it been touch and go today?"

"Touch and go," June admits. "Sometimes it's better than others. Right now, I'm hungry more than anything else."

"I'll make sure we get you some Zofran for the nausea," I say.

I chat with her about her birth plan while checking the monitors, noting that both June and baby look great. Her vitals are within normal limits, and the baby's heart tones are reassuring, with contractions consistently around five minutes apart.

"It appears you were last checked two hours ago. Do you mind if I recheck you to see how you're progressing?"

"Sure," she says, scooting down in the bed.

The boyfriend finally tears his attention away from his phone, his expression twisting into disgust before muttering, "I'm hungry. I'll be back."

The callousness of his tone rubs me the wrong way, but I keep my expression neutral for June's sake.

I muse over the thought of tripping him as he walks by. Of course, I wouldn't, but the idea is funny. I should tell him he's not allowed to bring food into the room. He'd probably be pissed that a woman told him what he couldn't do. I have to stifle a chuckle as I check June's cervix. Just as I expected, she is six centimeters, the same as two hours ago.

Next, I take inventory of the supplies in her room, ensuring I have everything we could possibly need.

"Can I ask you something?" June asks with a bit of hesitancy.

"Of course," I say, turning my full attention to her.

"Are you a mom?"

The question shifts my focus to Imogene. I feel an urge to check her location on my smart watch, but I push myself to focus on June instead.

"I am. I have a fourteen-year-old daughter."

"Wow! That's great," she says.

As I appraise June, I notice more than just the physical discomfort. She is uneasy, and there is a reason she is asking.

"It is great, but what's up? You asked for a reason." My head tilts as I wait to listen.

June looks down, considering what she wants to say, then looks up again, biting her bottom lip. "How do I know if I'm ready? How do I know if I'm going to be a good mom?" She chuckles as she says this—an attempt to keep her worry light-hearted.

Her vulnerability strikes a chord in me, and with a reassuring smile, I share, "The fact that you're asking that question shows you're more ready than you think. Being scared is part of becoming a parent. All you can do is do your best with what you have."

She nods and rests her hands in her lap, staring at them as she contemplates.

I add, "You're going to be a great mom, but to do that, we have to get this show on the road. I'll be right back." I step out of the room.

In the little kitchen area, I nab a granola bar, applesauce, and yogurt. On my way out, I make eye contact with Jackie, the charge nurse. She watches me, and her eyes narrow as I walk by.

Back in June's room, I hand her the snacks. "It's not a meal, but it'll hold you over."

Her eyes become saucers. "I thought I wasn't supposed to have food."

"The evidence that supports that practice is weak. I would rather you have the energy to push because, mark my words, we will be doing that very thing in the next couple of hours. Eat and relax for a few minutes. When I return, I want to try a different position. Do you need anything else?"

June shakes her head. "No, I'm okay. Do you know where my boyfriend went? I thought he was only going to the vending machine."

"I'm not sure, but don't worry. We'll make sure he's back before anything too exciting happens."

With a satisfied grin, I head to room twelve to see my second patient. Unlike June, Alison displays calm excitement, smiling and looking fresh-faced. Beside her stands a man who could easily be mistaken for Patrick Dempsey, gently massaging her shoulders. The scene warms my heart. "I'm Stacy. I'll be taking over for Lucas. How are you feeling?"

She beams. "Excited."

"Excited to no longer be pregnant or to meet your baby?" I say with a playful smirk.

With a light laugh, she says, "Both," and gazes at her husband. "It's been quite some time since we last did this."

I start checking her vitals. Everything looks good.

"You mentioned that it's been a while?" I respectfully show my interest in the conversation without being intrusive.

"Yes, our youngest just started her first year of high school and our older two are in college."

"Planned?" I ask, smiling.

Her husband chuckles and shares a look with his wife. "It seems the birth control took a vacation during our first kid-free vacation in over a decade. But given how the first evening of our trip unfolded, we're not exactly shocked."

A blush colors Alison's cheeks, a reaction as endearing as the story itself.

"I'm just happy to experience this with my beautiful wife once more," he continues. "Although, I don't think I can manage as many horsey rides this time."

The lines around his eyes crinkle as he reminisces. They are so sweet, and it makes me ache for how Garrett and I used to be all those years before life caught up with us. Together for sixteen and married shortly before we conceived Imogene—we used to be so happy.

I finish charting and ask, "Is there anything specific you need? Do you have a birth plan you want to discuss? Have you decided on pain management?"

"Oh, we're old-fashioned," she says. "I've done this before, you know."

"Yes, I know. Well, you look great. If you don't need anything else, I will leave you to it."

I return to June's room, and her boyfriend is back, digging into a double bacon cheeseburger from the shop down the road. Those burgers are amazing. I want to snatch it out of his hands, but I turn my attention to June. "You doing okay?"

"The food helped. I feel a lot better," she says, a hint of relief in her voice.

"Good. Could we try moving you into a new position?"

"Sure." She nods her consent.

I explain how to use the blue peanut ball, positioning it between her thighs. While she lies on her side, I guide her hips, showing her how to rock to encourage fetal descent and cervical dilation.

"You might get tired of the peanut ball, but it will help move things along. At least, I hope so. Try to get some rest."

She closes her eyes, attempting to find comfort in the new position, and my gaze drifts back to her boyfriend. I glare at him as I leave the room. Spinning forward, I come around the corner and nearly headbutt Jackie.

"Oh, hey. Sorry about that. Didn't see you there," I say, trying to sidestep her.

"Did you give your patient food?" Accusation colors her tone.

Not today.

I keep my response nonchalant. "No. Her boyfriend was starved, and she didn't want him to leave." If I tell the truth, she'll spend the next fifteen minutes lecturing me on hospital policy, and I'll probably receive another verbal warning. I don't have the time or patience for that.

Jackie's lips tighten. "That's interesting because he was just at the desk complaining about a slice of cheese left on the hood of his car and holding a brown paper bag of what I assumed was food."

"Cheese? That's bizarre." My brows knit together as I try to steer the conversation away from her initial question.

"Someone was cheesing cars last night, probably just some teenagers, but that doesn't answer my question. Was the food really for him?"

"Sure was," I say with a strained smile.

Jackie folds her arms in front of her. "We follow the rules on my shift."

"Sure. As long as the rules coincide with my patients' needs, I'm totally good with that." I brush past her, tension building in my shoulders in that all-too-familiar way whenever dealing with her.

Jackie and I have never seen eye to eye. I prefer to work independently, but she's a relentless micromanager. Several years ago, when we first began working together, she insisted on reviewing everything I did, although I had already been a nurse for more than a decade. At first, I shrugged it off as her just being thorough. But it didn't stop there. During a complicated delivery, the doctor called for a C-section. I understood the concern, but I also knew we still had options. I suggested repositioning the mother to improve circulation, trying to avoid the C-section. Jackie bulldozed right over me, barking orders to prep for surgery instead.

But the breaking point came when I refused to discharge an inmate who'd just given birth. I wanted the mother to have more time with her baby before she went back to jail, but Jackie ensured I was written up for insubordination. Since then, she has reported anything I do that she disagrees with. It has gotten to a point where her voice alone causes the hair on the back of my neck to rise. At this point, I have to be careful because I might actually lose my job. I've received more verbal and written warnings working with Jackie than at any other time in my career. I should have learned by now to let things go. But she pisses me off every time.

The next couple of hours are quiet. My thoughts drift to Imogene, torn between worrying about her and what I need to accomplish for her today amidst my hospital routine. I also mentally run through my personal to-do list: visit Dad at the nursing home, sort through our bills, remind Garrett to change my oil, shop for cheaper car insurance, and call about lowering the interest rate on a credit card.

It's just after 1:00 PM when I leave the floor to take my break in the cafeteria. As I walk down the hall, Dr. Kilpatrick is standing at a computer in the sleep room with a perplexed grimace on his face. I know that face. He is battling the EMR. His fingers jab at the keys, and he mutters his disdain for technology under his breath. My eyes flick up as I thank the universe for giving me this opportunity.

I approach him and gingerly place a hand on his shoulder. For eight years, I have worked alongside Dr. Kilpatrick, an OB/GYN doctor who has been here for forty years. He's a brilliant doctor, but technology is his Achilles' heel.

Dr. Kilpatrick relaxes at my touch. "Oh, Stacy, I'm so glad you're here. I have a patient in room fifteen, and I was trying to access her medical history, but this stupid thing won't work. I did exactly what you showed me."

I tilt my head and smile. "May I?"

He steps to the side, and I take the mouse. I feign confusion, a little theater to spare his pride. "Hmm, that's strange."

"What?" Dr. Kilpatrick asks.

"There seems to be a glitch, but don't worry, I've got a workaround. Let's get you what you need, and I'll sort this out with IT later," I reassure him.

"Thank you." He lets out a long breath.

I open his patient's history and read it aloud. With the information he needs, Dr. Kilpatrick turns away. I stare after him. His back is rounded from years of shouldering the weight of his patients' worries and woes. Although he probably should retire, I'm glad he is still here. I need him. Imogene needs him. I clench my fists and breathe in deep.

Today is a good day.

When Dr. Kilpatrick is out of sight and I'm sure there is no sign of anyone else, especially Jackie, I turn back to the computer and search for my name, pulling up my patient record.

I scan my surroundings one more time before filling a script for leuprolide—a medication used to treat endometriosis. I do not have endometriosis, but the diagnosis is present in my chart.

I started with monthly injections to monitor for any side effects, but after several months without any issues, we moved to a three-month injection. Now, I'm ready to fill a script for a six-month injection, which means I won't have to do this again for six more months. The thought fills me with relief. I hate that I'm using my friend and colleague in a way that feels exploitative, but I don't have a choice.

When I'm done, I leave to have lunch.

CHAPTER 2

DROPS OF JUPITER

Imogene

In space, stars are born from chaos, their light reaching across the void to touch other realms. They exist within a collection, a family, a community, a constellation, and they have the privilege of belonging. One day, I hope to belong the way the stars do.

My class is at the Bishop Museum of Science, where we drift from one exhibit to the next. It looks like we're all together, but really, everyone's split into cliques. Groups of girls giggle in tight circles while the boys act like peacocks, pushing each other and telling crude jokes. And I exist on the edges. Isolation clings to me like a shadow.

As I walk by my classmates, trying to go unnoticed, I wish for what they have. For as long as I can remember, my heart has felt disconnected from my body. I'm also disconnected from everyone else. I imagine being one of the girls, sharing sticky lip gloss and gossiping. To wear dresses or strappy sandals and for no one to look twice. I also yearn for friends, though I've never had many—just one, but not anymore.

For lunch, we eat at the museum cafeteria. A group of nearby girls whisper and glance my way, making me feel like an exhibit. I keep my head down, munching on my turkey sandwich and chips until my name cuts through the noise.

"Hey, Imogene," McKenzie, a girl who used to be my best friend, calls. I point to myself, puzzled, because she hasn't spoken one word to me since the summer before eighth grade.

She nods, and the other girls smile and nod.

"Come here. Come sit with us."

I hesitate. I've known McKenzie my whole life, but everything is different now. We're different now. I study the girls. They appear friendly and hopeful. It looks safe, so I sling my backpack over my shoulder and pick up my food.

As I take a seat, McKenzie says, "I like your shoes."

My navy canvas sneakers, painted with clusters of white dots to resemble galaxies, peek out from under the table's edge. "Thanks," I say. My anxiety makes it difficult to give more than one-word responses.

What if I say the wrong thing? Should I say more? I don't want to seem so desperate for friendship that she decides to cast me back out into the void.

"I was just telling Stormy about the star party your mom threw for us. Remember?" McKenzie asks, gesturing to the girl beside her from our class. Of course I remember. Those parties were a cornerstone of my childhood.

"Yeah." I bring my fingers to my mouth to chew on the rough edge of my thumbnail.

She turns to the others. "That was before Imogene thought she was a girl."

The way she says it sends a pang of hurt through my chest, but at least she is using my name and pronouns.

McKenzie uses her pointer finger to move her blonde curtain bangs from the front of her face. "Her mom made star-shaped cookies and themed drinks. I still have the planisphere she gave me. Oh! And your telescope!" McKenzie looks back at me. "What was the name of that planet we saw at your last party?"

"Jupiter. It was in opposition, so it was brighter and closer to Earth that day," I mumble quickly.

"Oh, yeah! Will you ever have another one?" Her eyes twinkle like the stars as she says this, and it takes everything within me to stifle my eagerness so that it's not off-putting.

"Maybe," I say, allowing a small smile.

"You should!" Her enthusiasm is contagious. I can feel my guard dropping.

The girls nod in unison, and my smile widens.

"Of course, you'll have to get a handle on your mom."

I look up at the suggestion.

"Her mom *hovers*," McKenzie accuses. Pity laces her tone, but her facial expression suggests amusement. "I swear, her mom would stay for every birthday party, refused to let Imogene go to camp, and she used to sit and watch us play at the park even though we were, what, twelve? Respectfully, it was kind of creepy."

I dip my head, embarrassment warming my cheeks. Mom worries a lot. About everything. "I just want to keep you safe. It's my job," she will often say to me, but sometimes it is too much. I often resent her constant worry, but I wouldn't call it creepy.

I stare down at my shoes, the heat crawling down my neck as laughter spills from the other girls.

"She just . . . worries." The words taste bitter in my mouth.

"No wonder you ended up this way." McKenzie's words slice through the air like a cold draft. I flinch but swallow the hurt, locking it away in a tight bubble inside my chest. She is criticizing Mom, not me.

I wonder if I'm making excuses for McKenzie when I shouldn't be.

After lunch, we go to the planetarium together. They include me, as if this is the way it's always been, and it feels nice. It feels like when McKenzie and I were friends.

Sitting in a chair next to McKenzie, with the others arranged in a wide semi-circle, we recline and face upward. The first stars flicker to life on the ceiling in the dim, hushed dome. Though I've been here several times before, the awe never fades. The narrator's voice takes us across the universe, and I try to take in as much as possible. The anxiety that boiled over earlier turns to a simmer, and I let out an exhale.

Today is a good day.

Leaving the museum and walking to the bus, McKenzie asks, "Want to sit with me?"

"Sure," I say with a smile. Out of the corner of my eye, I catch sight of Jonah, a boy who often shoulder checks me in the hallway at school. He is exchanging a knowing look with McKenzie. My stomach churns with unease, but I push it away and take a deep breath of the salt-stained air. I'm being paranoid. McKenzie talking to me again is a big deal. I can't afford to lose this.

If I worry too much, I'll ruin it, and I'll be alone again.

Usually on the bus, I fold into myself and put on my headphones to drown out the sounds of the other kids. However, the girls still talk to me, so I stay alert.

McKenzie faces me and says, "Is it true you had bottom surgery?"

I stiffen. "I don't think that's something I should talk about," I manage, attempting to steer the conversation away from what's in my pants.

But McKenzie, either oblivious to or ignoring my discomfort, presses on. "So, like, if you don't have a penis anymore, how do you pee? Did they create a new hole when they cut it off?"

I can feel eyes on us. The volume of the attention restricts my airway.

"I didn't get it 'cut off,'" I correct her, keeping my voice low.

McKenzie's left eyebrow arches, and a smirk flickers on her lips. "You still have a penis?" Her voice is too loud, and I wish I could silence the words before they reach other ears.

My cheeks burn. "I don't want to talk about this."

"I thought you had the surgery. That's why I've been calling you Imogene, but I guess you're still *Charlie*." She draws out the name, so it seems to last forever. The name sounds like nails on a chalkboard, and I flinch.

From behind me, I hear Jonah's voice. "He pretends to be a girl just so he can use the girls' bathroom. Pervert."

Every word lands like a slap. It stings, but I can't let them see how much it hurts. Anger churns in my stomach, burning its way up, but I swallow it down before it escapes. If I stay calm, if I play along, maybe they'll stop. Maybe they'll still let me stay.

McKenzie gasps in response to Jonah's accusation, but I'm uncertain if it's genuine. "Is that true?" She holds her hand to her chest and presses her lips together in concern. I don't understand. Why is she doing this to me? My question clings to my throat, while her question sends ripples of laughter through the bus.

"No," I say, my voice quivering. I fight the heat building behind my eyes, refusing to let the tears spill. *Don't give them more reasons to laugh.* "I'm not even allowed to use the girls' bathroom."

"That's because you've been labeled a predator," Jonah chimes in again. "The other parents don't want you raping their daughters."

"I would never do that." But even as the words leave my mouth, they feel hollow, like they don't carry enough substance to convince them. I can feel the doubt lingering in the air, and it tears me apart.

I want to scream, to tell them I'm a good person, that I'm not a threat to anyone. I want to explain myself in a way that makes them believe me—makes them see that I'm not what they think I am—but I can't find the words.

"That's what all rapists say," Jonah retorts.

Rows of students laugh, and I stare at McKenzie. Her eyes sting with the same hurt I feel, although her lips are stretched into a satisfied grin.

I realize that engaging only fuels their hate, so I fold into myself. Imaginary silver tape stifles my voice, and regret washes over me for believing McKenzie wanted to be my friend again. The drive from Bradenton back to our school in Sarasota is only thirty minutes. I just need to survive twenty-five more minutes before I can escape this situation.

When the bus pulls into the school, I scan the parking lot for my dad's truck. Desperation rises, but I don't see him. The pit in my stomach grows, and I try not to panic as I climb down the bus stairs onto the sidewalk. With my jaw clenched tight, I squeeze the straps of my backpack, pulling it forward as I put some distance between me and the other kids trickling from the bus.

Eventually, I stand alone at the edge of the school parking lot, while the last few cars drive away. Only a few kids remain, including Jonah and his friends. I try to stay invisible, hoping to avoid any unwanted attention. As the minutes tick by, familiar anxiety creeps in—I'm alone, exposed and vulnerable.

My palms sweat as I pull my phone from my pocket to text Dad. Before I can finish my text, Jonah and a few other boys approach, their intentions clear in their swagger.

"This guy is a rapist," he tells the other boys, both of his arms raised and pointing toward me.

The boys pretend to be outraged.

"No, I'm not!" My voice cracks as I say it.

Jonah's laughter, cold and mocking, pierces the humid air. "Looks like I hit a nerve. If you aren't a rapist, then why pretend to be a girl?"

"I am a girl." My head juts forward as I make my point. It takes everything in me to keep my threatening tears at bay.

"Girls don't have dicks," another boy challenges.

I refuse to let them define me. I'm a transgender girl. Not a predator.

They have encircled me now and seem to revel in their perceived power. I search for an escape, but the ring of boys tightens, and I'm trapped.

The building pressure finally reaches a point at which I can't keep my anger from bursting out. Confidence and rage enter my body for a fleeting moment, and my words slip out before I have a chance to second-guess them. I surprise myself when I say, "Why are you so obsessed with what's in my pants? Are you gay?"

The air shifts as Jonah's friends react, their jeers now directed at him. But Jonah, undeterred, steps closer. "Nah, man. I'm just tired of all you freaks shoving this shit down our throats. If I had it my way, you'd all be dead. Fucking freaks."

Jonah's face is close enough that I can feel the heat of his breath. I can't back away. It is as if my sneakers have melted to the sidewalk. What happens next is an out-of-body experience as my hand balls into a fist, and I swing. I hear the unmistakable crunch of bone hitting bone and pain shoots through my hand following the contact.

Chaos erupts.

In a flash, I'm on the ground, being pummeled by a flurry of kicks. The boys' voices merge into a single, hateful chant. "Rapist."

From a distance, a voice yells, "Hey, hey, hey, back off right now!"

I freeze, shock shackling my limbs.

A moment later, Mr. Alvarez, our biology teacher, appears just as Jonah kicks me one last time. He grabs Jonah by the collar and yanks him back. The boys scatter like birds startled by an approaching storm.

Jonah protests, "That asshole punched me!"

Mr. Alvarez, still holding Jonah's collar, asks me, "Is that true?"

I nod with regret.

Mr. Alvarez's jaw ticks as he looks around the parking lot, considering his next move before speaking again. "We'll settle this tomorrow. Now, either go home, or I'll call your parents."

Once Jonah is gone, I push myself to sit up, my body and my ego bruised. Mr. Alvarez stares out at the parking lot. He removes his glasses, running a hand across his forehead, before sliding them back on. He then turns his attention to me. "Are you okay?"

I offer only a shrug. My head throbs, and I don't feel like talking.

"Where are your parents? Do you usually walk home?"

"No," I mumble. "My dad was supposed to be here."

"Have you tried calling him?" He picks my bag off the ground and hands it to me. I glance around, searching for my phone. I spot it lying face down near the storm drain. My stomach tightens as I walk over to retrieve it, hoping for the best. When I pick it up, my fingers graze the rough edges of the shattered glass, tiny shards catching at my skin. I turn it over, and spiderwebs of cracks stretch across the screen. I press the power button, praying for some flicker of life, but the display stays black. It's broken. A sinking feeling settles in my chest. *Well, this sucks.*

"Is it broken?" Mr. Alvarez asks.

"Yeah." I stuff the stupid broken phone into my pocket.

"I could go get mine," he offers, gesturing toward the building.

"No, it's fine. My dad will be here soon."

"Can I wait with you?"

I want to say no. I want to be left alone. I want everyone to leave me alone. I wish a black hole would swallow me, but I shrug and sit on the ground instead.

Mr. Alvarez takes the spot beside me on the sidewalk. "I'm sorry they did that to you."

"It's whatever," I say. Talking about it is the last thing I want to do.

"No, it's not." He places his hands on his knees and peers out over the school parking lot. It's silent for a few beats before he adds, "I had a sibling a lot like you."

I turn my head to stare at him. He said sibling and I'm curious to know if his sibling was trans, but I don't ask.

Mr. Alvarez sighs, staring down for a moment. "It was a long time ago, but . . ." Mr. Alvarez stops and changes the direction of his sentence. "The thing is that when other people bully you because you're different, it's most often because they have something to hide. Often, it's fear. Sometimes it's something else. Something they're ashamed of. Exposing you can feel like a way of protecting themselves."

"That's dumb," I say. *How does bullying help hide the parts of yourself that you're most ashamed of?* If what Mr. Alvarez says is true, it's ridiculous.

"Yeah, it really is," Mr. Alvarez agrees just as Dad pulls up and rolls down the passenger window.

"You ready to go?" Dad calls out.

"Yeah," I say, pushing myself up from the cement.

Mr. Alvarez rises alongside me, turning to my dad with an affirming nod. "You've got an incredible kid here. She's really cool."

The use of my correct pronouns is a balm for my heart. I manage a grateful nod toward Mr. Alvarez before walking around the truck.

"I do," Dad says. After a pause, he adds, "Garrett."

"Ramon," Mr. Alvarez says back.

When I'm inside the car, Dad rolls up the window, and the truck accelerates.

"How was the museum?" he asks, looking over at me when we come to a stoplight.

"Fine," I reply flatly.

"Just fine? What happened to your face?" Concern creases his features as he takes in the swelling.

I bring my shoulders to my ears, unable to muster the energy to explain. Sensing my reluctance, Dad falls silent, offering me space.

I should have known better. I shouldn't have wanted to belong. I'll never belong, but gosh, I'm so tired of hiding.

A moment later, he adds, "Damn. I'm sorry."

CHAPTER 3

ROAD RAGE

Garrett

"Get out of the way!" The words escape my lips in a burst of frustration, reverberating through the confined space of my pickup. I slam my hand on the horn, a sharp clamor cutting through the air, as the car in front of me—a shitty white sedan crawling fifteen miles under the speed limit— swerves into the passing lane. My foot hammers the gas. As I drive alongside the white car, I raise my hand to give them the bird, but then I see the driver.

Behind the wheel of the sedan is a kid barely a year older than Imogene, his eyes wide with terror. Beside him, a man, presumably his father, throws his hands up and mouths, "He's learning, you jackass!"

The realization pierces me with regret so severe it's physical. A lump forms in my throat as I'm confronted by my impulsiveness. I keep screwing up.

Stacy has reminded me more than once that I needed to pick up Imogene today, and I forgot. I wish I had a legitimate excuse, but I'm begging for jobs right now, so I can't blame it on my booming business. As I navigate the familiar route to Imogene's school, my mind rehearses an apology to Imogene and Stacy.

I craft and recraft my words in a futile attempt to soften the blow of disappointment. Like so many others, I know this mistake will be another log on the fire of our disintegrating marriage. It seems no matter how hard I try, I can't reach Stacy like I used to. Each day, I tiptoe around landmines, afraid to make a move, terrified of the fallout. And that has made me numb most days.

I pull my focus from Stacy and back to the road, stepping on the gas.

When I pull up, Imogene is sitting next to a man about my age in a purple plaid button-up and khaki pants. Likely a teacher. A thread of guilt tugs at me.

"You ready to go?" I attempt casualness, but a hint of tension exists in the back of my jaw.

"Yeah," Imogene says, and I notice her red, blotchy face. I open my mouth to say something, but the teacher overshadows my question.

"You've got an incredible kid here. She's really cool," he offers, and something in his tone causes me to pause, but I introduce myself before rolling my window back up.

While I wait for Imogene to buckle her seatbelt, I inspect the angry welts swelling on her face. She was in a fight or, more likely, she failed to stand up for herself. A tightness clenches my chest, a mix of protective fury and heartache.

"How was the museum?" I ask with caution as I approach a stoplight.

"Fine," she says.

"Just fine? What happened to your face?"

She shrugs. Imogene is a fortress, and her shrug is a drawbridge pulling up, leaving me stranded on the other side.

I resist the urge to push her further. I don't want to be like Stacy, who would have probably called the National Guard at the sight of our daughter. As much as we want to fix it for her, Imogene has to learn to stick up for herself.

Imogene has spent more than a year sitting on the outskirts of society, ridiculed by those on the inside. I fucking hate it, but this is her fight. I know being trans wasn't her choice, but socially transitioning was—and she's got to stop letting people walk all over her. It's not fair, but the world isn't fair. She doesn't have to be alone either. Other kids at her school are gay or nonbinary, but she refuses to try. She's always been shy, but she needs to get over it. I realize I'm blaming her, and that doesn't feel good. Ultimately, I feel awful that she has to deal with all this crap.

The wave of conflicting emotions that comes with my stream of consciousness forces an exhausted sigh.

I shake my head and utter, "Damn. I'm sorry."

She doesn't reply, but that's par for the course. Imogene has a habit of sucking up into herself like a turtle pulling into its shell, unreachable when things get tough. I once could pull her out, but it's become harder in recent years. Just like with Stacy, I can't reach her.

If Imogene knew how I reacted when I first learned she was trans, she'd probably have retreated so deeply into herself that I'd be locked out forever. I still think about the night Stacy told me. It was all so overwhelming that I had to push it away, turn it into a joke.

"He thinks he's a girl?" I asked Stacy as we laid in bed, facing each other. The day had been a blur—opening the shop for Barnett Woodworks had drained me, and my exhaustion only made what she was saying harder to process. The words felt absurd, like she was telling me aliens had landed and were ready to live among us. I blinked, trying to wrap my mind around the new information.

"She doesn't think she's a girl," Stacy corrected, her voice edged with frustration. "She is a girl."

I didn't know what to say, so without much thought, I blurted out, "That explains why he's so emotional."

"Garrett." Her voice held a warning.

As the information sank in, it became more ridiculous. Our son? A girl? I remember thinking, *None of this existed when I was a kid. This has to be some weird trend.* And, with that thought, I dismissed Imogene's truth.

"You're getting too worked up about this. The kid thought he was allergic to peaches for an entire year after watching Daniel Tiger. It's a phase," I told her.

Stacy looked horrified. "This isn't a joke, nor a phase." Her chest inflated with worry. I pressed my lips together, realizing that any further argument would end badly for me.

To be honest, I was being mentally lazy, using jokes to cope with something that made me uncomfortable. I'm still a little uncomfortable. I still sometimes think about the son I expected to have rather than the daughter I got. And as much as I try, I struggle to understand Imogene. I struggle to meet her where she is because I don't relate. No matter how hard I want to, I'll never know what it's like for Imogene. I'll never understand how she feels.

Sometimes, I still wonder if it's just a phase. I'd never say that to her or Stacy. Instead, I focus on accepting Imogene as she is today, even if that means she might not be the same tomorrow. The simple truth is that I love my child—boy, girl, it doesn't matter. Imogene is my kid, and I'll do whatever is necessary.

When I pull into our driveway, I put the truck into park and turn to my daughter. The engine's quiet hum lingers between us.

"I'm not in the mood," she dismisses me, anticipating what I'm about to say, but I push forward anyway.

"If you don't want to tell me what happened, that's fine. I won't press." I suck on my teeth for a minute while I decide my next words. "Ignoring things . . . doesn't make them go away. You can't let these kids torture you. Fight back."

Imogene's jaw sets, and I can hear her back molars grinding.

The air between us crackles with her unspoken frustration. "Sure, Dad, because fighting back always solves everything, doesn't it?" A bitter edge of realism laces her voice.

"It could," I offer. "Maybe if you showed them you're not an easy target, they'd think twice before coming at you."

"Or maybe standing up for myself is what will get me killed."

With those words, she steps out of the truck, leaving me grappling with what may be the truth. The stakes are incredibly high, but I worry that if she doesn't grow a backbone now, worse things will happen when she goes out into the real world, especially if this isn't a phase but her forever.

I just want her to be okay.

I walk into the house, her words heavy in my chest. I scan the living room, searching for a way to make things better, but there isn't anything I can do, so instead, I sit and do nothing.

CHAPTER 4

YOU'VE BEEN CHEESED

Stacy

June is ready to push several hours later. As we are practicing a couple of pushes, a sudden wave of nausea hits her. I tear open an alcohol wipe and tell her to smell it. She holds it to her nose and takes a deep breath in.

"That worked," she says with a tentative smile that builds on itself as she finds comfort.

June and I find a position she wants to push in while I watch the monitors simultaneously. Minutes later, the on-call doctor, who had just transferred here, enters the room. I was hoping for Dr. Kilpatrick, but he must have another patient.

"I'm going to need you on your back," he tells June.

June glances over the doctor's shoulder—a silent plea for advocacy, and I don't hesitate. "She's comfortable on her hands and knees. If you can't deliver the baby like this, I'll find someone who can."

The doctor's brows shoot up, but he yields. Meanwhile, June's boyfriend stays glued to his phone, completely disengaged. I shake my head—so subtle it's barely noticeable. *This poor girl.*

Over the next hour, I guide June through pushing, monitoring her progress and the fetal tracing for signs of descent or distress. Her sweat-slicked face sits in a constant grimace as she breathes raggedly between pushes. "Just a while longer. You're doing great." She shakes her head and grunts as she pushes, just as the doctor returns.

She's progressing, but slowly. Fetal heart rate is stable. Contractions are strong. We're not quite crowning, but we're getting close. I page the doctor. He returns a few minutes later, slipping on gloves.

A moment later, one of our nurses, Carmen, interrupts.

"Your patient in room thirteen is ready to push," she says, slightly breathless.

Without meaning to, I respond sharply, "She can't be ready."

"She is." The nurse's brows push together. Two assigned mothers, pushing at once, with the same nurse—freak coincidence.

I glance at the doctor, who is now fully engaged in June's delivery. He doesn't have time to check on Alison.

"Do we have another doctor?" I ask.

Carmen shakes her head. Her lips press into a thin line.

"Where is Dr. Kilpatrick?"

"H-he went home about thirty minutes ago."

I grit my teeth. "Call him."

"I already did. He didn't answer."

I shift my gaze between June, the doctor, and Carmen as I weigh my options. June is close but not crowning yet. If I time this right, I can check on Alison before June gets to the final stretch.

Then, Carmen's pager beeps. She looks down at it, then back at me, suddenly torn. "Shit. They need me now."

I swallow hard. Now, it's just me and the doctor. If I stay with June, I'm leaving Alison without anyone.

I consider all possible solutions. I could call Jackie, but I don't want her anywhere near my patients. I should have anticipated this. Veteran moms can progress unpredictably fast.

"Go," I tell Carmen. "I'll check on Alison myself."

Carmen hesitates. "Are you sure?"

I nod, already moving toward the door.

Rushing into Alison's room, I wash my hands. Tremors crawl up my fingers, the same tremors I've had in stressful moments since the day I almost lost Imogene, and I squeeze my fingers together to get them to stop. Then I snap on a pair of gloves before saying, "May I?"

At the base of Alison's bed, I slip in two fingers, and sure enough, she is complete, plus two. She is ready. The urgency of birth doesn't discriminate.

"There isn't a doctor available. They are helping another patient, but it should be only a minute. Can you hold on for just a little while longer?" I ask, hoping for some leeway.

Alison's face glistens with sweat, and the hair around her temples is stuck to her face. Next to her, her husband holds one of her hands in both of his. She shakes her head emphatically. "This baby is coming right now, so either you catch it or my husband will."

I exhale, repositioning my fingers, trying to confirm what I already know. The baby's head is too low to stop this now.

I try to ground myself. I almost always know what to do, but right now, I'm struggling. There is no time to think. I go into reactive mode and brace myself to deliver a baby.

Four times. That was all. Alison pushes four times before her baby boy makes his way into the world. I have seen it before, but it always amazes me. I set him on his mother's chest while we complete delayed cord clamping. There's a profound sense of accomplishment and relief in delivering a baby, a momentary high. However, with June in the other room, my high doesn't last long.

The list of things that need to be done before I can leave the room overtakes the euphoria.

A notification comes across my smart watch. The family tracking app we use indicates Imogene has arrived back at school, but I haven't seen a notification for Garrett come through. My chest seizes with worry that he forgot to pick her up, and I want to call and check, but I can't. This simple limitation makes me irritable, but I push it away.

When I've done everything I need to do for Alison and the baby, I head back to June, checking my watch as I walk.

As I near June's room, the distinct sound of wheels comes into earshot. June emerges from the room on a hospital bed accompanied by Jackie and several other members of our team.

"Where are you going?" I call as I speed-walk after them.

"Shoulder dystocia. She is hemorrhaging," Jackie says over her shoulder.

Holy shit. I run along June's bedside. Her eyes are wide, and her chin trembles.

I place a hand on her arm, and with as much sureness as I can muster, I say, "I know this is scary. We are going to get you through this. Trust me."

For the next hour, I coordinate as we work to stabilize June. Baby is with the boyfriend, and my heart aches at the separation between this mother and child.

Once June is stable, I use my watch to call Garrett. He doesn't answer. The app shows he arrived at the school, but twenty minutes after Imogene.

I shove down the frustration that builds over Garrett's lack of responsibility. There's nothing I can do about it. I'm here, at work, and I can barely handle what's here.

Hours later, June is back in her room, and a baby girl, who she has lovingly named Amelia, lays peacefully on her chest.

"You were totally worth it," June breathes as she smiles at Amelia. Her boyfriend is now by her side rather than ignoring her, and I hope this experience opened his eyes—although I know it probably hasn't.

"I have a question," June announces to me.

"Yes?"

"Do you think she got stuck because he made me lay on my back to deliver?"

My eyes widen. Rage fills my veins. That shit stain of a doctor. How dare he? While I can't say for certain whether the outcome of June's labor was caused by her delivering on her back, what gave him the audacity to force a laboring person to deliver in any position other than the one she chose?

"He what?"

"Yeah, after you left. Do you think that is why she got stuck?"

"That's unlikely," I respond, but my blood is boiling. I charge out of the room, determined to confront Dr. Shit Stain, but once again, Jackie is there as I round the corner.

"Can we talk?" she asks.

"I have something I need to deal with."

"What?" The toe of her shoe taps the speckled linoleum floor.

I let out an exaggerated breath and cross my arms.

"I need to go talk to the on-call doctor—Dr. Shit Stain. He made my patient deliver on her back," I say reluctantly.

"That can wait. Come on." She spins on her heel and makes for the breakroom. I shake my head and relax my arms before following her. When the door to the break room shuts behind us, she turns on me.

"I'm going to recommend to your manager that you are written up."

"For what?" I flick my hands up.

"Violating hospital policy by giving your patient food, lying to me about it, unprofessional behavior in front of a patient, and jeopardizing patient safety." Jackie's voice is stern.

"Unprofessional behavior? Jeopardizing patient safety?" My mouth hangs open at the accusations.

"Did you not question Dr. Johnson's ability to do his job in front of the patient?"

"Yes, but . . ." I clench my fists.

"No." She cuts me off, her hand slicing through the air to emphasize her point. "You literally just called him Dr. Shit Stain in a space where anyone could hear you. You don't think that's problematic?"

"Fine, but I didn't jeopardize a patient's safety." I cross my arms.

Her steady stare pins me in place. "Yes, you did." She speaks in a steady, unwavering tone. "You could have asked me for help, but instead, you tried to handle both births. It's well known around here that you won't take help. I understand your need to control the situation, but today, your need for control put a patient at risk."

I step back and swallow hard. My jaw tightens as I process her words. I want to fight her on this, but I know it is useless. I thought I was doing what was best for my patients, but I might have made a bad call. I just hope it doesn't cost me my job. I can't afford to lose my job. I can't afford life without a job.

I nod and lower my head, muttering, "You're right. I'm sorry." Admitting fault and accepting defeat makes my lungs feel paralyzed, but I have no choice. I can't risk everything for the sake of my pride.

I finish the final hour of my shift. By the time it is over, the inside of my cheek is sore and raw from biting it in thought and annoyance.

After my shift, I walk out to my car, drained and defeated. The humidity clings to me—thick and oppressive—as I replay the day's events, analyzing every move and interaction. My mind shifts between acceptance and rage. I climb into my car and shake my head, trying to dismantle the stress gnawing at me. Inhaling a deep breath, I look forward.

There, on my windshield, is a single slice of yellow sticky cheese. It's glossy, plastic-like sheen mocks me.

I was cheesed.

Manic laughter erupts from my mouth, and I scream, "Motherfucker!"

The scream lasts an eternity, but when the remnants of the sound dissipate, I feel a little better. I glance to my left and realize my car door is still open. Through it, an unsuspecting elderly lady stands frozen, staring at me with a mix of terror and shock written across her face.

CHAPTER 5

WEAPONIZED INCOMPETENCE

Stacy

The lights are on inside, and Garrett, visible through the living room curtains, is slumped back in his recliner with his legs stretched out. A headset covers his ears, and a controller rests in his hands. His fingers fly across the buttons and toggle the joystick. I'm already annoyed, as I'm almost 100% certain he has done nothing since he came home, including make dinner.

I roll my eyes before I walk through the door. The moment I do, I spot piles of screws and other odd bits he leaves around our house. His work boots—covered in sawdust—are discarded in the foyer, and when I peer past the entrance to the kitchen, a pile of dirty dishes from this morning are visible in the sink. I'm not surprised, but after the day I had, I would have appreciated some effort. Any effort.

Garrett has a habit of playing it all off as if it is not a big deal. Make him a list, he says. He'll get to it. But I don't want to make him a damn list. I want him to use the brain God gave him and do the things that need to be done.

At the sight of me, Garrett flicks the headset off one ear and says, "Hey, babe. How was work?"

I don't answer his question, but instead say, "Dinner?" One of my brows arches, and my voice drips with accusation.

His face drops. "Sorry, long day, and I just needed to blow off some steam."

"We have talked about this a million times. On the days I work, you're responsible for dinner. I get home after you." I cross my arms over my chest. My body language is similar to my stance when talking to Jackie earlier today.

"I know, I know," he says, putting his hands up and lifting himself from the recliner. If he knew, he would have taken care of dinner. "Work ran late, and my whole day was messed up. Pizza?"

I want to tell him that won't work. We can't afford pizza, but I don't. "Fine. I need a shower."

"Do you want me to order it?" he asks as I walk away.

It takes everything in me not to yell as I say, "Yes, please."

In the shower, I try to relax my shoulders and let the heat of the water loosen the knots within them. I've been in a constant state of stress for nearly a year, stuck in an impossible situation.

We'd always only scraped by, bad luck a constant drain on our savings, but Garrett fucked us over when he suddenly quit his job as an assistant superintendent for one of the biggest construction companies in Florida. He threw our stability away rather than opening his mouth.

It started off as little things—disagreements with his boss and corporate when they started cutting corners, all in the name of profit. But then, it got worse, and he'd come home venting about how safety protocols were being ignored and how workers were being pushed past their limits to hit deadlines.

But instead of standing up to them or reporting what was happening, Garrett just complained. He let it fester until, one day, he quit. No warning. No backup plan. Just this raw, misguided conviction that he could start his own business from scratch, with no business experience and no safety net.

He walked away from everything, and I had to clean up the mess. Late at night, I'd find myself sitting at the dining room table, staring at bills that never seemed to end. Garrett would come in from the garage, covered in sawdust, and go on about the next big job or a plan to expand his business.

"It's just not working, Garrett," I'd say, my voice thin with exhaustion. "We can't afford this."

But he never listened. He'd start talking about renting a shop, hiring people—things we didn't have the money for, but he'd always finish with, "Just trust me, Stacy. We can do this."

Unfortunately, there was no "we" Even after we opened the shop—an investment that drove us into soul-crushing debt—it was me who had to figure out how to keep us afloat.

When I turn off the stream of water, the muscles in my shoulders are no more relaxed than when I got in. I stretch my neck to the ceiling to relieve some of the tension there. Out of the shower, I wrap a large bath sheet around me and look toward the mirror, which is fogged over. That is exactly how my brain feels—foggy.

In the bedroom, I dress into my pajamas, already longing for bedtime. At least I have tomorrow off, which I'll use to visit Dad.

Garrett comes into the room while I dress. He feels like an intruder. I hate for him to see me naked. I don't know when this happened. It seems like yesterday we were a new couple, living together, naked more than we were dressed. Now, I feel he shouldn't be here, so I rush to pull my pajama shirt over my head to hide my exposed breasts.

He sits on the bed. "Stacy?"

"Hmm?" I reply, purposefully not responding with words.

"I don't want to fight."

"Who said we were fighting?" I am fully aware of the tension between us.

He sighs. "I feel like I'm always disappointing you. You're never happy, no matter what I do. If I put in effort, it is the wrong effort. If I take a step back, I'm lazy. No matter what I do, I feel like you view me as incompetent."

That is because you are. I turn to him, now dressed and guarded. "I don't want to come home from a twelve-hour shift and worry about dinner. That's all."

"It's more than that, Stacy. I know it is, but you won't let me in. You won't talk to me. I don't feel like your husband. I don't even feel like your roommate. We don't have sex anymore."

This bothers me more than it should, because he is right. When he touches me, I can't reciprocate because I don't have it in me. I'm stressed out about caring for Imogene, caring for my father, and keeping us above water. Sex is the furthest thing from my mind, but he doesn't get it.

"That's great, Garrett. Of all the things to be concerned with, sex is top of mind. Is there anything else you want to say? Anything else you want to complain about?"

"Never mind," he says, getting up to leave the room.

Relief washes over me, but a tangle of panic and anxiety I cannot explain quickly replaces it. Sitting on the edge of the bed, I try to steady my nerves. I don't want us to be like this anymore. But I can't seem to change it. I know what the root of the issue is, but I can't communicate it in a way that makes sense. And when I do communicate, he never hears me. Yes, he listens, but there is a difference between listening and hearing.

I'm just so tired of feeling like everything is on my shoulders. But when I ask him for help, I don't even want him to follow through because I'm afraid he'll just make things worse.

I retrieve the prescription bag I picked up from the pharmacy on my way home and go to Imogene's room. I take a deep breath and shimmy my body to expel my frustration. Taking one more deep breath through my nose, I exhale and lift the corners of my mouth into a smile.

Not letting Imogene see my struggle is important to me. It's my job to protect her from worry. It's my job to provide her with stability. Being distressed in front of her doesn't help me do either of those things.

At her door, I knock lightly.

"Come in!" she says over the music coming from the speaker in her room.

I slip inside, and peer up at the projection of swirling clouds and stars on Imogene's ceiling. Imogene's room is a universe unto itself. Her shelves are overflowing with books on astronomy and models of planets. Across from her bed, dominating the wall above her desk, is an image of a galaxy, its spiraling arms cast in shades of blue and silver.

Imogene sits hunched over her laptop, working on something for school. She wears a beanie, which is odd because it is already unusually warm for the end of May in Florida.

I walk up and, as I always do, pull her face toward mine to kiss her temple when she recoils with an "Ow!"

"What was that? Are you hurt?" Leaning in to examine where I touched her face, she pulls away with angst.

"I'm fine," she says.

"I don't think so." I put my hand under her chin to turn her face to me. Under the edge of the beanie, a bruise is forming, and I lift the hem to reveal more.

"What happened?"

"Nothing!" She jerks away from me again.

"Oh, no. This is not nothing. Who hurt you?" I lower myself and search her eyes, forcing eye contact. Imogene bites her lip in refusal.

"Imogene, do I need to go to your school?"

Her face drops.

"Imogene?" I say again, more firmly.

"I don't want to talk about it," she says.

"I'm not giving you a choice. Tell me what happened to your face."

Minutes later, after I pulled information out of Imogene and administered her meds, I march into the living room to stand before Garrett, who has reclaimed his spot in the recliner. "You told me work went late, and I chose not to say anything about you being late to pick up Imogene, but did you know?"

"She told you." He shifts his body weight, his face falling in response to my accusation.

"She was pushed to the ground and kicked by a group of boys. Her cell phone is broken, too. How could you not tell me?" My hands cut through the air, fingers splayed, grasping for an explanation.

"I didn't know that!" The pitch of his voice increases.

"Which part?" My face shakes with frustration.

"About her cell phone!" He hesitates. "Or any of it, really. She wouldn't talk to me." His defensive tone sends hot frustration to my cheeks.

I let out a gust of air. "How can you be so apathetic when it comes to our daughter?"

He lowers the recliner's footrest and sits up, now on the offense. "Imogene needs to learn to stand up for herself."

"Oh, my God! Do you hear yourself? Placing the blame on Imogene rather than everyone else? What do you expect her to do?" I demand, my eyes brimming with angry tears.

"Life as a trans person is harder. If this is the path she has chosen, then she has to own it," he argues.

"You realize she has no choice, right?" I scream. "Sometimes, you're just as bad as everyone else."

Garrett stands and grows larger. "This is my son we are talking about!"

Although he is taller than me, I don't shrink back. Instead, I straighten my spine. "Your daughter!" I correct him, and he shrinks back.

"You know what I mean, Stacy. Please don't police every word that comes out of my mouth. I'm doing my best."

"How often do you slip up in front of her?" My eyes narrow.

"Never," he claims, but his eyes betray him.

I continue to glare at him. "Never? Really?"

His chin dips, and his gaze falls. "Sometimes," he mumbles.

"Garrett! It's been a year and a half, and you're still not trying. Do you know what she told me? She said that when someone uses her dead name or misgenders her, it feels like they are cutting away at her heart. With each chunk of flesh cored out from within her, she isn't sure how much longer she can go before she is empty. Is that what you want to do to our daughter?" My hands tremble.

"No, that's not what I want. I'm trying." His brows come down, and he shakes his head.

"Could have fooled me." My tone is cold.

"What do you want from me? Really? And don't try to placate me by being vague or saying nothing. Tell me. What am I doing wrong?"

The frustration builds and then snaps, shoving me over the edge. "Everything! I feel like I'm always nagging you just to help me. I'm carrying everything on my own, and you don't care. Our lives are falling apart, and I can't shoulder it on my own anymore."

"First, you're being dramatic. Our life is not falling apart. Second, you won't let me help you! None of this is my fault!" Garrett says.

I lower my voice and embed venom in every word. "Of course. It's never your fault."

He continues, now on the offense. "You're right. It's always my fault. Even before Imogene came out, I was never good enough. You've always blamed me for every bad thing that has ever happened and used it as leverage to control everything."

Every part of me is screaming to fight back, but I know it won't change anything.

I turn my back on him. I'm about to yell back that I'm done. Done with everything, but then the doorbell rings.

Pizza is here.

CHAPTER 6

THE CENTER OF ADVOCACY

Stacy

I use concealer to hide the dark circles sitting under my eyes, blush to wake my dull skin, and mascara to make my puffy lids look less tired after crying myself to sleep last night.

As I stare at my reflection in the mirror, I see myself fourteen years ago. The wall behind me was orange rather than light gray. My face had a youthfulness that was exasperated by the swelling of pregnancy. My husband's tender kiss grazed my shoulder as I applied lip balm.

"Nervous?" Garrett asked. It was Imogene's induction day. We were headed to the hospital in a few hours. Garrett's light brown hair was longer than usual, and he had the tiniest bit of stubble on his chin. I liked it when he neglected shaving for a few days. I rubbed the side of my face along the prickly space on his jaw. He planted another kiss on my temple.

"A little, but mostly, I'm ready to be done. I don't think I can handle another day of this. How about you?"

"Not nervous." His hands encircled me and caressed the sides of my baby bump.

"Not even a little? Having a baby is a big deal. Nighttime feedings, diaper changes, colic." I arched a brow at him. "And you're not nervous at all?"

"Oh, I thought you were managing those things, and I would be the fun parent."

My brow dropped, and I narrowed my eyes. He leaned his head back with a laugh.

"I'm kidding! I plan to be a full and present participant in childrearing, but I'm not nervous at all. We are going to rock this parenting thing. I mean, look at us." He gestured to our reflection.

The daydream evaporates, and I say, "Yeah, look at us," but it's only me staring at my present reflection.

Out of habit, I say aloud, "Today is a good day." I shift my gaze to the ceiling and blink rapidly to keep threatening tears at bay. I leave the bathroom to check on Imogene.

When I knock on Imogene's door and crack it open, she is stretching the black beanie from last night over her head.

"You about ready?"

"Are you taking me?" she asks. Garrett usually takes Imogene to school since it is on his way to the shop.

"Yes, I want to have a word with your principal."

The corners of her mouth sink with dread. "Mom, please don't."

"Don't, what? Advocate for you? That's my job," I tell her.

"It will just make things worse," she responds, with a plea in her eyes.

"I promise I will not make it worse. I will ask the principal to be as sensitive as possible to prevent any potential backlash."

"It's not going to work," she whines, and it makes her seem even younger.

"I understand you're scared, but if these kids don't learn a lesson now, there's a good chance they never will. Do you understand that? It isn't about justice for you as much as it is about preventing this type of behavior in the future."

"Fine." She stands to collect her things.

In the kitchen, Garrett is packing his lunch as I make for the coffee bar to fill my thermos. I have a terrible caffeine addiction, but who doesn't these days? Life is chaotic and the only way to cope is with copious amounts of caffeine.

"You're up early," he notes.

"I'm taking Imogene to school." I screw the lid onto my thermos and wipe the spilled coffee from its silver side with a paper towel.

Garrett raises an eyebrow.

"I'm going to go talk to her principal."

He looks like he is trying to decide what to say next. Like Imogene, he probably wants to discourage me from doing this. Although they are so different, they are very much alike.

"What does Imogene say?" Garrett asks.

"Does it matter? Those boys can't just get off because she's too scared to speak up for herself."

"While I agree Imogene needs to stick up for herself, going to the principal? Come on, you know that is just going to make things worse."

"That is the type of thinking that allows their behavior to continue."

"I mean, she should address things head-on. She can't hide behind other people for the rest of her life." Garrett stuffs a sandwich into a plastic bag and places it into his lunchbox.

My shoulders rise. "Garrett, she's a child." My statement is a criticism of his worldview.

Garrett raises his hands and bows his head. "Fine then. Did Imogene mention her teacher was there?"

"Teacher?"

"Yes, when I got to the school, a teacher, or at least I assume so, was sitting next to her. He probably saw what happened."

I see now that Garrett is offering an olive branch, and my shoulders rid themselves of an ounce of tension. "Do you know his name?"

"He told me, but I don't remember," he says with a shrug.

"That's fine, I'll ask Imogene." She didn't mention him, and it makes me wonder what else she isn't mentioning.

Garrett crosses the distance and puts an arm around my lower back. I tense for a moment before remembering the olive branch and let my guard down.

"Just be easy on her. She might need more support than other teens, but she is still a teen who needs some level of independence and space," Garrett says, staring into my eyes. I want to protest, but he continues speaking, recognizing the look on my face. "I know. We are her parents, and it is our job to protect her, and you do such a good job at that, but balance. She needs balance, and I think you know that, too."

I nod slowly, and Garrett comes in for a kiss. I can tell he wants it to be more than a peck at the way he lingers, but I pull away to grab a banana and throw it in my bag. He is so quick to sweep things under the rug, but I can't.

On our way to the school, Imogene is quiet, and I can tell she is unhappy.

"Music?" I ask her, but she shrugs. Gosh, I swear shrugging has become her only form of communication. I have learned what these shrugs mean by the length of the invisible string that connects her shoulders to her ears.

This shrug communicates, *I want to crawl into a hole and hide.*

I bite my bottom lip, thinking about what to say next. I change the subject temporarily.

"How are you doing with the six-month dose? Have you noticed anything unusual? Any side effects?"

"You just gave it to me last night."

Okay, that wasn't what I was hoping for. I just want her to talk to me—say something, anything. I hate not knowing what's going on in her head.

"I thought maybe we could go camping in a couple of weeks. I hear a meteor shower is happening. There are supposed to be like forty meteors or something like that."

"Okay," she says, shrugging again. This shrug says *although I very much want to go camping, I'm mad at you, so I'm not going to show any interest.*

I take the conversation in a different direction. "Your dad said a teacher was there when he picked you up. You didn't mention that last night."

She exhales sharply. "It wasn't relevant. You asked how my face got bruised. Not why the boys eventually stopped."

Teenagers. I roll my eyes, but she doesn't see me.

"I'm glad he showed up. It could've been much worse. Who was it?" I tap my blinker, the steady *click, click, click* marking my lane change.

"Who was who?" Imogene says, and it is apparent she's not listening.

"Who was the teacher?" I repeat calmly, even though my child is definitely pushing my buttons right now.

"Mr. Alvarez," she finally reveals.

"Oh! I know him. Doesn't he teach science?"

"Yeah. Biology."

"He's one of the ones you like, right?"

"I don't know."

Imogene's lack of or limited responses makes me want to stop the car and demand answers, but I keep driving.

When we pull into the school parking lot, Imogene takes her backpack, decorated with far too many enamel pins, and slings it over her back. She dashes toward the school, leaving me trailing behind.

"Today is a good day!" I yell after her, but she doesn't acknowledge me. It stings because it was always our little ritual at school drop-off when she was little, but I guess all good things come to an end. I shake my head and watch as Imogene rushes toward the school.

Garrett's words replay in my mind. *Balance.*

Upon entering the school, I approach the reception desk and request to speak with Mrs. Higgins. Within minutes, someone directs me toward the principal's office, where I sit in front of her desk. Mrs. Higgins regards me with a composed demeanor as I settle into a chair that has likely accommodated countless concerned parents before me.

She laces her hands on top of her desk and says, "How can I help you, Mrs. Barnett?"

"Stacy is fine."

"All right, Stacy, how can I help you?"

"Well, there was an incident with my daughter Imogene yesterday outside the school after the field trip to the museum," I explain.

"I'm aware. Mr. Alvarez called me last night to let me know." Her face is stone as she speaks.

"Can I ask why there wasn't a teacher present to supervise until the students were picked up? Also, why wasn't it reported yesterday?"

"These are high school kids, not elementary students. Most of them drive themselves now. As far as reporting, I have already spoken to Mr. Alvarez. He believed it was fine to handle it during regular school hours." She sounds bored as she speaks. "I do want to inform you that I have reviewed the camera footage, and Charlie—"

I interrupt, my voice steady but firm. "Imogene."

The principal lets out a weary sigh, her eyes briefly flicking upward before meeting mine again. "Your child threw the first punch."

"Yes, but that's because they were bullying her. She was defending herself."

"To defend oneself does not come after you've already assaulted one of your classmates," she replies sharply, her tone implying an end to the argument, but then she changes her mind and continues. "I can see how that may be hard for a family like yours to understand."

My head snaps back. "A family like mine?"

"Look, Stacy." She leans back, crossing her arms. "I'm going to level with you. You're lucky if Jonah's parents don't press charges for assault and, given we have a zero bullying and violence policy, I'm inclined to expel your child."

I haven't even registered that she mentioned expulsion or charges because I can't help but notice the words she chooses not to use.

"Why won't you use her name? Since I corrected you, you have resisted the urge to use her pronouns or her name."

"I'm attempting to show you respect, and I hope you'll show me enough respect to understand that these types of things are quite uncomfortable. Please, let's stay on task."

My face heats and the familiar tremors that consume my hands when I'm overwhelmed emerge. I want to zero in on her refusal to use Imogene's name but turn my attention to the reason I'm here.

"Are you expelling her?" My chin dips as I ask the question.

"Mr. Alvarez has asked me not to. He thinks we can find a different solution, but I can't do anything if Jonah's parents decide to press charges. All I can control is what happens at school."

I scratch my head. I didn't expect the conversation to go this way. I came here expecting the school to be on my daughter's side because she was assaulted, but instead, I'm sitting in front of a principal who's treating her like the problem. It feels as if the ground has tilted, and I place my hands on the desk to keep myself from falling sideways.

Mrs. Higgins sits up a little straighter. "There are less than two weeks of school left, so I have decided we will offer Imogene after-school detention for the rest of the year and for the first three months of next year. She will serve detention with whichever teacher is assigned this year, but next year, Mr. Alvarez has volunteered to allow her to do detention with him while also completing community service here at the school."

"Community service?"

"We'll call you to set up a time to go over the paperwork by the end of the day. I wasn't prepared for you to come in this early. Also, you'll need to schedule progress meetings with the school counselor to manage your child's progress."

Blindsided by the sudden turn of events, my voice catches in my throat, and I struggle to form words.

"Anything else?" the principal asks, her tone brisk. Her eyes shift to her computer screen.

The question snaps me back. Gathering my resolve, I straighten in my chair, my voice firmer. "How do I ensure my child is safe at this school?"

Mrs. Higgins has already checked out of the conversation and stares at her computer screen. "What you mean to ask is: How do we ensure the other students at this school are safe around your child?"

CHAPTER 7

HER NAME IS IMOGENE

Stacy, A Year and a Half Before

Sometimes, I'd have this nightmare where Imogene was floating through space, reaching out to touch the stars. Her hand stretched out tentatively, her face lit with curiosity. I stood on Earth's surface, watching her drift higher, mesmerized by her graceful movements. But as she floated further away, dread would seize within me.

I'd call out, "Come back! You've gone too far." She'd glance back with a sly smile on her lips. But then she kept playing among the cosmos.

My yelling grew desperate as she drifted. Eventually, she paused, her shoulders dropping as if she realized this game couldn't go on. She swam through the void, trying to come back to me. But with every stroke of her arms, she seemed to be carried even farther away. I tried to launch myself from the ground, desperate to reach her, but no matter how hard I pushed, I couldn't escape gravity's pull.

She became smaller and smaller, a shrinking figure against the vast, unending sky. I cried, yelled, jumped—anything to close the distance—but she shrank to the size of an ant. Then vanished. Gone.

I woke from the nightmare drenched in a cold sweat, my body trembling, remnants of my screams still raw in my throat, and tears clinging to my cheeks. It was just a dream. But it haunted me nonetheless.

This nightmare had only started in the last year. I could feel my child slipping away from me. She rarely spent time with us anymore, isolating herself like a hermit. Her friend McKenzie didn't come around anymore, and any conversation with Imogene had dwindled to "Fine," "Okay," or a shrug. I kept trying, kept asking if she was all right, but she would only respond with silence. A silence so overwhelming it felt like she was being pulled into some galaxy within her mind, drifting away where I couldn't follow. And before long, I feared she'd disappear.

So, when she called me while I was at work—her voice urgent and vulnerable—saying, "Mom, I need you," I didn't hesitate. I found a colleague to cover my patients, muttered something about a family emergency that couldn't wait, and hurried out the door.

As I drove to Imogene, my hands drummed on the steering wheel, my stomach twisting into knots. I tried to anticipate what was so urgent but couldn't.

I did not anticipate that she would tell me her name was Imogene.

"Imogene? You want to change your name to Imogene? Why?"

I laced and unlaced my fingers over the fabric of my scrubs. I was trying—really trying—to understand why my child wanted to change her name to Imogene.

"Because, Mom." Imogene's reply bounced off the walls. The word "because" sounded like the end of a discussion she was tired of having. Her restless pacing could have burned a trail into the carpet. She opened her mouth to continue, but my words tumbled over hers.

"I just don't get it. Your name is Charlie. Charlie is a perfectly good name. I gave it to you." The words were a defense against a truth I could sense but wasn't ready to face. "I named you after Grandpa Charles," I explained, even though she already knew.

Imogene's chest deflated, and her gaze dropped. I saw my sweet child. Sunny afternoons felt like yesterday, when she would nestle into my lap, the light filling the house with warmth. Clutching a fidget spinner and a book, she would lean back against me, the quiet hum of the spinner's whir serving as background music while I read.

But that version of Imogene had been gone for some time. Over the past year, she started pulling away—from me, from everyone. She spent hours shut away in her room, emerging only for dinner, where she ate in quick, silent bites before retreating again. Her change had crept up, like a shadow growing longer, until she became a ghost of the person she used to be. The harder I tried to connect with her, the more distant she became, leaving me frozen and terrified.

Now Imogene sat before me, staring at the floor, while my thoughts raced faster than I could process. The silence between us was deafening.

I scanned the room, searching for something to anchor myself to, but it was impossible.

"Why Imogene? Imogene is a girl's name."

When she lifted her face, I saw a tear tracing her cheek.

"I am a girl."

Something big was happening, and I didn't know how to handle it. I reached for understanding, desperate for something to hold on to.

"A girl?" I repeated, my voice betraying my bewilderment. The notion splintered my understanding of the world. Imogene had always been different from other kids, but I thought that difference was her quiet, inquisitive nature. She was always in her head, keeping to herself unless she was with her friend McKenzie. Sure, she was a little nerdy and softer than other boys, but I had never considered this possibility.

Imogene rushed to kneel before me, gathering my hands in hers. Tears brimmed in her large blue eyes, and she nodded with determination. I could see how important this was to her and, by default, I wanted it to be important to me, but I still struggled with the shock of it.

"Yes, Mom. A girl."

My brain short-circuited. A girl. What did that even mean? I understood the concept of being transgender, but I didn't understand all it came with, how it would impact our family, how it would impact my child.

"Charlie . . ." I said breathlessly, unsure of what to say next.

"My name is Imogene. Not Charlie." She corrected me—gentle, but firm.

I shook my head, trying to reboot my brain to make sense of the tangle of thoughts running through it. Imogene. Not Charlie. Imogene. My child's identity, once as familiar to me as my own, now felt foreign.

"Why Imogene?" I asked because, despite everything, I couldn't unstick myself from the name. When I look back at that day, I can't believe how fixed upon her name I was. There she was, telling me she's trans, but the name felt like the most confusing part of it all.

Imogene pressed her lips together, furrowing her brows in a familiar way, creating a soft indentation between them.

"Imogene." Her chin dipped with certainty. "It comes from the Gaelic name Innogen, which comes from the Gaelic word inghean. Inghean means maiden . . . or daughter . . . or girl. I chose Imogene because I have no choice but to feel as if I was always meant to be a girl."

The power in her words struck me like lightning.

A laugh escaped me—awkward, misplaced, a reflex to the surreal. I slapped a hand over my mouth, afraid my laughter would be mistaken for mockery.

"I didn't mean to laugh," I told her.

"It's okay, Mom," Imogene said, trying to reassure me, even though she was the one who needed reassurance. I just wasn't where she was yet. She had a head start, and I was racing to catch up. But eventually, I saw it in the determined set of her jaw and the earnest plea in her eyes.

Imogene was a girl. My girl.

And I would do whatever it took to keep her close, to make sure she never drifted away from me again.

CHAPTER 8

ANTISEPTIC AND DEATH

Stacy

The air smells of antiseptic, floral-scented air freshener, and impending and unavoidable death—a smell I know all too well. It's the same one that greets me every time I visit my dad in the nursing home.

My dad was diagnosed with dementia less than two years after we moved to Florida from Colorado to be near him. He got confused on his way to Imogene's sixth birthday party, driving twenty miles under the speed limit and failing to notice the flashing police lights behind him. When I got the call he'd been arrested for refusing a sobriety test, I was furious, certain he'd been drinking again. I remember exchanging a glance with my friend Melissa, who stood across from me in the kitchen while Garrett and Imogene play-fought with balloon swords in the living room. I felt so betrayed. But when I learned it wasn't alcohol, my anger turned to something much heavier—grief.

It wasn't the kind of grief that crashed down, raw and all-consuming, like when I lost my mom. This was slow, creeping, and cruel.

Now, every visit is a reminder of what was stolen from us. I check in at the nursing home before making my way down the brightly lit hallway to my dad's room.

Passing one nurse, she offers a warm, if tired, smile—a familiar face.

"How is he today?" I ask, pausing in stride.

"He's been asking for you," she replies in a gentle voice. "Seems good today."

Reassured, I nod my thanks and continue. Maybe today he will remember me.

After his diagnoses, he rapidly declined, and Garrett and I had to cover the cost of his care. Thankfully, we were accepted into a subsidized program that reduces the cost. Key word is subsidized because it is still expensive. But before Mom died, I promised I'd always take care of Dad, and the Medicaid-approved homes here don't cut it, so I make it work.

Dad never planned for the future, always floating through life, assuming things would work out. It was part of his charm, but also what I resented. Because I had to pick up the pieces.

Ironically, I married a man just like him. Garrett and my dad are so alike they hit it off immediately, often spending time together even when I wasn't around. I used to tease Garrett about liking my dad more than he liked me. But despite how close they once were, Garrett rarely visits him now. He says it's too hard, and as much as I wish he would, I understand.

It is hard.

I knock on Dad's door and open it just enough to peek inside.

"Darby, is that you?" Every time I walk into his room with hope, and he calls me Darby, it feels like losing him all over again.

"No, Dad. It's Stacy, your daughter." It's been months since he has recognized me. I always come with a level of optimism that it might be different, but it never is. Most often, he thinks I'm my mom. And given it's been over two decades since she died, I know what timeline his brain is stuck in.

As I move through the doorway, the room feels warm, but I think little of it.

Dad sits at the small card table next to his bed and works on a puzzle.

"Can I join you?" I ask.

He grunts—a sound I understand as affirmation.

"How are you today?" I ask, pulling up a chair across from him.

He looks up at me and smiles. "You look beautiful today."

"Thank you, Dad."

"Where's Stacy? Is she around here somewhere?"

I press my lips together, never certain how to answer this question.

"Is she okay?" he asks, and I force myself to pretend.

My shoulders sink a fraction. "She's fine. A little stressed out right now." I pick up a puzzle piece and hold it between my fingers, examining it against the rest.

"What does a seven-year-old girl have to be stressed out about?" He scratches his chin.

The one thing I've come to appreciate about my dad's dementia is that he is a safe person to vent to because he rarely passes judgment and he doesn't repeat what I say.

"Well, life isn't going the way she thought it would. It sometimes feels like the entire world is out to get Imogene, and she can't figure out how to keep her safe."

"Awe. That's a pickle." Dad nods, his focus drifting back to the pieces scattered on the table. He picks up a piece, puts it down, and picks up another. Putting puzzles together takes him a lot longer than it used to.

"It sure is," I agree.

I study his profile. He sits slightly stooped, and the translucent skin under what used to be a strong jaw sags. Although it would be safe to assume this is the most vulnerable state he has ever been in, it's not. He is stronger now than he was in the aftermath of Mom's death.

Mom passed away at home while in hospice after battling stage four breast cancer that metastasized before we caught it. I was only fourteen years old, the same age as Imogene today. My dad let me miss an entire semester of high school just so I wouldn't miss a moment with my mom.

While my friends went to school dances and complained about homework, I sat by Mom's bed, playing cribbage with her.

The thing was, Mom believed she would beat her illness even though it had gone too far to be treated. When I confessed to her how scared I was to lose her, she would say, "I'm going to beat this."

Her conviction was my gospel, and knowing very little about cancer at that age, I held it close to my chest.

I glance across the table at Dad now, his fingers fumbling over a puzzle piece. The room feels stifling hot, but he seems unaffected, lost in his own world. I wipe the sweat from my neck and look away.

What I remember most about my mom's last weeks is that her nurses wanted to move her from her bedroom to a hospital bed in the living room, but she refused, wanting to stay close to my dad and the life they shared. Although caring for my mom was more difficult in the tight space between her bed and the adjacent wall, the nurses allowed her this last bit of agency over something no one could control.

I wanted to be like them—a source of comfort for people like my mom.

The day before her departure from this world, she conceded to the hospital bed, a white flag raised not in defeat but in acceptance. That first and last night in the living room, she slipped away.

Dad's eyes shift up to me. "I can't figure out where this piece goes." He holds out the piece.

"Hmmm," I say. "I think it may go here." I take the puzzle piece out of his hand and place it in the proper space.

"Thanks, Darby."

"No problem," I reply, managing a tight smile.

After Mom died, Dad wasn't okay. Grief filled him to the brim, leaving no space for me. His carefree nature turned against him, and instead of being happy-go-lucky, he was sad and despondent. He took to drinking, and although he eventually got sober, those couple of years where he was drunk more often than he was sober were hard. So, I had to grow up. Take control.

I cooked. I cleaned. I made sure he got to work, and the bills were paid. And through all that, I learned I liked having control. Because when I was in charge, the world ran as it should.

After several more minutes inside Dad's room, I feel sweat dripping down my back. The heat feels unbearable now, making it hard to think straight.

"Is it hot in here?" I ask as I fan myself uselessly. I scan the small room as if the heat is visible.

"Hmmm," he says as he examines another puzzle piece.

I stand and walk over to the thermostat. It read a stifling eighty-one degrees—a baffling temperature for such a small room. I fiddle with the controls, switching the system off and then on again, toggling from "fan" to "auto." Still, nothing.

"I'll be right back. I need to find building maintenance."

At the nurses' station, a familiar man stands at the counter where I checked in just fifteen minutes earlier. He wears thick-framed dark green glasses and a lime green bow tie. I catch myself staring, struck by a strong sense of déjà vu. Sensing my gaze, he looks up and offers an award-winning smile.

He recognizes my struggle to place him and puts out a hand. "Ramon or Mr. Alvarez. I have Imogene in my biology class."

It all comes together at once. He is the teacher who stopped those boys.

I give a weak laugh. "Oh, yes. Sorry. Seeing you in a new context took me for a loop," I say, feeling a wave of embarrassment wash over me. I want to talk to him about yesterday, but given we are at a nursing home and not the school, it might be inappropriate.

Instead, I ask, "How are you?"

"No worries. I'm as good as I can be. I hope it's okay if I ask, but how's Imogene?"

I'm relieved he brought her up. "As good as she can be, too, but I'm concerned. I met with the principal today." I wonder if Mr. Alvarez shares the same views as Mrs. Higgins, but he did ask about Imogene, so maybe not. I still can't believe the woman blamed Imogene for what happened yesterday.

His face falls in understanding, and it's enough for me to know he is aware of and disheartened by how Mrs. Higgins feels.

"How was that?" he asks. His gaze is intense through the glass of his lenses, and I feel disarmed by him.

I let out a large breath. "Not good. Mrs. Higgins was completely unhelpful and borderline hateful. She thinks Imogene could face charges." My voice cracks with worry.

He nods. "I know. I did what I could."

"Why didn't you report it sooner?" I ask. I try to keep my tone from being accusatory, but I'm uncertain if I'm successful. Ramon doesn't seem phased though.

He scratches the side of his head. "She threw the first punch, and . . . I don't know. I felt like it would be best for Imogene if we handled it differently." He grimaces. "I'm sorry."

"No, you're okay. It's okay," I say. He was doing Imogene a favor, which is much clearer now that I've met with Mrs. Higgins. I'm grateful.

He studies me for a moment, as if he is deciding on his response. "Tell you what. Let me give you my number. If you or Imogene need anything, call me. I know all this can feel lonely. I don't know what I can do to help, but I'm here if you need it. Plus, I'm taking the last week of school off, so I won't be there if she needs me."

Ramon recites his phone number while I enter it into my phone, though I'm unsure what I might need from him. After he finishes, I save the number and hold my phone up for him to see. "Got it. Thank you."

"There's no need to thank me," he says with a small smile. "Just call or text if you need anything."

I nod in appreciation, and a woman appears from the office. "Here's the form you need to sign. You can pick up your mother's things in her room," she says to Ramon.

Realization floods my system, and my eyes widen. "Your mom?"

Ramon's face tightens. "She died—the reason I won't be at school. I'm headed to Jacksonville. She still has a house there."

"Oh, I'm so sorry." I think about those days after my mom died and what that felt like.

He waves off my concern. "It was time. She was suffering, and now she isn't."

I respond with a strained but knowing smile.

The woman who handed Ramon the clipboard stares at us, waiting. Ramon notices, quickly signs his name, and hands the clipboard back to her.

"I can take you to her room," she says.

I turn to her, not wanting to miss an opportunity to report the issue with the air conditioning.

"Hey, sorry to interrupt, but I believe the air-conditioning unit in my dad's room isn't working. Can we call someone to fix it?"

"I will call maintenance as soon as I'm done with Mr. Alvarez."

"Thank you," I say, bringing my hands together in front of me.

Ramon walks behind the woman and although I need to go in the same direction, I don't follow quite yet. Instead, I take a moment to reflect on our conversation. To be going through something like losing a parent and still find it in your heart to offer a helping hand . . . It's the most positive interaction I've had all week.

Eventually, I head back to Dad's room. When I open the door, the warmth hits me again. He's still at the small card table, his focus on the puzzle, oblivious to the heat.

I sit across from him again, picking up another puzzle piece.

"Here," I mutter, slipping the puzzle piece into place.

He doesn't look up, but smiles. "Thanks, Darby."

I nod, my throat tight. "No problem, Dad."

CHAPTER 9

ON WEDNESDAY, I WEAR PINK

Imogene

On Monday, my classmates chanted "rapist" and kicked me.

On Tuesday, I received three months of detention and community service that will bleed into next school year. Later that day, I found a magazine page shoved into the vent of my locker. Someone had pasted my face onto the image of a muscular man with tan, oiled skin. The imaginary scream that echoed in my head was deafening and stayed with me for the rest of the day. Mom has never allowed me to have social media, citing it as a platform for bullying, but she doesn't realize bullies will always find a way.

What bothers me most is that I've wanted to belong so badly that I've tempered who I am. Dressing androgynous in T-shirts and jeans, keeping my hair shorter than most girls but longer than most boys—I do everything possible to reduce the discomfort others inevitably feel in my presence.

But not anymore. I'm done.

So, on Wednesday, I wear pink.

"Are you sure you want to wear that?" Dad asked when I came out into the kitchen that morning. He looked impressed when I said I was sure. And I was sure because today, I was 100% percent going to be *that girl*.

I stride into my high school wearing a light pink dress with little white flowers. Instead of the light makeup I usually use to feminize my appearance, I have a full beat on. It's the most makeup I've ever worn. The only thing out of place is my constellation-painted shoes because I own nothing else except gym sneakers and slides.

As I walk through the halls, the murmurs are louder than usual, but I keep my head up and my back straight.

If being trans bothers them so much, then that's what I'll give them. I'm tired of hiding.

I watch closely to gauge how I am received. Pockets of students laugh and chatter until hushed voices announce my presence. They turn and point, their conversations now reduced to whispers. I'm torn between embarrassment and indignation but choose to lean into the fire inside me.

The only one oblivious to me is a teacher's pet who trudges down the hall with purpose, clutching a model of a DNA strand—a project for finals. Two boys play rowdily nearby while also staring and nearly collide with this oblivious student who steps back just in time. With each step, the power of the whispers and stares ebb, and I realize this feels good.

I'm a comet, blazing my trail across their sky. I'm done living on the edge to make other people comfortable. I deserve comfort, too.

I search for McKenzie, hoping she is nearby. I want her to see me. I want her to see I am a girl, and no matter what she does to me, I'm not going to change. But I don't see her.

At my locker, I slide the lock numbers into place. If I rush the process, I will mess up and have to start over, so I force myself to breathe. When I pull on the lock, the anxiety that was building in my chest releases.

Today is a good day.

"Come with me," a voice says from behind me, and I swivel around to identify the source. Principal Higgins stands in her frumpy floral shirt and too-tight dress slacks. An annoyed and expectant look rests on her face.

I stare for too long—confused by her presence.

"I said come with me," she repeats. Her sharp tone startles me, and my face flushes as collective snickers bounce off the locker-lined walls.

Did Jonah's parents decide to press charges? Am I going to jail? Shit. I'm going to jail. I suck on my teeth, nervous energy creeping back in.

Following Mrs. Higgins, we bypass her office and head to a conference room on the far side of the admin offices.

I'm definitely going to jail.

Another woman dressed in business casual already sits at the small conference table. She doesn't look like a cop. Higgins gestures for me to sit across from the woman. Anxiety rattles through me. I'm certain if they speak to me, I won't hear them, but Mrs. Higgins's words cut through the noise.

"This is Ms. Dixon. She is here from the Department of Child and Family Services and has asked to speak to you."

My brows arch as I try to understand.

"How are you doing today, Charlie?"

The use of my dead name sends a dagger through my chest.

"I go by Imogene," I tell her, though correcting her is hard.

"Imogene," she repeats with a slight nod and a smile, communicating acceptance. "I'm here because it was reported that your mother might be giving you a medication not prescribed to you by your doctor."

"What?" I say, knowing full well what she is talking about.

"Have you ever heard of leuprolide?"

I shake my head. The speed matches my heart rate. Who could have reported it? No one knows. Not even Dad.

"Are you sure?" Ms. Dixon's face softens further, her eyes warm with genuine concern. The corners of her mouth lift in a small, reassuring smile.

I dip my chin. "I'm sure. I don't take any medications."

"Hmm. Well, the medication I'm referring to stops you from going through puberty."

"Okay?" I say, trying to sound clueless. My palms are sweating, and I try to dry them on the fabric of my dress.

"Imogene, you are fourteen, right?"

My nod is almost imperceptible, but she recognizes the slight movement.

"At this age, you should present some signs of puberty, but after speaking with your principal and a few of your teachers, they have all reported you seem to be a late bloomer."

I fidget, tapping my foot against the floor. "I can't help what my body does. It sounds like I'm being targeted because I'm trans."

My principal speaks up, "No one is targeting you."

"Oh yeah? Two days ago, a bunch of boys pushed me to the ground and kicked me because I'm trans, but I'm still the one with after-school detention." My voice cracks, my frustration spilling out.

"You instigated that fight," Mrs. Higgins says.

"They were calling me a rapist. I'm not a rapist." I lift from my seat, nearly about to stand.

The DCFS investigator clears her throat. "That is not why I'm here."

I glower at my principal, but she tightens her lips coolly.

"We received a report from the police that your mother might be providing you with this medication," Ms. Dixon says. "It was reported by her place of employment, and they are undergoing an investigation right now."

"What? What's going to happen to her?" My voice rises in panic. I knew what we'd been doing wasn't allowed, but I never thought for a moment she'd get caught. As annoying as Mom can be sometimes, I don't want her to get in trouble.

"So, your mom is providing you with gender-affirming care?" Mrs. Higgins jumps in.

Ms. Dixon holds up her hand to stop my principal from saying more.

"Could you give Imogene and me a moment alone, please?" She turns and gives Mrs. Higgins a pointed stare.

Mrs. Higgins's eyes widen, but she gives a curt nod and stands from the table. "I'll be in my office if you need me."

When the conference room door swings shut and the mechanism clicks, Ms. Dixon speaks again. "Imogene, your mom might be in a lot of trouble. She altered her medical history and has been taking advantage of a colleague to prescribe herself medication for endometriosis. Now, that does happen, but most often, if a nurse commits prescription fraud, it's for painkillers. Not this drug. Based on the information we have, it appears she is providing you with gender-affirming care."

"She has endometriosis," I say, not fully understanding what that even means, but knowing if it's the story my mom has come up with, then it's what I need to stick to.

"The police don't believe that is the case."

Waves turn to sirens over my ocean of unease. I might be sick. Mom once said the more I taught her about outer space, the scarier it became. She didn't like the unknown. I imagine this is how she feels.

"Providing gender-affirming care to a minor is currently illegal. What your mom is doing is considered child endangerment. Her colleagues knew about you and were the ones who suggested you might be receiving the medication."

"You don't understand. My mom would never do anything to endanger my life. My mom is just trying to help me."

"I know that's what you and your mom think, but it doesn't change the law. As stupid as it is. Although I don't agree with it, I'm obligated to investigate these things when they are brought to our attention."

"What's going to happen?"

"I don't know quite yet. I'm going to talk to your mom and dad today, and the hospital and police will continue their investigation. But I need to ask you again: Did your mom provide you with the medication?"

I shake my head. I need to call Mom—warn her, but I don't have a phone. Mine is broken and we haven't replaced it yet. I wish I had a friend who would let me borrow theirs, but I don't.

"Okay," she says. "You can go to class. Here's my card. If there is anything you want to tell me, call me. I can help you, but only if you allow me to."

CHAPTER 10

BEANS FOR BREAKFAST

Stacy, Nearly One Year Before

The house was quiet, and Garrett had already left for an early meeting with a potential client. He rarely worked weekends, but he couldn't afford to pass up jobs. His shop had only been open for six months, and I knew these things took time, but Barnett Woodworks had yet to turn a profit.

I was elbow-deep in pantry chaos, sorting through food we never used, trying to create some kind of order. I could have sworn I had just cleaned out and organized our pantry, but cans were coated in dust and loose packets of instant oatmeal had fallen victim to the Florida humidity. I had a system: take everything out, wipe down each item, and as I put everything back, write down what needed to be used. Wasting food was not an option.

"Mom?"

I dropped an armful of cans, and they clattered to the floor, one of them bouncing off my foot.

"Shit!" I yelped.

Imogene's eyes widened, and she rushed toward me. "I'm so sorry, Mom. I didn't mean to scare you."

We both knelt to pick up the cans, working together, though my toe still throbbed.

Once we gathered the cans and placed them on the kitchen island across from the pantry, I turned to Imogene. "You hungry? We got beans," I joked, holding up a can of black beans.

She smiled, but there was something heavy behind her eyes. "Can we talk?"

My heart sank. The last time she asked me that, she told me she wanted to change her name to Imogene. I tried not to make assumptions but braced myself. I had learned from that conversation to slow down, to listen.

"Of course," I said, placing the can of beans, its label soft and deteriorating, on the counter before taking a seat on a stool at the kitchen island. "What's on your mind?"

Imogene hesitated, her hands fidgeting with the hem of her oversized shirt. She couldn't quite meet my eyes. I tried to stay calm as I waited.

"I've been thinking about . . . puberty blockers."

I took a breath. I had anticipated she might come to me with this, and I thought I was prepared. "And?" I asked, careful not to take over the conversation, even though I wanted to.

"I need them. I can't . . . I can't do this." Her voice cracked, and I could see the desperation in her eyes.

"Are you sure?"

"Yes," she said quickly, her voice firm but trembling.

I paused, remembering the hours I had spent at my computer after Imogene came out, clicking through websites and absorbing as much as I could about what it meant to be transgender. Research was my way of gaining control over something that felt so out of my control. But the more I learned, the more helpless I felt. I found out trans teens are 7.6 times more likely to attempt suicide, and transgender people are over four times more likely to experience violent victimization, including rape, sexual assault, and aggravated assault. She had already drifted so far from us and, although she had come out, she had yet to return fully. Therefore, those numbers were not only statistics. They were warnings.

My heart had shattered for my child, and I struggled to breathe, gripped by all the what-ifs. What if someone hurt her? What if she hurt herself? What if she changed her mind about transitioning later? What if puberty altered her body in ways that would make her hate herself forever? Every possible negative outcome circled in my brain, feeding my anxiety.

But then I came across a Stanford article that said teens who receive hormone treatment experience fewer thoughts of suicide. Hormone therapy could also help trans people move through the world with less scrutiny, reducing the risk of being victims of violence. That was something I could control. And although blockers seemed like the perfect solution, I was afraid of pushing Imogene in the wrong direction. So, even though every instinct in me screamed to act, I held back. I had to. But now that Imogene was asking to stop puberty, it was crucial I did more research and made sure this was the best option for her.

"We should take some time to think about it," I said gently. "I've done some research, but there's a lot I don't know. Let's learn more, okay?"

Imogene nodded, though her expression remained tight with worry. "Okay. How long will it take?"

"I'm not sure. But soon, I promise."

She nodded again, her relief visible, though the tension in her shoulders hadn't completely melted away.

As Imogene walked away, I tried to refocus on organizing the pantry, but my thoughts drifted back to those months before, when I had spent hours reading stories about trans people and learning about the negative outcomes. The names and faces of those lost to violence or suicide still haunted me.

When I finally finished the pantry and sat at my laptop, a quick Google search revealed something I hadn't been ready for. Florida had passed a law restricting gender-affirming care for minors.

My heart sank.

And Georgia? They followed suit shortly after. The closest state where we could get her the care she needed was Arkansas. I kept reading, desperate for a loophole, but the more I dug, the worse it got. All those anxieties from months ago flooded back.

Because of the way the law was worded, there was a real risk that families in Florida could face legal action, threats from child welfare services, even custody disputes if a parent sought care for their child out of state. The thought of losing Imogene to the system paralyzed me.

That night, I sat with Garrett, determined to figure out a way to leave Florida. Maybe we could go back to Colorado or even Canada, where I was born—somewhere Imogene could legally get the care she needed. But Garrett met my urgency with caution.

"It doesn't make sense," he said, shaking his head. "I'm not even sure I want Imogene on hormone blockers, let alone willing to uproot our entire lives for it."

"You don't understand," I countered, my voice tight. "The effects of puberty on her body will be much harder to reverse later. If we just slow it down now, we can give her time to decide. The risk is greater without them."

"And then what?" Garrett challenged. "How long are we talking about puberty blockers? What happens after that—actual hormones? Full transition? I feel like starting this is opening a can of worms Imogene might not fully understand yet."

"We're not rushing her into anything," I said, trying to keep calm. "I only want to put her on blockers until she is older. Let her have time to make an informed decision about transitioning."

Garrett sighed, leaning back in his chair. "I get that. I really do. But we can't just move. We just opened Barnett Woodworks."

"Then sell it," I said, my desperation creeping in. "Get a regular job again. We can start saving and get out of here."

"Stacy, it's not that simple. If I sold the business, wouldn't we lose all the time we invested? And what about your dad? He's here. It's not just about us. It's about the whole picture."

I sat in silence, my frustration growing. I knew it wasn't simple, but could he not see the urgency, the importance? The more I thought about it, the more I realized he would never sacrifice for her the way I was willing to.

For the next several weeks, I worked through different options, trying to figure out how to help my child. However, we were stuck. We had no money, and my dad was in a nursing home we were lucky to get him into. We couldn't leave, and I didn't know how I would get her access to the care she needed. The statistics and stories spun in my head, along with dollar signs and numbers holding our family in place. Finally, I decided we just needed to buy a little more time until I could figure out a permanent solution. Just for a little while.

And I didn't care if it wasn't legal. I had to protect her, no matter the cost.

CHAPTER 11

THE CONSEQUENCES OF CARE

Stacy

The hot, bitter liquid feels good on my tongue as I drain the last of the coffee from my thermos. I'll need more before my shift starts. After yesterday, and my second visit to Imogene's school, where they gave her after-school detention and community service next year, I couldn't shake the doom resting in the pit of my stomach. Last night, those feelings haunted my dreams, and I woke up exhausted.

I head straight for the scrub vending machine. Scanning my badge, I input my size, and a fresh pair of scrubs appears. On my way to the locker room, my manager steps out in front of me.

"Hey, Peter!" I greet him, attempting to be friendly because I know Jackie has probably already recommended my write-up.

"Stacy, I need you to follow me. We have a meeting with Linda." The disappointment in his voice is heavy.

My shoulders drop at the mention of Linda, our HR director. I'm getting written up for this bullshit.

"Come on! All I did was give a very hungry woman some food."

"Stacy, please."

Peter turns on his heel and heads toward the admin offices. I rush after him, trying to keep up with his long stride. I can't get written up again. Pretty soon they are going to fire me, and then what? Just the thought of trying to pay our bills without my income makes my heart erratic.

I can fix this. I can say life has been stressful, and I allowed my personal life to bleed into my professional life, but I will be better. I'll follow hospital policy, take orders, and ask for help. I can fix this.

When we reach the office, Linda and someone from legal—whose name I can't remember—are waiting for me. The presence of legal raises the hairs on my arms.

Linda's office is meticulously organized with neutral beige walls adorned with framed certificates and tidy stacks of papers. The overzealous air conditioning leaves my already sweaty skin feeling clammy.

"Have a seat," Linda says. She sits up straight, although it doesn't help her. She is a petite woman with small round features. If I didn't know better, I would think she is harmless.

I sit, keeping every muscle in my body tense, ready to run at any moment.

"Thank you for meeting with us."

I nod curtly.

Linda folds her hands together and breathes in deeply. "There isn't an easy way to say this, so I will just start. We recently instituted an alert that sounds when the chart for a non-admitted patient is accessed. Two days ago, you accessed your own medical file, which on its own violates HIPPA."

"Let me explain," I rush, but then I realize what she said doesn't match my expectations for this conversation. I stop and wait for her to finish.

"Since then, we have conducted an investigation. Thus far, we have detailed records showing each time you scanned your badge, including the exact locations and timestamps over the last year. These logs match up with camera footage and activities recorded in the EMR. It's evident you accessed your own medical record, entered a diagnosis of endometriosis, and prescribed and refilled medication for yourself using Dr. Kilpatrick's credentials. We have cross-referenced all these activities, and the evidence is clear."

My eyes bulge, and a rock lodges itself in my throat. My head swims with all the potential reasons, rationales, and excuses I could make. As the woman before me talks, I try to come up with something, but my thoughts are chaotic, bouncing off each other and back.

This is bad.

My phone goes off in my pocket, and I try to ignore it, but it only adds to the noise and increases my panic. I pull it out to check who is calling. Garrett's name flashes across my screen. My mind immediately shifts to Imogene. Is she okay? Did something else happen at school? They would have called me, though. Right? Imogene can't call me. She doesn't have a phone. My hands shake.

"Stacy, please silence your phone. We'd like to get through this conversation."

I want to object, but I listen and put it on Do Not Disturb before slipping it back into my pocket. "Sorry," I mutter.

"Thank you. Do you understand the implications of your actions?"

I stare blankly as I try to decide how to respond. *Think. Think. Fuck.* There is no excuse that could save me. *Think. Deny.*

"I never used Dr. Kilpatrick's credentials. I only ever helped him when he struggled to navigate the EMR. That's all," I finally say.

I'm met by three tight faces. They don't believe me. I focus on breathing through my nose and out of my mouth.

"You're saying someone else did this? That they went into your medical record, gave you a diagnosis, and prescribed medication?"

"What other explanation is there? I would never," I lie.

"It's come to our attention that you have a son."

"Daughter," I correct.

"Yes, my apologies. A trans daughter who is an adolescent. The drug prescribed was leuprolide, which is often used as a hormone blocker."

My breath catches in my throat as my mind drifts back to the day Imogene asked for hormone blockers. The desperation on her face. I wanted to play by the rules to get her the care she needed, but it was so much harder than it should be. I felt terrible when I used my relationship with Dr. Kilpatrick to get her medication, but I didn't know what else to do. I feel like a trapped animal, but I force myself to calm down, exhaling a long and steady breath.

"So?" I say, staying off the truth.

"Stacy, please don't insult our intelligence."

Peter speaks up. "Stacy, lying won't help you. There's no point."

Denying isn't going to work. They have me backed into a corner. I need to get them to see my humanity. The wall I've built to protect the truth falls, and with it, a flood of tears spills.

"You have to understand, Imogene is my whole world," I plead, my voice breaking. "I would do anything for her. She just needed a little time. That's all. Please understand. I felt like I had no other choice."

My breath hitches as I search their faces, hoping for a flicker of empathy, some sign that they understand. But all of their faces remain stony.

"You did have a choice, and you chose to take advantage of your position to commit fraud. Even more, the hospital doesn't condone treating a minor without the oversight of a licensed physician. It's dangerous and unethical. Because of the choices you have made, we are suspending you without pay, immediately. We have reported your misuse to the Florida Board of Nursing and to the police."

For the second time this week, the room tilts. Linda's words echo in my head. I can barely breathe now. I was doing what was best for Imogene, but everything is falling apart.

"The police?" My heart pounds in my chest, but the question is a whisper.

"Stacy, what you have done is fraudulent. I'm sure an officer will be in touch soon."

I swallow hard, but my mouth is dry. Fraud? The police? I blink, trying to force my brain to catch up, but nothing makes sense. What am I supposed to do?

My job, my license, my life—it's all gone, just like that.

CHAPTER 12

THE LAKE HOUSE

Stacy

Sarasota Lake is nestled in the heart of Sarasota, Florida, reflecting the vibrant hues of the surrounding area and the blue sky above.

As I approach the lake, I reach into my pocket for my phone to call Garrett back but then change my mind.

I can't face him. My pride won't let me. Instead, I toss the phone onto the passenger seat, anger bubbling just below the surface.

I pull into a parking space and shut off the engine, staring out over the water. I come here anytime I feel lost. The water is where I feel closest to my mom. Maybe being here now will calm my anxiety and bring some clarity.

Before Mom died and we moved to the States, Mom liked to sit by Okanagan Lake. She would say, "Water is the source of all good things." My mother was so . . . positive? Uplifting? I try to think of the perfect word to describe her.

The water is quite beautiful today. Ripples of soft waves glimmer in the sun. It comes to me. The word I was looking for. Buoyant. My mom was buoyant.

"Mom, I don't know what to do," I say aloud, looking toward the sky. "We could run away. I could take Imogene, stay with Aunt Marge, maybe convince Garrett to come, and we could figure out how to make it back home." Aunt Marge is the only family I have, though I barely know her.

I want to be closer to Mom, so I leave the car to sit on the damp ground. The sun intensifies the deep, earthy scent of decaying leaves and grass mixed with the salty aroma of the nearby ocean. I breathe it all in through my nose and out of my mouth.

But what would going to Canada really solve? Maybe it would just give us some time, a little space to breathe.

Right now, everything feels too imminent—arrest, job loss, the financial and legal chaos we're drowning in. If I could get some distance from the storm that's coming, maybe I could figure out a way to fix things. In Canada, I wouldn't have to worry about the police showing up at my doorstep right away. Extradition would catch up with me eventually, but not right away. I could think. Clear my head. Even if it's only temporary, maybe that's enough.

For Imogene, it could mean the difference between getting the care she needs or losing it entirely. I just gave her a six-month injection of leuprolide, so she's okay for now, but our time will run out. Everything I've risked can't be for nothing. She deserves proper care, not this constant, dangerous balancing act.

I reach into my pocket, thinking about checking how long extradition might take, wondering if that's even something I could find out. But my phone's still in the car. I'll look it up later.

My father's face floats to the forefront of my mind, and I feel a pang of guilt.

"I know, Mom. I promised I would take care of him." I bite my lip, considering my options. "I won't leave, but gosh, I wish I could."

The longer I sit, the more aware I become of the ache in my hips, but I don't get up. Instead, I'm beholden to the water and remember when it almost took Imogene from me.

Imogene was only four and a shy and meek child. Still, when surrounded by trees and water, she moved with an untamed spirit, weaving through the aspens framing the lake house we rented in the Colorado mountains, just a few hours from home. The property owners had a large telescope setup on the front porch. In the late evening hours when darkness finally had fallen, Imogene would stand at the scope, a single eye glued to the lens.

"It's a sar! It's a lot of sars!" she'd repeat. The "t" missing from her speech amplified the charm of the genuine awe in her voice.

On the last full day of our trip, Garrett and I sat in wicker chairs and ate breakfast. Garrett cradled his plate, heaping a generous portion of scrambled eggs and potatoes before guiding them past his lips. "Thanks, babe. This is good," he said, albeit clumsily, through a mouthful.

Oblivious to the world around her, Imogene used a stick to draw lines in the soft dirt outside the edge of the grassy patch of land, her little sun hat casting a shadow over her dirt-smudged face.

"I think we'll go fishing today," Garrett said.

"Charlie would like that," I agreed and filled my nostrils with the crisp morning air.

He turned to me with a hopeful look. "You coming?"

"Not today. I was thinking of taking the day to read a bit. It's been, what, four years since I could just sit and read?"

"Is that a long time?" he asked, cracking a smile.

"Sure is." I smiled at the easy banter.

When we finished breakfast, I rose to clean the kitchen while Garrett continued watching Imogene.

I still remember feeling the hot, soapy washcloth in my hand when I heard a child's cry. Instinctively, my heart skipped a beat. It was an unfamiliar, intermittent wail. I abandoned the dishes and hurried into the living room with big bay windows overlooking the porch and lake. I found nothing but the empty space where Garrett and Imogene should have been. A wave of panic washed over me. I raced through the front door, my eyes darting left and right, searching for any sign of them. The crying had stopped, and the quiet was unnerving. The world seemed to be holding its breath.

Then, a gasp for air, a cry from the lake. My gaze snapped to the water, where a ripple signified where my child was.

I ran, and although the distance was short, I couldn't get there fast enough. My voice tore through the air. *"Help!"*

The icy lake water resisted my frantic pace as I waded toward the ripple signaling where Imogene had vanished. Garrett's voice, laced with confusion and alarm, cut through the chaos. "Stacy! What are you doing? Where's Charlie?"

Then a small head broke through the water's surface, and Garrett's questions ceased.

When I got to Imogene, I scooped her from the lake's grasp and went to the shore. She slumped against me, and my heart pounded in response. I needed to get the water out of her lungs. Suddenly, Garrett was beside us, and he took Imogene from me. His pace outmatched mine, swiftly carrying our child to the bank.

I followed, and as Garrett reached the dirt along the shore's edge, he gently laid Imogene's little body on the ground and started rescue maneuvers. When I reached his side, I took over. Working as fast as possible, I tempered my movements, cognizant of Imogene's slight form.

The moment Imogene coughed, releasing the water threatening her, relief flooded me, immense and unyielding. I enveloped her in my arms, and as the terror and adrenaline subsided, I realized what had happened and how it could have ended. Tears streamed down my face.

Garrett moved to comfort me, but a rising tide of anger eclipsed my relief. I lashed out at him. "How could you let this happen?" The words were out before I could stop them. "Where were you?"

His brows knitted together, and his mouth opened and closed as he tried to figure out how to respond. Then he said, "I just went to unload the fishing equipment. I was literally gone for three minutes."

"And you didn't think to tell me or take Charlie with you?" The incredulity in my voice was sharp.

"It was only going to be a minute. I didn't think . . ." His voice trailed off.

"That is the problem, Garrett. You never think." I turned away from him and held Imogene closer to my chest just before she began crying.

I never stopped hearing her cries that day. Even now, sitting by this lake, I realize it's a wound that never healed. And I can't let it happen again. I won't lose her, not to this place, not to anyone.

Once again, looking out over Sarasota Lake, that familiar feeling of fear over losing my child settles in my stomach. I have to close my eyes to ward off the nausea.

Hours later, still consumed by my thoughts, I pull into the driveway and step out of the car. While walking up to my house, I grab my phone and bring the screen to life, only to see thirty-four missed calls from Garrett and twelve text messages. It takes a moment for me to wrap my head around the volume, but before I can, a car door slams. I turn to see a woman walking toward me. I was so consumed by my thoughts I didn't notice the white SUV parked along the sidewalk.

"Hello? Mrs. Barnett? My name is Lilly Dixon. Can I have a moment of your time?"

CHAPTER 13

GONE GIRLS

Garrett

"What were you thinking?" I ask, my voice tight.

Stacy leans forward in the oversized upholstered chair in our living room. Her elbows rest on her knees, pressing her fingers into the skin above her brow. I can't wrap my head around just how reckless my wife has been. She made decisions about our child's medical care without me. She risked everything. Her lies hurt more than anything else. We used to tell each other everything, and she kept this from me.

"You don't understand. Imogene just needs a little more time." she pleads.

"Stacy, do you get it? You're going to lose your job and your nursing license. DCFS is investigating. You might go to prison." I struggle to keep the volume of my voice in check.

Stacy's hands fly away from her face as she speaks. "I know, but what else would you have had me do?"

"Not lie to me. Let me be a part of the solution."

She scoffs. "Oh, that's rich. You, a part of the solution."

"Dammit, Stacy!" I yell. She always does this, turns everything around on me. I didn't do any of this. I just want us to be a team like we used to be. I don't want to be the villain in her story.

She sits back, startled by my outburst, and I remind myself to rein it in. I can't stop thinking about this morning when Lilly Dixon, an investigator with the Department of Child and Family Services, walked into my shop. At first, I thought she was there to place an order. She looked so unsuspecting.

"Stacy, I'm really trying here. You have no concept of what it was like to be blindsided. I was in the middle of working when that woman came in to question me about whether we were shooting up our kid with drugs."

Stacy's eyes widen. "What did you tell her?" That's her biggest concern, of course. What I told the investigator. She has probably already convinced herself I said the wrong thing.

"I told her I didn't know what she was talking about."

She sits back and lets out a breath. "Did she believe you?"

"Probably because, unlike you, I wasn't lying."

"I lied to protect our child. I can't be complacent like you, Garrett."

"Complacent?" The accusation sends heat crawling up my neck.

"Yes, complacent. You have never cared about Imogene's well-being the way I have. All you care about is yourself."

She's nuts. She has lost it. My fingers twitch, and I press my lips together until I can feel my teeth about to cut into the inside of my mouth. I want to shake her, shake the crazy out of her, and because of that feeling alone, I know I have to end this conversation before I do something I'll regret.

A slight tremor in my jaw grows as I say, "I can't do this anymore. I can't be the villain in your made-up story. You're fucking crazy."

"Mom? Dad?" Imogene stands in the threshold between the kitchen and the living room, wide-eyed.

My jaw loosens as I realize she just heard me call her mom crazy. I try to save face, but before I can, the doorbell rings, followed by a loud knock.

All three of our heads turn toward the door. The seconds pass, and not one of us makes a move. One, two, three, four . . . another knock . . . five, six, seven . . . the chime sounds again. On the second doorbell ring, I bite my lip and stand.

Imogene and Stacy freeze as I open the door and see Lilly Dixon.

"Hello, Mr. Barnett," Lilly says. Her voice wavers and her eyes peer past me into the house in search of something.

"Can I help you?" I ask. She is just as unassuming as when she entered my shop this morning, and I nearly forget she's the threat.

"Is your wife available to talk?" She clutches her purse, hugging it to her side as if she is worried about being mugged in this quiet suburban neighborhood.

"What is this about?" I use the full size of my body to block the doorway, unwilling to allow her the license to look into my home without a good reason.

She recognizes my defensive stance and holds up a hand. "I'm only here to warn you. My supervisor is pushing for emergency removal. Based on our investigation, they feel there is a case of medical neglect and emotional abuse."

A chill creeps up my spine and takes hold of my lungs, making it hard to breathe. I try to process what she's saying, but it's too much. The instinct to protect my family flares, and all I want to do is tell her to leave us alone. I also want to pretend like none of this is happening. I want to ignore the problem, but I can't. However, I don't know if I can trust her. I don't know what to believe.

I stare at her for a long moment, measuring her with my eyes. Despite her shallow breath, her eyes are steady. If we're going to survive this, we can't afford to turn away help. I need to hear what she knows.

"Come in," I tell her, opening the door and stepping back.

Stacy comes into the entryway, and Imogene follows on her heels.

"Why are you here?" Stacy asks.

"To warn you," Lilly holds up a hand again to communicate she is an ally.

Stacy turns to Imogene. "I need you to go to your room."

Imogene shakes her head. "No, if it's about me, I'm staying."

"Imogene, I asked you to—"

I cut Stacy off. "She's right. Let her stay."

I'm tired of Stacy calling the shots. Imogene is fourteen, and it's time I stop letting Stacy coddle her. Imogene is smart, but she needs to face the harsh realities of life. If she doesn't start now, she'll be unprepared for the day she's no longer a child.

"You sure?" Lilly asks, her eyes sympathetic as she takes in our family dynamic, and I nod. Stacy's lips form a thin line, but she doesn't argue.

"Okay." Lilly takes a deep breath, letting it out through the small "O" of her mouth. "If anyone finds out I did this, I'm good as fired. I've tried to advocate for your family, but my supervisor feels it is best we remove Imogene from the home. I have orders to do so tomorrow if the judge grants it."

"What?" Stacy gasps, her face reflecting the horror I feel in my gut. I teeter between anger at Stacy because this is her fault and undeniable helplessness because I don't know what to do. How do you even fix a mess as catastrophic as this one?

"I'm sorry," Lilly offers.

"Why are you telling us this?" I ask. My question holds an undercurrent of skepticism. If she could be fired for this, why is she doing it?

"Because I don't agree with this decision. My job is to ensure the well-being of children, and in my opinion, this decision doesn't do that. But my hands are tied. I thought the least I could do was give you a head start on finding an attorney. Maybe even have a family member lined up for kinship care?"

"So tomorrow?" Stacy asks.

"Most likely. We are just waiting on the judge, but yeah." Lilly's eyes drift to her feet before returning a pained look to us. "I better go. I shouldn't be here, but I wanted to let you know."

She turns on her heels and hurries to an SUV parked on the street. I want to call her back to ask her more. I want to ask for advice. How do we navigate this? What can we do to prevent it from happening? But I realize she laid out our options.

We need to find an attorney and arrange for kinship care. The problem is, we don't have any family nearby to arrange care with. Maybe there's something else we can do? I spend too long stuck in my thoughts, and by the time I finally find my voice again, Lilly is gone.

Imogene interrupts my trance.

"Remove me?"

I turn to stare at Imogene. She is going to have to grow up quick, so I don't see a point in trying to soften the blow. "Yeah, DCFS will take you to live somewhere else tomorrow." My voice is calm and measured despite the storm brewing inside my chest.

"Garrett!" Stacy yells, her eyes bulging.

"What? She was right here. She heard the investigator. What good is lying going to do?"

"And this is how I know you don't care."

I do care, but I'll never convince Stacy of that. I messed up all those years ago when Imogene almost drowned. Stacy doesn't say it—not anymore, at least—but I know she doesn't trust me when it comes to parenting because of that day. I've beaten myself up for my negligence. It was a mistake, and I just wish she would give me a second chance. She never will, though. She's so damn convinced she's the only one who can care for Imogene.

"Believe what you want." I walk away before I blow up.

In the kitchen, I grab a glass from the cabinet and pour myself a healthy helping of whiskey. As the alcohol hits my lips, I welcome the burn and anticipate the forthcoming slow, pervasive warmth. I firmly massage my forehead and try to calm the sense of doom that lingers after Lilly's warning.

Stacy has single-handedly ruined our family because she can't stand not being in control. I can't trust her and knowing that feels like a hydraulic press crushing my heart. I tilt my head back to stare at the ceiling, trying to come to terms with everything I know to be true. I'm so angry with her, but I also love her. Love and anger are such intense emotions, and I don't have the capacity for both at the same time, so I swing between the two. It's exhausting and leaves me depleted. I want us to be okay, to be a team, but is that even possible at this point?

It has to be. I don't know if I can navigate this without her.

That night I sleep in the guest bedroom. I toss and turn, unable to quiet my worries. Despite my terrible sleep, I'm disorientated when I wake up. The edges of sleep cloud my memory as I walk downstairs into our living room. I expect to see Stacy, but she isn't there. In the kitchen, I start a pot of coffee and put my whiskey glass from the night before in the dishwasher.

I step back into the living room and peer out the window. The morning condensation blurs my view, but I can make out just enough. Stacy's car isn't in the driveway. My heart quickens as the night before comes into full focus.

My bare feet pound against the hardwood as I climb the stairs to Imogene's room. I fling the door open with such force that, for a glimmer of a moment, I think I will see her in bed, but no.

Her backpack is not hanging on its hook next to her closet, and her laptop is missing from her desk. I run to our bedroom, and when I lunge through the doorway, I see the bed is made and Stacy is gone.

Although I know the truth, my mind won't accept it. I sprint back downstairs, calling for them.

"Stacy! Imogene! *Stacccyyyy!*"

The only sound that returns is the echo of my own frantic words. I run out the front door and stand on the edge of our driveway in my boxer shorts. Realization slams into me.

They're gone.

CHAPTER 14

WHO IS AMBER HAGERMAN?

As dawn breaks, I admire the soft features on Imogene's sleeping face. We were in the car for less than an hour before the engine's hum lulled her to sleep. The landscape of east Florida passes by with the occasional palm tree silhouetted against the softening sky.

The adrenaline from Lilly's warning and Garrett's response has nearly worn off. I fight to keep my eyes open despite the increasing light of day. Rolling down the window, the fresh air wakes me up for only a moment before I feel sleep's pull again. My phone vibrates in my pocket, and I can only assume it's Garrett, who has probably realized we are gone by now.

Shame and regret mix with my assurance that this was the only choice I could have made. I push the feelings away, not allowing myself to dwell on them. When the phone ceases to vibrate, I let out a rush of air, a false relief, as if I had entirely avoided the conversation. But I know I can't avoid him forever. I'll call him back when I have some privacy.

The second time my phone rings, I grab it from the cup holder and hit the end button before powering it down. He'll have to wait. I know he's going to be pissed. I can't blame him, but I'm not turning around.

We continue to drive, the pale morning light casting long shadows across the empty highway. I pull on my sunglasses and go through the events of the last several days. Circular reasoning. I go round and round in my thoughts, questioning what I could have done differently to prevent this and landing on nothing each time. There was nothing I could have done.

"Mom?" Imogene's voice pulls me from my spiraling thoughts. I peek over at her. She rubs her eyes and looks out to see where we are.

"What's up?" I ask.

"I have to pee," she tells me. I scan our surroundings, but I'm not entirely sure where the nearest restroom is, so I power on my phone and, keeping one eye on the road, quickly use the maps app to find the closest rest stop. At least with Imogene in the bathroom, I can call Garrett back.

About ten minutes later, we pull into a mostly empty rest area. A camper, which belongs to a family with four small children, is the only vehicle in the lot. Imogene gets out of the car and heads inside. I watch her stand before the doors, trying to decide which restroom to use and finally deciding it is safe to use the women's restroom. If only other people like me, cis people, understood the mental energy we never have to exert when faced with such choices. "Cis" once was a new term for me. It means identifying with the gender assigned at birth.

I watch the mom of the family across the lot use a wet wipe to clean a child's face as I hover over Garrett's name in my phone's call log. I remember those days when life seemed simple. It was all a hoax. There's nothing simple about life.

Inhaling a deep breath, I tap the screen to call Garrett. It doesn't finish ringing once before he picks up.

"Where the fuck are you going?" he screams into the phone.

"Garrett, calm down."

"Answer the question, Stacy. Where are you taking my daughter?"

"Our daughter," I correct, but I know my correction is meant to distract him. I glance toward the rest stop building again to make sure Imogene is still inside.

"I'm not playing games. Tell me."

"We'll be back. I promise. Can you please take care of my dad until then?"

"You shouldn't have done this."

"I shouldn't have done this? You and everyone else gave me no choice."

"You had a choice, and you chose wrong. You can't just leave. Where are you going? Don't make me ask again!" My free hand taps on the steering wheel.

"You know, I had full intentions of telling you where we are going, but with how you are acting, I don't think I should." I don't know if that is entirely true, but I say it anyway.

"You took my kid!"

She is my kid, too. My circular thoughts from before spin again, and I reach for the only thing I know for sure. "I'm saving our child!"

My voice rises and echoes in the confines of the car. I press my lips together, trying to regain control.

"Are you sure that's why you're doing this? Is it for Imogene, or is it because you don't want to end up in prison for the shit you did?"

Garrett's question hits like a punch to the gut, forcing the air out of me, which is quickly replaced by a reality I've yet to address. Of course I don't want to go to prison. But I'm not doing this for selfish reasons. My motivation lies in protecting our daughter, which I can't do if she's in a group home and I'm behind bars.

The silence on my end stretches too long. Garrett screams into the phone, his voice raw with frustration. "I want you to come back home right now! Come back home right now!"

I swallow hard. I can't reason with him.

"I can't talk to you when you're like this. Call me back when you calm down." I end the call and let out a shaky breath. My fingers tingle and I ball my fists to stop the oncoming tremors. I try to pull apart the tangle of emotions within me, which include pride, anger, fear, protectiveness over Imogene, and an overwhelming urge to run.

Imogene emerges from the rest stop, and my phone vibrates in my hand again before I can process what emotions are driving me forward.

My eyes dart back and forth across the area of the rest stop. I don't know what to do. I want to avoid Garrett, but he is the one who avoids things. I can't. I hop out of the car and walk toward Imogene. "Hey, I got to go, too. Just sit in the car for a minute."

Inside a bathroom stall, I answer my phone before it has the chance to stop vibrating.

"Hello?"

"Stacy, I'm begging you. Just come back. We can figure this out together." His anger has turned to desperation. I don't trust it.

"You know why I can't do that."

I study the graffiti inside the humidity-stained walls of the stall. *Kimmie was here*, and *J.B. and S.Q. forever* are emboldened in black permanent marker. Little white spots decorate the pen strokes due to the brick's uneven surface.

"Please, Stacy," he begs.

"You may hate me right now, but I know you still love Dad. Please take care of him. I'm going to fix this, you'll see."

"Just tell me where you are going." Garrett's voice is sad and soft. It pushes my wall down, if only for a moment. His desperation tugs at me, but it's not enough for me to tell him the truth. So I lie.

"Melissa's house, but I promise we are just going long enough to make a plan. Okay? I just want to get Imogene to safety. Once I do, we can figure out a way to fix this."

Melissa, my best friend and old roommate, lives just outside of Utica, New York, so if Garrett checks my location, for now, it will appear that's where we're headed. I haven't told Melissa about this plan, but I won't need to. She is my friend more than Garrett's, and he won't feel comfortable calling her. I'm banking on his inaction more than anything else. But I can't bank on it enough to tell him the truth. If he knew what I was actually planning, he'd try to stop me.

Garrett's frustration comes out in the static of his heavy breath.

"Two weeks." His words come out clipped and authoritative.

"What do you mean?"

"You have two weeks to figure your shit out. I'll come up with an excuse for why you're gone and keep DCFS and the police off your back. But two weeks—that's all I'm willing to give. If you don't return by then, I'll report you for kidnapping, and we'll do things my way."

His threat annoys me.

"Please." I roll my eyes, although he can't see that.

"You know what? Fuck you, Stacy. I was trying to be nice but fuck you! I'm calling the cops, and I'm coming for my kid. Mark my words, Stacy. You'll be sorry you did this," he screams into the receiver and hangs up.

When I lower the phone, my hands shake so violently, I drop my phone on the tile floor. Would he call the cops? What did he mean when he said I'll be sorry? I try to convince myself that Garrett isn't going to do anything. Taking the initiative has never been his strength, but what if I'm wrong? What if I'm underestimating him this time?

My jaw clenches as I try to sort out all the information. He gave me two weeks, which is more than I need to cross the border. But what if I don't even have a single day now? I can't be certain.

I bend to pick up my phone, and when I stand, I take a deep breath. My fingers fly over the screen as I rush to turn off location sharing. Thank God Imogene's phone is broken because he can't track her either. Next, I hover over Garrett's contact, thinking and then, without allowing myself to think much more about it, I block Garrett's number. It's only temporary. We just have to get to Canada, and once we do, we will be safe, and I can figure this all out then.

In Canada, I plan to go to my Aunt Marge's house. She and my mom were never close, there was too much of an age gap between them. Also, I've only met her once, at Mom's funeral.

This morning, before we left, I found Aunt Marge's number online. I almost called. Almost. But I didn't know what to say or how to explain our situation. I also worried that she may say no to taking us in. So instead, we're just going. If she turns us away, I'll figure something else out.

I get back in the car, forcing a smile for Imogene. "All set?"

She nods, and I start the engine.

"There's a cooler full of food in the back if you get hungry," I tell her.

I wait for her to grab a muffin and a banana.

Once she is back in her seat and buckled, I pull back onto the highway. I occasionally glance at Imogene through the corner of my eye, and I can't help but wonder if she truly understands the lengths I will go to protect her. I will do whatever it takes.

As we drive, I try to rid myself of the sound of Garrett's anger, but I can't. He has never quite understood the way I need him to understand.

Imogene never got the chance to come out to her dad because I did it for her. She wanted to do it herself, but it was important that I was a buffer. And based on how he reacted, I'm glad I stepped in. That's the part no one seems to understand. Garrett thinks I'm controlling, that I'm a helicopter parent, but more often than not, I'm right. I knew how he would respond. What I had hoped for was that it wouldn't take him so long to stop misgendering her and calling her Charlie.

My thoughts shift to the day we chose the name Charlie—the name that came before everything. That day, my baby kicked within my womb, and the skin of my stomach stretched outward in this weird alien-isk monster manner.

Garrett laid in bed beside me, his head propped up on his hand, watching and mesmerized by the child inside me. We tossed around baby names. Each name flew into the air and hung there as we analyzed it.

"Jordan," Garrett suggested. The imagined string of letters spelling the name hovered for only a moment, a sign that it was not right for us.

"Malakie," I countered, and Garrett shook his head, destroying the ethereal word.

"Hmm," I said in thought. Who knew it would be so difficult to come up with a name for your child? "How about Preston?"

"Preston is a douchebag's name."

I laughed. "No, it isn't. I went to school with a boy named Preston. He was sweet."

"Sweet? So, we're naming our child after an ex-boyfriend?"

"You are insane. I went to school with him. I didn't date him."

A smile twitched on his lips, and I knew he was only giving me a hard time.

"Still sounds like a douchebag."

"How?"

"What was his last name?" Garrett asked.

"Prescott," I said.

"Preston Prescott. *That's terrible!* Why would his parents do that to him? Did they want him to grow up with a superiority complex? He probably grew up to be an avid golfer who sells real estate and frequents strip clubs."

"Fine. Come up with a better name."

"I can't," he said.

"You can't?" I asked incredulously.

He shook his head. "It is way too hard sitting here next to you to concentrate on baby names when all I can think about is recreating the moment we made this baby."

"What are you talking about?" I asked, looking down at myself dressed in a stained sports bra and cotton shorts. A bowl of chocolate ice cream sat atop my large belly. I went to take a bite at the same time Garrett nuzzled into my neck. The sudden attack caused me to drop the spoon, and the sticky chocolate dessert landed on my bare stomach.

"Look what you made me do!"

He gave me a smoldering look, picked the spoon off my stomach, and took the half-finished bowl out of my hand. He rolled behind him to put the bowl and spoon on the nightstand and greeted me with hungry eyes.

I reached over to grab a tissue to clean up the melting ice cream, but he said, "May I?"

When he kissed the ice cream away, I grabbed the collar of his T-shirt and brought his lips to mine. They were cold and sweet.

"I love you," he whispered between kisses.

"I love you more," I said.

He pulled back, and his eyes narrowed in on my face. "Take it back."

"No! I'm not taking it back."

"Take it back!"

"But why?"

"Because loving me more is impossible, and therefore, it is a lie. We don't lie to each other."

"Fine. I take it back," I said with a smile.

Garrett pulled me close and pressed his lips into my hair. "How about Charlie? After your dad? But instead of Charles, it will just be Charlie."

I looked up at him. "Really?"

"Yeah. I like that name."

The memory is bittersweet. The name we chose reminds me of my dad and those tender moments with Garrett. But that name also hurts my child deeply, and therefore, hearing another person use it hurts me.

Another couple of hours into our drive, I start drifting again. I close my eyes tightly and force them open, fighting the sleep that wants to overtake my body. I take a deep breath to help carry oxygen to my brain.

I am so damn tired.

Then I jump. A piercing, urgent siren blares through the car speakers.

Imogene puts her hands on her ears, and I swerve a bit. A car next to me honks its horn in response. I hit the button on the stereo to silence the noise, but it continues, just quieter, from my phone. I glance at the screen—an Amber Alert. Garrett called the cops. My vision is clouded by disbelief.

He called the cops on me.

I glance between the road ahead and the phone, trying to wrap my head around our circumstances when I realize . . .

The alert was for someone else. None of the information on the alert belongs to me.

My shoulders slump, the tension freeing from them. He didn't report me, but he could. I didn't think he was capable of it, but what if I'm wrong? The next Amber Alert could be about us. It will be my daughter's name, the make and model of my car. My plates would be on display for the whole world to see. And then what? A high-speed chase? An arrest for kidnapping my own child? Losing Imogene forever? And then this—all of this would be for nothing. We can't keep going in this car. It's too dangerous.

Imogene breaks me out of my train of thought. "That was terrible," she says, referring to the sound. "Couldn't they make that sound a little less intrusive? Also, why is it called an Amber Alert?"

"Because of Amber Hagerman," I tell her. However, I'm still considering the possibility Garrett could call the cops. Maybe I'm being paranoid, but what if I'm not?

"Was she kidnapped?"

"Yeah. Hey, I think we need a new car."

"Why? Wait. Do you think DCFS will put out an Amber Alert for me?"

"They might." I don't want to tell her I'm more worried about what her father may do. I scan the road for an exit and spot one just a quarter of a mile away.

Imogene sits straighter in the passenger seat, staring at me expectantly, but I don't explain further.

As soon as we take the exit, I locate a shopping center and quickly maneuver into the parking lot. I drive around until I stop behind the building near the large garage doors meant for freight deliveries.

"Mom, maybe we should go back."

"Not now." I put my hand up to stop her worry. "Let me think."

Imogene sinks in her seat, visibly perturbed.

We need another car. I could try to steal one. In the movies, they take wires and tap them together and the car starts. But if I steal a car, and I get caught, I'll go to prison for prescription fraud, kidnapping, and grand theft auto.

I scan the area, trying to determine where we are. Still, the surroundings don't offer an immediate answer, and my desperation heightens. I fumble for my phone. The tremors take over, and I drop the phone into the crack between my seat and the center console.

"Shit!" I yell.

"Mom, calm down," Imogene says, and I realize I'm scaring her, which makes sense because I'm currently living in a state of terror myself.

I take a deep breath and force myself to meet her eyes. "I'm sorry. The alert just startled me, that's all."

But even as I apologize, my hands won't stop shaking as I bend to retrieve the phone. When I have it again, I analyze the maps app. We are in Jacksonville.

The city's name is familiar. *Jacksonville.* I repeat it to myself, trying to remember why it feels so significant. My chaotic thoughts finally settle. I know what I need to do.

I go to my contacts list, scrolling through contacts before I find the one I'm looking for. I tap the screen to dial. It rings twice before connecting.

"Hello?" a man answers.

CHAPTER 15

MOURNING CRASHERS

Stacy

We pull into a quaint residential area where cars line both sides of the street. I peer out my window, searching for the house number Ramon gave me. As I scan the houses, I realize one is bustling with activity. Cars are bumper to bumper in the driveway and along the curb. People sit on the porch, plates of food in their hands.

Did he have us come to a party? It's barely mid-day. I glance at Imogene, and we exchange confused looks. I have to circle the block to find a parking spot, which ends up being two blocks away. Putting the car into park, I turn to Imogene.

"Stay here," I tell her.

"But, Mom—"

"I'll only be gone a minute. I'll be right back," I say as I leave the vehicle.

As I approach the house, I expect someone to ask why I'm there, but the people on the porch are engrossed in a conversation in Spanish.

"Hi, I'm looking for Ramon."

"You his girlfriend?" one woman asks.

I flush. "No. Just a friend. He told me to meet him here." I don't think I even qualify as a friend. In fact, Ramon and I are strangers, but to say so would be weird.

The woman gets up and goes to the door. "Ramon, your girlfriend is here!"

Flushing again, I stand awkwardly as they assess me, occasionally glancing down the street to where my car is parked. Imogene is out of sight from this vantage point, which unsettles me. An impulse to tap my foot on the wooden porch grows, but I suppress it, recognizing it would be rude. Instead, I let my nervous energy simmer, consuming my thoughts.

A sense of relief washes over me when Ramon comes out of the house. I'll be back with Imogene in just a moment.

"Stacy," he greets, waiting for me to explain my presence. On the phone, I provided no details, only mentioned it was urgent. I wonder if this is a mistake, but I don't know what else to do.

"Is there somewhere we can go to talk?" I ask. My hands are shaking, so I shove them in my pockets to disguise it.

One woman whoops. "Talk? You know what that means. And the day after Mami's funeral." She shakes her head dramatically.

My face blanches. How could I be so stupid? I knew why he was in Jacksonville, but I was so consumed by my fear that I didn't put the pieces together. I now realize that all the people I thought to be partygoers are mourners. I've never wished I could disappear from existence more than I wish it in this moment, but it's too late. I'm here.

"Bianca, please." Ramon rolls his eyes and ushers me inside.

We navigate the throng of people there to celebrate and grieve the life of Ramon's mom. He leads me to a bedroom on the left side of the house. As we walk, I realize I can't ask for his help. At least not now. I have to figure out a different plan.

The bedroom is neat, filled with old furniture, a beautiful handmade quilt, a rocking chair, and perfume bottles lining the dresser. It has the comforting scent of a well-lived, tidy life.

"I'm so sorry for interrupting your mom's funeral. I wasn't thinking," I blurt out.

He puts his hand up. "You're fine. The funeral was yesterday. We just have family in town, and this is what we do. We eat. When I said to call anytime, I meant it. What's going on?"

My heart stops as I try to find the words, and suddenly, I realize I'm on the verge of tears. I breathe in deeply and blink hard. Then, taking off my sunglasses, I make eye contact.

"DCFS has been investigating our family, and today, they were supposed to come to remove Imogene from our home."

His expression drops. "Oh, my God. Why?"

I suck in my bottom lip as I decide how much to tell him. But what does it matter? The secret is already out.

"I've been giving her hormone blockers. I thought I was doing what was best, but . . ." I shake my head, unable to finish the thought.

"And now they want to take her?" he asks, his tone a blend of empathetic and curious.

I cry, "I can't let them take Imogene, so I left this morning. We had plans to go to my aunt's house in Canada for a few weeks so that I can clear my head, and figure out a plan, but I need a new car. I can't drive mine."

"What's wrong with it?" he asks. He places a hand on my arm. I find the touch comforting.

"Nothing. I'm being paranoid. I just need to get us across the border, and I keep thinking: What if there isn't enough time? What if she's reported as kidnapped before I can get there? I just . . ." As I speak, I realize how crazy I sound. Garrett may have been right.

His eyes grow with concern. He lifts his hand from my arm, takes a deep breath, and looks around. My heart is pounding, and he must hear it in the silence. Then he brings his attention back to my face.

I open my mouth to explain further, but he cuts me off.

"It's okay. Don't explain." He takes in one more hesitant breath and says, "How can I help?"

At his offer to help, I remember just how wrong it is that I'm here. His mother just died, and here I am, crying about my problems when he has his own. I don't know what I'm doing anymore. I need a car, but gosh . . .

"This was a mistake. I was desperate, and I wasn't thinking. I should go." I turn away from him, but his fingers graze my wrist, bringing me back to face him.

His brows come together above his thick green frames. "Let me help, please."

I shake my head.

"What do you need?" He ducks his head, examining my face for answers.

"A car. I need to borrow a car." It pains me to tell him this. I really shouldn't be here.

"How much further is it to where you need to go?"

"It's about fifteen hours from here. We just need to get to Toronto, but I shouldn't have come here. I'm so sorry." I am sorry. This was stupid and inconsiderate.

He takes a shaky breath. "I'll take you."

I'm caught off guard, and a part of me wants to grab hold of the lifeline he's offering. But deep down, I know it's not fair to let him shoulder this burden. Inside, there's a fierce struggle between desire and consideration. I want to protect my daughter. I would burn entire cities to the ground for her. Yet, taking advantage of someone's kindness feels wrong, even though it hasn't stopped me before. I go back and forth, unable to decide. I have no idea which side of me will win.

"No, I don't need you to do that. I just need to find a car. I don't have a lot of money, but if I could, I don't know, borrow something?" I shake my head. I don't know what I was thinking coming here.

"The only car I have is my car."

"I understand." I go to pull away again.

"No, no. Let me think." He stands before me, his eyes searching the room for a solution.

The sounds of family talking and laughing, celebrating the life of Ramon's mother, seep through the bedroom door, and deepen the quiet between us.

Ramon shifts his gaze to my face. "I have the time to take you. I'm off this next week because I thought my family would need more from me, but honestly, there are enough of us that I think they'll be okay. I want to help you. Let me."

"Ramon, I couldn't ask you to do that. What if they report her as kidnapped? Then what? You're going to help me kidnap my daughter?"

He presses his lips together and studies my face. After a moment, he says, "If that is what you need, then yes."

I sit with his words for a minute.

"Do you understand how much you would be risking for us?"

Ramon exhales, his face softening. "I haven't always been a good person. I've done a lot of harm, and I promised myself a long time ago I would do whatever it took to make up for it. This is an opportunity for me to do just that. Is it stupid?" He swallows hard. "Very. But you need help, and I want to help you."

"Okay," I say with a bit of uncertainty.

"Where is Imogene?" he asks, his tone shift indicating he doesn't want to talk about the things he regrets any further. He only wants to focus on what he can do now.

"In my car. We are parked just down the street."

"All right. Give me ten minutes to say my goodbyes and grab my things. Go get Imogene. My car is parked on the west side of the street. It's a silver Impala." He reaches into his pocket and pulls out his keys. "Load everything inside, and I'll be right out. We should probably drop your car off somewhere. There's a parking lot often used by people selling vehicles. No one will think much of another car sitting there. I'll grab some paper and a Sharpie to make a sign."

Without thinking, I throw my arms around him. "Thank you. Thank you so much!"

He allows the hug, placing his hands on my sides, signaling that while he doesn't know me well enough to fully embrace it, he understands and accepts it. I pull away, tears wetting my cheeks. "I will figure out a way to repay you."

"Let's not worry about that now."

As I leave the house to head for my car, my sunglasses are back on my face to disguise my tears. As I walk down the street, I'm a little less worried now that we have a plan.

But when I get close enough to see into the car, Imogene is gone.

I run to the car, hoping my eyes deceive me, and fling the door open, looking inside and into the back seat. I whirl around, scanning the street, but she is nowhere to be seen. "Imogene!" I call out. I spin again. *"Imogene!"*

I run back to the house, unsure how Ramon will help me with this one. I don't wait on the porch this time, but rush past the people into the house. I weave through the crowd, searching for Ramon's face, but I can't find him. Finally, I enter the backyard, where a higher concentration of family and friends are gathered. Imogene sits with a plate in her hand, eating food with Ramon's family.

Relief floods through me before a surge of irritation appears. I march over to her, and she looks up, surprised to see me.

"Imogene," I say, trying to keep my voice steady, "you scared me."

"Mom! Have you ever had an empanada?" she asks with a smile, holding one out to me.

I stand still and blink as I take in Imogene and her surroundings. The people around her laugh.

"Eat more," an older woman encourages, plopping a pile of rice on Imogene's plate. "You're too skinny."

"You were supposed to stay in the car," I tell Imogene.

"I had to use the bathroom again, and I tried telling you before you left the car, but you wouldn't listen."

"And then what? You invited yourself to eat? We have plenty of food in the car." I place a hand on my hip.

"No . . ."

Before we can go back and forth any further, Ramon interrupts us. "Looks like my tia found you without a plate in your hand."

The woman who served the rice nods in agreement.

"We have to go, Imogene," I say, reaching to take her plate.

"Oh, no, no, no. Let the girl sit and eat. I'll get you a plate. You're too skinny, too." The woman ushers me to a chair.

Ramon presses his lips together to hold back a laugh, and I take a seat while his tia hands me a plate. I try to resist, but her reaction is severe, and I'm too afraid to say no.

"Tia, we have to go," Ramon says, but she gives him a look. He raises his hands in defense. "Okay. They'll eat, but then we need to go."

She gives an agreeable nod and leaves me with my plate.

"I think she may have been hungry," Ramon says, watching Imogene spoon a heaping forkful of rice and beans into her mouth. She's a teenager. She's always hungry.

CHAPTER 16

HEATSTROKE

Stacy

Empty food cartons, to-go coffee cups, and what appears to be random school papers litter the floorboards of Ramon's car. He gives me a nervous smile, clearly embarrassed about the state of the sedan, but I wave off his concern.

"Mine is usually worse," I say warmly. Imogene arches a brow at me, knowing my statement is far from the truth.

We had just dropped my car off in the parking lot Ramon suggested, and I sit with my bag in my lap as he puts the car into drive.

I reach for the AC dial on the dash, but before I can adjust it, Ramon admits, "No AC." He rolls the windows down to provide a bit of relief from the Florida heat. Temps are already climbing, but I tell myself it will be okay. As we ascend north, we'll find lower temperatures and the lack of air conditioning won't be a problem.

As we drive, I pick at my cuticle, unsure of what to say. I still struggle with the guilt of pulling Ramon away from his family. Imogene makes up for my awkward silence with constant chatter about space and science. She always comes alive when science is involved. Ramon, being a science teacher at her school, is happy to entertain her with conversation. A bead of sweat rolls down the side of my face, and perspiration sits atop Ramon's forehead.

"Did you know we have biological evidence that helps us understand why some people are transgender?" Ramon asks Imogene.

"You mean like chromosomes? I saw somewhere people can have an extra Y or X chromosome," Imogene replies.

I can't help but smile at the topic Ramon has chosen for our car ride.

"Yes, chromosomes can play a role, but there's more to it than that. Some studies suggest certain regions of the brain differ in size and structure between cisgender and transgender people in a way that corresponds to gender identity."

"Bet," Imogene says, expressing her approval. I laugh. *Bet*—Gen Z slang cracks me up. I look back at her with a smile, only to find she is unbuckled and leaning forward in her seat.

"Imogene! Seatbelt." She rolls her eyes but sits back and buckles herself back in. I don't appreciate the teenage eye-rolling, though. I shake my head.

Ramon raises his voice so Imogene can hear him over the sound of the open car windows. "There have also been studies showing that hormone levels during fetal development or epigenetic factors also could play a role in developing gender expression."

He raises one finger in the air, as if he is checking the weather. "But being transgender isn't something science can fully explain, and it's crucial we don't rely too heavily on it. Even though it's interesting, there is a lot we don't know, and at the end of the day, people deserve respect and acceptance for who they are, no matter what."

I'm in awe of Ramon. I knew he was a nice guy but watching him have this conversation with Imogene . . . it's more than I expected.

When Imogene tires of talking, she recedes back into her seat. After a few minutes of silence, she asks, "Can I call Dad?"

I glance back. "I don't think that's a good idea," I say. I hadn't quite worked out how I was going to tackle this question, and at this moment, I wish I had.

"Why?"

I groan internally, knowing I can't avoid her question. "He's mad we left, but not at you. He's mad at me. Just give him some time. We'll call him as soon as we get to Canada, okay?"

Imogene shrugs, and I glimpse her biting her nails.

Ramon glances over at me.

"So, is it DCFS or your husband that you're worried about?" he asks in a hushed tone. I realize then that I glossed over Garrett in our earlier conversation. I'm not sure if it was intentional or not.

"Both," I say, deciding on honesty.

Ramon presses his lips together and gives a tight nod but continues to drive.

The open windows do little to combat the oppressive heat. Beads of sweat form on my forehead, and I can feel the sticky dampness on my back as I shift in the seat. I reach into my bag that sits at my feet for a bottle of water.

Handing one back to Imogene, I say, "Drink this. I don't want you to overheat."

Mentioning overheating—must have jinxed us because several minutes later, barely two hours into our drive as we near Savannah, Georgia, Imogene asks, "What's that smell?"

I breathe in through my nose and am met with the smell of burning metal.

Ramon glances at the dials on his dash. "We're overheating. We just need some coolant. I'll stop and get some."

I pull the smell through my nose again. This can't be good.

"It smells like burnt metal," Imogene says.

"Sure does," I reply, peeking at the gauges on the dash and seeing the little arrow sitting in the orange section. What if we break down? I try to hold in my panic.

Imogene perks up in the back seat.

"Did you know space smells like burnt metal? Well, maybe not all of space, but astronauts say that when they get back from a spacewalk, that's what it smells like. It's because when astronauts open the hatch, particles exposed to the vacuum of space are released into the airlock. The particles undergo high-energy interactions, and when the astronauts re-enter the spacecraft's pressurized environment, the particles produce a series of chemical reactions that cause a burnt metal smell."

As she talks, her voice blurs into the background. My focus doesn't stray from the dashboard or the rising heat. My hands fidget in my lap. I glance at Ramon, who's fully engaged in what Imogene is telling him.

"I didn't know that," Ramon admits with a grin. I keep my eye on his temperature gauge, worry creeping in that we may not make it.

"Yeah! There is a whole, like, section of astrochemistry dedicated to learning more about the smell because it helps them develop materials for spacecraft and spacesuits."

"That's super interesting," Ramon responds. Then he points ahead. "There's a gas station there. We can stop and get some coolant. I should have checked it before we left."

The gas station only being a mile away relieves my worry. Still, the dashboard thermometer edges higher, creeping toward the red zone.

As we inch closer to the gas station, the engine's hum becomes a strained growl. The temperature gauge on the dashboard comes perilously close to the maximum. I try to will it to stay in the safe zone just a little longer, but the needle doesn't obey.

Suddenly, a plume of steam erupts from under the hood, momentarily obscuring the windshield. The car shudders, and the engine's roar turns into a sickly sputter.

"What's happening?" Imogene asks, but we don't answer.

Instead, Ramon shakes his head and mutters, "Oh, no."

"We just need some coolant?" I ask skeptically.

Ramon glances at me, frowning as he maneuvers the car into the gas station parking lot. Before he can park, a loud hiss accompanies the final gasp of the engine, and the car jerks to a stop. Ramon switches off the ignition, and the silence that follows is deafening.

The familiar panic from earlier rises again, along with the acrid smell of antifreeze and burnt oil stinging my nostrils. Simultaneously, Ramon and I push our doors open and exit the car.

The sun blazes overhead, reflecting off the asphalt in shimmering waves. I join Ramon at the front of the car. I watch, unspeaking, as Ramon pops the hood. A cloud of steam billows from within. He reaches into the hood and pulls his hand away. The metal is too hot to touch. The engine hisses, as if scolding us for pushing it too hard.

"Mom?" Imogene calls from inside the car.

"What's up, sweetie?" I ask, though I'm screaming inside.

"I need to use the bathroom."

I swear this child has to pee every five minutes. I look around at the busy lot and say, "Fine, but in and out. Got it?"

"Got it."

Sweat drips down my face, and I wipe it away with the back of my hand, feeling a mix of frustration and helplessness. The cars pulling in and out of the parking lot seem indifferent to our plight, their drivers casting curious glances but not slowing down. The reality of the situation sinks in.

We are stranded. Maybe asking for Ramon's help was a mistake, but what else would I have done?

Ramon heads to the back seat and comes back with a T-shirt. I watch as he works. I can't be angry with him, but I'm angry at the situation. I was naive to think we were home free. That it would be easy to get to Canada.

Ramon, under the hood, looks out with apologetic eyes. "We might need more than coolant."

"Look, Mom!" Imogene comes out of the gas station with star-shaped purple sunglasses.

"Imogene," I say with a stern look. "I said in and out. Can you just please listen to me?"

She doesn't even try to hide her eye roll before she gets back in the car. When she was little, not every interaction was met with an eye roll or a shrug. She doesn't know this, but it hurts my feelings when she responds to me with such indifference. I just have to tell myself, over and over again, that this is developmentally appropriate.

"What do we do?" I ask Ramon.

He turns to me. "We need a mechanic." Ramon exhales. "I'm sorry I have such a shitty car."

"You teach high school in Florida. I think you get a pass."

I close my eyes and try to think of a solution. We need to keep moving, but we have lost our car again. They say things happen in threes, but it feels like we are in the middle of a landslide, being pummeled as we fall.

Ramon lowers the hood and wipes his hands on the T-shirt. "If you and Imogene want to sit tight, I can see if someone nearby can give us a tow."

A few minutes later, Ramon emerges from the side of the gas station with a heavyset man in an orange trucker hat and a blue button-up shirt too small for his frame.

"He's going to pull us up the street. There's a motel we can stay at until we figure out what to do. The car is not going to be fixed today."

I sit in the car with Imogene as a pickup truck backs up to the nose of the car. Ramon and the man he recruited work to secure the two vehicles together using straps. With the car in neutral, I steer while Imogene sits in the back.

As we approach the motel, the pickup truck pulls us into the parking lot. The place looks rundown, with faded paint and a flickering neon sign. The man helping us unhooks the straps, and Ramon hands him some cash. I head inside with Imogene and check us into two rooms at sixty dollars each per night—a third of the money I have.

Inside the motel room, the air is cool and stale. I sit on the edge of the bed to collect my thoughts. Ramon brings in the last of our bags before turning to me. "I'm going to head to the lobby and see if there's a mechanic they recommend."

I watch him leave, then glance at Imogene, who has turned on the television. She mindlessly flips through channels until she lands on a rerun of *iCarly*. The familiar sound of the show's theme song fills the room, and a wave of nostalgia hits me.

I can't help but smile. *iCarly*. It reminds me of a simpler time.

Suddenly, I'm back in our old living room. McKenzie and Imogene, no more than five years old, are sitting on the sofa in their pajamas, giggling at the same show. McKenzie was in Imogene's kindergarten class. I had worried so much about whether Imogene would make friends. She was so shy, but McKenzie broke through her shell. They were inseparable.

On screen, Spencer was making spaghetti tacos.

"Spaghetti tacos?" Garrett said, sitting on the edge of the sofa and then reaching for Imogene's feet in a playful attempt to tickle her. She squirmed away, moving closer to McKenzie to escape his grasp.

"Hey, don't knock it till you try it," I said just before taking a long sip of coffee from my favorite chipped mug.

"I want to try it!" McKenzie shouted, standing up on the couch. Imogene followed, and within seconds, both of them were jumping, chanting in unison, "Spaghetti tacos! Spaghetti tacos! Spaghetti tacos!"

I raised an eyebrow at Garrett, who got up from the couch and faced the kids, making a gentle downward-pushing motion with his hands. The children ceased jumping. "Okay, calm down. How about next time McKenzie sleeps over, we'll make *spaghetti tacos*?" When he said, "spaghetti tacos," the kids erupted again.

I pretended to be annoyed, breathing in deeply through my nose, but truthfully, I loved every second.

Then I noticed my dad's car pulling into the driveway. I craned my neck in surprise. I didn't know he was coming.

"Dad's here," I said to Garrett.

He stopped his playful teasing long enough to glance back. "Oh, shoot. I forgot."

"Forgot what?"

"I told him I'd go fishing with him." Garrett flashed a sheepish grin.

My shoulders sank. Garrett was supposed to hang the new gutters. He saw my disappointment and quickly put his hands up in surrender. "I promise I'll hang the gutters after fishing, okay?"

"Fine," I muttered, although I was tired of him putting it off.

"I wanna go fishing!" Imogene chimed in. Her eyes lit up with excitement. Garrett shot me a look, and my body tensed.

"Sorry, baby. Not today. You've got a friend over," I said gently. But before Imogene could protest, my dad walked through the front door, and both girls ran to greet him. McKenzie, who barely knew him, and Imogene wrapped their arms around Grandpa Charles.

Less than six months later, Dad would be diagnosed with dementia.

It's crazy how quickly things can change—how little control we have over it all. I wonder to myself whether Garrett will visit Dad. Probably not, and that makes my heart ache. I feel so bad for abandoning my father.

Twenty minutes have passed since Ramon left, and I can't sit still any longer. I decide to see how finding a mechanic is going.

"Stay here," I warn Imogene. She rolls her eyes at me for the second time today. "I mean it," I add.

"I know." Teenage attitude drips from her lips.

Standing at the front desk, Ramon says into his phone, "Three weeks?" He is in the lobby alone.

Ramon stares up at the ceiling, clearly frustrated. He sees me approaching. "Every shop I've called is backed up," he explains, holding his hand over the receiver as the attendant walks back into the lobby.

He spends a few more minutes on the phone before he ends the call. Turning to face me, his shoulders drop.

"If none of the shops can get you in, I just called my cousin. He can fix it, and he'll charge you half as much," the motel attendant offers behind us.

"Really?" I ask, redirecting my attention to him.

"Does he have a shop?" Ramon inquires.

"Not a shop, but he has access to my dad's garage. They'll fix you up good as new in lickety-split."

A mound of chew sits on the bottom lip of the attendant's mouth, coloring his teeth with a sticky brown residue.

"It sounds like our only option," I say to Ramon.

"All right," he agrees with a shrug.

After we learn a little more about the attendant's cousin, such as where this garage is located, and exchange contact information, we hand over the car key and walk back to the motel room. Ramon's room is next door to mine.

"Hey, can we stop for a minute?" Ramon asks.

"Sure." I halt immediately. Ramon seems surprised by the abrupt stop and stumbles into me.

He puts his hands out to steady himself. Standing far too close to him, I stare at his face, startled by the intimacy of our proximity, and take a step back.

"Yes?" I ask.

"Are you sure you know what you're doing?" Ramon scratches at the side of his face.

My brows knit together as I study him. "No, actually. I have no idea what I'm doing and haven't had any idea for a long time. I just know I can't lose her, and I'll do anything to keep her safe."

He studies my face. "I understand."

"Can I ask you a question?" I counter, trying to catch his eye.

"Of course."

"You mentioned you caused a lot of harm, but I still don't quite understand why you're helping us. Why?"

He pauses, glancing away for a moment before meeting my gaze again. "It's just finally my time to right some wrongs."

I want to ask more, to press him further and understand exactly why Ramon would risk everything for us, but we're interrupted by Imogene.

"Mom?" She stands just outside our motel room door.

"Imogene, I asked you not to leave the room."

"There's a roach in the bathroom."

I give Ramon a knowing and pleading expression. "I've got to go. Let me know if you hear anything from the mechanic."

He nods. "Will do."

CHAPTER 17

MOTEL ROYALTY

Imogene

In 1972, a spacecraft named Pioneer 10 traveled through the asteroid belt, which everyone thought was impossible until it happened. During its journey, the spacecraft had a very close encounter with Jupiter, crossed Neptune's orbit, and passed all the known planets at that time, making it to interstellar space.

What I find most fascinating about Pioneer 10 is the golden plaque it carries. It serves as a message for any aliens who might find it. Even now, Pioneer 10 drifts more than twelve billion kilometers from Earth. Although its signals are faint, it's still out there, carrying a tiny piece of humanity.

I imagine my path as moving further away from the familiar, much like a spacecraft drifting through space. I'm at the mercy of gravitational pulls from other objects, especially my mother. Without an active propulsion system of my own, I follow the trajectory she sets.

As I sit in the motel lobby, the air heavy with the scent of stale carpet and fried food from the diner next door, I pretend to be engrossed in an old pop culture magazine, but my ears are tuned in to Mom's conversation at the front desk.

"What do you mean it is going to cost $1,200?" Mom's voice rises like a rocket launching into space, fueled by frustration. I glance up, watching her face flush with worry and anger.

"I'm sorry, ma'am. Your head gasket is blown, and you got a cracked cylinder head. We're giving you a good deal," the greasy-haired motel attendant explains, his voice annoyingly calm. A wad of chew bulges in his cheek, making his words garbled.

Mom glances left at Ramon, whose face is empathetic. "How do we even know that this guy knows what he's doing?" she says, grasping at anything that might reduce the steep cost.

"Oh, he knows what he's doing. You don't have to worry about that," the attendant insists, shifting the chew in his mouth.

Ramon pats Mom's arm. "Maybe we should get a second opinion?" I see the tension in Mom's shoulders ease at his touch, but worry lines remain on her face. Dad knows a lot about cars. If he was here, he could fix this, but I heard the way he yelled at Mom. He's mad at her, and I can't help but feel responsible.

I skim an article about Johnny Depp and Amber Heard's divorce. McKenzie always liked Johnny Depp, especially in the pirate movies. The fact that I still think about her annoys me. I flip the page to some recipe before looking up at the sound of the lobby door's bell.

In walks the most ethereal person I've ever seen.

My chin snaps up as I take them in—a drag queen.

My gaze trails from her skirt to her head, and I hold my breath. She wears a tea-length dress of iridescent fabric that shimmers in shades of blue, purple, and pink. Tiny, sparkling sequins and crystals adorn the dress, creating a stardust effect. A plunging neckline is further accentuated by a statement necklace of large, opal-like stones.

A soft glow highlights her cheekbones, while her glossy, overlined light pink lips add a touch of glamor. Finally, perfectly arched brows point to a cascade of platinum blonde curls.

She notices me watching and gives me a wink, making me smile and blush. I've seen drag queens on TV and YouTube, but never in person. The magnitude of her presence is overwhelming.

"It's going to be at least three grand somewhere else," the attendant says to Mom and Ramon, who are still absorbed in their conversation about the car. They haven't noticed the queen, who waits for her turn.

"Do you have the money?" Ramon asks Mom.

"No. Not even close. You?" She looks hopeful.

He sighs and his shoulders sag. "No. I just paid off what I owed for the nursing home and the funeral. I also don't get paid for another two weeks. I'm mostly broke. I could maybe call my sister."

Mom shakes her head. "No… um, I don't want to bring another person into this." She pauses, glancing up.

The attendant takes this pause as an opportunity to address the drag queen. "Opal, you're back!"

The queen steps forward.

"Oh, you know, they can't get enough of me at the palace. We just got done with brunch," she says with a flirty grin, her voice a rich alto that fills the room. "What's a queen gotta do to get a room around here?"

Mom and Ramon glance at Opal, taking her in before moving to the side of the lobby to discuss the car situation in hushed whispers. I try to focus on my magazine, but Opal is magnetic.

Mom and Ramon's voices rise and fall as they discuss our money problems. I have a sinking feeling we'll have to go home. I don't know exactly how I feel about that option because I haven't figured out how I feel about running either. I don't know how I feel about anything.

When Opal finishes checking in, she turns to Mom and Ramon. "Excuse me." She sashays her shoulders with a dramatic flair. "I couldn't help but overhear you're having some money troubles. If you're interested, the Drag Palace, where I'm performing, is hiring. They're desperate, so if you tell 'em Opal sent you, they'll probably hire you on the spot."

My eyes widen. Work at a drag club? I recall the exaggerated expression of femininity from RuPaul's Drag Race on YouTube. I want to see it up close.

"Oh, thank you, but . . ." Mom begins.

"Sweetie, go or don't go. It's all the same to me. Just thought I'd offer." Opal gives a dramatic turn and lends me one last wink before leaving the lobby.

Mom and Ramon continue to discuss in hushed tones.

"Maybe we should consider it," Ramon suggests. "Just to get us through until the car is fixed?"

"Maybe we should take the bus." Mom pulls out her phone, and her fingers fly across the screen.

Ramon watches her, waiting. She looks up, disappointed.

"I don't have enough money for the tickets." She pauses, glancing to her left, deep in thought. "Besides, I wouldn't want to leave you here to figure out the car by yourself."

"What do you want to do?" Ramon holds my mom's gaze.

Mom hesitates, glancing at me but addressing Ramon. She lowers her voice further, but I can hear her. "I'll do anything, but what do I do with Imogene? I can't leave her here by herself."

I stand, my heart pounding. "I can go with you. I want to work there, too."

Mom gapes at me as if I've lost my mind. "You're fourteen. You can't even be inside a bar, let alone a drag bar."

The attendant, who has been eavesdropping, speaks up. "It's also a restaurant. Very family friendly."

Mom looks at Ramon again, her eyes filled with worry. "We'll talk about it in the room," she says, glancing back at the attendant, aware of his listening ears.

"Mom . . ."

"Stop, Imogene. We will talk about this later."

Mom plasters a polite smile on her face and turns to the attendant. "I'm sorry I got frustrated. Please tell your cousin we are grateful, and we'll figure out a way to pay for the repairs. I'll check in with you a little later."

She gestures for us to go outside, and we walk down the motel's exterior corridor until we reach our rooms. Inside, I plop onto the sagging mattress while Mom and Ramon take the two chairs that frame the exterior window on either side of a small, worn table with peeling Formica.

"We should consider it," Ramon says, leaning forward, his hands clasped together. "I know it's unconventional, but it's a solution. I could apply, and you two can stay back. I want to help."

"There is no way you are going to make enough money on your own. We'll be stuck here a month before we can pay for the repairs," Mom says.

"I just don't see a lot of other options," Ramon says.

"I have an idea," I start to say. "What if—"

Mom holds up her hand, cutting me off. "Imogene, please. Give me a second."

My unsaid words boil in my stomach. If we all worked there, we would make the money in no time.

Mom bites her bottom lip in thought. "We'll both go. Imogene, you will stay here in the room with the doors locked."

"Mom, please, I want to go with you. Please." The urge to see the palace and the drag queens pushes me to argue, which I rarely do. "Please."

CHAPTER 18

THE DRAG PALACE

Stacy

The heavy door of the Drag Palace swings shut behind us with a soft thud, cutting off the oppressive midday heat. The club is housed in what looks to be a restored historic building. Its exterior brickwork and cement steps lead to large wooden doors, with an added accessibility ramp tucked to the side. I wonder what this place used to be—a theater, maybe, or a music hall.

Ramon and I pass a hostess stand, and the space opens up. A large stage with a runway extends into the center of the room, surrounded by small, circular tables and chairs with an old-world charm, each covered in a plush red velvet. Dark maroon upholstered booths line the walls, each paired with thick wooden tables. Above each booth, mounted on the wall, hangs a large, framed photo of a drag queen. To the right is an oval-shaped bar.

The space buzzes with activity. Staff members dart around, prepping for the evening show. A tall, slender man with short, spiky hair directs a group of stagehands with brisk, authoritative gestures. His eyes narrow as they lock onto us.

"Can I help you?" Annoyance edges his tone.

"Yes, uh, we ran into one of your performers. Opal?" I say, my voice carrying a hint of uncertainty.

"Okay?" The man's disinterest is unmistakable. His tone makes me more apprehensive about our plan. We need to get on the road as fast as possible. We don't have time for this.

Ramon clears his throat. "They mentioned you're hiring."

"You're looking for jobs? Both of you?" He raises his brows.

Something about his attitude rubs me the wrong way. He's almost confrontational. Part of me wants to say "Forget it," throw up my hands, and walk out. But what other options do we have?

I step in to say, "Yes."

The man studies us for a moment. "You got experience?"

Ramon jumps in. "I waited tables through college. Mostly fine dining, but I know my way around a restaurant."

His confidence surprises me. It is the opposite of how I feel right now. I'm uncertain about everything except one thing: I need to get to Canada to save Imogene and myself.

The man shifts his attention to Ramon. "Can you dance?"

"I'm Cuban," Ramon replies with a hint of pride.

The guy tilts his head. "I didn't ask your race."

"I didn't give you my race. It's my ethnicity."

"Do you want a job?" His voice sharpens, clearly becoming impatient.

"Yes," I interject, sensing the tension.

The man's gaze shifts to me, trailing from my feet to my head, his expression skeptical. "And you?"

"No. I can't dance," I admit.

He pauses, still judging us as he asks his next question. "Where are you from?"

This is taking too long, so I take control. "We were passing through, and our car broke down. We don't have enough money for the repairs. Opal said you're desperate, and so are we. We need jobs, and I need to bring my daughter to work with me."

"Fucking Opal." He shakes his head. "Look, we don't offer daycare services for our staff."

"She's fourteen. She'll happily sit in the corner. She won't be a disruption. I just don't feel comfortable leaving her alone."

He cocks an eyebrow. "Fourteen isn't old enough to stay by herself?"

"Well, I . . ." I stammer, unsure how to explain. Yes, she's fourteen, but she's still a child, and Savannah is unfamiliar to us both. Also, Imogene doesn't have a phone. Even though the hotel has one, if she leaves and something happens, I won't be there, and she'll have no way to get ahold of me.

Before I can finish, the man lets out an exaggerated sigh. "We need the help. You're hired. I don't have time for paperwork, so I'll pay in cash," he says flatly.

"Really?" Ramon and I say in unison. Our pitch reveals our surprise.

"Don't get too excited. Just be back here by five. I'll figure something out for you then."

"So, my daughter can come?" I ask, needing to be sure.

He purses his lips. "Sure. It's fine. The show is PG, mostly comedy, and people do bring their kids, but I expect you to work, and I expect your daughter to not be a distraction."

"She's a good kid," Ramon offers.

"Yeah, but apparently can't be trusted alone," he mutters, rolling his eyes.

I ignore his comment. "Thank you. We'll be back. I'm Stacy."

Beside me, Ramon holds out his hand. "Ramon."

He glances at it before turning away. "Gary. See you soon."

Ramon and I exchange a look that says, *Gary's a real treat.*

As we leave the Drag Palace to walk back to the motel, I'm struck by the absurdity of our situation. I'm trying to get to Canada as quickly as possible, but I can't get there because we don't have a car, and the solution is a job at a drag club. It's ridiculous. It sounds like an opening to a joke.

"Is this how you envisioned starting your summer vacation?" I ask Ramon.

"I don't think anyone could've predicted this," he says with a chuckle.

I let out a large breath. "This is insane. I still don't understand why you're helping us."

He grins as he walks beside me. "Well, at this point, I don't have much of a choice. My car's out of commission."

His lighthearted response lifts some weight from my chest.

"When we get back to the motel, I need to do some research. Maybe there's something related to trans rights or parents' rights that I don't know about yet," I tell Ramon.

If we are stuck in this place, I might as well use the time to fix things.

"Have you considered finding an attorney?" he asks. The answer is yes, but what's the point of searching for an attorney when I can't pay for one yet?

"Of course I've thought about it. But even if I found someone to take my case, I can't afford to pay them." I sigh, kicking a stray pebble. "Maybe I can figure out the attorney part once we're in Canada. There's just so much I don't know yet. Garrett is furious with me, probably hates me. I have no idea what he's planning or if he'd help. I don't know if I'll have to fight this alone. I don't even know how much time I have, or how much I need."

I pause as I consider all the unknowns stacked beneath the one truth I can hold on to. "Right now, all I know is that I need to get Imogene to safety. Until then, I can try to find a loophole or a better solution, but right now, Canada's the only plan I can see."

He glances at me for a moment before staring forward.

"I know things aren't working out the way you envisioned. I'm really sorry."

My heart deflates at his apology. I want to get to Canada, yes, but our delay is not his fault. The last thing I want is for him to hold any guilt for the way things have turned out. "Hey, don't be sorry. I'm finally living my lifelong dream of working in a drag club." I laugh, and after a second, he does, too.

Several hours later, Ramon, Imogene, and I enter the club for our first shift. The moment we walk in, Imogene's eyes light up, and her entire focus is on the surroundings. Employees are busy preparing for the evening show. Technicians are on stage, checking the sound system with snippets of music and adjusting microphones, while others test the lighting, creating flashes of color and patterns that dance across the empty room.

I point to a booth that provides me with a visual from any place in the club and give Imogene a knowing look.

"Now?" she says.

"Yes, Imogene. Now."

She sulks over to the booth and slides inside. She might be mad, but at least I can keep an eye on her.

Ramon and I approach Gary at the bar. He's peering at a work schedule. Several men in robes, wearing wig caps and faces full of makeup, sit at a nearby table as they eat.

Gary first gestures to Ramon. "All right, since you have some experience, I'm going to put you on waitstaff." He then turns his attention to me. "Stacy, right?" I nod. "You'll host and bus tonight. Your job is to greet people as they come in and then clean tables as they leave. The show is usually packed by six-thirty, and we take to the stage at seven. People will expect to have their food before then, but sometimes, the kitchen gets backed up, which is fine because drag queens are always late. When the show starts, try to be discreet." He nods to himself. "Get your uniforms from Mary in the back. She will also show you the ropes. We don't have time for training, so hopefully, you learn fast."

"We do," I say eagerly.

"We'll see." Gary returns to the schedule.

After changing into a pink polo shirt and tying a black apron around my waist, I'm instructed to set the dining room for the evening dinner and performance. As I wipe down tables, a loud voice breaks the silence.

A queen in a black leotard, with dramatic arched brows and gold glitter shadow wearing a wig cap, stomps across the stage in red stilettos, screaming, "Where's my prop hat?"

"Chill, Illusion," one of the stage techs says to her.

"I am not going to chill when my prop hat is missing. Where am I supposed to pull the rabbit from? My ass?"

Imogene giggles, and I look over at her to see she is no longer in the booth but standing several feet in front of it. I shoot her a look. She sneers before returning to the booth, slouching deeper into it with a shrug.

Just then, a different queen, a heavyset one with large breasts, comes out on the left, with the missing top hat on her head. "What in the Sam Hill are you shoutin' about?"

"Steve, you bitch!" Illusion puts a hand on her hip.

"Now, sugar, that's a mighty strong word. Also, if you'd open your eyes, you'd see I'm not Steve currently. Care to try again?" The heavyset queen's voice drips with exaggerated Southern charm.

Illusion's voice drops several octaves as she puts her character aside. "Give me my hat, Peach."

In her over-the-top costume, complete with big hair, a gingham top, and daisy duke cut-off shorts, Peach winks at Illusion. "Well, fine then. Suit yourself." She removes the top hat with a flourish and hands it over with a playful bow, her exaggerated gestures drawing laughter from the crew and myself.

I watch the queens' interaction out of the corner of my eye as I clean the tables, but I also watch Imogene's reaction to them. She is completely enraptured. I've never seen her this curious or excited about anything outside of astronomy. The brightness in her excitement reminds me of her light.

Imogene's shoulders sink when they walk off stage in opposite directions, and she folds into herself again. Her light fades, and my heart aches for the brightness that's slipped away.

Twenty minutes before the doors open, a line of people wait outside. And even though it is Friday, it amazes me how this place draws such an audience.

Either the food or the performers must be top tier—or maybe both. I'm curious to find out. I glance at Imogene to make sure she's still sitting in her booth.

Seeing her in the same place I left her, I give myself a small nod of reassurance. With a crowd like this, maybe between the tips and our pay from the club, we'll earn what we need sooner than expected.

As I'm busy seating people, Gary comes over to me, wiping his hands on a bar towel. "I need your kid to find a new spot."

My eyes widen. "What?"

"We always fill up, and I can't have the booth used for babysitting. She can go backstage."

The lack of supervision makes my chest thud. I can't do that.

"She can't go back there. Isn't there important stuff backstage?" I ask.

"You said she wouldn't be any trouble."

"She won't, but . . ."

Ramon notices our conversation and comes over. "Hey, what's going on?" he asks.

"Look, I'm thankful for the extra hands, but if your kid can't be trusted to sit tight backstage, I don't know if she should be here at all." Gary flings the bar towel over his shoulder and looks at us expectantly.

My stomach tightens, and a flush of panic creeps up my neck. Before I can respond, Ramon steps in. "Whoa. She'll be fine backstage. Would it be all right if Stacy takes a break to take her back there?"

"Whatever," Gary grumbles and walks away, pulling the towel from his shoulder. He mumbles something under his breath, but I don't catch what he says.

"Ramon, I don't feel good about this."

"It's going to be fine. Just go back with her. Find a place she can sit and maybe even watch the show from behind the curtain. She's a smart kid. She'll be fine. Okay?"

My jaw is still tense, but I breathe through my nose and nod. Turning to Imogene, I gesture with my hand to follow me. "Come on."

Once she is next to me, I say, "I know this is super exciting, but I need you to be on your best behavior. Just sit backstage and don't talk to anyone. All right?"

"Okay," she says, elongating the "a" in a way that tells me she's annoyed with being told what to do.

When we get backstage, the area is bustling with activity. Sequined costumes hang from racks and mirrors with bright bulbs line the walls, reflecting the faces of queens in various stages of preparation. The air smells of hairspray and makeup.

Everyone is too busy to notice me, so I scan the room and find a spot where Imogene can sit without being in the way. A metal folding chair tucked into a corner next to a rack of costumes and props, provides a decent view of the stage through a gap in the curtain. It's secluded enough to keep her out of the way, but close enough for her to feel part of the action.

"You can sit here." I point to the chair. "You'll be able to watch the show from this spot. Please stay quiet and don't wander off."

Imogene nods.

"Got it?" I say, needing to hear her acknowledgement.

"*Gooot* it," she says.

This teenage attitude is something else. I huff as I walk back to the dining room. Sometimes, it feels like she thinks I'm doing all this for myself rather than for her.

Back in the dining room, I resume my duties of seating guests and filling glasses with water. The lively chatter of the audience and the vibrant energy is fantastic, but I can't stop worrying without eyes on Imogene.

I greet each person with a smile, and several times, I hear someone say, "This is my first drag show!" It is mine, too, but I smile politely and say, "Enjoy the show!" each time they make the proclamation.

I don't know what to expect from the show. They say family-friendly, but I find that rather odd. I try to think back to a time I saw even a snippet of a drag show, but the only thing that comes to mind is a clip of a queen twerking. That surely can't be what this is.

Once the room is full and everyone is seated, I feel like I can finally take a moment to absorb everything. Initially, I saw a restaurant, a bar, and a stage. Now, I notice the details I missed before. Photographs of drag queens, resembling beauty shots from the 80s, line the walls. The queens come in a variety of sizes and colors—black, brown, and white. Their costumes vary as much as they do, adding another layer of diversity. Some are glamorous, while others are more comical or whimsical, like the drag queen named Candyland, who wears a headpiece designed to resemble a stack of classic candy pieces.

Ramon stands at a table across from me, his back turned as he scribbles an order on a notepad. I'm still trying to figure him out. My lips lift into a smile when I think of how he chatted with Imogene in the car or how he uses his index finger to push his green frames up the bridge of his nose. He's sweet, and although we are close in age, it seems like life hasn't compromised him yet.

I go back to the hostess stand to see where I'm needed. While I stand at the entrance, I'm forced to turn people without a reservation away because it's a full house. Then the music playing overhead changes. There is a distinct beat that repeats, and I watch as all the waitstaff come out from the back, each holding a fan. They hand out fans to several audience members and then step back, beginning to snap their fans in rhythm.

Snap, snap, snap.

People clap to the beat. Ramon is among them, snapping his fan. I watch as he tries to smile and snap, missing the beat. His hip juts out a second after each snap, like he cannot synchronize the movements. He catches my gaze, and his eyes widen, the whites around his irises visible. I can't hold back my laugh.

The curtain opens, and an emcee announces a Black queen as Flora Fatal—pronounced with a long "a," like "fate-al." She is stunning. She commands the stage with every step. The crowd's energy shifts when she raises a fan high above her head and snaps it with a resounding crack that echoes through the room.

The music swells, and she begins to lip-sync with perfect precision. Her movements are crisp and expressive. Her costume is a full-length green body suit with floral designs wrapping around her arms and legs. Her bright pink hair is set in large bouncy curls and two cone-shaped buns atop. I stare, trying to place where I've seen this costume before.

Poison Ivy. How clever.

The waitstaff and audience members with fans join in, creating a symphony of snaps and claps that fill the space. The rhythm is infectious, and soon, the entire room is alive with the beat. Halfway through, Flora Fatal steps off the stage, grabbing a handful of carnations and exchanging them for tips from the audience members.

When her number is over, I find Ramon grabbing plates for a table in the kitchen. "I thought you could dance?" I say.

"I said I'm Cuban, not that I had rhythm."

I chuckle, finally realizing why Ramon answered Gary that way. He preferred not to lie.

"Thanks for doing this," I say.

"I'm glad to. I'm actually having fun," he says as he loads a large tray onto his shoulder.

I refill pitchers with water and return to the floor, but my mind is still on Imogene. I have no idea what she is doing backstage, and the thought of her being alone in such a chaotic environment makes my chest tighten.

As I move between tables, I try to catch glimpses of the backstage area. Is she sitting quietly like I told her, or is she wandering around and getting into things she shouldn't? The unknown gnaws at me, making it hard to focus on my tasks.

The lights dim, and the stage is reset for the next act. Next comes out the queen who was missing her hat, Illusion. Illusion's act is part magic, part comedy, and her timing is impeccable. She interacts with the audience, and the resulting banter is genius.

During her act, she brings an audience member onto the stage. "I will now make our friend here levitate!" she announces. However, as Illusion flicks her wand, she is dragged into the air. Her surprise and flailing arms and legs cause laughter to erupt from the audience. "Get me down!"

The whole dining room is full of smiles and laughter. I can see why this place is so popular. The show is most definitely top tier.

Several more acts take the stage, including Opal, who delivers a heartfelt ballad in a dazzling ball gown. Georgia Peach follows, riding a miniature tractor to the tune of "She Thinks My Tractor's Sexy." Her exaggerated gestures and silly Southern ad-libs have the audience roaring with laughter.

As the night progresses, the energy in the room builds. I move between tables, refilling drinks, taking plates away, and watching the performance out of the corner of my eye. Still, the worry about Imogene never leaves my mind.

When the lights come up and the performers take their final bows, the emcee thanks everyone for coming and invites the audience to return for future shows. The dining room soon empties, and I bus the tables with increasing urgency. The moment the activity lulls, I rush backstage to check on Imogene.

When I walk back, I'm surprised—even though I shouldn't be—to see Imogene is not in her chair. Instead, Illusion and Flora Fatal are teaching her to vogue.

"Vogue is sharp. It's precise," Flora Fatal instructs, their voice smooth and commanding. Imogene stands, feet shoulder-width apart, hands on her hips. She extends one arm out. The movement is tentative yet earnest.

Illusion jumps in. "Keep your fingers together. You're a blade, not a noodle."

Imogene walks forward, placing one foot in front of the other.

"Swing those hips, girl!" she directs. Imogene swings her hips from side to side, nearly tripping over her feet but staying upright when she spins back around to face them.

"You got it," Illusion praises, but then pauses as she notices Imogene staring at me, mouth open in surprise.

"Imogene, I told you not to bother them," I say, my voice wilted with slight disappointment.

"Respectfully, ma'am, no one puts Baby in a corner," Illusion says.

My brows raise, but I hold my tongue. I'm not mad. Only worried. Gary was clear about Imogene not being a distraction, and I don't know these people. But at the same time, I see something I rarely do. Imogene is alive here. My shy child, the one who struggles to connect and express herself, is vibrant in their presence.

I soften, letting my stern demeanor melt away. "I don't want to interrupt, but we are about to leave."

"Do I have to?" Imogene asks.

I nod gently.

"Fine." She breaks eye contact and walks ahead of me into the dining room.

CHAPTER 19

LESSONS IN ASTRONOMY

Imogene

I always knew I was different. Although other kids had interests, few love anything as much as I love astronomy. Still, there was something else that only I seemed to experience. It wasn't until the fifth grade that a sense of dread accompanied my difference.

At school, they separated the boys from the girls, and we went into different classrooms to learn about puberty. I thought the whole thing was weird and dumb. I remember looking longingly at McKenzie as she was herded off with the other girls. I felt like I was supposed to be with her, with them, not with the boys.

When the lights dimmed and the video began, I realized that by dismissing puberty, I had ignored it to save myself from it. The video showed the physical changes boys would undergo: muscle growth, facial and body hair, voice deepening, and growth spurts. The video combined footage of boys playing sports with skits about hormones, especially testosterone, to highlight how my body would change.

By the time we got to the part about personal hygiene, I was in the middle of an existential crisis. I didn't want my body to change, especially in those ways. A growing anxiety gripped my chest, and I knew there must be a mistake. There had to be.

Sometimes, I still think the body I was born into was a mistake. It just doesn't make sense to me. How can I feel so different on the inside from what I am on the outside? I often regret existing at all because existing the way I do hurts, and it's lonely.

After I realized I was trans, my life got even lonelier. I'm constantly torn between feeling disconnected from the body I was given while embracing my trans identity. Navigating those two things feels impossible. How do you deal with a part of yourself that feels so wrong when another part of you finally feels right?

The drag queens chatter as they apply their makeup. I watch them in awe of their confidence and skill. The camaraderie they share is beautiful and unlike anything I've ever witnessed before.

Mom tried to make me stay in the booth again, but Illusion—who I've learned goes by Bryce when not in drag—rescued me before the show.

"Didn't I tell you? We don't put Baby in the corner," Bryce said to Mom before flexing his pointer and middle finger to signal me to follow. I jumped up from the booth, eager to go backstage again.

"Imogene, don't move a muscle." Mom turned to Bryce, her body shifting into full-on protective mode. "She has no business being backstage while you're getting ready."

Bryce tilted his head, confused. "Hasn't she told you? She's my new apprentice. How is she supposed to learn if she's out here?" Bryce gestured to the dining room.

Mom's eyes narrowed, and her lips tilted down. She was trying to decide whether to let me go. I wish she would just let up. Sometimes her worry is suffocating.

Bryce continued, "We have dressing rooms back there. She won't see anything except for a bunch of queens plastering their faces with makeup and contouring their chests."

Ramon approached from the side of the room, glancing at her with a hesitant look. "Hey, I got a call from the mechanic. It's going to cost a little more . . ." His voice trailed off, and he shifted uncomfortably as he shared the news.

Her face immediately soured. "Really?"

"We should go," I said to Mom as I pointed a thumb over my shoulder toward the stage.

"Imogene . . ." I heard her mutter, but I was already following Bryce backstage.

I glanced back, and she shook her head before turning to Ramon. I'd won. I don't win a lot with Mom. Her word is usually final, but tonight, I got my way and because of that, I get to watch the queens transform as I am now.

"Baby, will you pass me my wig? That one up there." Opal points to one of several blonde wigs on display. I stand to get it and hear Georgia Peach say, "Just 'cause Illusion done made Baby some kinda apprentice don't mean she's your servant. She ain't being paid."

"Baby, you don't mind, do you?" Opal glances at me in the mirror as she applies a bit of blush to her cheeks.

"No. Not at all." In fact, I'm eager to help in any way I can. I bring the wig to Opal, where she sits before one of several vanities.

"See?" Opal says to Peach.

Flora Fatal emerges from the dressing area a moment later, wearing only sweatpants. When they see me, they scream and cover their exposed chest.

Illusion rolls her eyes.

"What? A warning would be nice. This is a child!" Flora exclaims.

"Oh, come on, girl, you don't have any fat around those nips," Illusion retorts with a smirk.

"Question: Is it the fat or the nipple that's inappropriate?" Opal chimes in.

Confused, Flora asks, "What are you talking about?"

"Think about it. Men's nipples are fine because they don't have fat, but women can show the fat but not the nipple." Opal places a finger on her cheek thoughtfully. "So, is it the fat or the nipple?"

"I reckon it only applies to women," Peach chimes in, grabbing at her chest. "I got nipples and fat, and ain't nobody says a thing to me when I'm topless on the beach."

Peach is a large round man, who goes by Steve when not in drag. Unlike some of the other queens, Peach doesn't have to use a breastplate or contouring to create a feminine chest.

"That's because they're afraid you may sit on them," Opal quips, causing a burst of laughter.

Peach gasps theatrically. "This is 2024. Fatphobia is a thing of the past."

"Not when the phobia stems from a genuine fear of being suffocated," Illusion teases.

"Oh, don't listen to them. You are gorg—every inch of you," Flora says.

Peach strikes a pose and lets her hand drift over her curves. "Bet your boots I am," she says with a grin.

As I watch the queens' banter, I don't feel as lonely as I usually do. I sit and listen intently, trying to catch every moment of their conversation. If I could bottle it up and keep it forever, I would.

Illusion calls to me from her chair. "If you're going to be my apprentice, it is time you learn to block your brows."

My eyes widen because I don't know what that means, and I don't ask.

"Come here," she encourages.

I stand so quickly I almost lose my balance.

Illusion scoots her chair and gestures at the folded chair in the corner where I sat on my first night. "Grab that and come have a seat."

I get the chair and unfold it next to Illusion.

She shows me how she uses a purple glue stick to paste her brows to her face. When she's done, she hands the glue stick to me. I stare in the mirror, pressing the glue into my brow hair.

"Now, we wait for it to dry, and add two more layers," Illusion instructs. She turns her attention to her vanity, turning various lipstick shades over to read the label. I study my face in the mirror.

The purple glue stiffened my brow hairs, making them stick straight up and giving me an incredibly ridiculous look. Despite this, I feel at ease. In fact, the longer I'm here, the more comfortable I am—comfortable enough to start asking questions.

"Is there such a thing as a girl drag queen?" I don't know what the rules of drag are, and it's been killing me. Can I do drag if I'm trans? Do I need to identify as a man outside of drag for it to be legit?

Illusion stops organizing her cosmetics and turns in her seat, placing her hands on her lap. She studies me. "How do you identify?"

I glance at my lap, a knot of fear tightening in my stomach. This is the first time anyone has asked me that question, and although I know the answer, I feel like I might get it wrong.

"I'm trans," I whisper.

"Mm-hmm?" she prompts, encouraging me to continue.

"I'm a girl," I say with uncertainty, even though there is no uncertainty to be had.

"She/Her pronouns?" Illusion's voice lifts at the end of the word pronouns.

"Yes." My voice is stronger this time.

"Well, Baby . . ." She tilts her head. "Is it okay that I call you Baby? I guess I never asked."

"Yeah, it's cool," I say. Truthfully, I've thought about it a lot. I worked so hard to get everyone to call me Imogene, and now all these drag queens are calling me "Baby." But I don't mind. If anything, I like it.

"A drag queen presents as feminine. A drag king presents as masculine. It doesn't matter what your gender identity is off stage. Opal is also a trans woman and Flora is nonbinary. You can do whatever you like. Drag is for everyone—all identities and orientations. This is an art, and there are no rules when it comes to art."

"So, I can be a trans girl and also a drag queen?"

"Baby, you can be a cisgender heterosexual man who fishes on the weekends and works in finance and be a drag queen. It doesn't matter."

Peach speaks up, "Y'all talkin' 'bout me?"

"Just because I said the word 'straight,' you assume I'm talking about you." Illusion shakes her head.

Opal pipes in, "Oh, she was totally talking about you." Opal leans over. "Peach is our token straight guy." She winks at me.

When McKenzie was more friend than bully, we had the kind of friendship the queens share. In fact, she was my only real friend, even though she had many others.

McKenzie often stayed the night at my house. She said my house felt different and more welcoming, and she liked it. Our goal was always to spend the entire night on my trampoline, lying side by side under the endless expanse of sky. But inevitably, I'd hear a noise, get scared, and beg to go inside.

We often hosted star parties, and McKenzie would invite all the kids from school. They wouldn't have come if I had invited them, but McKenzie was popular. I often compared myself to McKenzie, and though I loved her, deep-seated envy constantly gnawed at me. Now I recognize I was jealous of her femineity more than anything else.

One night on the trampoline, the cool night air brushed against our skin, and a rhythmic chirping of crickets surrounded us. "I'm getting eaten alive," I grumbled, sitting up, and swatting at my legs. "Let's go inside."

"Charlie! You said you wouldn't chicken out," McKenzie whined, her voice tinged with playful blame.

"But I'm going to be covered in bug bites tomorrow, and they itch," I retorted, already scratching at an itchy welt forming on my skin.

"Oh, it's not that bad. I don't want to go inside. I like looking at the stars. Can you tell me about that one again?" She pointed up, her finger tracing a path to Orion's Belt, a trio of twinkling stars that seemed to wink at us from the sky.

I followed her gaze and launched into a familiar explanation about Orion's Belt.

"Orion's Belt comes from a Greek myth where Orion, a hunter, said he could hunt and kill any animal. This made Mother Earth, or Gaia, mad, so she sent a scorpion to kill him."

"Did it work? Did the scorpion kill him?"

"Yeah. There are other versions of the story, too. Also, the stars you see are bigger than the sun. That's why we can see them, even though they're far away."

"You're such a nerd." McKenzie grabbed my hand. The warmth of her touch was comforting.

"You're my best friend," I whispered.

"Is that all?" she asked, her tone shifting to something serious.

"What do you mean?" I asked, turning toward her. The moonlight illuminated her face.

"Like, what if we were more than friends one day?" Her eyes searched mine for something I wasn't sure I could give.

I thought about it. "Maybe when we're older? I think I need to be older." I tried to placate her with a compromise. I was confused about how I felt about myself, girls, dating—all of it, really. It felt too overwhelming to figure out, so I didn't want to deal with it.

"Okay, maybe when we're older," she conceded, but the seed of her question lingered in my mind.

How did I feel about dating, and would I want to date McKenzie? She was my best friend, but the thought of it made me uncomfortable. I couldn't quite pinpoint why, but maybe it was because McKenzie felt more like a sister than anything else. Or maybe it was the mystifying envy I often felt when I looked at her.

A year later, that mystifying envy made more sense. I had realized I was trans a few months earlier, though I hadn't told McKenzie right away. The day I finally told her, I had been at home, watching a trans person on YouTube—a creator I'd discovered not long after my initial realization. Their story fascinated me—the ability to swap genders, to change what felt inherently wrong. It awakened something in me that had always been there, lurking beneath the surface. I'd always felt uncomfortable in my skin. I'd always felt different from the other boys, and learning about trans people helped me understand a little more about why I had always felt that way.

When McKenzie walked into my room, I shut my laptop, hoping she hadn't seen what I was watching.

"What were you doing?" Suspicion was clear on her face.

"Nothing."

"Were you watching porn?" she asked, crossing her arms and raising an eyebrow.

"What? No! That's gross," I shouted, my face burning.

She stepped closer. "Then let me see."

"No," I said, my voice cracking.

"Charlie . . ." she said, her tone stern.

I looked down, shame washing over me.

"Why are you being so weird?"

I thought about the turmoil that had been churning inside me for as long as I could remember. I struggled to put it into words. "Have you ever felt like you were born into the wrong life?" I asked.

"You mean like you were supposed to be born into a different family? Sure," she said, confusion clear in her voice.

"No. Like you weren't born in the right body," I tried to clarify, my heart pounding.

"Are you a wizard, Harry?" McKenzie said in an exaggerated British accent. She laughed, but I could see the confusion in her eyes. I screwed up my face, trying to find the right words.

"I think I'm transgender," I finally said, my voice trembling.

Her face twisted in disbelief. "What?"

"Transgender," I repeated, more firmly this time.

"No, you're not," she said, shaking her head in denial. "That's crazy. Why would you say that?" She seemed disgusted. It broke my heart.

She left my room that day and never came back. From then on, McKenzie acted like I didn't exist. She'd always been there, and then she wasn't. What hurt most was not knowing why she was so disgusted by me.

I couldn't comprehend how I went from being her best friend to someone she treated as subhuman. I was still me, but maybe she never saw me until I came out to her. Her response made me feel like I should hate myself. Self-loathing and loneliness together are a toxic cocktail.

But, for the first time since she left, I feel a little less alone here with the queens.

CHAPTER 20

'TIS BUT A SCRATCH!

Stacy

Ramon sits at the bar after drag brunch with a beer in front of him. He is engrossed in a conversation with Gary.

"No way! You played for the Gators?" Gary shakes his head and laughs.

"Sure did. Center fielder here." Ramon sips his beer and smiles proudly.

When I approach the bar, I sit beside Ramon and gesture to his beer. "Hard shift?"

He glances at the pint glass full of amber liquid and then gestures toward Gary, who has just drifted away. "Gary and I got caught up talking about college ball. He insisted on buying me a beer. Hope that's all right?"

My eyebrows squish together. "Of course. Why wouldn't it be?"

"I don't know," he mutters, a blush creeping up his cheeks. I chuckle, unable to resist.

"Where's Imogene?" he inquires, glancing toward the back.

I lift my brows. "Backstage, sewing beads onto Opal's dress. She's having the time of her life."

I had just come from backstage where I was helping a queen who sprained her ankle this morning. While I wrapped the ankle, Opal told a story about how her wig got stuck in a window and someone walking by her house was concerned a woman might be trapped. The room laughed wildly as Opal said, "And they told me, 'There's a lady stuck in your window!' I thought some crazy woman had broken into my house, so I grabbed a baseball bat." She mimes walking the perimeter of her house with a bat in her hand.

As I secured the bandage, I said to the injured queen, "Make sure you keep this elevated with ice and use ibuprofen rather than Tylenol. It will help with the inflammation."

"Guess I'm not performing tonight," they said with a disappointed sigh.

"Don't worry, sugar. I got ya. I always got ya," Peach said.

I recount the story to Ramon.

"Do they know you're a nurse?" Ramon asks.

"Imogene must have told them. They came and got me right after the show."

"Hmh." Ramon takes another sip of his beer.

I adjust myself on the barstool. "If you would have asked me what I would be doing on a random Monday, it would not have been this, but . . ." I consider my words. "I'm glad it's all happening this way." Ramon gives me an amused but curious stare. I put my hands up to explain further. "I'm not happy we are in the situation we are in, but I'm glad Imogene seems happy. It's been a long time since I've seen her smile in this way."

"Really?" Ramon says.

"Yeah. She's struggled for a long time, and even though I've tried, I haven't known how to help her." Admitting my failings as a mother is hard, but I feel comfortable talking to Ramon.

Ramon nods in understanding as he leans further forward. "Tell me more," he says, placing one of his forearms on the edge of the bar.

I gaze at the ceiling, then focus my eyes on the bar's back wall, not looking at anything in particular. "She was about twelve when everything changed. For a year before she came out to me, she withdrew into her own world. She became a loner. She'd never had a lot of friends, but she had one good friend. Suddenly, they stopped talking, and the only thing Imogene continued to find some level of enjoyment in was her interest in astronomy, but even that seemed tainted in some way."

"Who was the friend?" Ramon asks.

"McKenzie Michaels. Did you have her in class?"

"Yeah." He looks at me thoughtfully. "She's a smart girl, but she's unsure of who she is. She has this mask she puts up. Maybe that mask is the reason they stopped being friends? Of course, I could be off base. Teenagers are confusing. It's a hard age for everyone."

"Being a teen is hard, but it's more than that for someone like Imogene."

"Because she's trans?" He swirls the amber liquid inside the pint glass, watching the foam catch on the sides before looking at me.

"I don't know. Imogene started pulling away before she came out, so I assumed her reclusiveness would stop after she came out. I thought maybe the reason she had been struggling was because of this secret."

"But it didn't get better?"

"Barely. I've literally tried everything, too. I tried to get her into therapy, but she refused. She didn't want to talk to a stranger about her problems. So I made sure she had the family support she needed, and the medical care." I roll my eyes at myself and sigh. "I genuinely thought that if I could accept her and make sure everyone around us also accepted her, she would return to herself again. But she stayed withdrawn, and I don't know how to help her. To be honest, it is terrifying. But being here, it's like she has finally come back."

"That's good," he says.

"It is good," I respond, biting my bottom lip.

"But?" He nudges me with his shoulder.

I sigh as I try to discern my feelings. "I don't know. I was in such a hurry to get out of Florida, out of the United States, because I thought it would be safer. I was scared, and now I'm stuck here, and that safety I was looking for . . . well, it's here. Is that dumb?"

"No. I can see it. That's the whole point of a drag club, actually."

"Yeah, I guess you're right." I trace my fingers across the bar top, leaving marks in the thin layer of water left from when Gary wiped it down.

"So? Canada's off the table?" Ramon teases. "You're going to hide in a drag club until the end of time?"

"No, we can't stay here forever, but at least Imogene is having a good time." I throw my head back in thought. I don't know when Garrett will get tired of waiting and come after us, or worse, send the police. Every time I let myself think about it, a rush of anxiety floods my system, making me want to run at full speed. But I can't run. Not yet. For now, all I can do is make money and try to find a way out of this mess.

"You don't look happy about that," Ramon says, referring to Imogene having a good time.

I sigh. "I'm not unhappy. It's just . . . I don't know." I shake my head, searching for the right words. "It feels like . . ." I falter, unsure how to articulate the unease. I love seeing Imogene so happy, but something gnaws at my gut.

"Like she's growing up too fast, and maybe you're not the center of her world anymore? That you're not the only one who can make her feel safe?" Ramon suggests.

I snap my head up, startled. It's as if he's reading my mind.

"That sounds selfish, doesn't it? Maybe even a little crazy?"

He adjusts his glasses and studies me. "I'm not a parent, but I get it. I hang out with teenagers for a living, and they change a lot between starting high school and graduating. Change is hard, so yeah."

He smiles, his warm brown eyes offering comfort. I hold his gaze, feeling an indescribable emotion. Perhaps it's a deep respect? Respect for a person willing to put their life on hold to help someone who was but a stranger only days before. He transitioned from living his life to staying in a motel room and waiting tables. I think back to yesterday morning. Imogene and I clapped while he tried to snap his fan to the rhythm we set. He was always a second off, and we laughed so hard. Admiration for Ramon mounts within me.

I lean against the bar to escape the intensity, changing the subject. "So, college ball?"

"Yeah. College ball. I probably wouldn't have gone to college if I hadn't made it onto the Gators." He traces the grooves in the bar with his fingers. I divert my eyes from him, feeling myself edging on something I shouldn't and don't want to address.

"Why? Aren't you a huge science nerd like Imogene?" I ask.

"Sure. I am now that I'm no longer a punk."

My mouth nearly drops open. "Oh, gosh. I cannot imagine you being a punk!"

"You met my aunt, right? Saw how pushy she was? My mom was worse."

"And that made you a punk?"

"We were told we had no choice but to go to college, which made me want nothing to do with the place. Instead of studying like she wanted me to, I spent my time ditching class and hanging out with friends." Ramon gives a half-hearted shrug. "My mom was an immigrant, and the pressure of being an immigrant's kid is intense. Under pressure, I rebel. But I got lucky. I got picked, went to college, and made my mom proud."

"Awe . . . I also don't like being told what to do," I tell him.

"That's obvious," he says, and I lightly smack his arm with the back of my hand, chuckling.

As my fingers brush his arm, I'm reminded of Garrett. The way I used to touch his arm was just like this, especially when he made an off-color joke or said something outrageous. I used to love it. Love his jokes. Love that he always said what was on his mind. But, over time, it got tiresome. I needed him to be serious, but he couldn't be bothered. I never imagined our marriage would turn into what it became. I push the painful thought away before it can spread to my heart.

"Mom, mom, mom!" Imogene runs up from behind us, startling me. I swing around at the same time as Ramon, and the rush of the movement causes my elbow to hit the beer glass in his hand, which lands on the floor.

"Oh, shoot! I'm sorry!" Imogene says, and behind her follows Illusion.

"You scared us," I tell her.

"Is everything okay?" Ramon asks.

"Mom." The excitement is radiating off of Imogene. Illusion behind her holds a big Cheshire cat grin.

"They have invited *me* to perform! They want me to perform with them. Not tomorrow, but Wednesday night. Can I please? Mom?"

I look at Imogene, shocked by this information. "Um, let me think about it."

"No. Mom, please, just say yes. We have a lot to do, and we don't have time for you to think about it."

"Isn't she a bit young for drag?" I ask Illusion.

Illusion steps forward. "It's just a little lip sync number at the mic. Nothing fancy."

I shake my head slowly. "I don't know. Imogene, we aren't here for this. We're just here to make money to fix the car."

Imogene turns to Illusion. "I'll get tips, right?"

"Of course, Baby. We'll put you in the split."

Imogene attempts to give me puppy eyes. "Mom, please?"

"It's not about the money. I need time to think about it. You just sprung this on me." Worry creeps in. What if the audience isn't kind to her? What if something happens?

She doesn't see the things I witness on the floor. People sometimes grab at the queens as they walk around or make mocking jokes. While the dining room often seems filled with love and joy, I've observed a slight undercurrent of hate. It's not as loud but still lurks beneath the surface.

"You never let me do anything!" Imogene exclaims in a way that I've never seen and then she marches away. My chest clenches at the accusation. They always said the teen years were hard, but I don't think anyone prepared me for quite how much Imogene would test my patience.

Illusion covers her mouth with her hand. "I'm genuinely sorry. I thought I was doing something nice but may have over-stepped."

I put my hand up to my forehead. "You're fine. I just want to think about it. That's all."

"That's fair." Illusion rubs the back of her neck before dropping her gaze to the shattered glass on the floor. "Do you need some help? I can grab a dustpan."

"No, thank you. I think we got it," I say, gesturing to Ramon.

I bend over to pick up the larger pieces of glass while Ramon fetches a dustpan and broom. An unsettled feeling churns within me, like a persistent ghost I haven't been able to shake for years.

Deep in thought, I continue to lay pieces of glass in my hand.

"Hey, after this, if you want to head back and work on doing some research, I can walk Imogene back," says Ramon from behind me.

His voice breaks my thoughts, and a shard of glass slips through my fingers, cutting my skin. I suck in a breath and cradle my hand in front of me.

"I'm so sorry!"

"It's okay. It's not your fault. I was lost in thought."

He hunches to help me, and we butt heads. I fall back, and he remains hunched, but brings his hand to his forehead. "Ow."

"Gosh, what is with me today?" I say.

"You mean me." Ramon laughs, and I laugh with him.

"You got me good," I say.

"If I wanted this type of abuse, I would have stayed back in Jacksonville," Ramon says.

"You're abused?" I hold out a bleeding finger.

Ramon steps closer and takes my hand in his. His touch sends a shiver down my spine. He carefully examines the cut, but blood obscures it. His proximity causes my breath to catch and my heart to race. I feel a little lightheaded and lean back on my heels to steady myself.

"It looks bad. How does it feel?" he asks, his voice filled with concern.

I focus on my bleeding finger, trying to ignore the intoxicating closeness of Ramon. "It hurts a lot, which probably means it's not as bad as it looks."

"Really?"

"Yeah. Usually that's the case," I say with a half grin.

"Hmm." He's considering something, and I don't like not knowing his thoughts.

"What?"

"Maybe if that's true for cuts, it might also be true for other things. Maybe sometimes the things we worry about the most aren't as bad as we imagine."

I glare at him, but he might be right. Regardless, I need time to think.

CHAPTER 21

HOW GARRETT MET STACY

Garrett, Sixteen Years Before

The day I met Stacy was also the day I became a carpenter.

One afternoon, while chopping firewood for my uncle, I swung the axe with all my strength. The blade bit into the thick log, and with a sharp crack, it split clean in two.

"Hey, Garrett! How 'bout you take a break? Let's go have a beer," Uncle Ernest's voice cut through the mild evening air. My uncle's property sat on the outskirts of Denver. After being laid off, I'd moved in to save money and help him with his property.

I wiped the sweat from my forehead with my wrist and followed him into the house. Inside, the scent of pine and earth clung to us like a second skin. I grabbed the handle of the old fridge, an antique from the 50s with an icebox the size of a shoebox and pulled it open. The clinking of keys and the rustle of fabric stopped me. Uncle Ernest dropped the keys in his pocket before grabbing his hat.

"Road beer?" he joked. His laugh was raspy from too many cigarettes smoked in one lifetime.

"Are we leaving?" I asked, a hint of surprise lacing my tone.

"Yeah, I need a change of scenery. Thought we could hit up Cruisers," he replied.

Cruisers was a dive bar on the edge of town. It promised three-dollar well drinks and a bathroom that smelled of old urine cakes and mildew. Oddly enough, the blend of unfortunate smells added to the bar's charm.

We hopped in his truck and took the county road to the bar. The truck's tires kicked up clouds of dust. Once we arrived, the dust storm behind us settled into a hazy cloud.

Inside the bar, the transition from the bright, unforgiving daylight into the dim, dusky interior was jarring. I blinked several times to force my eyes to adjust. Dust-laden windows scattered the sunlight, and the dim lighting did little more than accentuate the bottles of liquor lining the wall.

"Hey, Ernest!" a comrade of my uncles from the VFW shouted from the other end of the room. Uncle Ernest went over to chat with him while I took a seat at the bar and ordered a beer.

Leaning forward, my shirt slid across my back. Starched by dried sweat, it felt stiff against my torso. When the bartender delivered my beer, I lifted the glass for a drink. My lips were salty and dry, so the beer felt good.

My gaze drifted across the dimly lit bar, landing on a man and woman playing pool. His shots were precise, each movement calculated. Hers, though less accurate, were as enthusiastic. She seemed unbothered by her misses, her laughter ringing clear against the backdrop of clinking glasses and murmured conversations.

She tossed her pretty brunette hair, and something in the way she moved caught my attention. Her natural grace made it impossible to look away. Her wide and genuine smile reached her eyes, crinkling at the edges in a way that told me she loved to laugh.

The guy she was with seemed like a tool. He showed off as he played, and although she appeared to be having fun, his show didn't impress her. She must have felt my gaze because, for a fleeting moment, she made eye contact with me. Hastily, I looked away and sipped my beer.

"Sorry about that," my uncle said as he took the stool beside me. He grunted as he lifted himself. "Haven't seen good ol' Greg in a while."

"You're fine," I assured him and signaled for another round.

"Listen," Uncle Ernest began, his tone carrying a weight that demanded attention, "it's time."

"Time?" I echoed.

"Time for you to find a job," he stated plainly, as if it were the simplest thing in the world. He took a large gulp of his beer and wiped his mouth with his sleeve.

"We're in the middle of a recession. No one is hiring."

His chuckle was soft, more reflective than amused. "No one is hiring because you're set on nothing but car sales. You're boxing yourself in."

"I'm good at selling electronics."

"And you're also good with your hands," he pressed, undeterred. "You need something solid, Garrett. A trade that'll hold up regardless of the economy's ups and downs."

I couldn't help but scoff, my skepticism showing through. "Tradespeople get laid off, too. Construction is doing terribly right now."

"Sure, but it's less permanent for them."

I sighed, knowing I wouldn't win this fight.

Uncle Ernest's eyes held mine in a steady gaze. "My friend Greg over there is hiring. He's willing to let you apprentice with him." He says this as if he'd already set the pieces in motion before we'd even walked into the bar.

"Apprentice? Is it paid?"

"Yes, it's paid. It isn't much, but a job is a job. It would be good for you to learn carpentry."

His arrangement made more sense now. Since high school, I'd built furniture when I had time. "I don't want to be a carpenter." The thought of turning woodworking into a career seemed to threaten its very essence. "Woodworking is a hobby. Turning my hobby into a job . . . that just . . . makes it a job."

"Look, you got to get a job. Try it out. Keep looking if it doesn't fit, but sitting by and waiting for an opportunity to hit you in the face isn't an option."

Before I could muster another word, Uncle Ernest motioned for Greg, who seemed to be waiting for the invitation. Greg approached and extended his hand, offering a firm handshake.

An hour later, I had marching orders for my first day of work. With the talks about my eventual job out of the way, Greg and Uncle Ernest started barking—as these old men did—about the state of our country and how everyone's want for a participation trophy is the reason for the current recession. Opting not to listen to them talk about everything wrong with my generation, I stepped outside.

The parking lot was mostly empty, save for the woman and man from the pool table earlier. They seemed to be having an intimate moment, so I stepped around the corner of the building to give them some privacy. That was until I heard her protests.

"I'm not getting in the car. You're drunk," she said.

His response came out slurred but insistent. "Get in the car," he shot back.

"Please, can't I drive?" she pleaded. Desperation tinged her voice.

But he was immovable. His decision was final. "Either you get in now, or I'm leaving you here."

I rounded the corner just in time to witness the car door slam and the harsh scrape of the tires against gravel as he reversed out of the parking lot.

"Dammit!" She kicked at the earth, hopping a little with frustration.

"You okay?" I asked, stepping closer.

Her laugh was bitter. "If you call being stranded by your date in the middle of nowhere 'okay,' then sure." She shook her head. "I knew I shouldn't have come out here. Stupid Melissa. This is all her fault."

"Melissa?"

"My roommate." She sighed. "She set us up, and when he asked to get a drink, I didn't think he would take me to a rundown bar in the middle of nowhere."

"Well, this isn't the middle of nowhere. I know it smells like cow shit, but there's a Target ten miles from here."

A weak chuckle escaped her. And I wanted to make that happen again.

"Where do you live?"

"I'm not telling you. I don't even know you." She jerked her head back, and a small line appeared between her brows.

"Easily remedied. I'm Garrett." I extended my hand.

"How am I supposed to know that's your real name?" She crossed her arms. I couldn't tell if she was joking or serious. Either way, she was cute.

"How am I supposed to know you didn't stage all this to rob me?" Humor embedded my words.

Her laughter was fuller, richer, and brighter this time. She looked at my hand and hesitated before taking it, her grip firm yet gentle. "I'm Stacy," she said, and the corner of her lips turned upward. "I live in Aurora."

Her admission felt like a small victory.

"I'm pretty familiar with Aurora. If you agree, I could give you a ride to this place—Aurora." I cocked my head to the side.

Her smile turned sheepish, her defenses visibly lowering. "Fine, you can take me home, but no funny business, okay? You try anything, and I swear, I will not hesitate to defend myself."

I put my hands up. "Noted. I will do my best to be as unfunny as possible."

She laughed again.

I'm unable to contain my grin. "And I'm already failing."

She laughed harder.

"I don't think this is going to work out between you and me." I motioned between us with my finger.

Her laughter subsided into a playful glare. "Oh, so you're planning on leaving me stranded, too?"

"No, I just meant that if I keep making you laugh, I'm not sure I'll make it back home in one piece."

"You know what I meant," she replied, shaking her head lightly.

"I do," I conceded with a smile. "Let me check with my uncle. We came together."

She nodded.

"Wait here."

Bursting back into the bar, my urgency got the better of me, causing a slight stumble over both my feet. I quickly explained the situation to Uncle Ernest. "There's this woman outside, and—"

Without hesitation, Uncle Ernest dangled his keys in the air, a knowing smile on his face. "Take it. Greg's got me covered for the ride. Right, Greg?" His gaze shifted to Greg, who nodded in agreement, his beer halfway to his lips.

"Thank you, Greg, for everything. I appreciate it."

Stepping back outside, I found her in the dim glow of the parking lot lights, hugging herself against the chill of the late evening.

"You okay?"

"Yeah. I usually plan for this sort of thing, and I'm pretty irritated that I didn't this time."

"You devise a plan for when your date gets drunk at a dive bar in the Mojave Desert and leaves you stranded? This way." I gestured toward the truck.

"I thought you said this wasn't the middle of nowhere," Stacy quipped.

"Hey, I just work here," I shot back with a grin.

"You work here?" She raised a brow and peered over my shoulder at the bar before eyeing my white tee, dirty jeans, and work boots.

"Looks like I finally nailed being unfunny." I headed to the driver's door and climbed inside. She followed suit, sliding into the passenger seat with a cautious grace. When she reached for the seatbelt, it refused to budge.

She frowned. "Your seat belt is broken."

"Sorry. This is my uncle's truck. He was alive before seatbelts were standard practice and still believes the government has no right to tell us we should wear one. The middle seatbelt works, though."

She climbed to the middle seat and took the seatbelt, placing it across her lap, buckling it in, and tightening it around her waist.

Her loose sundress was now cinched in at the middle, and I allowed myself the quickest glance at her figure before turning my eyes to the road. *Keep it respectful, Garrett. She just had a horrible date. She doesn't need your pervy eyes checking her out.*

As we pulled onto the main road, she asked, "So, if you don't work at the bar, where do you work?"

"I'm a carpenter," I said. Although I haven't started yet, it wasn't exactly a lie, and it sounded better than being unemployed. Her reaction was unexpected. She smiled wide.

"What?" I said and stole a glance at her.

"My dad is a carpenter. Maybe this night was meant to be."

Her words hung in the air between us.

"I guess the universe has its ways," I mused, allowing myself to entertain the thought that perhaps there was more to this evening's events than mere coincidence.

When we got to Stacy's apartment complex, she turned to me with a small smile. "Thank you for the ride."

"I would love the chance to attempt to be truly unfunny again."

She bit her bottom lip and looked at me through a fan of soft brown lashes. "As you said, 'the universe has its ways,' If it is meant to be, it will happen."

With that, she scooted to the passenger seat and climbed out of the truck. I watched her walk up to the apartment building and open the door. She turned back, her sundress catching slightly in the wind, and gave a small wave before disappearing into the building.

After that, I couldn't stop thinking about her. Two weeks later, the universe spoke, and I bumped into Stacy at the hospital after I cut my hand at work and needed stitches. She was a student nurse and happened to have clinicals that day.

CHAPTER 22

READY, SET, SHINE

Stacy

"Imogene! Please slow down," I yell after her.

She slows enough to placate me, but not enough for Ramon and me to catch up. Ramon shoots me a sympathetic look but doesn't interfere.

"Look both ways," I remind her before she crosses.

The sun shines bright and casts dappled patterns on Savannah's brick sidewalks. Blooming flowers emit a sweet smell that blends with the faint saltiness from the nearby ocean.

We are walking back to the club for our second shift, and Imogene is staying several steps ahead, her shoulders tense, and her movements are sharp. Reaching out, she brushes her fingers against the wrought-iron fence as we pass, but otherwise acts as if she is blind to the world around her.

She is mad at me for needing time. I feel like I'm always begging others for time. Just enough for me to figure things out before the inevitable happens. But maybe it's not time I need, but a pause, because regardless of how hard I try to slow or halt time, time is a general, a ticking tyrant. I'm at its will. It controls me. I do not control it. I beg for time to slow so I may untangle the chaos, but it never does.

"What am I going to do with her?" I ask Ramon.

His mouth stretches into a grin. "Let her."

I shake my head. Letting her is exactly what she wants, but not something I'm comfortable with.

When we reach the Drag Palace, Imogene darts ahead, vanishing into the building before I can say a word. I quicken my pace to catch up, but Ramon's hand lands on my shoulder.

I face him, and his compassionate expression catches me off guard. My heart beats harder with no prompting. His warm brown eyes tilt at the corners, and his lips are parted as if he is about to say something but has lost his train of thought. I wait, one, two, three beats, for the reason he stopped me. But he remains silent, the moment stretching between us.

He clears his throat and shifts his gaze. "I'm not trying to tell you how to parent. It's just that, from my experience, when we try too hard to control someone, especially a teenager, they push back. Maybe it's okay to let her be angry. Whether you let her perform is your decision, but if you decide not to, let her have her feelings about it."

I press my lips together, and he gives me a moment to process his words. "You're right." My shoulders drop, and I move my gaze to his face. "Thank you for everything. I know I keep saying that, but I don't know how I would have done any of this without you."

"You would probably already be in Canada," he jokes.

I chuckle, but his statement also makes me think. We have been gone for five days. When Garrett and I ended our last call, I was certain he wouldn't give me this time, but he has. Part of me wants to believe the time is his way of giving me grace, but it's more likely that he has returned to his habit of not following through. Either way, I need a plan by the end of these two weeks.

Although our progress toward Canada has halted, I have tried to use the time to plan. I've read everything I could on extradition law, custody rights, and protections for families like ours, hoping I could find even the smallest loophole that might save us.

Unfortunately, I have yet to find anything useful online.

We're making nearly $200 per shift combined, and although it will be tight, if the car gets done in the next couple of days, we should have enough money. The lingering uncertainty that exists beyond getting to Canada makes my fingers tingle, so I push it away. I still have time. I can still make it work.

Once we walk inside the club, I keep my head down and work. The moment with Ramon outside has unsettled me. My thoughts feel tangled, but I push them aside. Getting distracted now would only make an already complicated situation worse.

My mind drifts instead to Garrett. We've been in a rough spot for a long time. However, there has always been this lingering desire for what we had when we first started our lives together. A desire strong enough to keep an ember of our love alive even when it felt like the world was collapsing around us. Even through all the resentment and pain, there was still hope. That hope no longer exists. Garrett and I will never be the same again.

I feel the steady tug of grief on my heart and think it may pull me under. But grief is a luxury I can't afford. Not now. Not when there's so much at stake. I force myself to let it go, to clear my mind of everything—Ramon and the moment outside, Garrett and our broken marriage, the stress pressing on my chest. I channel all of it into work, letting the rhythm of the night drown out the noise in my head.

Tonight's show is phenomenal. They changed the setlist, and Peach welcomed five guests to the stage for a pie-eating contest. The contestants had only sixty seconds to devour their pies, an impossible task. The penalty for not finishing the pie is a face full of whipped cream. Seeing Peach playfully shove people's faces into the pie tins filled with fluffy, sweet white cream made me laugh until my sides ached.

The best part was when Peach scooped a dollop of whipped cream off a man's face with her finger and licked it clean. She then exclaimed, "Damn boy, that's finger-lickin' good!"

The crowd roared, and their laughter was infectious.

When all the guests are busy eating and enjoying the show, I weave through the backstage maze to the bathroom. The stark fluorescent lights flicker, casting an eerie glow on the cracked tiles. In the stall, the confines of the bathroom are quiet, and I allow my worries and my indecision to creep back in. What is going on with me and Ramon? Why am I even asking myself that question? Why won't I let Imogene perform? Is it about protecting her, or is it something else? The uncertainty is a persistent itch I can't scratch. The music from the dining room permeates the bathroom, and it's a few minutes before I convince myself to exit the stall.

As I emerge, I'm startled by the sight of Flora Fatal. Their towering presence and impeccable makeup are striking under the harsh light.

"Oh, my god, you scared me," I say, holding a hand to my chest.

"Girl, you scared me! You're in the men's bathroom." Flora imitates me, putting their hand to their chest and inhaling an exaggerated breath.

I look around as my cheeks flush. "I'm sorry. I'm a little distracted tonight."

"Oh, it don't really matter here at the Drag Palace, but still didn't expect to see you in here. I don't normally use this bathroom, but Peach is occupying the one backstage. Too much Taco Bell." Flora sneers in a playful display of disgust, then turns to the mirror to primp their hair. I turn on the faucet and wash my hands. The cool water soothes my thoughts.

"You know, that girl of yours is wicked smart," Flora says.

"Has she been bombarding you all with facts about space?"

Flora gives off a throaty laugh. "Oh, yeah. Between that and her questions about drag, she doesn't stop talking, but we love her. She's got genuine star quality, that girl."

I smile, a slight but genuine curve of my lips. "You think so?"

Imogene has always been shy. Apart from her fascination with astronomy, I've never seen her so electric. That includes her sudden outward petulance toward me.

Flora takes a tube of gloss from between their breasts and swipes some on their lips. "I do think so, but it's no wonder she's obsessed with outer space. She's been looking everywhere for her kind."

"Her kind?" I ask.

"Yes, girl. Her kind. Like I said, she's a star. All she needs now is to stop hiding her sparkle because, in my opinion, it's quite stunning."

I smile at the sentiment. "It is," I agree.

"Well, ta-ta, darling," they say before sashaying out of the bathroom while I dry my hands.

I stand at the sink a moment longer, absorbing the myriad signals around me. Ramon says I worry too much about things I don't need to worry about. Flora thinks Imogene is a star.

Maybe it is just me.

Garrett has long accused me of coddling Imogene, teasing me about being a helicopter parent. It infuriated me, but perhaps he was right on some level. I've had my reasons, though. I almost lost Imogene once, and that experience rewired me as a mother. But maybe I can allow Imogene to shine. With only a few more days before we go, perhaps it wouldn't be so bad to let Imogene leave on a high note.

After I finish work at the end of the night, I find Ramon cleaning the prep station across from the kitchen line. He's crouched, scrubbing the doors on a cooler.

"How much longer do you have?" I ask.

He looks up, his face flushed from the effort. "Ten minutes?"

"Is it okay if we head back without you? I want to talk to Imogene."

"Sure thing. I'll see you at the motel."

I nod and go backstage, where Imogene places rollers in a wig. The familiar scent of hairspray mingles with the heady aroma of sweat. She holds several pearl-tipped pins in her mouth and when she gets the roller where she wants it, she removes a pin from her mouth and pushes it through the hair and the soft mannequin head underneath.

"It's time to go."

She ignores me, her focus unwavering.

"Imogene," I say more firmly, but she ignores me again.

Peach speaks up from where she sits at a vanity. "Hey, your momma's callin' you. There might be no rules to drag, but ignoring your momma is quite impolite."

Imogene's face blanches, her boldness faltering. Without a word, she stands and walks over to her backpack to pick it up.

"Love you, Baby!" Several of the queens shout in unison, their voices a blend of affection and jest.

Imogene's face turns bright red. Though it pains her, maybe she needed a little embarrassment to humble her. We step out into the humid night. The soft glow of streetlamps casts long shadows.

We walk in silence for a few minutes. Imogene crosses her arms, but at least she is not walking ahead of me this time.

I let my mind wander back to the scariest day of my life—the day at the lake. After the incident, I was so shaken that I wanted to go home immediately. We packed up our car and left the lake house.

Imogene slept the entire drive, but as we got closer to home, she began coughing.

When we arrived, I lifted her small, sleepy body from the back seat and felt her shallow breathing against my chest.

"Something's wrong," I said to Garrett. Without hesitation, I buckled her back into the car seat and told him to drive to the hospital.

At the hospital, they assured me she was fine. Totally okay. But what if she hadn't been? The what-ifs haunted me then, and they still do now. A shiver runs up my spine.

I glance over at Imogene as she walks, her arms crossed and her body tense. I just don't want anything bad to happen. Since that day at the lake, endless what-if scenarios have filled my mind. What-if this and what-if that. Now, I don't even need to imagine a what-if to feel fear. But I can't let my fear and worry hurt Imogene when my purpose has been to protect her. I have to find balance. I'm just not sure how.

When we're almost at the motel, I speak up. "Will you please stop ignoring me?"

She tightens her arms around herself.

"Imogene," I say sternly.

She spins to face me and, with all the moodiness she can muster, asks, "Can I perform?"

"I just wanted some time to think about it," I reply, trying to sound calm, though I know she can hear the tension in my voice.

"And did you think about it?"

"I did."

"And you decided I can't." She flaps her arms down and rolls her eyes.

As wonderful as this new, more assertive side of Imogene has been, it is also extremely trying. Part of me wants to say she can't perform just because of her attitude, but I push forward with my decision, determined to stay rational.

"I'm sorry that I couldn't give you the answer you wanted right away. I felt like I was being rushed. I'm not trying to be mean. I just needed time to think about something as big as you performing in front of a crowd at a drag club."

Imogene turns away, her shoulders tense. I gently touch her arm, hoping to convey my sincerity.

"Please understand," I continue softly, "I just want to keep you safe."

She spins around, and I can see the defiance in her eyes. "Nothing is going to happen!"

"Maybe you're right, but what will we do if something bad happens?" I ask, the anxiety clear in my voice.

"Like what?"

"I don't know," I admit, trying to get her to understand the dangers without laying them out explicitly—mostly because I don't have a strong grasp on the potential risks myself.

"So? I can't perform?"

I take a deep breath, and she can see the conflict in my eyes. Finally, I exhale and nod. "You can. But I have stipulations."

"Really?" Imogene's eyes widen in shock. "Oh, my god! I can't wait to tell Illusion! Opal said she'll help me put my persona together. What about my hair? I bet I can use one of their wigs. What am I going to wear?" She jumps for joy, her excitement bubbling over.

"Imogene," I interrupt, hoping to calm her down. "Listen. You can perform, but I don't want you to leave that stage. You come out, lip-sync your song, and then go right backstage. Don't come onto the floor. Don't interact with the audience. Do you hear me?"

"Yes, yes, I hear you! This is going to be amazing!"

I stare as she bursts with excitement. My jaw tenses. I hope I know what I'm doing.

CHAPTER 23

STELLAR METAMORPHOSIS

Imogene

"Look at this!" Bryce pulls down the zipper on a garment bag, revealing a black dress with a tulle skirt. The tulle gives a voluminous and airy appearance. The off-the-shoulder bodice has layers of ruffled tulle, creating a soft, cloud-like effect around the neckline and shoulders. As Bryce pulls the dress from the bag, multiple layers of sheer fabric cascade in varying lengths.

I move closer to caress the dress. Silver stars of all shapes and sizes cover the tulle. My eyes trail from the dress to Bryce, wide in disbelief.

"How did you . . . Where did . . ." My words trail off as I gape at the dress. I'm stunned by its perfection.

He places the garment bag on a chair and holds the dress away from him to examine it. "I made it. Last night."

"What? How? Why?"

"Oh, Baby. I couldn't let you make your debut in just any dress. Also, tulle requires no hemming, and I already had this fabric."

I run to Bryce, hugging him tight around his waist. He makes an *oomph* sound, signaling that I knocked the air out of him. A single tear slides down my cheek, and I stare at him. His smile is wide. After McKenzie rejected me, I thought I'd always be alone, but I am far from it here. Having people who care about and accept me outside of my parents somehow makes me think that one day, I might fully accept myself.

"Thank you!" I say.

"Baby, it's my pleasure. Your mom told me you're leaving soon, and I have a thing about making my mark on the world." He looks at the ceiling thoughtfully. "It's really about me." Bryce gives a one-shoulder shrug that coordinates with a knowing smirk.

I turn to the dress and grab each side. Bryce steps back, watching me admire the dress.

"Can I have it? Like after the show when I leave?"

"Baby, that dress was made for you. I don't know another queen who could wear it, first because of the size and second because they would never do it justice. Speaking of, I guessed a lot when determining the sizing, but I have a pretty good eye, and the style is forgiving. It should fit."

This dress feels like more than just fabric. It's as if Bryce sees me even before I fully see myself. I hug the dress to my chest, feeling the excitement bubble inside me. "I have to show my mom and Ramon. Can I?"

Bryce waves me off. "Go, just don't rip it. I don't have time to repair it."

I nod eagerly and rush into the dining room where Mom and Ramon are sitting at a table with stacks of cash spread out in front of them. Ramon counts the bills carefully while Mom is hunched over my laptop, her face tight with concentration. She's been like this for days—focused on reading federal, state, and Canadian laws. I can see the stress etched into her features as her fingers glide over the mouse pad.

But my joy is too big to let it be tempered by her stress.

"Mom! Mom, look!" I call out, unable to contain my excitement.

Mom looks up, her brow furrowing as she takes in the dress. It takes her a moment to register what I'm holding.

"Is that what you're wearing?" she asks, her eyes widening.

I beam. "Bryce made it for me."

"When?" Ramon asks, glancing up from his counting.

"Last night." I can't help but grin and hop in place.

Mom's shoulders visibly soften, and a smile spreads across her face. "That was incredibly kind. Did you say thank you?"

I pause, feeling my initial excitement fade. The way she asks—it feels like she can't just let me have this moment without trying to control it. I feel a sudden wave rise in my chest.

I scoff, rolling my eyes. "Yes. Gosh, Mom, can't you just be happy about anything?"

The words come out harsher than I intended. Mom's face falls, and I regret my words. Despite how much her hovering gets to me, I don't want to hurt her.

"I'm sure your mom just wants to make sure Illusion's—I mean Bryce's efforts are appreciated," Ramon offers, setting aside the money in his hand. "That's all."

"I'm sorry," I say, feeling a pang of guilt.

"It's all good," Mom says, quickly changing the subject and fixing her face to disguise her hurt as she always does. "Are you hungry?"

"I'm fine. I just wanted to show you. I'm going to go back so we can prepare."

"Sounds good," she says, exchanging a look with Ramon. He tells Mom how much money they have so far, and they return to work. I head backstage, my excitement overshadowing the lingering guilt in my chest.

For the rest of the day, I focus on perfecting the rest of my outfit. In the dressing room, I try on wig after wig, searching for the perfect one. Wigs litter the vanity table, each one not quite right.

Dipping my head, I scoop my forehead into a red curly wig and bring it up, adjusting the lace to sit at my hairline. I stare at myself in the mirror, examining the new persona staring back.

Opal walks in, still in her street clothes. She does a double-take at the sight of me surrounded by a multitude of discarded wigs. "That's the one," she says with a confident nod.

"For real?" I ask, my fingers brushing the synthetic curls.

"Yeah, it goes with our song."

I look back at my reflection, and with this wig, I kind of look like her—Chappell Roan. I only discovered her music a few days ago, but I knew it was perfect for my debut.

My chest rises as I inhale a deep breath, a smile spreading across my face. The red curls frame my features, transforming me into someone bold and vibrant. Today, I'm not just preparing for a performance—I'm stepping into an unknown part of myself. As Illusion told me, it's not about the transition, but the transformation.

Today is a good day.

Minutes before I'm to step out on stage, I stand before a floor-length mirror. The other queens bustle around, making last-minute touches for the show, but despite the flurry of activity, I take a moment to push everything away and be alone with my reflection.

I sway in the black dress, watching the tulle move gracefully from side to side. This dress, the most feminine thing I've ever worn, somehow single-handedly soothes my dysphoria. I've spent countless hours scrutinizing my lanky, boy-like frame in the mirror, fixating on my flat torso. The sharp angles of my hips and shoulders, too square to belong to a girl, bother me.

But this dress, with its tulle neckline and cinched waist that flares into a wide skirt, creates an hourglass figure. And for the first time, I almost feel connected to myself.

Flora comes over and places a hand on my shoulder. "You look beautiful."

I find their eyes in the mirror's reflection. "Is it time?"

"Yep, Illusion told me to come get you."

I'm directed to stand on stage behind the curtain. The lights are off, and despite the noise of the audience in the dining room and the music playing overhead, I can hear my own nervous breathing. My heart pounds like a drum. The air is thick with anticipation, and I feel the crowd's energy beyond the curtain.

I never thought I'd be brave enough for this. If only my dad were here to see it. I'm doing what he wanted me to do. I'm being brave.

The music quiets, and the curtains part, revealing a sea of expectant faces. I imagine the exhilaration I feel is similar to how astronauts might feel when the spacecraft's hatch first opens, revealing space. My body is like a coiled spring, ready to snap at any moment.

I step up to the microphone and place my black glove-covered hand on the stand. I'm moving in slow motion with zero gravity. The lights above, blazing like the sun, illuminate only me, and I squint as my eyes adjust.

A piano melody flows overhead, like a stream of cool water, just before the opening lyrics of "Pink Pony Club" play. I take a deep breath. The audience falls silent. Their attention is wholly on me.

With the mic off, I sing softly, still new to lip-syncing. The lyrics hit deep, speaking to parts of myself I'm still trying to understand. There's something about wanting to belong and finding the freedom to be who you are that makes my chest tighten—in a good way.

I feel every eye on me, but instead of being scared, I feel free. This is my moment.

As the music builds, my confidence swells. Then, as the song reaches its climax, the stage explodes with light and color. One by one, the drag queens join me on stage, their vibrant costumes a stark contrast to my black dress. They surround me, and the audience erupts in applause and cheers.

Amid the performance, I scan the crowd and find my mom standing beside Ramon in the back. Her eyes are bright with pride and tears, her hands clasped together as if in prayer. She is not hovering or worrying. She is just there, beaming with pride. That's all I've ever wanted.

As the song fades out, the drag queens strike dramatic poses. The crowd roars, the applause thunderous. I stand in the center of the stage, the spotlight still on me, my chest heaving with emotion more than exertion. An intense sense of belonging, a connection as I've never felt before, washes over me, and for the second time that day, a tear escapes and falls down my face.

CHAPTER 24

TODDLERS IN TIARAS

Stacy

As Imogene steps onto the stage, the gasps from the audience are audible, and in my naivety, I believe they mirror my own—awed by her presence. She stands unmoving at the mic, one hand gripping the stand as she leans in. The song that comes over the speakers is one I've never heard before. I focus on the lyrics and Imogene, intently listening. Immediately, I understand her song choice.

As I watch her mouth move along to the words, my eyes mist over. The song is a dagger. The lyrics speak of wanting to be free, of belonging somewhere far from home, where she feels seen and accepted. As I watch her, eyes bright and determined, it hits me. She's telling me something, something I've been too scared to acknowledge. It hurts because I realize how far she feels from me.

Watching her perform, embodying the struggle I've been desperate to shield her from, I see I have done very little to lessen the blow of life's disappointments, but instead, have stifled her growth. Part of the reason she cannot shine is that I have been standing in the way. I intended to protect her, but I obstructed her path.

When the other drag queens join her on stage, my emotions overwhelm me, and I raise my hands to my mouth. Their collective energy is stunning. As their performance ends, I feel like my heart might leap from my chest. I glance over at Ramon, standing next to me, but I'm puzzled by the concern etched on his face.

Then I hear it—a few tables away are mutterings of disapproval. "That was a child!" a middle-aged man shouts after the curtain closes. He points his finger accusingly at the stage.

"What's your point?" a woman with short, spiky hair retorts from behind his table, turning to face him.

"It's bad enough they can watch, but to perform, too?" the man continues, his voice rising.

Anger and dread settle over me, and my pulse quickens. Is he talking about Imogene?

"Why are you even here if this offends you so much?" another man interjects, irritation clear in his tone. "No one forced you to be here."

The tension escalates with overlapping voice. "I'm an adult. That's a kid. Those groomers are recruiting kids now. Don't you see how that's a problem?"

"And you probably have no problem with toddlers in beauty competitions, but you have a problem with a girl singing with a bunch of drag queens. Check your internalized homophobia," the man shoots back.

The argument seems on the verge of spiraling out of control, with people shifting in their seats and others murmuring in agreement or dissent. Ramon steps closer to me, his hand hovering protectively near my back. The original naysayer finally mutters, "Whatever, man," and turns away. Still, the uneasy atmosphere lingers, and the echoes of his words hang in the air.

I should leave it alone, let it blow over, but I can't. His words claw at me. I glance at the stage where Imogene and the queens were only a moment ago. The queens have only been kind and accepting, so hearing that man twist their relationships into something ugly feels like a personal attack. It enrages me. How dare someone reduce their love and support to something so malicious?

Compelled by an inexplicable urge, I approach the table that started the commotion. "Can I get you anything before the next act?" I want to dump their food on their laps, but I hold my composure. I need to be close by so I can control any potential chaos.

"Our check," the man snaps. They barely touched their plates, abandoning their half-eaten meals due to their discontent. The two women with him look embarrassed, their eyes avoiding mine.

I deliver their check, and they leave soon after. Their reaction is exactly what I had feared—not the specifics, but the hostility. I'm just grateful their departure spares most of the audience from witnessing any further confrontation. It would have shattered me—shattered Imogene—if she had heard their vile words. But with the performance over, the immediate risk has passed.

At the show's end, I leave my duties to check on Imogene.

"Did you like it?" she asks when she sees me, still breathless and in her costume. Her bright red lips stretch into a wide smile, and her eyes sparkle with post-performance joy.

"Yeah, it was great."

Sensing the tension in my tone, although I tried to disguise it, she frowns and asks, "What? Was it bad?"

I try to save face. "No. It wasn't bad at all. It was quite beautiful. I loved it." I force a reassuring smile.

She waves off her concern, focusing on her excitement. "Illusion says we can do it again tomorrow if it's okay with you."

Illusion steps forward, extending a hand. "Not trying to overstep, but it was a fantastic addition to the show."

"It's best we don't," I say, trying to keep my voice steady.

"But, Mom," Imogene protests.

This time Illusion comes to my defense. "You know what? Now that I think about it, we had to swap Opal's ballad for that spot. She might be mad if we do it a second time."

Imogene's shoulders slump.

I approach her tentatively, placing a gentle hand on her arm. "You did such a wonderful job tonight. Truly, I'm proud of you. I need to go clean, but maybe you can clean up, too, and I'll come get you when I'm done."

She nods, but the disappointment stains her expression. As I turn to return to work, I glance back at her, and a pang of guilt blooms in my chest. I want to protect her, but it's hard to balance that with letting her shine.

I'm in the dining room, cleaning menus when Illusion comes out. She approaches with a gentle smile.

"Hey," she says. I stop cleaning and face her. "I want to thank you. I remember being Baby's age, and it wasn't easy. You're a much better mother than mine was. God rest her soul." Illusion voice drips with drama. "She would have died a whole decade sooner if she had seen me on that stage at Imogene's age tonight."

"Yes, of course. Thank you for inviting her. You made her whole year."

We stand there for a moment too long. I stretch the washrag in my hand while mulling over my mixed feelings. I want to see my daughter happy, but being out there so visible puts a target on her back, and I don't want to make it easy for anyone to aim. Why would Illusion?

"Why did you invite her to perform with you?" I ask.

"Because no one puts Baby in the corner." Illusion winks.

"You keep saying that," I respond, tilting my head.

Illusion peers into the dining room, her gaze thoughtful, then turns back to me. "I remember what it felt like to not belong, and here at the Drag Palace, I've only known belonging. This place is special, unlike any other. I wanted to make sure Imogene got a taste of what that feels like because, if she knows what to look for, then she'll find her people just as I've found mine."

Illusion heads backstage to become Bryce again, and I sit with her statement, letting it sink in.

When I finish cleaning the dining room, I notice Ramon laughing and talking at a table with a group waitstaff and cooks. I considered joining them but decide to collect Imogene.

Backstage, several of the queens sit around chatting. I turn my head from side to side as I search for Imogene, but she is nowhere to be seen.

"Imogene?" I say aloud, but no one answers.

My heart thuds, a physiological response I'm no stranger to.

Steve walks through, already dressed in his street clothes.

"Have you seen Imogene?" I ask, my voice tinged with worry.

"Not since 'bout thirty minutes ago," Steve replies, the corners of his mouth turned down.

Alarm bells ring in my ears, but Flora steps in before panic can take hold. "She's on the roof. I told her I would let you know, but I ripped a hole in my suit and got distracted."

"*The roof?*" I echo, bewildered. "Why would you let her go to the roof?"

"I'm sorry, I didn't think . . . The stairs are through that door," Flora says, their eyes full of apology as she points toward a door marked *Exit*.

I spin around, push the door open, and start climbing the stairs.

When I reach the top, Imogene is sitting alone, her neck craned as she stares at the stars. The night sky stretches above her, an expanse of twinkling lights.

"Hey, what are you doing out here? Star-gazing?" I ask, approaching her cautiously, trying to determine if I'll be the recipient of teenage anger tonight.

She breathes in deeply, her shoulders rising and falling. "I'm sad," she breathes.

"Why? Because you can't perform tomorrow?" I ask, sitting beside her, trying to read her expression in the dim light.

Imogene shakes her head. "No, it's more than that. I don't want to leave here." She pauses. "I also miss Dad. He would have been proud of me."

My heart deflates. "He would have," I agree.

She adds, "I also miss McKenzie."

When McKenzie disappeared from our lives, I tried to ask Imogene about it, but she would only shrug me off. I thought maybe they had a stupid fight and would resolve it. But they never did. I tried to get Imogene to tell me what happened between them. I probably pushed harder than I should have, since it just made Imogene recoil away from me in a way that set my anxiety on fire.

This was the first time Imogene has talked about McKenzie willingly. I want to press, to ask more, but I'm afraid.

I sit quietly and decide to move forward with honesty, just as Imogene has.

"Hey," I whisper. "I want to ask about what happened with McKenzie, but I also don't want to upset you. If you decide to share, I'm here to listen."

She lets out a long sigh.

"I told her I was trans." Heartbreak sits in the curve of her lips. "That was the last day of our friendship."

At this revelation, I learn that McKenzie was the first person to know the real Imogene, and she rejected her. My heart aches for my child.

I snuggle up next to Imogene and hold her hand, bringing it into my lap. The warmth of her fingers intertwines with mine. "I'm sorry." I don't offer a solution because, frankly, I don't have one. There are going to be so many people who turn their backs on my daughter simply because of her gender identity. People will go out of their way to tell her she is a man and deny her existence.

But to have her closest friend reject her . . . that's hard, and I don't think there is anything I can do to make that pain more bearable. Therefore, an apology is all I can offer.

Together, we sit, our necks stretched, and our chins pointed as we stare at wisps of clouds decorated by scattered stars.

After a long moment, Imogene changes the subject. "Did you know that stars come in different colors? There are green, blue, and even red stars?" Her voice holds a flicker of wonder that pierces through the melancholy of her heartbreak.

"I do now," I reply, even though I'm certain she has told me that fact before. I've always admired her fascination with the universe. To be so smart and inquisitive. However, the thought of space and its expansiveness makes me uneasy. Terribly uneasy. It feels so unknown and unpredictable. And the thought of space beyond what I can see before me makes my chest hurt almost as bad as when I'm afraid for my daughter. Imogene once told me I have astrophobia, or an irrational fear of outer space. I denied it, but she was right.

Imogene continues her lesson on the stars. "It depends on their temperature. Guess which ones are the hottest?"

"Hmm. Red," I say, playing along.

"Blue. Red stars are the coolest."

"You are the coolest," I say, squeezing her hand.

She chuckles, a soft sound that melts any lingering tension between us. "Thanks for letting me perform and not overthinking it for too long."

"I'm sorry I said no to a second night. You know I only want to do right by you, don't you? That everything I do is for you?"

Imogene bites at her fingernails. "I understand, but I need you to be my mom, not just my protector. I don't want to be saved. I just want to be loved."

"I do love you. That's why I try so hard to protect you."

"I know." She leans into me, and my heart stops.

I lift to look at her face, illuminated by the faint glow of the streetlights. "What do you think about *Toddlers & Tiaras?*" I ask her, trying to lighten the mood.

Her brows scrunch together. "Fine, I guess. That's random."

I laugh, and she shakes her head with a small smile.

When we walk back down, the backstage area is empty. Music pulses from the dining room, and Imogene and I look around, trying to understand what's happening and where everyone has gone.

As we open the door to the dining room, we are amazed to see someone has moved all the tables and chairs. Multicolored lights dance along the floor, reflecting off the feet of everyone in the club. The queens and several waitstaff are dancing with abandon, their movements free. Illusion sees us and waves us onto the dance floor.

Imogene takes in the crowd, her eyes wide with wonder. "What's going on?"

"We're celebrating!" Flora yells back, their voice full of exuberance. Bryce shimmies playfully as Flora swings their hips.

"What?" Imogene and I say together, puzzled.

"Your debut, Baby! Now get out here and dance."

Imogene releases my hand and joins the group, her movements gaining confidence as she swept up in the celebration. I watch her, a smile tugging at my lips. The exuberance and energy radiating from her is blinding. Ramon stands across from me on the other side of the dance floor, standing with a few others who have chosen not to join in. I walk over to him.

"Told you everything would turn out all right," he says, gesturing to the dancing crowd.

"Yeah, but it also could have gotten out of hand." I know everything feels like it's okay, but I need to stay realistic.

"But it didn't," he argues.

"Maybe not this time, but one day it will. There is so much hate in this world, and we aren't always going to get lucky."

"If you're looking for hate, you'll always find it." Ramon gives me a pressed smile.

I give a one-shoulder shrug. "I guess."

"Just say it. I was right."

"Never."

Amused by my stubbornness, he holds out his hand and looks at me with a warm, inviting smile. "You want to dance?" He wiggles his eyebrows.

I tilt my head. "I thought you couldn't dance."

"I'm Cuban," he says with a grin. I laugh, taking his hand so he can lead me onto the dance floor.

The other dancers move to make room for us, and we are submerged into the collective energy. Through the crowd, I catch glimpses of Imogene. She is glowing, her laughter echoing above the beat, her joy unmistakable.

Ramon's dancing is charmingly awkward. He steps out of sync with the music, but his enthusiasm is infectious. He sways and twirls me with a playful grin, and I can't help but laugh at his earnest effort.

Ramon stumbles, and I quickly correct before we both end up on the floor. We laugh large belly laughs. "See? Not so bad, right?" he says.

"Not bad at all," I agree. A lightness I haven't felt in a decade lifts my soul.

CHAPTER 25

THE SPACE BETWEEN

Stacy

Savannah is a beautiful city. Silvery tendrils of Spanish moss drape the historic oaks lining the streets. Ramon insists we take different routes to work each morning, each one sharing something a bit different about the city. Today, we pass through a park full of trees and sweeping green spaces.

Ramon pulls his phone out of his pocket and glances at the screen before answering it. "Hello?"

I walk beside him and Imogene, enjoying the leisurely pace. Imogene plays an old Game Boy that a queen gave her while she walks. I've warned her about watching where she walks, but she doesn't care. Plus, I feel bad she still doesn't have a phone. I can't afford to buy her one right now. And even if I could buy her a cheap one, I'm scared she'll call Garrett. I just need a little more time to get her to safety before she calls him. So far, I have found nothing that will definitively help us, except the small relief that extradition could take ages to go through.

"It's done?" Ramon asks. There's a glimmer of enthusiasm in his expression.

I watch Ramon as he walks, one hand in his pocket while the other holds the phone to his ear. The easy way he carries himself. Unapologetic, kind, and cheery, but also responsible and self-sacrificing. His button-up shirt is a little snug, and his top buttons are undone, allowing for sparse chest hair to peek through. He looks so much more relaxed than the day I met him at the nursing home when he wore a bow tie and dress slacks. I've enjoyed getting to know this other side of him. He's good people.

"No, that's great. Of course. Thank you. We're headed to work right now, but we can come get it after our shift. Is two o'clock okay? Great!" Ramon says.

As he hangs up, he turns to me with a broad smile. I can sense the relief in his posture.

"What did they say?"

"It's done. The car is ready." He tucks his phone back into his pocket.

I let out a contented sigh, and my shoulders relax. "Finally."

"Does that mean we're leaving tomorrow?" Imogene asks.

"Um. We could leave today," I say.

Imogene's arms drop to her side, the Game Boy still clutched in her hand. "No, please, Mom. Can we just stay one more night?"

I glance over at Ramon. He shrugs, a smile tugging at his lips. "What's one more night?"

We still had time to spare, the extra money would be good, and it would allow Imogene time to say goodbye to all the queens working today because not all of them work both shifts. "Okay, then. Tonight is our last night."

"Dope," Imogene says, returning her attention to her game and only glancing up intermittently to check her path as she walks.

The morning air feels fresher, and the path ahead seems brighter. Maybe everything will work out. We have enough money, Garrett hasn't tried anything, and maybe in a couple of days, I'll be in a place where I can concentrate on mending this mess.

An elderly man walks his dog ahead of us, and from the back, he looks a little like my dad. My heart aches at the thought. Since he got sick, I have visited at least twice a week, and now I haven't seen him in over a week. I doubt he's noticed, but I'm also anxious to find a way through this so I can find my way back to him.

At the club, I hum to myself while I work. Beside me, Ramon works in comfortable silence. The morning light filters through the windows, casting a warm glow over everything.

Ramon nudges me playfully as he helps me set tables in the dining room. "You seem different today," he notes.

I pause. "I don't know. Seeing Imogene on stage last night, the car being fixed today, and us having enough money to pay for it—I finally feel like things are going to be okay."

Ramon places a stack of plates on the table before turning to me, his expression sincere. "They will be, and even if they're not, you'll make it through. I've only met a few people as determined as you."

Warmth spreads through me at his words. "I don't think I've ever met someone like you."

He chuckles softly while adjusting a chair. "I hope that's not a bad thing."

"It's a compliment."

Blush creeps along his cheeks. Ramon's modesty is sweet, and it makes me smile. He clears his throat, clearly flustered, and changes the subject. "Gary said he can give us a ride to pick up the car after brunch."

I stop in my tracks. He always does that. He always takes the initiative.

"Thank you. I mean it. Most men are not so proactive."

I turn my attention back to setting the table and glimpse Ramon's bashful smile from the corner of my eye as he says, "No problem."

When brunch is over, I instruct Imogene to stay put with Illusion until we get back. Gary drops us off in front of an open garage, housing Ramon's car.

I watch Ramon count out the cash and hand it to the mechanic.

In the car, Ramon puts in the key, and I have a moment of doubt before I hear the engine come to life. Then, the most miraculous thing happens. Cool air comes from the vent. Ramon rolls the window down.

"Did you fix the AC?" he asks the mechanic.

The mechanic, wiping his hands on a rag, nods. "This morning. After one ride around town to make sure it ran smoothly, I thought it would be cruel not to fix your AC, too. I didn't charge you, so you can thank me."

Ramon's grin widens. "Thanks, man."

On our drive back to the club, my phone vibrates in my pocket. I pull it out to check who is calling. Sarasota Memorial Hospital flashes across the screen. It disrupts my good mood and anchors me back to reality.

I'm not ready to face it. I block their number like I blocked Garrett's. In fact, every time I get a call from a number that seems suspicious, I block it. It's only temporary.

When we pull up to the Drag Palace, we sit in the car. We're finally going to leave this place. It's only been a week, but the connection I feel to the Drag Palace and the people inside is undeniable.

For the first time, I saw Imogene come to life in a way I never had before. Here, she can truly be herself. Part of me doesn't want to take that away from her. Leaving feels like it might somehow diminish her light, but staying also isn't an option. We've already been so incredibly lucky that nothing has happened yet. But just because it hasn't—just because the police haven't shown up to arrest me, Garrett hasn't reported me for kidnapping (as far as I know), or Imogene hasn't been placed in foster care—doesn't mean it won't. So, we have to go.

With a little space and time, I believe I can make things right. But I'm also not ready to say goodbye to Ramon. He has been such a breath of fresh air—someone who takes responsibility for a burden that isn't even his to carry. I still don't know why he does this. He has nothing to gain.

Ramon breaks the silence, his voice tinged with nostalgia. "It's going to be strange leaving this place."

"Yeah, it is," I agree, glancing at him. He grabs his phone from the center console and thumbs Toronto into his GPS app.

"If we leave in the morning at around seven, we can get there by midnight with breaks." He adjusts his fingers' pinch to zoom in and out on the screen. I study him as his brows pull together, studying the route on his phone.

"I don't know how I will ever repay you for all you have done for us."

"I don't need to be repaid. I'm happy to help," he says.

"But why?" I adjust myself in my seat, sitting straighter to communicate I'm serious about my question.

"Why what?" he asks. I can tell he doesn't want to reveal his motivations, but I feel a need to understand.

"Why are you helping us? Normal people don't help other people like this."

"Sure, they do." He puts his phone down and makes eye contact with me.

I chuckle. "No, they don't! Ramon, tell me. Why are you helping us?"

I'm surprised when his face drops. He lets out an exaggerated breath. "I had a sibling a lot like Imogene."

My brows pinch together.

He rubs the palms of his hands on his pants, uncomfortable. "They were different. This was a time before people had the awareness and the language to talk about things like gender identity. So, I guess she may have been my sister in a different reality, but back then, I couldn't see it. I didn't understand it, and . . ."

"I understand. I didn't quite react in a way that I wish I had when Imogene came to me," I say.

"No, it's not that. I was cruel. I was their older brother, and because I couldn't understand it, I was a real asshole."

I realize then he said his sibling may have been. Past tense. "Wait, did they pass away?"

"Yeah, they did. I just thought if I could help Hector man up . . ." He pauses, taking a deep breath. "But I don't want to pretend my intentions were good. I was honestly embarrassed by Hector."

He glances at me briefly, then looks away, his expression full of regret. "Hector was only two years younger than me, and it was so apparent they were different. Growing up, Hector drew a lot of attention, even when they didn't want to. Hector was the only name I knew them by."

He considers his words. "I felt more of a need to be accepted by my peers than to protect my sibling the way you protect Imogene. Because of that, I was their biggest bully. So much so that I looked for opportunities to expose them. Bringing attention to them felt safer than ignoring or concealing."

"What happened?" I ask, imagining the worst.

"I don't know for sure if Hector was transgender. They never said. They probably didn't know themselves. And with how awful people were to them, they started drinking, I'm guessing, as a way to cope."

Ramon's eyes mist over, and he balls his hands to fists. "I went off to college and left Hector behind. In their senior year and my second year of college, Hector was in a car accident. They were drunk, not wearing a seatbelt, and died on impact when their skull hit the pavement."

I reach out to touch his clenched fist. "I'm so sorry."

Ramon lets off a melancholy chuckle. "It was the same semester I took a psychology class that covered trans issues. During that class, something just clicked, and I knew. I had matured a lot in college and realized what a jerk I'd been. I planned to go home to apologize for how I treated Hector." Ramon's shoulders sag as he finishes. "But I never got the chance."

"It's not your fault," I try to reassure, but I know that if this were my experience, the guilt would eat me alive.

"It is, but I can't go back and change any of it. That's why I . . . why I jumped at the opportunity to help you. I want to do better, but I don't know if I'll ever do enough to make up for what I've done."

I reach for his face, caressing the soft stubble on his chin. "I'm so sorry, Ramon. If Hector was trans, and in fact, your sister, I know she's very proud of you now."

He looks at me, his eyes watery, and leans in. The smell of his skin is tantalizing, and I can't help but want to be closer to him in this moment of vulnerability. Before I know it, his lips are on mine. While we are hesitant at first, once he feels I'm reciprocating the kiss, he kisses me more fiercely.

But then I pull away from him, stricken and not sure of what I'm doing. A swirl of conflicting emotions fills my chest, and I'm trying to process what just happened when I catch movement out of the corner of my eye. Imogene is standing at a 45-degree angle from the car.

Panic consumes me. "Oh, my god!"

Ramon echoes my alarm with a single word. "Shit."

I lock eyes with Imogene. Her gaze is watery and filled with a hurt that mirrors Ramon's, yet different. Her hurt is angry, not remorseful. I leap from the car, rushing toward her.

"Imogene, wait! I can explain," I call out, even though I have no explanation to give.

She pivots on her heels and runs down the road.

CHAPTER 26

THE SEVEN LETTER WORD

Stacy, Eight Days Before

The night Lilly came to warn us about the emergency removal, I sat on my bed, trying to think of a way to fix everything that had gone wrong.

I rocked back and forth, hands pressed to my forehead, repeating, "I can fix this, I can fix this." My breathing was shallow, my heart pounding, and tears blurred my vision.

But how? My mind strained for a solution, but nothing came. There was no way. They were going to take her away—away from me, from us. My baby. Imogene would end up somewhere awful, with people who didn't understand her, alone and vulnerable. I couldn't let that happen. Every muscle in my body believed something terrible was going to happen to Imogene if they took her away.

It was all my fault. Everything was falling apart. I was going to lose my job, my license, my career. I'd be arrested. I'd go to prison. And Imogene . . . what would happen to her then? Garrett? He couldn't even take care of himself, let alone her. She would be stuck in foster care until she aged out of the system.

I was drowning, barely keeping my head above water, and no matter what I did, I kept getting pulled under.

My heart raced, my mind spinning out of control. We had to go. That was the only option left, right? We couldn't stay here, not after this. If we waited, the police would come knocking, and I wouldn't be able to protect Imogene. I couldn't let that happen. I wouldn't let that happen. We needed to leave. Flee Florida and get to Canada. Stay with my aunt. I hadn't talked to her in years, but she would take us in, wouldn't she? Maybe then we'd have a chance.

I started to pack just as Garrett entered the room and shut the door behind him. Before he could say anything, I cut in with an abruptness that stopped him in his tracks.

"We have to leave."

"Leave?" His brows shot up with the sharpness of his question.

"Yes, leave. We can't let them take Imogene." I could tell by the way Garrett looked at me he was offended I'd already made up my mind. But I didn't care.

"Oh, no, Stacy. You're already in enough trouble. We need to go about things the right way. The legal way this time."

"There is no right way!" I yanked open the dresser drawers and grabbed handfuls of clothes, tossing them onto the bed. "Do you think a group home is going to be better for her? You think DCFS is going to put her somewhere safe?"

"Calm down. You're being irrational." Garrett's calm demeanor was in such great contrast to the storm inside me. The contrast deepened my frustration.

"Irrational?" I snapped, desperation rising. "This is our daughter's life we're talking about. We need to act. We're leaving."

"Stacy, listen to yourself. You're nuts." Why is it whenever a man disagrees with a woman, he calls her crazy? I'm not crazy.

"Don't you dare call me crazy again." I slammed my dresser drawers shut and walked around the bed to stand in front of him.

"But that is how you're acting." Tension spiked his every word. "We are not leaving."

"Yes, we are!" I screamed. The room felt like it was closing in on me, suffocating me. My face felt hot. He regarded me as if I were a wild animal, and I let my shoulders fall, breathing heavily.

"I want a divorce." He stepped back, his words sucking the heat from my face and chilling me to the bone.

For a moment, the only sound was the quiet hum of our air-conditioning unit. We had promised we would never say that word unless we meant it. It was one of the ground rules we set before we got married. Never had either of us uttered it. And now . . .

"You don't mean that," I said, my voice barely above a whisper.

"Yes, I do." His voice was steady now, and the calmness in his eyes sent a shiver down my spine, making me feel more uneasy than his anger ever did.

I shook my head, refusing to believe this was what he wanted. He was so lazy that he would rather get a divorce than help me. Seriously. Of all the times he could have asked for a divorce, he does it when we had so much at risk. He didn't care about Imogene like I did. He would rather abandon us than fight to protect our daughter.

A sense of betrayal washed over me. The room spun as I tried to make sense of the emotions crashing over me—fear, sadness, anger, and a profound sense of loss.

I wrapped my arms around myself, trying to hold together the pieces of my heart shattered by his words. *Why now?* When we needed him most. *Why would he leave when the world is crashing down around us?*

My words stuck in my throat, but I finally muttered, "You're really going to leave us now? When everything is falling apart?" Tears welled in my eyes, but I refused to let them fall. "Why would you do that to us?"

"Because of you, Stacy! You've ruined our family. You hover over Imogene so much she probably waits for your permission to breathe. You do things behind my back, you don't respect me, and I'm always the bad guy." He stared at me like it was all so obvious. "I want a divorce because I fucking hate you."

I stood silent. I could no longer stop the tears streaming down my face. He was right about one thing: I had gone behind his back. At the time, I'd been scared. I was terrified he'd try and stop me. That was wrong. But I couldn't change it. All I could do was think of Imogene.

Finally, I said, "What about Imogene?"

"Fuck, Stacy. Do you hear yourself? You don't give a shit about me or our marriage. I'm telling you I want a divorce, and you still think I'm going to want to take part in the fucked-up nonsense you've created?"

He stepped closer, his physical presence threatening. "I'm going to tell DCFS everything. And then Imogene will come live with me—away from you."

My heart dropped. My chest tightened as if I couldn't get enough air. "You can't. You can't take Imogene from me," I said, my voice trembling with disbelief. Could he? He had to be bluffing.

"I will. I promise," he sneered. "You've made her anxious and afraid of her own shadow. She's a shell of the person she could be, who she *wants* to be, because of you. You're a terrible mother."

His words stung, and I gasped for air as if I'd been punched in the stomach. Terrible mother? No, he was wrong. *I've done everything for her.* I did what I had to do to protect her, to keep her safe.

He was the problem, and I wanted him to hurt the way I did.

"Good. I'm glad you want a divorce because I want one, too. You're lazy. You don't care about anyone but yourself."

"You mean I don't care to control anyone but myself."

"Don't twist this around." My voice trembled with a mix of anger and desperation. "All I've ever done is take care of Imogene. I've kept her safe."

"Safe? You've smothered her. She's not living, Stacy. She's just surviving, and that's because of you."

I stood silent, tears streaming down my face. When I finally met his gaze, his eyes were dark and narrowed, his expression twisted with contempt.

After a long pause, I said, "You don't care about us."

I searched his face for any sign that he might prove me wrong. But his expression was cold, unmoved, as he bent down to retrieve the pajama pants he'd carelessly left by the bed that morning. Then he turned to his nightstand and unplugged his phone charger before grabbing his phone.

"I care about Imogene, and that's why tomorrow, I'll make sure I do everything I can to get custody, so you don't fuck her up any more than you already have."

Fear crashed over me. "You're bluffing," I said, though my voice cracked with doubt.

"I'm done with you. I'm divorcing you, and I will take Imogene."

The door slammed behind him. This was real. My hands shook, and I clenched them into fists. The man who had once been my best friend was now my enemy.

I started pacing the room. *Could he take Imogene from me? Would he?* The thought clawed at my insides.

All day, my thoughts had spun in circles, and I couldn't slow them down. They spun with such force that each fact, each variable, each contributing factor seemed stuck to the inside of my skull, and the centrifugal force made freeing any of them impossible.

My mind spiraled, searching for a way out, and all I could see was the day Imogene almost drowned. The image replayed itself with gut-wrenching clarity: the echo of my screams, her tiny frame motionless in Garrett's arms as he waded to shore, my hands trembling as I pushed down on her chest.

That day changed everything. In the weeks that followed, I couldn't stop replaying it—the moment I saw her little head break the lake's surface, the lifeless stillness of her body, the icy water, the fragility of those breaths as she came back to us.

The fear never disappeared. If anything, it grew stronger. I imagined scenarios where she was hit by a car or diagnosed with a life-threatening disease. The thoughts spiraled, each more terrifying than the last.

Behind closed doors, I hid the panic attacks, wiped away the tears before Garrett saw them. My brain replayed those moments by the lake faster and faster until it was all I could think about. The tremors in my hands started soon after. I hated them. They made me feel weak and vulnerable, as if I was falling apart, piece by piece.

From that moment on, I couldn't stop hovering. I couldn't stop worrying. I had almost lost her once, and the thought of ever coming that close again was unbearable.

My chest heaved as I relived that part of my life, but I forced myself to control my breathing. I didn't have the luxury of breaking down. I wiped the remaining tears from my face and sucked on my teeth, scanning the room until my brain worked well enough to come up with even the shell of a plan.

I couldn't lose Imogene. I needed a lawyer. But a lawyer would take time, time I didn't have. DCFS was coming for Imogene tomorrow.

There was only one option. My pulse quickened as the decision solidified in my mind.

I didn't care what Garrett said. We were leaving.

I grabbed a suitcase from the closet and shoved the clothes from the bed inside. Then, I grabbed toiletries from the bathroom and tossed in whatever random items I could find—a belt, a notebook, even a flashlight. I wasn't sure how we would fix this mess, but staying wasn't an option anymore.

I would figure it out. I had to. For her.

With trembling fingers, I zipped the suitcase. There was no going back.

CHAPTER 27

THE SHOW MUST GO ON

Stacy

"Imogene, Imogene, come back!" I shout, my voice cracking as it echoes down the street. Onlookers turn their heads, and I rush past them, unconcerned with their curiosity.

"How could you do that?" she yells, still walking away from me.

"It was nothing. I promise. We've just been spending so much time together, and it was a mistake. Just a mistake."

"What about Dad?" she demands.

"I said it was a mistake."

She spins around and narrows her eyes. "Are you going to tell him?"

"Who? Your dad?"

"Yes, Dad. You have to tell him."

I hesitate. I want to tell her everything—that her dad and I are over, that he wants a divorce, and worse, that he may use all this against me to get custody. But I can't. I can't destroy her perception of him. So, I say whatever I think she wants to hear.

"I will. I will tell him what happened."

Imogene crosses her arms and says, "Good."

"Good," I repeat, but it isn't enough for Imogene because then she says, "I'm not going with him. I want nothing to do with him."

"Ramon? Imogene, he's our ride. We don't have a car!" Her defiance is infuriating.

"So?" She glares at me.

"What do you mean 'so'? Imogene, we are almost there. Do you understand?"

"Almost where, Mom? What are we doing? All you've told me is we can fix this once we get to Canada. How? It doesn't even make sense. You won't even let me call Dad. How do I know I can trust you?"

"You can trust me. It's just . . . I . . . You don't understand," I say, even though I know much of what I'm doing is driven by fear rather than reason. I just haven't wanted to admit it.

"Help me understand. If you have such a brilliant plan on how you can keep me out of foster care, then reveal it."

Having nothing to offer her, I say, "I'm not doing this right now. We will leave tomorrow with Ramon, whether or not you like it."

"This isn't fair. None of this is fair. You don't care about me—about my feelings. You've never cared about me. It's always about you. Always!"

Her statement hits a chord.

"Now that's not fair. Everything I've done, everything I've risked, has been for you. I lost my career, I could go to prison, and I had to leave my home and my dad. Your father wants a—" I stop myself before I say anymore.

"He wants a what?" She crosses her arms over her chest and waits for me to fill in the blank, but I don't. She does it for me. "A divorce?"

I press my lips together and stare at her with watery eyes. "Imogene, please understand that everything I'm doing is for you."

"No, you're doing it for you. You have to control everyone and everything. Even Dad. That's why he wants a divorce. It isn't my fault. It's yours." She talks with her hands, illustrating the point she is making.

I shake my head. "I'm not saying it's your fault."

At this, Imogene throws her arms down and walks ahead again. I feel myself losing control, and, as always, my hands shake in response.

I yell after Imogene. "Think whatever you want, Imogene, but we are leaving tomorrow with Ramon. Now, either you follow me back to the Drag Palace, or we can go back to the motel and miss saying goodbye."

She spins on her heel, and I can tell by the set of her jaw she wants to continue tearing into me, but she marches back to the Drag Palace. I let out a shaky breath. It seems like every effort I make to set things right only pushes us further into chaos. And what nobody seems to understand is none of this is for me.

I march behind her, keeping pace but giving her just enough space so she can cool off. I don't want her to hate me, but I also don't know how to change it.

As I pass Ramon, he looks at me with concern in his eyes. I don't stop to talk to him and instead mouth the words, "I'm sorry," as I continue following Imogene.

Inside the club, Imogene is already gone, probably backstage.

Gary, who returned after dropping us off, stares at the place where Imogene must have blown past him. "Did something happen?" he asks.

I laugh it off, not wanting to bring more attention or further complicate an already complicated situation.

"Teenage angst," I say, and he nods knowingly.

He leaves me to tend to the kitchen. I stand frozen, staring at the door leading backstage. Feeling a wash of regret, part of me wants to go back there. I just wish she could understand, even for one minute, how much this has worn me down.

As I prepare for our last shift at The Drag Palace, I think about Imogene's anger. I wish I could explain the kiss with Ramon so she would understand, but I don't understand it myself. I don't know why I kissed Ramon back. He's great, but I don't know what I'm doing. Often, Ramon helps me set the dining room, but I avoid him. I need to clear my head, and when he's around, things become more confusing than they already are.

I'm nearly done when angry voices travel through the walls of the club. I stop and listen at the same time as several other employees, including Gary.

"Do you hear that?" Gary's voice is tinged with concern. The regular chatter inside the restaurant comes to a halt, and we all stand alert as we listen. The door swings open, and the bouncer who works at the front door comes in, looking flustered. "We've got protesters."

"Are you fucking kidding me?" Gary exclaims. He throws his head back and walks over to the bar.

My eyes widen. "Protesters?"

"Dammit," Gary mutters as he reaches around and grabs a bullhorn before barging outside.

I hear his voice carry over the crowd, and I move to look outside. A group of about a dozen individuals hold various signs. One reads, "Don't Exploit Children," while another states, "Drag Queens R Not for Kids." They chant in unison, but I can't distinguish what they are chanting over Gary's bullhorn. I move closer to the front door.

"Go home, or I'm calling the police!" Gary's voice is forceful.

"We have a right to protest!" one of them shouts back.

The chanting resumes, louder and more aggressive. They are saying, "Protect our kids." Gary throws his arm down, the bullhorn swinging wildly, and storms back inside.

"You . . ." he says, pointing at me. His eyes are wild.

"What?" I ask, my fingers twitching, ready to tremble.

"Your kid brought them here. They're pissed about a kid performing. I knew I should have put a stop to it."

"Wait, what?" I don't understand how people can get so worked up about something so harmless. All Imogene did was lip sync a song.

Gary paces back and forth, running his hands through his hair, trying to think.

"What do you want to do, boss?" someone asks.

Gary stops abruptly, a decision made. "Business as usual. It's a small group, and I'm sure after tonight, they'll go back to their caves and take their homophobia and hate of all things joyous to the internet where they belong." I want to believe him, to hope this will all blow over, but what if they don't go away? What happens then?

He shouts at Ramon, "You're off tables and bouncing tonight. The likelihood is we won't have a full house with those asshats out there, and we'll need the extra muscle at the door."

"I can do that," Ramon says. He nods and takes off his apron before heading toward the entrance.

I take a deep breath and head backstage to check on Imogene. The news has already spread among the queens. Pockets of them whisper to each other as they get ready. The atmosphere in the club has changed drastically.

"Imogene, I need to talk to you," I say as matter-of-factly as possible.

"Then talk," she replies with attitude, organizing heels on a shelf.

"What did I tell you about disrespectin' your momma?" Peach chimes in from where she's buckling a platform heel.

Imogene rolls her eyes and walks over to me.

"What?" she says.

"There are a group of protesters outside. They are upset about children being at the club."

"What? That's so stupid!"

"Yes, but it's what is happening right now. Look, I need you to promise me you'll stay back here. I want to leave now, but it's probably best we wait until after the protesters leave. Can you please just promise me to stay put?"

"Yeah, okay," she says, letting her guard down so I know she is sincere in her promise.

CHAPTER 28

I'M HIS WIFE

Stacy

Only half our reservations show, which is likely because would-be patrons turned back at the sight of the protesters. The last table I seat belongs to a husband and his pregnant wife. "Sorry about that," I say, gesturing outside.

"You have the best chicken wings in town. It's all I can think about. Nobody messes with me and my chicken wings right now," the wife says.

I offer a small laugh. Seeing her so close to term makes me miss my patients. For a moment, I let myself feel the loss of my career and the life I'd built. Grief wells up, raw and overwhelming, threatening to spill over. When it edges too close, pressing against the line of what I can bear without breaking, I swallow it back down. That part of my life is gone, a sacrifice I made for Imogene. For her, I'd trade a hundred careers.

The evening show starts as usual, but the queens increase their energy on stage, quieting the volume of those outside. However, even though they give the show everything they got, the protesters are louder than earlier, their chants and jeers seeping through the walls. I look out a window to find the crowd has tripled in size.

The atmosphere is completely different inside. Although the audience is smaller tonight, they feed off the energy on stage with enthusiasm. I spot the pregnant woman from earlier having the best time. She is clapping along to the music and handing money to Georgia Peach, who is riding her miniature tractor to the tune of "I Play Chicken with the Train."

I shake my head when Peach does the splits on the tractor while it spins in circles in the middle of the dining room. Even in the craziest times, these queens can make anyone smile. I head to the other side of the dining room to refill drinks. But when I hear a commotion, I double back, concerned for Peach, but instead, I see the pregnant woman's face contort in pain. She clutches her belly, her eyes wide. Her husband jumps to her side, panic etched on his face.

"Help! Someone, please help!" he shouts.

The music stops abruptly, and all eyes turn to the couple. Peach is the first to react, hopping off her tractor, and rushing to their side.

"Stacy!" Peach yells, but I'm already on my way.

I'm nearly there when the woman gasps, trying to speak between waves of pain. "This feels wrong," she says.

I push through a small crowd of people who have gathered in front of the couple's booth. "I'm a nurse," I announce, my voice steady despite the surrounding chaos. "Let me through."

Her husband speaks up. "You're a nurse?" He doesn't believe me, given I brought them to their table.

Ramon is beside me now and says, "This is her summer job."

I give him a look because of the absurdity of his statement, but it is fleeting because I shift my attention to the pregnant woman. "My name is Stacy. I'm a nurse. Is it okay if I examine you?"

She nods, but fear is alive in her eyes.

I place my hand on her abdomen, feeling for any unusual firmness or tenderness. Her abdomen is rigid, and she winces in pain. Agony contorts her face, and beads of sweat are forming above her brow.

"How long have you been in pain?" I ask, keeping my voice calm and reassuring.

"Just now." She gasps, her breathing shallow and rapid. "It hurts so much."

"Everyone, turn away from the pregnant woman," I say in my most authoritative voice. I'm unsure if they listen, but I don't have time to worry about them.

"Can I please look under your dress?"

When she nods, I lift the hem of her dress and see blood staining her underwear. My heart races as I recognize the signs of a serious complication.

"What's your name?" I ask.

"Maya," she tells me.

"Maya, you're going to be okay. Your baby is going to be okay. Do you trust me?"

She gasps again. "Yes."

The tone of my voice changes, and I yell at those behind me. "We don't have time to wait for an ambulance. We need to get her to the hospital now."

The queens help clear a path to the door, their hands moving quickly and efficiently. The crowd parts, murmuring, the tension inside the club reaching a new peak. My mind pivots to Imogene, but I push it aside, focusing on the woman in front of me. The woman's husband and I support her, guiding her outside to get her to a nearby car. Her face is pale, and she winces with every step, clutching her belly tighter.

When we get outside, the crowd of protesters feels far larger than it had from the window. Their voices are a cacophony of hate and anger. Signs bob in the air, and their chants are relentless. Flora Fatal comes up beside us and takes my place, supporting the pregnant woman's weight. Ramon runs up behind us.

We keep our heads low as we try to go around the throng of people who block the sidewalk to the parking lot on the side of the building. However, they move to stay in front of us.

"Move out of the way," I say to one belligerent man, trying to keep my voice calm but firm.

"What you're doing in there is sick!" he sneers at Flora, who is standing hunched in six-inch platforms to save a pregnant woman's life.

Maya's husband signals to Flora that he's about to transfer Maya's weight to her. Flora braces themself, ready for the added burden. Her husband tries to help me navigate through the crowd, but the bodies make it too thick. Agitation takes over, and he shoulder-checks the man in front of us. The man staggers, losing his balance. Another guy pushes Maya's husband, and he stumbles back, colliding with me. Flora attempts to pull Maya back from the chaos, and I use all my strength to steady them. Ramon holds the back as we try to move through the crowd.

I guide our group, trying again to go around them, but another man stands in our way, his face twisted with anger. A fist comes out of nowhere, and Ramon's hand crashes into the nose of the man blocking us.

The sound of bone against bone is sickening, but it creates the opportunity we need. I take the gap in the crowd to get Maya safely to the edge of the parking lot. My heart races. I regret not calling an ambulance, but I didn't realize the crowd would be like this.

Behind us, tensions continue to rise as Maya's husband and Ramon are stuck in a struggle. Shouts and scuffles break out, but I can't worry about them. I can only worry about Maya.

Then, when we are only thirty feet from the crowd and so many more feet from the car, a sound rings through the air—an unmistakable, terrifying sound. A gunshot. I twist to see where it came from. At first, everything seems fine. Everyone is standing back, and the lack of movement makes me think I must have imagined it. But then Ramon grabs his torso and bends over. Blood is evident between his fingers.

My heart sinks.

A man holding a gun stands back, eyes wide with shock. "Oh shit, oh shit. I didn't mean to . . ."

"Someone help me right now!" I scream, my voice breaking. "I have a woman with a possible placental abruption and a man with a gunshot wound. Both of these people are going to die if no one helps me. Do you understand that? My car is right there. Get these people to my car now!" My voice is a deep growl.

The pregnant woman's husband rushes forward to take his wife. Flora Fatal runs back for Ramon. Everyone else scatters. We move quickly, adrenaline driving us as we half-carry and half-drag them to the car. The chaos around us fades into a blur of movement and noise.

We pile into the car, the urgency of the situation pushing us beyond the limits. My hands tremble as I fumble with the seatbelt, my mind racing.

"I need directions!" I yell into the car.

"I can drive," Flora offers, but we are already in our seats. We don't have time.

"Just tell me where I'm going!" I snap back. Flora starts spouting directions.

I order Maya's husband to call 911. "Tell them to rendezvous with us." I bite down on my bottom lip with the same force with which I press the gas pedal.

I glance at Maya in the rearview mirror. Her face is paler than before and twisted with pain. Her breathing is shallow and rapid. My mind flashes back to her enjoying the show just minutes before. How quickly things can change.

I don't know if we will make it in time. Looking at her now, I believe we're too late, but I keep this thought to myself.

Ramon's expression is a mask of torment as he presses his hand to his wound. The blood seeps through, and the dark stain on his shirt grows each second. "Hang on, Ramon," I yell, more to myself than to him.

The car's engine roars as I push it to its limits, weaving through traffic, not giving a shit that I'm breaking every traffic law in existence. Cars honk at me as I look left to right before running a red light, and everyone in the car groans when I take a corner too sharply.

"Ramon, I need your wallet. Someone, get me his wallet," I yell to those in the car.

"Got it," Maya's husband says.

"Read me his driver's license."

"What?"

"Read it to me!" I repeat, my voice edging on frantic.

He reads Ramon's driver's license to me.

"Again!"

He reads it several more times between Flora cutting in with directions to the hospital.

We are only a few blocks from the hospital when I see the ambulance, but there is no time. Maya has lost consciousness, and I can't stop. I blow past the ambulance. At the hospital, the car skids as we come to a stop, and the medical team rushes out to meet us, their movements swift and practiced.

Ramon is also no longer conscious, and I push my personal feelings down as they pull him from the car. Maya's husband goes with her as the medical team takes over. I follow Ramon, walking backward into the emergency room while shouting instructions to Flora for Imogene.

"What is your relation to the patient?" one of the medical staff asks me. I can't bear the thought of being separated from him.

"I'm his wife."

CHAPTER 29

LIGHT AS A FEATHER

Imogene

"They were kissing! Like, I just don't understand. Why would she do that . . . to my dad?" Illusion gently combs some stray hairs from her wig in place while listening.

"Baby, sometimes people make mistakes," she says, spraying edge melt under the hairline of her wig before pressing it down with the tail of a comb.

"I just don't understand how she could do that to him." My voice cracks.

Illusion straps a band around her hairline and turns to me. "People are complicated. Attraction complicates things further, and honestly, Ramon's very attractive."

"Eww." My face twists. "He's my teacher!" I like Ramon. He's a cool guy, but he kissed my mom. He knew she was married, and he still kissed her. Maybe he isn't as cool as I thought. Also, Dad might want a divorce, but they are still married. It's just wrong.

Illusion smiles, but before she can tease me further, shouting from the dining room bleeds through the walls, and the music pauses. Illusion stands. "Stay here. Let me see what's going on."

I strain my ears to hear what is happening, but I can't make out much. Mom said to stay here, and part of me wants to see what's going on out there to spite her. But Illusion also told me to stay, so I comply.

Sometimes, it feels as if I have no say over what happens in my life. Things just happen, and I'm a puppet, and Mom is the puppet master. However, I can't blame it all on Mom. Sometimes, life forces us both to move in a direction we don't want to travel.

Like DCFS's plan to remove me from my home. I was never convinced running was the answer, but what choice did we have? The thought of being taken from my parents terrified me. I didn't know where I might end up. Worse, what if I never got my puberty blockers again? The idea of my body changing in ways I can't control scares me.

We weren't trying to do anything wrong when we started the puberty blockers. We just needed more time. If we could buy ourselves that time, eventually, things would be okay. But it felt like fighting against orbital decay. No matter how hard a satellite resists, gravity always pulls it back. Sooner or later, it reenters the atmosphere and burns up.

The world was our gravity, determined to drag us down. And Mom? She took drastic measures to keep us from falling.

The morning we left, I was hesitant to leave without Dad, but Mom reassured me we just needed time. That morning, before I got in the car, I peered at the second floor where Dad was sleeping. I didn't blame him for not coming. If anything, I was glad he'd chosen not to let my issues run his life, unlike Mom.

A loud sound like fireworks jolts me out of my daydream, and I strain my ears. I can't sit here not knowing what is happening outside.

I walk into the dining room of the club, and Illusion spots me the moment the backstage door swings shut. She rushes toward me. The patrons there for dinner are in various states of disarray. Some huddle together, speaking in hushed tones. Waitstaff rush between tables, trying to maintain some semblance of order. Still, the atmosphere is thick with fear.

"What's happening?" I ask.

Illusion glances around the room, worry etched on her face. Some of the staff stand at the windows, watching what's going on outside.

Impatience guiding my question, I ask, "What was that sound?"

"A gunshot," she admits.

"Mom? Is my mom okay?" I swivel my head, trying to locate her, but I can't see her anywhere. I make eye contact with Illusion. Please say my mom is okay. I might be mad at Mom, but I don't want her to be hurt.

"Your mom is fine. But she's not here. She's headed to the hospital. A pregnant woman had an emergency, and the protesters got out of hand, but everybody is okay. You're safe. We're safe. Everything is going to be fine." At this moment, Illusion's promises sound a lot like Mom's, and it makes me feel uneasy.

"When you say it like that, it makes me think nothing will be okay. Like, when is Mom coming back? Did someone get shot?" I bring my fingers to my mouth to chew on my nails.

"I understand you have a lot of questions, but right now, I don't have the answers. If I did, I would give them to you. Remember—nobody puts Baby in the corner."

After that, I stayed backstage for hours, waiting while the police took everyone's statements. One by one, the queens came into the dressing room to change into their street clothes, wash off their makeup, and remove their wigs. They are all quiet and somber.

I want to ask each of them for information about what happened, but I don't want to intrude. I also mentally note each queen, knowing there were gunshots. It makes me wonder if any of them were hurt, and I feel sick whenever I consider who it could have been.

As each queen comes backstage, I mentally mark them as safe.

When Illusion finally comes in, the only queen working tonight who I haven't seen is Flora, and I have this sinking feeling in my gut.

"I just talked to Flora. Your mom asked me to keep an eye on you tonight. You're coming with me." I breathe out a sigh of relief after hearing Flora's name.

"Wait. My mom said that. She said I could stay the night at your house?" I ask, disbelief in my voice.

"She did," Illusion confirms. "But we need to go by your motel first so we can grab your things."

"Uh-huh," I say, still reeling from the first part. "My mom doesn't allow me to stay anywhere with anyone."

"She must like me," Illusion says with a wink.

I feel skeptical but knowing that I'm not my mom's priority for the first time is somehow freeing.

"This is my first sleepover," I tell her.

"So, what you're telling me is you've never played Light as a Feather, Stiff as a Board?"

I scrunch my face. "Played what?"

CHAPTER 30

ODD TIMING

Garrett

At that moment, I meant it—every letter, every syllable. I wanted a divorce. I wanted to be free from the crazy woman tearing our family apart, the woman who lied to me.

The morning I woke to an empty house, I called Stacy over and over again. My anger from the night before only intensified, and I felt like I would explode. I paced each time the phone rang, burning a trail into the tile floor.

When she finally answered, I felt a mix of hatred, panic, and relief. I pleaded, threatened, and pleaded again. But a small voice inside me urged caution, warning that acting in anger would lead to regret. I still wanted a divorce. I couldn't do this anymore, but I never wanted to take Imogene from her. I'd spoken out of anger to hurt her the way she hurt me. So, on the phone with her that morning, I gave her an ultimatum. "You have two weeks."

She said she was going to Melissa's house in upstate New York. It was uncomfortably close to the Canadian border, but I chose to trust Stacy enough to let her go. Part of me thought if I didn't give her a little leeway, she might panic and take Imogene across the border. But then she pissed me off again with her condescending tone, and consumed by rage, I flew off the handle once more.

This wasn't like me. I rarely got angry, but after everything we'd been through with Imogene, her betrayal cut deep. Yet, despite it all, I couldn't truly hate Stacy.

Just as Lilly had warned, DCFS arrived at our house that morning. At around 10:00 AM, I opened the door to find two women standing there—

one was Lilly, and the other introduced herself as Francis. Francis looked like she hadn't smiled in years.

"Can I help you?" I asked after the introductions.

"Is your wife or son home?" Francis asked.

"My daughter," I corrected.

"Are they home?" Francis continued, her eyes narrowing as she spoke.

"They are not."

"Okay. When will they be back?"

I took a deep breath, steadying myself. "They're in New York, staying with a friend. Imogene had an altercation at school, and we thought it best for them to get away for a bit with everything going on."

Lilly's eyes flicked up to mine. Disappointment etched along the features of her face.

Francis narrowed her eyes further. "Kind of odd timing, don't you think?"

"How so?" I leaned against the doorframe, trying to appear relaxed.

"Wasn't your wife recently suspended from her job?"

I gave an exasperated sigh, then waited for a beat before continuing to speak. "Yeah, she was. She needed her friend this week. It's been hard on her."

Francis pulled out a small notebook and a yellow No. 2 pencil from her bag. "Can you provide me with this friend's address?"

I smacked my lips together and made a show of pausing to think. "I'm sorry. I don't feel comfortable doing that. She has nothing to do with any of this. Can I ask why you're here? I've already talked to Lilly. I answered all her questions."

Lilly pursed her lips and swallowed. Maybe she was afraid I would reveal her visit from the evening before.

Francis placed her pencil in the center of the notebook and gave me a no-nonsense stare. "Mr. Barnett, we are here to investigate whether there is a legitimate case of child endangerment, and I don't have the patience for games."

"I'm not playing games, and neither my wife nor I are endangering our child. If someone says so, it's because they're transphobic, which is pretty shitty. Now, if you don't have any other questions, I have a meeting I need to get ready for."

"Uh, Mr. Barnett . . ." Francis tried to respond, but I had already shut the door.

When they were gone, a shaky breath escaped through my lips. I sat down on the bench in our foyer and placed my head in my hands.

The day before, Lilly had said that if the judge granted orders, they would be here to remove Imogene. However, based on my conversation with Francis, they must not have gotten the orders they'd hoped for.

I thought about calling Stacy. I probably should have updated her, but I didn't want to fly off the handle again or accidentally make things worse than they already were. I also just didn't have the energy to deal with her.

For the next several days, I went to work, ate dinner alone, and hovered over Stacy's number in my phone, unable to press the button to call her.

I logged into the family tracking app periodically. Stacy had turned off her location. After what I had threatened, I wasn't surprised, but I wish she'd turn it back on.

I logged into our accounts. It was the first time I'd logged in for some time. There was one withdrawal of $400 on the morning they left. However, looking at our accounts, Stacy couldn't use any of our cards even if she wanted to. They were all nearly or completely maxed out. Even our business accounts were dangerously low.

As the days went on, my anger faded, replaced by loneliness. Memories flooded my mind—Stacy and I cooking together while Imogene played with Play-Doh at the kitchen table, Imogene's exaggerated laugh at my dumb dad jokes, and the way Stacy always gave a disapproving shake of her head even though I could clearly see the smile she tried to conceal. Those were the good days.

On the fourth day after they left, I thought about calling Melissa to check on Stacy. Melissa had been Stacy's roommate when we met, but that only lasted a short while because Stacy and I got an apartment together a few months into dating. But why would I call Melissa instead of Stacy? Melissa and I aren't close, and I don't know what Stacy has told her. In the end, I decided I wasn't in the mood to deal with it.

That's something Stacy has always hated about me. When things got hard, when conflict was inevitable, I did nothing. I didn't know why I was this way, and I couldn't seem to get over the hump. The moment anything got difficult, even things as simple as resetting a password, it took an incredible amount of energy to address it. It's part of the reason I quit my job. I was miserable, but instead of addressing the issue, I resigned and started my shop.

When tough conversations were on the horizon, I pretended everything is fine. Part of me wondered if it is why I asked for the divorce—because

I could no longer handle the conflict. I hated this about myself, and it was the very reason I tried to help Imogene be bold. To advocate for herself, yet Stacy, who was often the loudest person in the room, never allowed Imogene to speak for herself.

On the sixth day, two detectives came to the shop to talk to me. I saw them approach out of the corner of my eye but made them wait until my cut was complete. The saw's engine wound down with a high-pitched whine. I pushed my safety glasses onto my head and stepped forward, sawdust clinging to my work apron.

"Can I help you?" I asked, masking my unease with a polite smile.

"Do you have a minute? We have some questions about your wife, Stacy. It's our understanding she is out of town?" one of the men asked.

"Follow me," I said, leading them through the cluttered shop to my small office, where I entertained their questions for the next thirty minutes.

They asked exactly what you'd expect them to. Did I know my wife was committing prescription fraud? Had I ever seen the prescription for the medication in our home? Was I sure Stacy was coming back after her trip? I told the truth, but my truth was not damning. I didn't know she was committing fraud. I had never seen the medication, and I believed, genuinely, that she would be back. She only needed time, and I was giving it to her.

The detectives took notes, their expressions unreadable. They mentioned they'd called her several times but hadn't been able to reach her. I shrugged, unsure what to say.

Lilly and Francis returned in the early evening hours on the eighth day after I got home from the shop.

"Hey, what's up?" I walked up the driveway covered in sweat and sawdust.

"Can we talk inside?" Francis asked.

"I'd rather not."

"Why?" She pressed her lips together so firmly they nearly disappeared.

"It's a beautiful day," I said as sweat dripped down the hollow of my back. The sun set the world on fire, and it was difficult to breathe in the damp, heavy air.

"Are Stacy and Imogene here?" Lilly asked.

"I told you they won't be back for another week."

"We've tried multiple times to contact your wife but haven't been able to reach her."

"She's been busy," I say.

"Mr. Barnett, if we find out you're lying or withholding information, there will be severe consequences."

"I understand," I said, my voice steady but my insides churned.

As they left, Lilly looked back at me and nodded.

About an hour after they left, I sat at the kitchen table eating leftover spaghetti I had made several nights ago when my phone rang. I didn't recognize the number, but something told me I should answer it.

"Garrett?" The voice was familiar.

"Who is this?"

"It's Lilly Dixon. I'm sorry to bother you again. I thought you should know that my supervisor, Francis, is still pushing for removal. Unfortunately for her, the judge wants to wait until the police conclude their investigation into your wife's case. I don't know where Stacy and Imogene are, but this will go much better if they are here. Just a piece of advice: tell them to come back. I warned you so you'd have time to make arrangements or seek legal counsel, not flee."

I listened to her warning and thought about it.

"Okay. I'll see if they can come back early," I said. The call ended, and I let out a puff of air. I looked back down at my phone and found Stacy's number. My thumb hovered over the call button. Without the adrenaline of anger to drive me, I felt immobilized, stuck in a fog of hesitation and uncertainty.

Squeezing my eyes shut, I whispered to myself, "Just call her, Garrett. Just fucking call her."

CHAPTER 31

GOOD PEOPLE

Stacy

The fluorescent lights buzz overhead, casting a harsh glow. I've spent more than a decade inside hospitals. But being inside a hospital when someone you love or care for is hurting changes the ambiance of the place. So many people hate hospitals, and this is why.

I fidget in my chair, awaiting Ramon's return from an CT scan, hoping for a miracle. Good people deserve good things, and somehow, I disrupted what should be part of the natural order.

For the last hour, I've watched the medical staff work to stabilize him, my mind racing with questions. Did we get here in time? What damage did the bullet cause? Will he be okay? Will Maya be okay? Will her baby be okay? A tense feeling knotted in my gut, making me fear for their lives. This dread isn't based on anything concrete, just intuition, but regardless, it is unbearable.

I chose not to call an ambulance. I pushed through a group of protesters instead. What if the time it took to get through the protesters was the time she needed? If I hadn't made that choice, Ramon would be okay, right? These questions loop in my mind, and I dig my fingernails into my palms to stop the tremors. I chose not to call for help and tried to handle things on my own, as I always did, and therefore, I will be responsible for any life lost.

So much has happened in such a short time, and I feel this may be a sign. Maybe the universe is telling me I should never have left and, in fact, I should go back home, turn myself in, and await whatever future is ahead. I was so sure of myself. So confident that leaving was the solution, but it has been messy. When I was running, I couldn't see it, but the cracks in my plan are visible now.

The harm I've caused eats away at me, and there will be nothing left by the time this is all said and done.

I'm on the edge of my seat when Ramon's doctor comes in to talk to me.

"Mrs. Alvarez," he says.

"Yes?" I look to him, hopeful but also convinced of the worst possible outcome.

"The bullet fractured his rib, but it didn't puncture his lung or hit any major blood vessels. We don't need to operate. He just needs pain management and monitoring."

The relief moves like water through a broken dam and pours from my eyes.

When Ramon comes back into the room, he is still sedated. I watch him sleep for a bit before texting Flora, who volunteered to update everyone else at the club. We had been texting each other updates since I got to the hospital.

Me: Ramon is going to be okay. The bullet hit his ribs, so he'll need to take it easy, but he's okay.

Only a minute later, the phone pings.

Flora: Thank goodness. How about the pregnant woman? Any news on her?

Me: I don't have any, but I'll let you know when I do.

Given that Ramon is stable and asleep, I feel it's okay for me to leave him long enough to see if I can get an update on Maya. I fear the worst is true, and I already mourn the loss of life.

Walking into the labor and delivery unit, I'm transported. Although the unit's layout differs from mine, it's familiar enough to send a pang of nostalgia for a life I will never live again. A career I ruined. I've tried to avoid thinking about what I've either given up or destroyed because I feel as if I'm not allowed to regret what I've done because I did it for Imogene.

I spot Maya's husband at the nurse's station, and I'm thankful because I don't have to figure out how to get an update. I stand a few feet behind him, trying not to intrude. The nurse before him glances in my direction, acknowledging my presence. This prompts Maya's husband to turn around.

Recognition flashes across his face. "It's you."

"Hey, I'm so sorry," I begin. If Imogene hadn't performed, if I hadn't let her perform, if we had never gone to the Drag Palace, then the protesters wouldn't have shown up. If I hadn't put obstacles in the way, maybe Maya's chances would have been better.

I'm so consumed by guilt that it takes me a moment to process his words.

"Don't be sorry. You saved her life. My baby's life. She lost a lot of blood, but she's okay. They both are."

My mouth drops open, and my eyes mist over. "I'm so glad." I want to say more, but I don't know what else to say. I'm too overwhelmed with emotion.

"Thank you for everything," he says.

I want to wave him off and tell him not to thank me. Instead, I give a gentle nod and turn away. Although I'm so happy they are okay, I still feel horrible for all the ways I contributed to tonight's madness.

"Hey, wait," he says from behind me.

I spin back around.

"What's your name?" he asks.

"Stacy."

"You work here? You said you were a nurse."

"No, I worked at a hospital in Sarasota, Florida."

"That's awesome."

"Yeah. It was." I have to hold my breath to stifle the tears that threaten to emerge. "Have a good night. Congratulations on your baby."

The collective relief and guilt I feel turns into exhaustion. I check my watch, and it is 1:00 AM.

Back in Ramon's room, he is asleep, so I sit in the chair next to him and watch him until my eyelids are too heavy to keep open.

A couple of hours later, a nurse comes in to do her rounds, startling me awake. She checks Ramon's vitals, adjusts his IV, and makes notes in his chart. She then turns to me. "Can I get you anything to make you more comfortable?"

"I'm all right. Thank you, though." I offer a tired smile. As she leaves the room, I notice Ramon's eyes are open. He regards me with a mixture of fatigue and curiosity. I can't help but grin at him. "Always the hero," I breathe.

"Is she okay? The pregnant woman? The baby?" he asks. Here he is, in a hospital bed because he was shot, and his first thought is to make certain other people are okay. He is a hero.

"She is, and so is her baby, thanks to you," I reply. He sinks back into his pillow in relief.

"I didn't do anything except cosplay as a firing range target," he says with a hint of humor, a small smile playing on his lips. "How long do you think I'm going to be here?"

"They're keeping you for observation to ensure there are no complications, such as internal bleeding or a pneumothorax. It'll be a few days, but I promise you want to be here."

"I don't like hospitals," he admits, his expression clouding with discomfort.

"Yeah, I understand that."

"Can you? You're a nurse," he points out, raising an eyebrow.

"I was a nurse," I correct him. "And yes, I understand. In situations like these, I don't like hospitals either."

"You might still be a nurse," he says, his voice softer now.

"Highly doubtful," I sigh.

Ramon chuckles, then winces. "I know it doesn't feel like it, but everything is going to be okay."

"Says the man who just suffered a gunshot wound."

Ramon's mouth drops open, and he focuses his eyes on me. I think he's trying to make out my expression since he isn't wearing his glasses, but then he says, "When I say everything is going to be okay, I don't mean everything is going to line up the way you plan. What I mean is that regardless of what happens, even if your life falls apart, it may still surprise you. It might still turn out to be okay."

I study his face, and I don't know if it's his optimism in the face of this absolute shit show or exhaustion, but I can't stop myself from apologizing. "I'm so sorry I brought you into all of this. I feel like it's gotten so out of control. In my head, I thought it was simple, but it just kept getting more complicated. The kiss. You getting shot. I'm starting to think running was a mistake, and honestly, I knew it the moment I left, but refused to admit I could be wrong."

"I'm glad you left. I'm glad I got to help, even if we didn't make it to Canada. Don't worry so much. Don't worry about the kiss or what happened to me. I'm okay. Working at the Drag Palace, hanging out with you and Imogene—it's the most fun I've had in a long time."

He closes his eyes as the morphine drip begins to take hold.

I listen to him and hold his words in my heart. They aren't a cure for my worries, but they temper my concerns just enough. "You know how you told me about Hector and how that's the reason you wanted to help us?" I ask.

"Mmhmm . . ." His eyes are still closed.

"I think you've done enough. You're such a good person, and you don't have to do anything more than just exist the way you do," I say, but he doesn't hear me because he's already fallen asleep.

CHAPTER 32

FOUND IN THE ALGORITHM

Garrett

When I finally press call, it rings once before going straight to voicemail. For a brief moment, I'm relieved, but it's short-lived. I still need to reach Stacy, so I quickly type out a text instead.

Me: Can you please call me? It's important.

The message bubble turns green rather than its normal blue. She blocked me. She seriously blocked me! My jaw tenses, but I push down my frustration. I would call Imogene, but her phone is still in her room, smashed.

Because Lilly warned us and has kept me in the loop, I believe her when she says things will a lot better if Stacy and Imogene are here. Melissa is my only chance at reaching Stacy, so I find her number in my phone. I don't want to call her, but I need Stacy to come back. The phone rings several times before a woman picks up.

"Hello? Garrett?" Melissa's voice comes through the speaker.

"Hey, Melissa. How are you?" I say, as if calling her is a normal thing to do.

"Is Stacy okay?" she asks.

"Is Stacy okay?" I repeat slowly.

"Uh, yeah. Why else would you call me?"

"She's not with you?"

"No. Why would she be with me?"

The realization that Stacy never made it to Melissa's—and likely never planned to—washes over me like a monsoon.

"Uh, actually, never mind. Sorry. But hey, good talking to you. I gotta go, though. Bye."

I hang up before she could say anything else. If Stacy isn't at Melissa's, where is she? Did she take Imogene over the border?

Fuck. Stacy.

Shaking my head, I try to think past my irritation. While I've been here waiting, making excuses for her, and covering for her, she lied to me again. It isn't even possible to blame her at this point because I'm so damn stupid. What is she planning? Is she starting a whole new life in a different country? Canada had come up during our fight, but I chose not to believe it. How the hell am I going to explain this one to the cops and DCFS?

A rock wedges itself in my chest, and I feel stuck. My phone vibrates. At first, I think it might be Melissa calling back with questions, but the caller ID says Sarasota Memorial Hospital.

Great. They're probably calling about Stacy's case or something else I have to deal with because she's not here. I almost don't pick up. I watch the phone ring instead. Then, changing my mind, I hit the answer button and bring it to my ear.

"Garrett Barnett?" the person on the other end says.

"Yes?"

"We've been trying to reach your wife, Stacy, but haven't been able to get in touch with her."

"She went out of town. She'll be back in a couple of days." There I go, covering for her more. Why am I the one dealing with the aftermath of her decisions? She takes my kid to Canada, and I'm still doing this? Ugh. I run my fingers through my hair, pulling at the root.

"Well, maybe you could help me. Your father-in-law had a series of small strokes, and this time, he is in poor condition. I don't know how much longer he has."

That was not what I was expecting. I told Stacy I would go visit him, and I hadn't. I meant to, but I . . .

I need to stop making excuses. I didn't go, and now he doesn't have much time.

"I'll be right there," I say, standing before ending the call. Charles, Stacy's dad, is the last of Stacy's family, besides an elderly childless aunt in Canada whom Stacy barely knows. Regardless of what is happening between me and my wife, I would never take that out on Charles. Never.

Charles and I always had an interesting relationship. Before he got sick, he was one of my best friends. We'd golf on the weekends and host small football parties at his house. He loved to fish, and we'd spend hours on the water. He was a mess, but he was also a super cool guy.

Stacy constantly felt annoyed with her father, but she loved him. Twice a week, every week, Stacy had dinner with her dad, followed by a game of cribbage. Stacy said it was her mother's favorite game, and they played it to keep her memory alive. Although Stacy complained a lot about her dad, she had an indescribable attachment to him, almost as if it were her duty to ensure his well-being.

I admired their relationship, although it wasn't perfect. I didn't have parents, and Charles always liked having me around. I felt like a surrogate son of sorts and wanted to make that official.

The day I asked Charles for Stacy's hand in marriage, he told me "no." I've told this story so many times that it's ingrained in my memory. Stacy and I had been dating for hardly any time before I knew she was the one, and I didn't want to live a day without her. This was when we still lived in Colorado, long before we followed Charles to Florida.

My plan was simple. I invited him to a Rockies game, my go-to event since you could get tickets dirt cheap. I thought doing something we both loved would provide the perfect opportunity to ask him for his daughter's hand in marriage.

We sat in the bleachers in the rockpile, which are objectively the worst seats at the Coors Stadium, but also the most affordable. I had just purchased two overpriced hot dogs and drinks. I sat beside Charles, careful not to spill anything.

About an hour into the game, I finally worked up the courage. "I love Stacy," I said.

"Yeah, me too. Come on, ump! Are you blind?" he yelled, never taking his eyes off the field.

"And I want to thank you for being so quick to welcome me in."

"Go, go, go!" he hollered. Then he turned to me. "Are you trying to ask me if you can marry Stacy?"

I swallowed hard. "Yes, sir. I would like to ask for Stacy's hand in marriage."

"First of all, none of this 'sir' bullshit. Second, the answer is no."

"What?" I asked, blinking. Of all the responses, I hadn't expected that. Charles and I were friends. I thought he'd definitely say yes.

He adjusted in his seat and glanced around the stadium. "If you want to marry my daughter, next time you ask, get better seats. I can barely see the field. I'm not even sure if I'm yelling at the right team."

We finished watching the game as if the conversation had never happened. I appreciated that about him. He never lingered on anything for very long.

The very next week, we went to another Rockies game. I took nearly everything out of my measly savings that I hadn't spent on a ring for Stacy and bought club-level seats right behind home plate. That night, when I asked again, he said yes, but he also said, "She's a pain in the ass, so don't marry her unless you're willing to put up with it."

That memory feels like a lifetime ago as I walk into Charles's hospital room and pull up a chair beside his bed. "Hey, old man," I whisper. "I'm here."

He doesn't respond. His eyes are closed, and his breathing is shallow. I sit with him, and despite the discomfort, I'm glad I'm here. When Charles got sick, I couldn't bear to see him so disoriented. Stacy continued to visit him, but I kept my distance. Another example of how I avoid hard things.

I think about the only marriage advice he ever gave me—that bit about Stacy being a pain in the ass. She is, and the thought of her not being here to say goodbye to her dad sends a pang through my heart. If she knew he was here, she'd come back in an instant. But she doesn't know because she blocked me. My feelings regarding Stacy are so complicated that I push them out of my mind and focus on Charles.

After sitting in silence for so long, I become restless. The quiet of the room, outside of the machines, is overwhelming. I've had too much silence lately. I stand and search for the remote to the television. When I find it, I point it at the TV and watch as the screen flickers to life. It's only basic cable, but it's better than nothing. I scroll through a few channels until I find a baseball game. It feels like the right choice.

Leaning back in my chair, I watch for a bit. When the game ends, my stomach rumbles. I didn't eat dinner, and I'm starved. There are some vending machines around the corner, and although it isn't as sustaining as I would like, it's better than nothing. "Stay alive, old man. Don't die while I'm gone."

The machine takes cards, so I get something to drink, a chocolate bar, and a bag of chips. Back in the hospital room, I thank the high heavens he's still alive. I snap open the bag of chips and stare at the television. A news report covers a shooting in Savannah. I turn up the volume to listen.

The news anchor, a poised woman in her late thirties with sharp features and neatly styled hair, sits behind the desk.

"A peaceful protest at a Savannah drag club called the Drag Palace turned violent tonight when a shooting occurred. A bystander recorded the incident before posting it to social media. The video has already amassed nearly 2 million views in less than three hours."

The news plays the footage, and I watch as several people, including a very tall black drag queen, a pregnant woman, and a man who looks vaguely familiar, try to break through the crowd of protesters.

Then my wife's face comes on screen. She is among the group trying to push through.

I instinctively hold up the remote to pause the television, forgetting that I'm watching the most basic cable available. I have no choice but to continue watching, trying to make sense of what's happening on screen.

The familiar man punches another man in the face, and Stacy, along with the pregnant woman and the drag queen, successfully pushes through the crowd. Suddenly, gunshots ring out, and the familiar man clutches his chest. The crowd scatters, and the footage becomes shaky before it cuts off.

My heart slams against my ribs. Where's Imogene? I rush to pull out my phone and dial Stacy. It immediately goes to voicemail. "Stacy, please call me back if you hear this. I just saw you on the news. Is Imogene okay? Actually, just call me." I hang up, but then I remember. I'm blocked.

Desperation grips me. The clip came from social media. I search for the full video. I just need to find Imogene. Where was she in all of that? Is she hurt? I need to know what happened. I need to know if Imogene was with her.

I scroll through countless posts. There are numerous videos with commentary on the situation, but they only offer a few seconds of the clip. Finally, the full video appears on my screen. I watch it, my eyes scanning the footage, searching for Imogene, but she's nowhere to be seen. I replay the video, looking for additional clues. Stacy struggles to get the pregnant woman through the crowd. One man looks so familiar, and I think maybe my brain is playing tricks on me, but then it hits me. Imogene's teacher. What is he doing there?

My mind reels. I need to find Imogene. I need to find my wife.

I stand abruptly, my chair scraping against the floor. I glance at my father-in-law and realize I have a choice to make. He might be gone before I can get back. Placing a hand on his shoulder, I whisper, "You were right. She is a pain in the ass."

CHAPTER 33

I CAN'T DEFY GRAVITY

Stacy

"Stacy?" The familiar voice pulls me from a shallow sleep as I sit in the chair in Ramon's hospital room, having drifted in and out for hours. Morning light filters through the window, mingling with the distant beeping of monitors and the soft murmur of hospital staff.

My eyes flutter open, and Garrett stands in the hospital room doorway.

"Oh, my god, Garrett!" I nearly jump out of my seat.

He is the last person I expected to be here. His sudden appearance causes my heart to beat like a drum in my chest. His eyes slide over to Ramon, still asleep, before focusing back on me. How did he know I was here?

I wait for his anger, but it doesn't come. Instead of an angry man, I see someone who is simply tired. Dark circles and a downturned mouth are exacerbated by slumped shoulders.

"Can we talk?" His speech is quiet and slow.

I blink hard to wake myself as I stand. "Yeah," I say, breathlessly, unsure of what to expect. Following Garrett into the hallway, I stuff my hands in my pockets to stop any potential tremors.

"Where's Imogene?" he asks.

"She—she's staying with a friend. How did you know I was here?"

"You were on the news. The shooting. Someone got it on camera," he explains. "Once I could confirm it was Mr. Alvarez who was shot, I called all three hospitals here in Savannah and told them I was his brother."

"They think I'm his wife," I say. His lips tighten. I probably could have kept that bit of information to myself.

He looks at me with a watery, tired stare, and I don't know what to think. So, I reach for the most plausible thing. My jaw is tense as I ask, "Are you here to take Imogene from me?"

He shakes his head. "No." He hesitates. "I mean, yes, I want her home, but I won't take her from you."

I bite my lip, uncertain, because although his anger appears to have dissipated, a lot has happened, and I feel like we are from different planets at this point.

"Stacy." He reaches out and places a hand on my shoulder. I shift my gaze from his hand to his face. This interaction—it's confusing.

"Your dad . . ." With those two words, everything makes sense. His exhaustion. The gentleness in which he regards me despite everything.

"What? Is he okay?"

"He experienced several minor strokes, and they don't think he has much time left."

My eyes widen, and tears well up. "No. You're lying. You're saying that to hurt me." I don't want to believe it's true. Yes, Dad is old, and this is the natural order of things, but he's my dad.

"I'm not trying to hurt you. I know I've said a lot of hurtful things, and you deserved some of them. But that's not why I'm here. I came to find you so you can say goodbye."

I shake my head. After the night I've had, now this? I'm devastated. My vision blurs with tears.

"No," I say again. Garrett pulls me into a tight hug. Our marriage is so broken—so broken that he asked for a divorce and threatened to take our child, so broken that I kissed another man. But against his embrace and my heartache, I can't help but melt into him.

He whispers in my hair. "I'm sorry."

We stand like that for a moment, holding on until I feel his muscles tighten and his grip around me loosen. I step back and wipe the tears from my eyes. All this time, I have been trying to get to a perceived safety, but everything, including my regret, is pulling me back home. Part of me wants to keep going, to run from the inevitable, but Mom would be so disappointed if I left Dad alone in his final days. I'm not sure I could live with myself.

My heart is in the middle of a game of tug-of-war, and just when I think the choice may paralyze me, I decide. I have to go back. Dad needs me.

"Who is this friend Imogene is staying with?" Garrett's question catches me off guard, and I feel a pull to not answer it.

"Why?"

"So we can pick her up. You don't have a lot of time."

"She . . . she's with Bryce or Illusion."

"What?" he says.

"One of the drag queens from the club where the shooting happened," I say.

He blinks rapidly. "You let her stay the night with a drag queen?"

"I can explain, but hold on. Ramon was shot. I can't just leave him." I glance back at the room. Ramon represents another variable that makes this situation feel so impossible.

"Stacy, are you serious?" I can see his expression shift from confusion to annoyance.

"Hold on, let me think." I scrunch my brow. "Give me a minute, then we can go."

I walk back into Ramon's room, where he is still asleep. At his bedside, I squeeze his hand, hoping it will wake him.

"Hey," he says sleepily.

"Hey." I smile warmly and push a bit of hair out of his face. "Garrett, my husband, is here. My dad had a stroke and doesn't have much time. I don't want to leave you, but I don't know what else to do."

His lips turn down, and he searches my face. "Your dad?"

"Yeah, my dad." I press my lips together to stop myself from crying again.

"Oh, no," Ramon says.

I scrunch my brows and peer into his eyes. Leaving him here feels so wrong after all he has sacrificed.

"I . . . uh . . ." I don't want to abandon him.

"Go," he says.

"But—"

"No buts, just go. I'll still be here, but your dad might not be. Go be with him. He shouldn't be alone."

"Okay," I say breathlessly. I scan the room as I collect my thoughts. "I'll swing by the motel, check us all out, grab your things, and drop them all off here." Before I allow a to-do list to completely swallow up the guilt that is eating at me, I pause and ask, "You sure?"

"Yes, I'm sure. I can call my family, and they will be here within a few hours. Go. I'll be okay."

"I'm sorry, Ramon." Guilt laces my voice.

He squeezes my hand. "Thanks for the adventure. Call me?"

My heart deflates. "About the kiss . . ." Although I mentioned it before, I feel like it's still unsettled, and I can't leave without addressing it.

He studies me. "Not the right time or the right place?"

I shake my head and pull my bottom lip into my mouth. "I'm married, and even though that's rocky right now, I never should have. I'm so sorry."

Ramon lifts a hand. "It's okay."

I stand and sway from side to side. "Where does that leave us, then?"

"As friends," says Ramon with sincerity.

After I leave the room, Garrett and I don't speak until we are in the parking lot.

"Where's your car?" he says as I follow him to his truck.

I left Ramon's keys in his room, but that's not what he's asking me.

"In Jacksonville," I admit tentatively.

"What?" He stops walking to turn to me.

I put my hands up in defense as I explain. "I thought you would report me. Report that I had kidnapped Imogene, so I dumped the car. That's how I ended up with Ramon."

Garrett gives me a look as if I've lost my mind. "I still don't understand how Ramon is involved."

"It's complicated. I'll tell you in the car."

He shakes his head but continues on his way. I pull out my phone and text Bryce to let him know I'm on my way. Then I search previous text messages to find where he had sent me his address.

During the twenty-minute drive to Bryce's house, the tension in the car is palpable. I tell Garrett how we ended up with Ramon, and the story seems to put him on edge. The streets of Savannah pass by in a blur as anxiety builds in my gut.

"So, is there something between you and Ramon?" Garrett's voice cuts through the silence. I glance at him, his expression unreadable. My instinct is to deny it, but I can't lie to him anymore. Lying had already caused enough damage.

"It's complicated."

"You keep saying that."

"Well, it is."

"Unless he's your half-brother or something, it's not complicated. Is there or isn't there?" he presses, his tone flat, devoid of anger. I want to chuckle at his straightforwardness, but I stifle the impulse.

"We kissed," I admit, bracing for his reaction. Although Garrett has hurt me, I don't know where his heart is at, and I don't want to hurt him anymore than I already have.

He lets out a deep, heartbroken sigh that seems to echo in the confined space of the car.

"Did you kiss him, or did he kiss you?" His question is loaded with pain. We were so broken, the two of us, that his pain ignites an ember of hope. I've held so much resentment toward Garrett for so long, but I also remember what we used to be like. How much we loved each other. Still, there is an edge of pride that makes me not want to apologize for the things I've done because of the role he has played in all of it.

"Does it matter?" I ask, already knowing the answer.

"Yes, it matters."

"We kissed each other."

Silence envelops us for another five minutes, and the only sounds are the engine hum and the faint murmur of the radio playing. I love Garrett, and kissing Ramon was a mistake. I don't know if there's a way to mend our shattered marriage, but I'm sorry for the things I've done.

"I'm sorry," I finally say. My voice cracks.

"No, I'm sorry. I don't think I can be mad. I told you I hated you, that you were a terrible mother, and that I wanted a divorce." His voice is heavy. "I just never imagined you would be so quick to kiss someone else."

"Do you still want a divorce?" I ask, holding my breath for his answer.

"I don't know," he breathes.

When we pull into the driveway of an adorable little yellow house, I release a breath. Garrett reaches for the handle, but I place a hand on his arm.

"I know you don't want to do this right now, and we don't have a lot of time, but what about Imogene? What happens to her if we go back home?"

The familiar panic accompanied by thoughts of her being whisked away by DCFS infiltrates my heart. Garrett sits back in his seat and examines my face.

"I don't know. I can tell you that even though they have been pushing for orders to remove Imogene, they haven't succeeded. It sounds to me, and I'm only guessing, that the judge may be sympathetic to our particular case."

"But what if . . ."

Garrett cuts me off. "If they receive orders, we will cross that bridge when it comes. Together. As her parents. I need you to promise me right now that you'll stop going rogue and let me be an active participant in parenting our daughter. I love her just as much as you do." Garrett's voice breaks with heartache, but he goes on. "And the fact that you have hidden so much from me, that she has hidden so much from me—it kills me."

I study him. I want to justify everything I have done. I want to protect my pride, but he's right. The fear of losing Imogene has gripped me for so long. That fear has consumed me to the point where I can't operate without worrying about the what-ifs. This anxiety has taken over my whole being, and I don't know another way to exist.

Despite this, I know that Garrett loves his daughter, and I have to figure out a way to change.

CHAPTER 34

FOMO

Garrett

"Dad!" Imogene runs out of the yellow house toward me. I open my arms wide to catch her. Her bright eyes and broad smile light up her face. It's only been a week, but she appears taller, more confident, and self-assured.

She barrels into my chest, and I embrace her tightly. "I missed you," she says, her voice muffled against my shirt.

"I missed you too, kid," I say, my heart swelling.

I glance at Stacy, who is observing us with a mix of relief and tension. Her eyes dart to the door of the house, where a slim, tall man dressed in gray sweatpants and a black T-shirt stands. He must be the drag queen.

I'm still surprised by Stacy's decision. It's not like her. Stacy doesn't trust anyone. Ever.

Stacy steps over to Imogene, and I watch Imogene's face harden. There's something unresolved between them.

"Say goodbye. We're going home," Stacy tells Imogene. She reaches to move a bit of hair from Imogene's face, but Imogene pulls away.

"We are?" Imogene's face twists in confusion.

Stacy stares at me in a way that communicates she doesn't want to deliver the news, so I step in to explain. "Grandpa Charles doesn't have a lot of time left. We have to say goodbye."

Imogene's eyes widen, and her face pales. "What do you mean? Like he's dying?"

Stacy's eyes soften, and she moves toward Imogene again. "I'm sorry, sweetie." Stacy tries to hug Imogene, but Imogene sidesteps her embrace. The sting of rejection flashes across Stacy's face. I don't think Imogene's rejection is personal. It was only a reaction to the news combined with unanswered questions.

"What about DCFS? Will I be able to get the puberty blockers again if we go back?" Imogene asks.

I channel all of my energy into appearing confident. "We'll figure it out. I know that doesn't sound like an answer, and I wish I could give you a better one, but your mom and I will do whatever we need to do to ensure you stay in your home. As far as the puberty blockers, I don't know right now. It's another thing we need to figure out."

"Where's Ramon?" Imogene glances between Stacy and me, still trying to understand the sudden change in plans.

I glance at Stacy, unsure how much she's told Imogene. I know Stacy so well that I can see from her expression that she wants to lie. She wants to protect Imogene from the truth, but surprisingly, she changes her mind.

"He's okay, but last night . . ." Stacy swallows hard. "There was an altercation with the protesters, and he was shot. But I promise he's okay."

Imogene's eyes widen, but her lips press together. I suddenly understand the tension between her and Stacy. Imogene knows about the kiss.

It bothers me she knows, but what bothers me more is how quickly Stacy locked lips with Imogene's biology teacher. I feel like I have no right to be mad, but couldn't she have waited more than a week? I'm not usually a jealous guy, but boy, would I love to punch Ramon right where that bullet hit him.

That's a violent thought. I should box that up and put it away.

I turn my attention to Imogene. "We should probably get going."

"Let me get my bag," Imogene says.

She turns to run back to the house, and the man on the small porch smiles at us as we approach.

I extend my hand to him. "Garrett."

"Bryce," he replies, shaking my hand. He regards me with familiarity.

Stacy says, "We have to go home. It's complicated, but Ramon is still in the hospital, and my dad isn't doing well." She rambles, trying to justify why she is leaving Ramon here, and I can tell it pains her.

Bryce raises his hand. "I got it. We'll take care of him. Don't worry. Call me when you get home? Let me know if you all made it safe?"

Stacy nods, and I can see a measure of tension lift from her shoulders.

Imogene comes out from the house, her backpack slung over her shoulder, along with a garment bag.

"What's that?" I ask.

"My dress. Dad, you wouldn't believe it, but I performed at the Drag Palace. Opening act!"

I turn to Stacy and Bryce for an explanation. My child, who struggles to say more than five words to a stranger, performed?

"Baby's a star," Bryce says adoringly.

It feels as if my daughter and wife have lived an entire lifetime without me, and there is so much I don't know.

Bryce holds out his arms to embrace Imogene, and she hugs him, just as she hugged me a moment ago. They pull apart, and Bryce gazes at her with a warm smile.

"Remember what I said, okay?" Bryce says to Imogene, and she nods in response.

Bryce then turns to Stacy. "Girl, don't you leave here without a hug."

Stacy laughs and hugs Bryce, their bond evident. We walk back to the car, and I can't shake feeling like an outsider to their recent experiences. Experiences that seem to have changed their DNA makeup.

Behind me, Imogene waves to Bryce as we drive away. We head to the motel to collect the rest of their things and also pick up Ramon's belongings.

Afterward, we drive back to the hospital. When we pull into the parking lot, Stacy asks Imogene, "Do you want to say goodbye?"

Imogene chews on her decision, glancing between me and her mom. She shakes her head, and Stacy's face falls in response.

I watch Stacy walk back into the hospital, and I don't know how I'm supposed to feel right now. I want to ask Imogene what's going on between her and Stacy, but I choose to let it be for now. Instead, I focus on something lighter.

"So, you performed?" I ask.

"Yeah, it was amazing. I wish you could have been there. Illusion, Peach, Opal, and Flora all helped me with it. I learned so much, like how to vogue or what campy means."

"Sounds like I missed out on a lot."

She smiles apologetically. "Sorry for the FOMO."

"FOMO?" I ask. Maybe that's another drag queen reference I don't understand.

"Fear of missing out," Imogene says slowly, as if it is the world's most obvious turn of phrase.

I chuckle.

"Dads," she says playfully.

"Illusion is Bryce's stage name? What are their pronouns?" I ask. I know nothing about drag culture.

"For Bryce, it's he/him when he isn't in drag, but she/her when she is in drag."

"Doesn't that get confusing?"

"No," she scoffs. "You just learn and kind of get used to it." She puts her hands on the center console as she explains.

"Is it like that for all the queens?"

"Anyone of any gender identity can be a drag queen. So, like, Opal is a trans woman like me, whereas Flora is nonbinary, but Georgia Peach is a cis straight man like you." Her pitch rises as she says, "like you."

"So, I could do drag?"

I'm teasing, but Imogene almost hits the roof of the truck with excitement. "You should do drag! I could do your makeup!"

I grin at her enthusiasm. "I don't know about that."

"Oh, come on, Dad. It would be so fun and good practice! I promise I'll make you look good."

"I don't think my self-confidence can handle it." I shake my head solemnly.

"Because you'll look bad?" she asks.

"Bad? Please. I'd be a total smoke show. You'd need a stick to keep the boys away!"

Imogene giggles, and I grin, pleased to hear her laugh.

Imogene continues to chatter about the Drag Palace and what it was like—the performances, the acts, the things she has learned. The only other time I've seen her this electric is when she rattles off facts about astronomy. It's nice to see that she has found another part of herself.

When Stacy returns to the car, she lets out a deep breath as she settles into her seat.

"Is everything all right?" I ask.

"Yeah, Ramon's sister is on her way, and one of the queens will be there shortly to keep him company."

"Good. Ready to go?" I say, looking back at Imogene before turning to Stacy.

"Yep," she replies, and I put the car into drive, heading back south toward home.

CHAPTER 35

GOODBYE

Stacy

As we drive back home, the same landscape that marked our escape blurs past the windows. Part of me feels like I'm surrendering, which makes me incredibly uncomfortable. But another part whispers that going home is the right choice and that maybe it will all be all right, like Ramon said. Life might surprise me. It's ridiculous and unrealistic, but that seems to be the theme of the last week.

During the first leg of our drive to Jacksonville, Imogene bounces between asking questions about Grandpa Charles and telling her dad about the Drag Palace. I wasn't always backstage with her, so some stories are also new to me. Then she sleeps. She's always been a car sleeper.

Garrett and I sit in heavy silence, the unspoken words between us creating a tangible barrier. We've reached a truce, a temporary ceasefire, allowing me the space to say goodbye to my dad. Regardless, the tension between us is thick.

When we pull into the parking lot where I left my car, Imogene wakes. "Are we home?" she asks, still half-asleep.

"No, just grabbing the car. Want to come with me?" I ask, hopeful.

She shakes her head and closes her eyes again, resting her head on a bunched-up hoodie against the window's glass. I exchange a look with Garrett and exit the truck.

In my car, I follow Garrett. It will be evening before we get to the hospital, and I pray Dad is still alive when we arrive. The rest of the drive is long, and as much as I know I should take the time to sort through everything I'm feeling, I'm too tired to do so. I can sort this out after I say goodbye to Dad.

When the hospital finally comes into view, a lump forms in my throat. I don't want to say goodbye, but there's no other choice. Another constant theme: choice.

Walking through the hospital corridors, memories of my suspension and the chaos that followed floods my mind. Just a week ago, I worked here. Now, I'm here under entirely different circumstances and feel as if I'm a completely different person. Imogene walks ahead of me with Garrett, and looking at her, I see she is a different person, too.

We finally reach my dad's room, and Garrett stands back to allow Imogene and me to walk ahead. I grab her hand and am relieved when she doesn't pull it away. The sight of Dad lying in bed hooked up to machines and monitors sends a sinking feeling through my stomach.

Imogene stands in the middle of the room, her eyes on her grandfather. He got sick when she was young, so memories of him before dementia are limited. However, when she was little, she was obsessed with him.

I gesture for us to move to his bedside, and Imogene nods. Kneeling beside him, I take his cool hand in mine. Tears blur my vision as I gaze at the man I call Dad, now so fragile. Garrett hovers in the middle of the room before moving closer to rest a hand on Imogene's shoulder.

"Dad, it's me, Stacy," I whisper, my voice trembling. "I'm here now, Dad. I'm so sorry I wasn't here sooner."

The door creaks open, and a nurse steps in, her expression soft. "You made it," she says. I recognize her, although I have never worked directly with her. I look at her name badge. Her name is Emma.

"We did," I say with a tight smile. I reach to touch Imogene, and she leans into me.

We sit by his side for what feels like an eternity. The minutes stretch into hours. Garrett moves to a chair by the window, watching silently. Imogene moves to sit next to him, but I don't leave my dad's side.

As the hours pass, I reflect on my relationship with my dad. After Mom passed away, he was such a mess, leaving me to pick up the pieces. I resented him for that, for making me the caretaker when I needed care myself. His love was always there, buried beneath grief and alcohol, but it wasn't enough. But as much as I resented him, I needed a sense of control.

Looking back now, I realize that taking care of him wasn't just about helping him, but it was about me trying to gain some assurance when everything else felt so out of control. His drinking, the overwhelming grief, and the unpredictability of life without Mom all felt like too much. But if I could manage our day-to-day, it gave me a sense of control, a way to convince myself things weren't completely unraveling.

Just like with Dad, taking care of the people I love, whether it's him or Imogene, has always been my way of dealing with the turmoil. In my attempts to protect, I've often smothered, thinking that if I could control every little detail, maybe I could prevent the worst from happening.

He stays with us through the night, and Garrett takes Imogene home to eat and sleep. For the second night, I sleep in a hospital room.

But the next morning, I wake to the sound of a continuous tone that accompanies a flat line. My breath catches in my throat as a nurse comes in, silences the alarm, and calls the time of death.

"Can I have some more time?" I ask.

I pull out my phone when she leaves and dial Garrett's number.

"We are leaving in ten minutes," he says when he answers.

"He's gone."

"He's gone?" Garrett clarifies.

"Yeah." I hang up the phone and return to my place next to him. "You know, you were a pain in my ass," I say. "Like a massive pain. But I wouldn't have had it any other way. I love you, Dad."

I sit for a moment, letting it all sink in. I know it was his time. I grieved my father once before, when dementia stole him from me, and now here I am, grieving him again. This time, it hurts even more because of the finality. I thought I was ready for this moment, but nothing could have prepared me for what it feels like to lose him a second time.

When Garrett and Imogene arrive, they each take their turns saying goodbye. I watch them, my heart aching with love and loss.

Eventually, once we've each had our time, we leave the hospital room, along with a piece of each of our hearts.

As we turn a corner and walk toward the exit, two men in suits walk toward us with badges visible on their belts. I dip my head to acknowledge their presence and am surprised when one of them addresses me by name.

"Stacy Barnett?"

"Yes?" I reply. We stop walking.

"I'm Officer Schenck, and this is Officer Kennedy. We have a warrant for your arrest."

"What?" I'm not sure I heard him right.

"You are being arrested on charges of prescription fraud and child abuse and endangerment. Please put your hands behind your back." They move toward me, one officer holding cuffs in his hand.

My world tilts on its axis.

"Are you kidding me? Her dad just died," Garrett says, stepping forward.

An officer holds his hand out. "Sir, I'm going to ask you to take a step back right now."

Garrett halts, his posture tense. Imogene's face is wild with distress, and I realize how traumatizing this moment is for her.

I fix my face and smile in her direction.

"It's okay. It's all going to be okay. I promise. Don't worry," I reassure as I turn to allow the officer to cuff me.

"We're very sorry for your loss," Officer Kennedy says. He sounds genuine, but he also has a job to do.

"Thank you," I say.

The officers guide me down the hallway, their grip firm but not rough. Onlookers glance our way, their eyes widening with curiosity and pity. One of them pulls out their phone to record. Their nosiness and my embarrassment are dehumanizing.

I hang my head and walk, focusing on putting one foot in front of the other.

CHAPTER 36

FIREFIGHTERS AND FAIRIES

Imogene

I drop my backpack and duffle on the bedroom floor and look around. The space feels foreign, even though I've spent most of my life here. Everything in this room is the same, yet nothing feels familiar.

I drift around the room. My hamper is overflowing with clothes piled in front of it rather than inside—something Mom hates. My bed is usually a mess because what's the point of making a bed you'll just mess up later? I push aside my comforter to reveal a patch of mattress covered in pink plaid sheets.

Taking a seat on the edge, I stare at a poster on my wall. The poster is of massive clouds of gas and dust that stretch into space. They look like towering columns and are illuminated by the glow of starlight. It's called the Pillars of Creation and was taken by the Hubble Space Telescope. The poster was a gift from Mom to mark the anniversary of the day I came out to her.

It's a reminder of how, even when she was doing things for me, it was about her. She never asked me if there was a date that felt more meaningful to me to mark the start of my transition. She just picked the one that centered her experience, the day that mattered most to her. I don't understand why she does it, but she always has.

She centers herself in my existence because I'm the center of hers. What she fails to understand is that I need more. I need autonomy, but even thinking about it makes me feel guilty. She's in jail because she broke the law for me, and I still manage to find ways to resent her.

A light knock on the door interrupts my thoughts. "Yeah?" I call out.

Dad pokes his head inside my room. "How does spaghetti sound? I made too much a couple of days ago and could use some help finishing it."

"That's fine."

"Do you want to eat with me?" We usually eat together, but he is offering me space. I appreciate having a choice, but I've missed him.

"Yeah, that would be nice."

"Ten minutes?"

I nod, and he leaves me alone with my thoughts. I go back to thinking about Mom. Although I knew what mom was doing was illegal, I was never concerned. I didn't think there would be consequences. All I knew was that puberty was knocking, and I didn't want to answer the door.

One time, Dad told me that teens have a hard time seeing past what's right in front of them. It's kind of like babies and object permanency. However, for teenagers, our brains are wired in such a way that we forget consequences exist, and even if we know they exist, we often think we are immune to them. I honestly believed Mom was immune to the consequences of my care.

But she wasn't, and now she's in jail. It wasn't until I heard the click of the handcuffs, the gravity of what she had done for me finally sank in. But she stood there, arms behind her back, and acted as if nothing was wrong. Her face was calm, as though she was trying not to spread panic. She constantly tried to shield me from worry and heartache, and I kind of wish she didn't do that. That she didn't feel like she had to do that. I lie back on my bed, legs dangling over the edge.

These feelings are overwhelming. After years of being coddled, as Dad says, maybe I'm not equipped to handle them.

"Imogene! Dinner's ready," Dad calls from downstairs.

I push myself up from the bed, leaning on my arms, and sigh. Today has not been good.

Downstairs, Dad is at the fridge, and two plates of spaghetti with a less-than-appetizing salad sit on the table.

"What do you want to drink? We have expired milk and Diet Coke," Dad says, rummaging in the fridge.

"I'm fine," I reply.

He shuts the fridge, holding a Diet Coke, and sits at the table with me. Something has been gnawing at me since we got back home, and I haven't asked because I assume I will be told it is none of my business, but I decide to ask anyway.

"Hey, Dad."

"What's up?"

"Did Mom tell you what happened between her and Ramon?"

He stares at me for a long minute, and I worry I'm the one who just blew the lid on the whole thing.

"She did."

I try to read his stony expression. I want to know what that means for them.

"Does that mean you are getting a divorce?" I ask tentatively.

"No. It doesn't. Your mom and I are not in a good place, but I don't want you to worry about that right now. I'm not mad about the kiss, but we have a lot we need to work out."

"Okay." I'm a little confused about him not being mad, but relieved, too.

I watch him twirl his fork into the pasta and take a big bite. He chews, staring at his plate, then glances at me. "Are you going to eat?"

I pick up my fork and poke at my plate.

"We didn't have insurance on your phone," Dad says between bites, "but I found a cheap smartphone online. It should be here tomorrow."

"Cool." I spin my fork in my hand.

"I know you didn't want to deal with that today. I'm sorry," Dad mutters.

I shake my head and bite my lip to keep back tears.

Earlier in the day, after Mom's arrest, Dad took action, which was something he said he was trying to improve on and called DCFS. He called Lilly Dixon, the investigator, and although it is Saturday, she and a woman named Francis agreed to meet with us. I told them the truth. Dad didn't know about the puberty blockers, and Mom and I had been keeping it a secret. Dad said honesty would lead to the best outcome, and I hope he is right. I don't want to go live in a group home.

Now we just wait to see what the judge decides.

Dad places his hand on mine and watches me as I stare at my plate. Tears. I didn't realize tears had fallen into my untouched spaghetti. After a moment, I look up, and he just keeps watching, giving me all the time I need to process my emotions.

I take a forkful of spaghetti and bring it to my lips, only to put it back down. "I don't think I can eat this. It kind of smells," I admit.

Dad lifts some to his nose, sniffs, and makes a face. "Yeah, you're right."

He orders Chinese takeout, and we watch a documentary while we eat. When the documentary ends, I head back to my room to think some more.

I wish I had someone I felt comfortable talking to. Sure, I can talk to the queens, but they're adults. Sometimes, no matter how hard they try, they just can't fully grasp my perspective.

Feeling a pang of loneliness, I reach for a photo album Mom made a few years ago, sitting on my bookshelf. The cover is navy blue with foam stars and planets. I open it and find a photo of me from before I knew my name was Imogene. In the picture, I'm standing next to McKenzie in our Halloween costumes. She's a fairy, and I'm a firefighter. I remember being envious of her translucent pastel wings, watching them bounce as she ran ahead of me trick-or-treating.

Mom walked behind us as we ran from house to house, collecting as much candy as our plastic pumpkin baskets could hold. When they were full and risked overflowing, we went back to my house to sort through the treats. Once we were done sorting and trading Halloween candy, I put on McKenzie's wings, held her fairy wand, and danced around my room. Then, we went into the backyard where we invented a new game.

Still, in my firefighter costume, we pretended I was a firefighting fairy. She'd point to imaginary fires in the backyard, and I'd skip over, twirling the wand until she announced the fire was out.

"You did it!" she'd cheer, jumping and clapping as if something magical had happened, though it was just a figment of our imaginations.

I turn the page to another photo of McKenzie and me. We're in our pajamas, watching cartoons on the sofa. It's one of those candid shots Mom took when we weren't looking. We both look so at ease.

Why did everything have to change? Why did my friend choose to leave me rather than stay by my side when I needed her most? This isn't a new question, but it feels like one. The night I stayed with Bryce at his house, I told him all about McKenzie and how our friendship ended.

"So, this isn't your first sleepover?" Bryce had asked when I told him how she used to always sleep over at my house. We were sitting on his sofa, a game of Monopoly balanced on the center cushion.

"Well, I had sleepovers at my house," I explained while straightening my play money.

"I feel like I've been lied to," Bryce teased, moving his game piece according to his dice roll.

"I wasn't trying to lie."

"So, why aren't you and this girl friends anymore?"

"Are you going to buy that?" I asked, and Bryce shook his head.

I picked up the dice. "I told her I thought I was trans, and she stopped talking to me until a couple weeks ago when she bullied me instead of ignoring me."

"Have you confronted her?" Bryce asked.

"No. What's the point?" I roll and both of my dice land on three.

"Because when you confront someone who hurt you, then it allows you to address your feelings rather than suppress them, which is almost never healthy. You'll never move on if you keep all that bottled up inside you."

CHAPTER 37

ONE MOMENT, YOUR HONOR

Stacy

My hands tremble, so I place them between my thighs to steady them. Cold air blasts through the room, exasperating the nervous chills that wreak havoc on my body. A camera is mounted in the corner, its lens fixed on me. I can't help but wonder if they're watching from another room, analyzing my every move. Are they scrutinizing my body language or how I breathe as evidence of my guilt?

When the officers enter, I shift in my seat, straightening my spine and centering my tailbone on the chair. *Stay calm, Stacy. Just breathe.*

Officer Schenck and Officer Kennedy sit across from me, and I sit rigid, waiting. Schenck wears a tailored gray suit, the fabric crisp and clean, with a navy tie neatly knotted at his collar. His leather shoes are polished, and his badge is clipped to his belt, just visible under his suit jacket. In contrast, Kennedy's dark blazer is too large for his frame and shows signs of wear. The open-collar shirt underneath is slightly wrinkled and also too large.

Kennedy's relaxed appearance mirrors his demeanor. Is this going to turn into one of those good cop, bad cop scenarios often seen on TV? My eyes narrow as I try to discern their tactic, but I remind myself to keep my face impassive and correct my expression.

"Mrs. Barnett, unfortunately for you, the hospital has a lot of evidence," Schenck says. He tosses a file folder on to the table. My gaze shifts to the folder. I want to see what's inside, to know exactly what evidence they have. But I also know they want me to want to see it. The only way they'll show me anything is if I offer them something in exchange.

I stare at the folder, chewing on my bottom lip. Then I remember that I can't afford to make any more mistakes. Anything I could offer will only incriminate me.

"I want an attorney." My voice comes out strong, which is quite at odds with how I feel.

Kennedy and Schenck exchange glances, and I stay unmoving and expressionless, waiting for their response. Schenck sucks on his cheek, creating a small divot where the flesh is pulled between his teeth.

"That quick?" he says.

He wants me to feel insecure about my decision, but I don't, so I repeat myself. "I want an attorney. I have a right to a state-appointed attorney. I will not speak to you without an attorney present."

Schenck grabs the folder from the table and walks out of the room. Over his shoulder, he mutters, "We'll arrange for a public defender." Kennedy follows him, turning to give me a stiff smile.

I sit in the frigid room by myself and try to think. Something I used to be so good at but haven't been able to do for some time. Everything is just so complicated, and it won't get any simpler.

A couple of hours later, a young man who looks too young to be a lawyer comes into the room and introduces himself as my attorney. His appearance is in line with Officer Kennedy, slightly unkempt and wrinkled, but his eyes are kind. He introduces himself as Brandon Hart.

We talk through the charges, and he asks me a series of questions about my case. As we near the end, I ask, "What's going to happen? I mean, what's the process?"

"You will have an arraignment either Monday or Tuesday. The judge will read off your charges and set bail. If a reasonable bail is granted, can you afford it?"

I shake my head. "No." There's no way I can afford bail.

"Noted."

"What about my dad? My dad passed away this morning. They arrested me at the hospital. If I can't make bail, will they let me out to attend his funeral?"

I'm hoping Garrett can handle the funeral arrangements. Although this type of thing is not his strong suit, I don't have anyone else to do it.

"We can file a motion for a temporary release, but it is ultimately up to the judge. You have no prior offenses, so it's possible. You ready?" he asks.

"For what?"

"Officer Schenck and Officer Kennedy have been waiting to talk to us."

"Oh, yeah." I bite my bottom lip and nod.

Both officers enter and sit across from us, a tension-laden silence stretching between us.

"Mrs. Barnett," Schenck begins, but Brandon cuts him off. "Before you start, it's important to know we're here to listen, but my client will not be providing any statements today."

Schenck's eyes flicker with irritation, but he maintains his composure. "Very well. We have substantial evidence regarding the prescription fraud. We'd like to give you the opportunity to explain your side of the story."

Brandon leans forward. "As I said, my client will not be making any statements at this time. We're here to hear what you have to say and review any evidence you wish to present."

Schenck opens a folder, pulls out a stack of papers, and slides it across the table. "These documents show a clear pattern of prescription fraud. Mrs. Barnett, would you care to comment on these?"

I look closer, scanning the several columns of dates and times, along with the EMR activity. I try to make sense of the information, but before I can, Brandon steps in smoothly. "As I mentioned, we're not providing any statements. We will review the evidence in due course and respond through the proper legal channels."

Kennedy interjects, his tone softer. "We understand you were trying to help your child, but this is a serious matter."

Brandon's expression remains neutral. "My client acted within her understanding of the law. We'll address these matters in court."

The officers exchange glances before Schenck closes the folder with a snap. "Thank you for your time. We'll see you at the arraignment."

The officers leave, and I turn to Brandon. "Why did we have them come back in here if that was all we were going to do?"

"It's called strategy." I watch as he takes his pen and slides it into an elastic loop in his pleather padfolio before closing it and tucking it back into his briefcase.

"That's it?" I ask. We barely talked. I told him what happened, we told the police we weren't telling them anything, but that was all.

"Yep, I have another client in the next room over. But I'll see you at your arraignment," he says, getting up.

I slump in my seat. The lack of clarity about what will happen next makes my head hurt.

Hours later, I'm transferred to the county jail. The process is cold and impersonal—fingerprints, mugshots, and the confiscation of my belongings. Instead of my own clothes, they give me a standard-issue beige scrub-like two-piece.

As I go through the process, one thought keeps repeating: I shouldn't be here. No one should be criminalized for doing what's right for their child. I know I broke the law, but Imogene needed more time.

I'm placed in a small cell with metal beds attached to the wall and thin mattresses. My cellmate, an older woman, looks up from her book and gives me a nod. The cell door clangs shut behind me, echoing in my ears.

"Dinner is soon," the woman says to me.

"Thanks." I take a seat on the bed opposite her. The other woman resumes reading, so I decide not to interrupt more than I already have.

As I sit on the bunk, I take in my surroundings and think about Imogene—how angry she's been with me, the distress she showed when they arrested me, and what I assume happened after they arrested me. I'm certain DCFS has already come to remove her. I imagine how scared she must have been, and my chest tightens. I hate knowing I wasn't there when she needed me most.

Where will they place her? In a group home, with strangers? People who don't know her? What if she ends up somewhere unsafe? She has been through so much. How is this even possible? The harder I try, the worse things get. I can't help but feel an overwhelming sense of isolation.

Tears slip down my cheeks as I grapple with the realization that I use my need to care for others as a way to control my environment. I want to protect, but in doing so, I often make things worse. Wouldn't it have been better if we stayed, if I turned myself in and she never had to watch me get arrested just minutes after saying goodbye to her grandfather?

Yes, Imogene wanted to stop puberty, and yes, I would have gone to any lengths to make that happen for her, but now she not only will no longer receive the care she needs, but she has lost her home.

The next day drags on as I wait for something to happen. It's Sunday, so I won't be called for my arraignment, but maybe Garrett will visit. But nothing happens except the monotony of jail.

By Monday morning, I've already convinced the world is better off without me. I've convinced myself of this narrative all day and all night. So much so that I'm surprised when they call my name for court.

The county jail is next door to the Sarasota County Courthouse, so although I'm not in the same building, we don't have to travel far. When I walk into the courtroom, I scan the room for any familiar face, and relief washes over me when I see Imogene and Garrett sitting together among the spectators.

Imogene is not in a group home. She's not in foster care. She's still with her father.

My lips part, and my brows rise as I make eye contact with Garrett and Imogene. Garrett gives me an awkward thumbs-up. I want to laugh but bite my lip and sit next to Brandon at a wooden table, resting my hands on my lap.

The judge sits at the front. Brandon hurriedly flips through the case files, looking increasingly panicked with each passing moment.

"Are you ready, Mr. Hart?" the judge asks.

"One moment, ma'am—I mean, Your Honor. Just locating the file," he mutters, continuing to rifle through his bag.

I lean over and whisper, "What's happening?"

"I left your case file in the office," he mutters back.

"What do you mean you left my file?" My eyes widen in shock.

"What are you being charged with?" he asks, clearly flustered.

"Prescription fraud and child abuse." We spoke two days ago. How has he already forgotten my charges? My first impression of his disheveled appearance may be a more prominent characteristic of his than the cool confidence in which he addressed the police the other day.

"Oomph," Brandon says.

The judge says, "Mr. Hart, how long are we going to sit here?"

"One more moment, Your Honor," Brandon says. Turning back to me, he whispers, "Um. It's fine, I'll just wing it."

"Wing it?" Panic surges through me. This is my life, and he's going to just wing it?

Brandon stands. The clerk reads out, "Case number 24-3678, People vs. Stacy Barnett. Charges include prescription fraud and unlawful distribution of controlled substances."

The judge nods. "Mrs. Barnett, how do you plead?"

"Not guilty, Your Honor," I say, my voice steady despite the fear coursing through me.

The judge makes a note on the record before turning to the prosecutor. "What is the state's recommendation for bail?"

The prosecutor, a stern woman with a no-nonsense demeanor, stands. "Your Honor, given the severity of the charges and the fact that Mrs. Barnett fled after it was revealed she was under investigation, we recommend bail be set at $200,000. She is a clear flight risk."

I feel my stomach drop. Two hundred thousand dollars? That's an impossible amount for us. I glance at Brandon, hoping he has some counterargument to make a difference. Although, I'm certain I can't afford any amount.

Brandon leans over to me. "Remind me: do you have a prior criminal record?"

"No. We spoke two days ago. I'm a mom, and I was a nurse. I didn't flee. My daughter and I just decided to leave for our trip early. If I was fleeing, would I have come back for my dad?" It isn't the truth, but I feel as if I need to spoon-feed him his argument.

"Right. Your dad died."

Brandon stands, adjusting his tie. "Your Honor, my client has strong ties to the community. She is a mother and a nurse with no prior criminal record. The trip she took was already planned. Mrs. Barnett returned early to be with her ailing father and has no intention of fleeing. She is not a flight risk."

I let out a relieved sigh. The competent lawyer I met with earlier is back.

The judge considers this for a moment, her eyes flicking between the prosecutor and Brandon. Finally, she looks at me, her expression unreadable.

"Mrs. Barnett, given the nature of the charges and the arguments presented, I'm setting your bail at $50,000." The gavel comes down with a resounding thud.

Brandon leans over. "Hey, that's doable. If you can come up with ten percent, you'll make bail."

I feel a mix of relief and despair. Maybe other people have $5,000 to tap into, but we don't. We were barely paying our bills each month, and the interest on our insurmountable debt continues to climb every day. Therefore, $5,000 is significant. So significant that I will likely be stuck in jail for the foreseeable future. I catch Garrett's eye as the bailiff escorts me out of the courtroom. He sets his jaw rigidly but gives me an encouraging nod. Next to him, Imogene stares at me with doe eyes.

Back in jail, I sit on my bunk, my mind racing. How are we going to come up with five thousand dollars? Do I even deserve to be bailed out? Probably not.

The walls feel like they're closing in on me, but I force myself to take deep breaths. I force myself to focus on what's good. Imogene is with Garrett. Not in foster care. Not in a group home, but with Garrett. I repeat this simple fact to myself, repeatedly, until I feel grounded. I still struggle knowing I won't be there to care for Imogene, but I have to put my trust in Garrett that he will do the job. I have no other choice but to trust him.

Hours later, the sound of the cell door opening jolts me from my thoughts. A guard steps in. "Barnett, you've got visitors."

CHAPTER 38

HONESTY IS THE BEST POLICY

Stacy

Garrett and Imogene's faces come into view as I approach the visitation booth, each separated by thick glass partitions. Inmates converse with their visitors at similar partitioned stations, their voices blending into a hum of overlapping conversations. The noise ebbs and flows, collectively loud yet subdued.

The guard gestures for me to sit, and I do, never breaking eye contact with my family. My hands tremble as I reach for the phone, but before I pick it up, Garrett presses a button on his side. A small red light blinks. On the other side of the glass, Garrett and Imogene wait. Garrett's face is lined with worry, but there's a softness in his eyes. Our temporary truce is still in effect. But there is something else behind his eyes. Shame.

What does he have to feel ashamed of?

"Hey," Garrett says, his voice crackling through the speaker.

"Hey," I murmur. Relief washes over me at the sight of them, but it's mixed with weariness and guilt.

I turn my attention to Imogene. "Hey, sweetie. How are you holding up?"

She shrugs, avoiding my gaze. Her silence is heavy. I hate being here. I hate not being there for her.

"We're okay," Garrett answers for her. "DCFS has decided to back off."

"Really? How? Why? I mean, thank God, but . . . how?" The tension in my shoulders eases just a fraction. At the same time, it's an additional layer of validation that running was a mistake. Had I stayed and held my ground, Ramon would never have been shot. I would have had more time with my dad before he passed.

"I have to tell you something." Garrett's face flickers with remorse. I can see there's something he doesn't want to say but knows he needs to.

"What?" I ask, my stomach tightening into a painful knot.

"Imogene talked to them. She . . ." He struggles for words, his gaze flickering to our daughter.

Imogene interjects. "I told them everything, Mom. I'm sorry."

I search her eyes, waiting for her to explain, but it's Garrett who continues.

He scratches at his jawline, and I can see the exhaustion in the lines around his eyes. He's tired. "I thought it was best to be honest from this point forward. We told them about the hormone blockers. Lying hasn't done anything but further complicate all of this."

"Okay, what happens next?" I ask.

"We got a call from Lilly this morning after your arraignment. The judge ordered a parenting plan instead of removal. Imogene will have to go to therapy, and so will you if you're released. There are some other requirements too, but Imogene gets to stay at home."

I exhale my relief and close my eyes.

When I open my eyes again, Imogene is watching me, clearly expecting disappointment.

"Are you mad?" she asks.

My first reaction to everything has been to run, hide, conceal, and lie. Now, I'm sitting behind a glass window, unable to be with my family. My way of doing things has only exasperated an already difficult situation. Garrett is right. Honesty is the best policy.

"No. I'm relieved."

"I'm sorry, Mom," she repeats.

"Don't be. You should have never been in this situation in the first place." At that, I feel my eyes mist over and I have to dig my nails into the palm of my hand to stop the tears.

Garrett regards me. "Neither should you. You did what you thought was best, and even though I don't agree with the way you went about it, I can understand how it felt like you didn't have any other options," Garrett says, placing a hand on Imogene's shoulder.

I don't deserve grace right now, but I'll take it. Every drop feels like a reprieve from drowning.

"I'm already looking into options for bail," Garrett continues.

I shake my head. "Don't." The thought of the financial strain makes my chest tighten.

"Stacy, I can't leave you in here."

I let out a long exhale and turn my attention to Imogene. "Honey, can you give your dad and me a moment?"

"What? Why? I thought we weren't doing this anymore—keeping things from each other."

"We aren't, but some things are not for you. You're still a child," I say gently.

Garrett looks at Imogene. "Listen to your mom. Go back to the waiting area. I'll be there in just a few minutes."

Imogene huffs, her frustration clear, but she stands and exits the visitation area. As she leaves, a guard follows her with his eyes, and it makes me uneasy. We are sending Imogene to sit by herself in a jail waiting room.

"Garrett, I don't think you understand. We are so far underwater. I've tried, but with everything—my dad and your business—I've been robbing Peter to pay Paul for years now. We have no money, and I'm not making a paycheck anymore."

"I know. I logged into our accounts after you left. I'm sorry. I've been hands-off and expected you to handle everything. You've tried to tell me, and I ignored you. I'm going to liquidate the business and use whatever I can to get us through. I'll get what we need for your bail and for your father's funeral. We'll file for bankruptcy or whatever else we need to do. But some of this is going to take time."

Listening to him lay out a plan is such a foreign experience, but I don't want him to worry about me. Though being separated from Imogene fills me with a lingering ache.

"Just worry about keeping you and Imogene above water. Dad doesn't need anything fancy, and I'm okay here. I'm so sorry for all of this. I thought I was doing what was best."

"I know."

Silence stretches out between us, and I'm hesitant to share what's on my mind, but I do anyway.

"Can I ask you a favor?" He nods. "Ramon," I say, not needing to explain further. His jaw ticks, but he exhales and keeps his eyes on me.

"I'll find out how he's doing," Garrett says matter-of-factly.

"Thank you," I whisper.

"Do you love him?" Garrett asks.

His question catches me off guard. I care for him, but love? I'm so confused by the question that I take too long to respond.

This frustrates Garrett, and he says, "You know what? Don't answer that." He stands to leave, the motion almost hesitant.

"Garrett, please."

He settles back into his seat. "We're being honest now," he reminds me.

"Not like that. I do have love for him, and I care for him. But this week has been insane. I'm so confused about what I'm feeling right now. I can't make heads from tails. So, excuse me if it takes me a minute to answer you."

Garrett looks at his hands, his fingers tense. He drops his shoulders. "I'll see what I can find out. I'll let you know when I do."

Our ceasefire resumes.

"One more thing. Will you let me know about Dad's funeral? My lawyer says I might get a temporary release," I ask.

I've never had to count on him this much, and it's hard for me to do, but I have no choice.

"Of course. Imogene and I will be back tomorrow, and we can talk more about the funeral then. I can't guarantee we will visit every day because there's a lot I have to take care of, but we'll be back tomorrow."

I nod gratefully, emotion getting caught in my throat, leaving me unable to say anything else.

"Bye, Stacy," he says, standing to leave. He lingers for just a moment longer than necessary.

"Bye, Garrett," I whisper as I watch him walk away.

CHAPTER 39

DESPERATE TIMES

Garrett

My pen dances across the legal pad, leaving a trail of scribbles and cross-outs. I stare at the laptop screen, jotting down numbers to understand the severity of our financial outlook as I sip a glass of whiskey. The more I pore over our finances, the worse it looks.

Our house has zero equity even though the market has been good because we already took out a second mortgage. The collective available balance across all our accounts is less than a thousand dollars, and no more money is coming in. The shop is working on a few jobs. Still, if I stop paying on all our accounts, there is barely enough to keep the lights on and food in the fridge because the profit margins are so slim.

The air in the kitchen feels stifling despite the AC working overtime. We should probably shut it off so we can afford our electric bill. I don't know how I can fix this. Selling the equipment in the shop and convincing the building owner to let us out of the lease would provide enough for Stacy's bail, the funeral expenses, and two months of our basic needs. Selling the house would eliminate the mortgage, but where would we live?

I have run these numbers several times but keep doing it in the hopes something changes. That I find room in our finances to make it all work without getting rid of the business, but there is no other way. Stacy tried to tell me Barnett Woodworks was pushing us further into debt than we could handle, that it didn't bring in enough for us to survive off of, but I didn't listen. I expected her to take care of it and believed it would all eventually work out.

The whiskey in my glass is almost gone. I gaze at the whisky bottle on the counter. It's more than halfway drained, and I won't be able to replace it once it's empty. I can't afford to replace anything.

We don't even have retirement accounts anymore. When I quit my job to start my business, I encouraged Stacy to drain them. I thought I could turn that money into something more, but I now realize she was right when she told me the risk was too great. I can blame Stacy for almost everything except for this.

I put my head in my hands and groan. She tried to tell me, and I didn't listen. Maybe that's why she did everything without telling me. She probably didn't see the point. She came to me once about the hormone blockers, and I shut her down. If she was that desperate to help Imogene, I would have liked her to say something more, but she probably thought I didn't care. I like to think I would have cared, but maybe after years of nagging me about money and being more proactive, she didn't think it was worth the effort to include me in other decisions.

I drain the glass, the burn of the whiskey a sharp contrast to the dull ache in my chest. My cell vibrates, breaking the silence. I glance at the caller ID, but I don't want to pick it up. Everything feels so wrong.

"Hello?" My back molars grind while I wait for their response.

"Garrett?" a man's voice says.

"Hey, Ramon. Thanks for calling me back. Sorry to bother you, but Stacy wanted me to check on you. How are you?"

"Still in the hospital, but I'll be okay. Where's Stacy? Did something happen?"

"She's been arrested. For prescription fraud and child abuse." I listen as he lets out a breath.

"Damn."

"Damn is right," I agree.

"How's Imogene?" Ramon asks. I feel a primal urge to protect my wife and daughter from another man's interest, but I push it down. The logical side of me understands Stacy didn't trust me and felt I wasn't someone she could rely on. And yet, Ramon risked everything to help my family. I want to hate him for it, but deep down, I know that if I'd been a different husband, there would never have been a world in which he and Stacy would have shared a kiss.

"She's fine. At least she will be. Again, thanks for calling me. Stacy asked me to reach out and . . ."

"Yeah, I'll be in here a few more days. I had an infection, but they said I should be out by the end of the week. Will you tell Stacy I'll visit when I return?"

Visit my wife in jail? I bite my lip, struggling to hold back a surge of jealousy. Maybe it's unfair to be angry with Stacy or Ramon, but it's not his place anymore. It's mine. I need to step up and be the man my family can rely on.

"You've done enough. I've got her," I say, and the line falls silent.

"Is there anything I can do to help?" he asks. I chew on his question.

"Not right now. Thank you for what you have done, but I can take it from here." I feel a boulder in my chest when I hang up the phone. I realize Stacy would love a visit from Ramon to see with her eyes that he is okay, but I need space from what happened between them.

A crash from upstairs makes me jump out of my seat. I put down the whiskey glass and run upstairs, yelling, "Imogene! Are you okay?"

"Yeah, I'm fine," she yells back, but the tone of her voice conveys distress. When I open her door, she is lying on the ground.

"What are you doing?" I ask. Her room is a mess. Her mattress is on its side, propped against a wall, her desk sits in the middle of the room, and her floor lamp is lying knocked over.

"Rearranging," she says, getting to her feet.

"Why?" I ask.

"Nothing in this room feels right anymore. I don't want to look at it."

She picks up the lamp, but a bin full of random items is in her way, so she tries to kick it across the room and stubs her toes. She sits on the ground, holding her foot. "Owe! Stupid, stupid, stupid!"

I head over and sit on the floor before her, my back against the dresser.

"Let me see," I say.

"I'm fine," she snaps.

I sigh. "No more of that."

"What?"

"No more hiding what you're going through and disguising it with shrugs and 'I'm fine' and huffs of annoyance. We aren't doing that anymore. So let me see and tell me what's wrong."

She glares at me, hesitating, but then allows me to look at her foot. She jammed her toenail badly enough to bleed.

I kneel closer and glance up at her face. She's staring down at her injured toe, her jaw tight, and her lips pressed together. I almost don't notice it—but then I see the look in her eyes.

It's more than just pain. There's this kind of wisdom that feels too heavy for someone her age. It's the look of someone who's used to gritting her teeth. The look in her eyes, stirs something within me, I've been avoiding.

I've always encouraged her to be bold in her expression of her gender identity. But now I realize it wasn't just about her. It was about me, too. I've been avoiding a small, shameful hope I've held onto. A hope I didn't even know was there.

I wanted her to express her gender identity so strongly because, deep down, I was still clinging to this hope that she'd be the son I had once expected. It's almost as if I needed her to overcompensate for something I couldn't let go of.

The realization is like a sucker punch. I didn't even know that hope was there, hiding under layers of self-doubt and avoidance. But now that I see it, I can't unsee it. I can't pretend anymore. That hope—it's been hurting her. It's been holding me back from being the dad she needs.

"Dad?" Her voice pulls me out of my thoughts. She's watching me with a look of concern.

"I'll be right back." I get up to grab a bandage. Once I'm back and sitting on the floor again, I pull Imogene's foot into my lap. When the antiseptic comes into contact with her toe, she sucks in a breath at the burn. Then I peel open the bandage.

"Are you going to tell me what's going on?" I ask. I want to do better. I want to be the dad she deserves.

She rolls her eyes.

I lift my brows at her. "I'm waiting."

"I don't know how to explain it," she moans.

"Well, try."

She chews on the tips of her fingers, and I want to tell her to get her hands out of her mouth, but instead, I sit and fix my gaze on her.

Finally, she starts to spill.

"Before we left, I was so lonely all the time. I felt like no one understood me, and the one person I thought understood me the most had abandoned me completely."

"McKenzie?"

Imogene nods. "I just miss having someone to talk to."

Stacy had been so worried when McKenzie suddenly stopped coming around. I told her it was fine, that she worried too much, that kids grow apart, and that it was normal. But I was wrong.

I nudge her. "I'm here. Your mom was here. Why didn't you talk to us?"

Imogene shakes her head. "Mom is always worried about everything, so I feel like it's my job to make her worry less, which means I can't talk to her. And you—you don't do touchy-feely very well. You tell me to toughen up, to be brave. And yes, I understand I need to be brave. I want to be brave, but it's hard when I feel so alone."

I think about Stacy, who lives in a constant state of worry. Her worrying has always annoyed me, and I've ignored her concerns rather than helping to soothe them. She never wanted Imogene to know she was worried, so she tried her hardest to pretend she was okay. Yet Imogene saw through her.

I remember when Imogene was in kindergarten. She didn't want to go to school, and so, on her first day, the teachers had to peel Imogene from Stacy's body. Stacy was a mess afterward and spent the entire day sitting in the school parking lot.

For years, Stacy wouldn't trust anyone with Imogene. She worked, but only on the days I was off, so we never saw each other and Imogene was never without her parents. I think Stacy's coddling made it hard for Imogene to adjust to school.

But Stacy figured out a way to relieve Imogene's anxiety. Every day, when she dropped Imogene off at school, she would tell her, "Today is a good day." That phrase eventually became their little ritual, and overtime, it was no longer necessary, but they said it anyway, even when they weren't together.

I want to ease Imogene's heartache and tell her it will be a good day, but I don't think it'll help. The platitude has been used so much that it now sits empty, so instead, I say, "I'm sorry."

"It's fine. I'm just explaining. Anyway, before we left, I was lonely, but then I wasn't when I was there at the Drag Palace. Now, I'm alone again, and I can't stop thinking about how it didn't use to be that way. I used to have a friend." Imogene's face screws up as she fights back tears.

"That's tough." I scoot closer to her. "Maybe you can make new friends?"

"I don't want new friends. I want the friend I used to have. Bryce thinks I should talk to McKenzie, but I don't know." She brings her knees to her chest and wraps her arms around them.

"Maybe he's right. What could it hurt?"

Imogene shrugs, and I want to tell her shrugging is not an effective form of communication, but I let this one go.

I look around her room. "I still don't quite understand how reorganizing your room helps any of this."

She chews on her lip. "I don't know. I just had an urge to change it. I thought maybe it might help. That's dumb, huh?"

I give it some thought. Maybe it's for the same reason Stacy reaches for control. Sometimes, when we are so distressed by our circumstances, we do things that don't make sense. We will go to any lengths to fix the thing that haunts us most, even if that means breaking the law, lying, and running away.

"It doesn't make sense, but somehow, I understand. Can I help?"

When Imogene and I finish rearranging her room, she steps back, taking it all in. The tension she has been holding onto dissolves before me. All we've done is change the orientation of the furniture to give Imogene more room to position her telescope at her window. It's not a big change, but it gives the room a new energy.

"This is way better. Thanks, Dad," she says. It's the first time in a long time that I feel like I've done something right.

I linger in the doorway for a moment, appreciating the small sense of calm this brought Imogene, before heading back downstairs to the kitchen, where my notepad and laptop wait. I stare at the door, feeling the magnitude of everything all at once. There's so much to be done, and our problems feel like a tangled mess with no plausible solution. Stacy has felt like this. Like Imogene, she has been dealing with this alone. Such desperate times would lead anyone to desperate measures.

I may finally understand why Stacy did what she did, but I'm not ready to forgive her. At least, not yet.

CHAPTER 40

DON'T SAY GAY

Imogene

As angry as I am with Ramon for kissing my mom, he may have been right about one thing: sometimes exposing others feels like protecting ourselves.

I was too angry at what happened the day of the field trip to the museum to understand it completely, but the more I think about McKenzie and her sudden shift from friend to bully, I have to believe that there is some truth in what he said.

When McKenzie pretended to befriend me again after nearly two years of zero communication, I was so eager that I jumped at the bait. I allowed her to exploit my vulnerabilities so she could draw attention away from her own—whatever they might be. She's ashamed of something, and I'm going to figure out what it is. Maybe if I try to understand what happened, it might remove some of the deep unnamed shame I feel.

I knock at her door and wait. The afternoon sunshine is intense, the heat almost unbearable. When no one comes to the door, I knock again, more insistently. Eventually, McKenzie's mom answers. It's the middle of the day, but it's apparent that I've woken her up. She stands there in her faded muumuu, her hair a disheveled mess, and eyes squinting against the sunlight.

"Charlie?" she says, and it slices through me, but differently than it used to before I knew what it felt like to belong. It still cuts, but not as deep.

"Imogene," I correct, and she blinks hard, trying to understand.

"Is McKenzie here?" My voice is steady despite the anxiety churning in my gut.

McKenzie's mom turns to yell into the house. "McKenzie, some person named Imogene is here to see you!"

I can't help but smile at what McKenzie's reaction to my name might be.

I hear McKenzie's voice from the back of the house, where her bedroom is, but her exact words are unclear.

"She'll be out in a minute," McKenzie's mom says before shutting the door in my face.

It's so hot that I pinch the front of my shirt, flicking it up to help cool myself off. I stand outside for what feels like an eternity, with the sun beating down on me, sweat trickling down my back. Doubts creep in. Maybe I was wrong to come. Maybe McKenzie is just going to leave me out here to roast.

Then I hear shuffling by the door, and the doorknob jiggles before she pulls it open. I feel the cool air from inside the house momentarily before McKenzie steps all the way out and shuts the door behind her. She looks different—tired, maybe, or just wary. Her eyes narrow as they adjust to the light, and she places a hand above her brow to shield her eyes from the sun.

"What are you doing here?" she asks, her tone sharp and defensive.

"I came to talk to you," I say, trying to keep my voice calm and collected, even though my heart is pounding in my chest.

"Why?" Her voice reveals so much disdain for me, but I don't believe it. Instead of letting her know I don't believe it, I pretend to be curious about it.

"Why do you hate me?"

The question hangs heavy in the air between us.

"Really? That's what you came here for?" She acts annoyed, but there's something else there, something she's trying to hide.

"McKenzie, you were my best friend in the whole world, and you threw that away. Why, because I'm trans? I might be trans, but I'm still me. I'm still your best friend. I was this person the whole time we were friends. I just hadn't accepted it yet because I didn't know I could, and accepting myself was a lot harder after you left. But, McKenzie, I've always been this person."

I've held this question inside me for so long, replaying every memory of us, trying to make sense of what I did wrong, why she abandoned me. Now that it's out in the open, I feel a strange mix of strength and vulnerability. Or maybe my vulnerability is my strength.

She looks at me, and for a moment, I see a flicker of the friend I used to know. But then it's gone, replaced by the guarded, defensive girl standing in front of me. The silence stretches on, heavy and uncomfortable.

She kicks at the ground and crosses her arms. "I know," she says.

"Then why? Why abandon me? Why torture me and sic your goons on me?"

"I don't want to talk about this." She turns to go back inside.

I reach out and grab her wrist before she can run away. "No, we are talking about it. It isn't fair that you can just pretend we were never friends. I can't. I think about how much I miss you all the time. And I don't want to miss you because you have been nothing but terrible to me. Lately, my life has been insane, and all I want is to have my friend back."

McKenzie's eyes drop to the hand holding her wrist, and I think she's going to yank it away, but she doesn't. She continues to stare. I hold my breath, waiting for her to acknowledge my words.

"Tell me, McKenzie. Why do you hate me?"

"Because I'm not gay," she says, tears springing to her eyes.

I look at her, confused, shaking my head slightly and letting go of her arm. "What? You don't have to be gay to be my friend."

McKenzie swallows hard and looks around, avoiding my gaze. "Because I didn't want to just be *your friend*," she confides, and I'm transported to all those moments. Those gentle touches, the times she would always hold my hand on the trampoline, each time she teased me about liking girls at school.

"Wait, what?"

"I don't want to be gay. I don't want to be like you." I realize then the vulnerability she was masking as she exposed mine.

"Do you still like me? Like as more than a friend?"

"I told you. I'm not gay." I lift my brows, realizing McKenzie is probably a little gay. I want to laugh. The giggle rises in my belly, and I have to push it down before it erupts from my mouth.

It all comes into focus. McKenzie liked me, really liked me, and when I came out, it confused her about her own sexuality. Being gay is not wrong, but it's scary. Especially when so many people say it is wrong.

I struggle with what to say, but then I remember what Bryce said to me before we left: the most difficult part of this journey is accepting ourselves, but when we reach that point, that's when we can find belonging. I look at McKenzie and realize she has yet to accept herself, and I can't force her to, but I can help her feel a little less lonely.

"I hear you. You're not gay. I imagine it's confusing because you liked me, and then I told you I was a girl. That must've been hard. Confusing. It was for me, too. I'm only asking for you to be my friend. Nothing else. Could we try that?" I peer around at her face, trying to discern what she's thinking.

"Maybe."

"Maybe? So, like, maybe if I set my telescope up tonight, you could come over and look at the Summer Triangle with me? I hear that Vega, Altair, and Deneb are all supposed to be extra bright tonight." I keep my gaze steady on her face.

"Maybe," she says again with a shrug. Maybe is better than no, and even if she never comes over again, at least I know I tried.

"Cool," I say, turning and walking back toward my house.

When I look over my shoulder, she is already back in her house. I don't know if she will come look at the stars with me tonight, but I'm glad I was brave enough to confront her.

I feel a flicker of hope, and maybe, just maybe, tonight will be a good night.

CHAPTER 41

WHEN LIFE GIVES YOU PEACHES

Stacy

I've only been in jail for four days, but I already feel an overwhelming sense of restlessness. I'm used to taking action—fixing things. But I can't do anything but wait, and it's driving me crazy.

Yesterday, Garrett and Imogene visited again. We spent the time talking through arrangements for my dad's funeral. I called my attorney this morning to ask about the special hearing for temporary release so that Garrett could plan the date, but my attorney wasn't available, so I left a message. Who knows if he'll even remember who I am. The helplessness gnaws at me, and I hate that I can't do more to move the process along, to ensure some type of certainty. The tremors, which usually only temporarily plague my hands, have become a permanent fixture.

The afternoon light filters into my cell, casting dim shadows that deepen my isolation. Like my cellmate, I've taken up reading to pass the time. I'm sitting on my bunk, a book open in my lap, when a guard approaches. "Barnett, you have a visitor," he says, and I look up, startled.

Garrett and Imogene weren't supposed to come today. They must have changed their plans. The unexpected shift makes me uncomfortable. Or maybe it's Brandon, my attorney, here to talk about the special hearing.

I rise from my bunk and follow the guard down the corridor to the visitation area. When I sit in the booth, I search for familiar faces, and then I see them. Flora, Opal, and Steve all parade into the area. Steve is dressed in a well-tailored dark suit, and Flora and Opal look as fabulous as ever.

A laugh bubbles up from somewhere deep inside me. I grab the phone, eager to talk to them. I didn't realize how badly I needed to see them, these friends who embody joy even in a place as bleak as this.

As they approach the window, Opal puts her hand on her waist and a foot forward, posing before she says something I can't make out because they haven't reached the booth yet. If I were to guess, it looked like she said, "Oh, girl, that color is not good on you."

I can't help but smile. It is a genuine smile that wakes up all the muscles in my face.

They all take a seat, their presence filling the room with warmth and familiarity.

Flora, realizing I can't hear them without the speaker, presses the button. The small red light blinks, signaling it's on.

"Yeah, it totally washes you out."

I gesture to my uniform, and they all nod. I just stare for several moments, at a loss for words.

"Cat got your tongue?" Steve says.

Finally, I find my voice. "Oh, my God, how did you know I was here? Did Imogene call you or . . ."

"Garrett talked to Ramon. I was visiting Ramon at the hospital, and he said you were arrested. So, I went to the club, and told Gary we were leaving," Flora says dramatically.

Opal interjects, "He wasn't happy about having a reduced set list, but I told him that if he didn't like it, he could put on a dress and dance." She flips her hair and smirks, pleased with herself.

"Can you imagine?" Flora responds, and they all laugh. The sound soothes my anxious soul.

I stare at the three of them, my heart swelling to have them here.

"Ramon told us everything about how you have been helping Imogene with her transition, even when it meant risking your job. Your life," Flora explains in a whisper.

Steve pipes in, his normal flirty southern twang, the one he adopts for Peach, is more masculine and less pronounced. "I was at the office when these two bimbos showed up during a meeting and dragged me out. I didn't know what could be so important, but we had to come when they said you were in jail."

I clasp my hands together, feeling a surge of gratitude. "Thank you, but you didn't have to. I'll be here for a while."

"Oh, honey, that's not happening. We're bailing you out today. We meet with the bail bondsman right after this," Opal says.

I'm floored. I put my hands up in protest. "No. I could never ask you to do that. It's a lot of money."

"How much?" Flora lowers her brows and stares at me through her large, fanned-out lashes.

"Just you coming to see me means the world to me, but I'm okay. Honestly."

"How much?" Flora repeats.

I breathe in deep through my nose. "Five thousand."

"That's nothing. Daddy Steve got you," Opal says, smiling at Steve.

Steve's eyes slide to the side where Opal sits, narrowing slightly. "You're real quick to spend my money, huh?"

Opal waves him off. "Oh, please."

Steve shifts his attention back to me. "She's right. Five thousand is nothing. I got you."

My eyes widen, and I shake my head in disbelief. "No, it—it's not."

"To him, it is. Fancy pants, finance guy," Flora says, their mouth pursed as she glances at Steve with a playful smirk.

"We thought about surprising you, but the bail bondsman couldn't meet with us for two hours, and it was visiting hours, so we came to see you here in all your beige glory," Opal says with a gesture to me through the glass.

I lean forward. "I'll pay you back."

"We can worry about that later. What we need to focus on is your defense. Do you at least have a decent attorney?" Steve asks.

"I have a public defender."

Opal shakes her head firmly. "That will not do."

"I can't afford anything else," I murmur.

"I can, and I will." Steve's tone leaves no room for argument.

 "No, you have already been too generous."

"Who do you think owns the club you've been working in?" he asks, raising an eyebrow.

"I don't know. Gary?" I guess with uncertainty.

Opal laughs loudly, the sound echoing in the room. "That guy? When he came to us, he was fresh out of court-ordered rehab and homeless. He wouldn't have a pot to piss in if it wasn't for the club."

"You?" I look at Steve, my mouth slightly agape. He purses his lips and nods.

"Most drag clubs can't afford to pay their queens enough to live. I wanted a place where everyone could make a livable wage and feel safe, including me. So, I bought it about fifteen years ago."

"Wow, how did I not know that?"

"Peachy here is so modest," Flora says in a baby voice, batting their eyelashes.

Steve rolls his eyes, but there's a fondness in his expression. "We're going to bail you out, and I'll contact my attorney. He doesn't do these types of cases, but he'll put me in touch with someone who can."

"Then we can get you out of that horrible beige thing," Opal says. "You look terrible, and I don't think I can handle another minute of it." She scrunches her face.

I laugh before a guard holds a finger to his lips to ask me to quiet down. Stifling my laugh, I clasp my hands together, trying to steady my voice. "Thank you. I'm so glad you're here."

"We got you, girl," Flora says, tilting their chin up. "But we should go. They only allow three visitors in, and we played rock-paper-scissors to decide who would stay outside. Bryce lost."

"Bryce is here? Does Imogene know?" I ask.

"She will soon," Opal says with a wink.

I watch them leave before a guard escorts me back to my cell. Disbelief washes over me. The Drag Palace, once a place I regarded as a means to an end, has become the place that will forever change our lives for the better. I felt guilty for leaving and making a mess of everything, but if I hadn't, I never would have met the queens. I don't know what the future holds, but the thought of being back home with my family, even temporarily, causes my lips to stretch into a smile. For the first time since I was arrested, I don't have to fight to keep my hands from shaking.

CHAPTER 42

DOUBLE SKUNKS

Stacy

I can't believe I'm standing here, only a few steps from home. Relief and anxiety twist together in my stomach as I look at our house, bathed in the soft glow of the evening sun. The familiar sight both comforts and unnerves me. Then my breath catches at the scene in the window.

Garrett and Imogene are at the kitchen table, deep in a game of cribbage. Root beer floats sit on the table, the long spoon handles and straws poking out of the frothy brown and cream concoctions.

It's been two weeks since I was home. On my last night here, I paced my room between bouts of packing as fear gripped my insides and I imagined the worst-case scenarios. My pulse quickens now, just like it did then, but with a strange, unexpected anticipation. It feels as if I'm coming home for the first time, but I'm uncertain how I will be received. My marriage, my life. None of it is as clear as it once was. I glance back to where Bryce, Steve, Opal, and Flora linger behind me in the driveway. They are giving me space to reunite with my family.

Taking a deep breath, I push open the front door and step inside. The familiar scent of home wraps around me, and for a moment, everything feels right in the world. That moment is fleeting because the fact is that my life may very well be over. Regardless, I'm happy to be home with Imogene. As I walk to the end of the entryway, Imogene and Garrett stand to see who it is. Imogene's eyes widen when her gaze lands on my face.

"Mom!" She jumps up to run toward me. The day we picked up Imogene from Bryce's, and she ran into Garrett's arms, I was so envious. She never embraced me like that anymore, and here she was, her arms tight around my waist. I hug her back, feeling tears prick at the corners of my eyes. The warmth of her embrace reminds me of when she was little. I had hoped she would never let go, and while she did for a time, she is back.

Garrett walks closer and looks at me, bewildered, as if asking, "How?" I turn and point through the open door. The queens' faces reflect the warmth of Imogene's hug.

Imogene stops her hug to look behind me. "You're here!" she shouts and darts outside to greet them.

"They're only in town for the night," I explain, stepping further into the house. "They bailed me out, and Steve is going to help pay for my attorney."

"Really?" Garrett asks, his voice filled with disbelief.

"Yeah, really," I confirm, nodding.

A moment later, the queens follow Imogene through the front door. They look around our modest house as they enter, their vibrant presence filling the space, painting it technicolor.

They each introduce themselves to Garrett, except Bryce, who says, "Good to see you again." Garrett shakes each of their hands and then stands awkwardly in front of the group, obviously unsure of what to do next.

He then remembers himself. "We were just playing cribbage. Do you want to join us?"

"Sure!" Bryce says, walking to the table while Imogene continues chatting with the others.

"Let me get the leaf for the table," I volunteer. We've had that leaf since we bought this table nearly ten years ago and have never used it before. Once I locate it in the back of a storage closet, Garrett and I pull the table apart and set up the game again.

The queens sit in the living room with Imogene, while Bryce helps us clear and reset the table. Their laughter travels to the kitchen. Garrett's eyes catch mine, and I try to understand the unspoken message, but the rift between us is still far too wide.

When the table is all put together again, everyone gathers around, and I have to look up how to play cribbage with six players. We play in pairs, taking turns at the cribbage board. The pegs clink into place as we count our points, "Fifteen-two, fifteen-four, a pair is six."

We play the game, stopping only to make root beer floats or to give space for Opal's storytelling. While in the kitchen, scooping vanilla ice cream into a glass cup, I watch Imogene and Garrett interact with the queens. Their competitive jests and jovial laughter fill the room. On the surface, this is the family I've been missing. The home I wanted to create.

However, I know now that our lives are so broken that this is only an illusion because we may be beyond repair.

About an hour into the evening, Imogene scores a double skunk, sending us all into a fit of laughter and groans. Then our doorbell rings. Everyone looks up from their cards, but Imogene jumps up. She runs to the door as if she was expecting company. I walk up behind her. The door swings open, and McKenzie stands on the step.

My heart stops at sight of her. I haven't seen her in nearly two years, and she has matured significantly since the last time she was at my house. I decide not to intrude and walk back over to the table. The queens and Garrett still hold their cards in their hands but look at me inquisitively.

"McKenzie," I announce as I take my seat.

Garrett's shoulders come down. "Really?"

"Yeah." I nod.

"She did it," Bryce says in awe.

"Did you have something to do with this?" I ask.

Bryce shrugs, a half-grin adorning his face as he looks back at his cards.

"Who's McKenzie?" Flora whispers. I crane my neck, not wanting Imogene and McKenzie to hear me. In a hushed tone, I say, "Imogene's long-lost best friend."

"Long-lost? Did her mother kidnap her, too?" Steve says, and my mouth drops open. "Too soon?" He grins.

Everyone at the table is silent for a beat until Garrett laughs wildly, and the queens join in. Humility isn't my strong suit, but the laughter is infectious, and I can't help but laugh too.

The girls walk into the kitchen, as if this moment isn't monumental. "Hey, is it okay if we take my telescope to the backyard?" Imogene asks. McKenzie stands with her hands in her pockets, taking in the group of people at the table.

Bryce lays down his hand. "I came all this way to play cribbage with you, and you're going to abandon me?"

Imogene scratches the side of her face. "Uh . . ."

Opal rolls her eyes at Bryce. "Not everything is about you."

Bryce wiggles his head and picks up his cards to study them again. "Last time I checked, it is."

"Is it okay?" Imogene asks again.

"Yes," I breathe. "Go. Have fun."

Both girls take the stairs to fetch Imogene's telescope, and Garrett and I exchange knowing glances.

CHAPTER 43

AFFIRM ME

Stacy

The next several months pass in a blur of preparations and arrangements. Garrett and I host a small funeral for my dad. The ceremony is intimate and somber, held at a quiet cemetery on the outskirts of town.

The sky is robin-egg blue, and a gentle breeze cuts through the morning humidity. Garrett stands beside me as they lower Dad's casket into the ground, a magnetic pull drawing me closer to him. I imagine his calloused, warm hand in mine, but we aren't in that place anymore, so I cross my arms to ward off the temptation. I tell myself the grief and looming uncertainty make me more vulnerable than usual, and I should keep my distance until there is some sense of clarity as to where life will take me.

After the funeral, Garrett and I continue to live together, but uncertainty clouds our future. We promise to put a pin in any major decisions about our marriage until the trial is over, and there are so many times I want to broach the conversation but choose not to. Garrett moves into the guest bedroom, and our interactions become polite, almost formal, as if we are both afraid to say or do something that might tip the fragile balance we have created.

Ramon texts me only once, but that single message tears me up. He risked everything for me, was shot because of me, and yet here I am, back in my home with my husband—even if our status is uncertain. It feels wrong, but I no longer know what "right" is. Things have spiraled into complication so quickly. Ramon's message is simple: *How are you?* It takes me days to respond with: *I'm okay. Thank you again for everything. I'm sorry.*

He doesn't text me back after that. I assume he is mad at me, or maybe he gets the message that right now—as selfish as it is—is not the right time.

Garrett liquidates his business and finds a job on a nearby construction site for a new shopping center. I get a job as a cashier at our local grocery store. Between us, it is enough to keep us above water while we wait for my trial. We also list the house and meet with a bankruptcy lawyer. Peach has been more than generous when it comes to paying for my criminal defense, my legal counsel for my case with the nursing board, and our bankruptcy. He offers to help us catch up on our bills, but he has already done too much. Helping with the legal fees is more than I could ever ask for.

Several weeks after my arrest, I meet with the attorney Peach recommends for my criminal case. Her office is warm and inviting, with dark wood furniture and shelves lined with books. The attorney, Ms. Coleson, is a large blonde woman in her early 50s who has a knack for speaking both plainly and eloquently. Her bright pink lipstick matches her pink blazer, which coordinates perfectly with her handbag perched atop her desk.

"Right now, they are charging you with child abuse as a second-degree felony and prescription fraud in the third-degree. You could face up to twenty years in prison. I can't create reasonable doubt in this case. The evidence is too strong."

I press my fist to my lips and stare at my lap. *Twenty years?* Newborns grow into adults in that time. Imogene will be in her 30s. It seems so unbelievable, but it could very well happen.

I'm going to spend the next twenty years of my life in prison, and I can't run. Not again.

"So, I'm screwed?" I ask.

"Not exactly. I recommend we focus on reducing time instead. Our best bet is to get the second-degree charges reduced down to third-degree, and hope the judge is lenient."

"What do you suggest?"

Ms. Coleson leans forward. "We're in Florida, and with the political climate being a minefield, there's a significant risk that a jury will be biased. Senate Bill 254 is relatively new. It directly restricts access to gender-affirming care for minors, and there's a lot of public opinion swirling around it. In fact, this case will set a precedent for future cases. I strongly recommend opting for a bench trial. A judge is more likely to be objective and rule based on the law."

I inhale a deep breath, considering her words. I'm transported back to the day I told Imogene we had to report her assault to the school. I told her it was about preventing this from happening to others. Although I don't want my life to be used as part of a larger battle because of all I'm at risk of losing, if risking myself means helping others like me, like my daughter . . . maybe it's a purpose I can accept. I'm just not sure it will work.

"You really think that's the best option?"

"I do," she says with a firm nod. "A jury trial could turn into a circus, and we don't want that. A judge will focus on the legality of your actions and the case's specifics. Given the circumstances of your actions, we can argue that you were acting in your child's best interest, and that should take some of the sting out of the charges. Additionally, if we can successfully get the prosecution to focus on the child abuse charges rather than the prescription fraud, we may have a fighting chance at a lesser sentence."

Ms. Coleson is the expert, and I have no choice but to trust her. Trusting others is still new to me, but I'm trying.

Over the next few weeks, I navigate the pretrial process with Ms. Coleson. The pretrial conferences are a series of meetings between Ms. Coleson and the prosecutor. We discuss the case, review evidence, and explore the possibility of plea bargains. Unfortunately, the prosecutor believes this is a slam-dunk case and is not eager to provide me with a deal.

During this phase, Ms. Coleson files several motions to suppress evidence, such as testimony made by Imogene at DCFS, which she believes was obtained unlawfully. Each motion is a small battle, with arguments made and decisions handed down. Some motions are granted, and others are denied. In addition to managing my criminal case, Ms. Coleson handles the nursing board for me. Thankfully, the board agreed to wait to hold my hearing until after the criminal trial to avoid any prejudice in the criminal case. God knows I can only focus on one problem at a time.

While navigating the legal charges, I also realize this might be my last summer with Imogene while she is still a child. Outside of my job and meeting with Ms. Coleson, I try to spend as much time with my daughter as she allows. I know I'm overbearing, so I try to back off while also soaking up every moment I can. We go to the movies, window shop in boutiques we cannot afford, bake cookies, and ride bikes. We celebrate her fifteenth birthday at home, and Garrett makes spaghetti tacos.

Following the pretrial conferences, we enter the discovery phase, in which Ms. Coleson explains each step, each document, and each legal maneuver. "We need to dot every 'i' and cross every 't' here," she insists. We spend hours preparing my testimony, anticipating the prosecutor's questions, and crafting truthful responses that mitigate the perceived severity of my actions. The evidence against me is so solid that I have a hard time believing I'll make it out of this. If anything, I'm just wasting Peach's money, but he insisted, so I'll fight the good fight.

One morning at her office, Ms. Coleson says, "I would like for Imogene to see a psychiatrist who specializes in transgender issues."

"She's already required to go to therapy by DCFS."

Ms. Coleson blinks at me. "I'm aware, but we will need someone on our side to put on the stand. I also want to have Imogene evaluated by a doctor, and I would like to start prepping her for testimony."

My chest tightens. "I don't know . . ."

"Do you want to go to prison?" Ms. Coleson asks.

"No, I just don't want to put any more on Imogene than I already have."

"Look, talk to her. See what she thinks, but without her testimony, you're not passing go, you're not collecting two hundred dollars, and you're going to jail." Ms. Coleson fixes her gaze on me with unwavering seriousness.

That night, I decide to talk to Garrett first. We sit on the back porch. I take a deep breath and broach the conversation. "She wants Imogene to testify."

Garrett nods. "I'm not surprised."

"She also wants Imogene to be evaluated by a doctor and to see a psychiatrist." I let out a sigh. "Don't you think she's been through enough? I don't know if I'm comfortable with all of this." I search his face in the glow of our back porch light, looking for any sign of agreement.

He remains silent for a long time, his gaze distant. When he speaks, his tone is thoughtful. "Imogene is stronger than you give her credit for. She is more than capable of being evaluated and taking the stand. I think you are reverting to past behaviors because this all feels so uncertain." He pauses, his expression softening. "And I don't think you should ask me what I think, but should ask Imogene how she feels."

A year ago, Garrett would have made fun of me for wanting to protect Imogene. To see him resist the urge to deflect with humor and give me an emotionally intelligent response is new. I want to tell him how much I appreciate it, but it doesn't feel like the right time. I turn his words over in my head. Am I justified in my hesitation, or am I doing what I always do? I know the answer, but I don't want to admit it. Regardless, the next day, I do what he suggests and ask Imogene if she would take the stand and be evaluated.

In the living room, she lies on her side, the remote in her hand. She moves her feet so I can sit on the sofa's edge.

"Whatcha watching?" I ask, trying to keep my tone light.

"Just some dumb movie. It isn't very good," she says, her eyes fixed on the screen.

"Can I talk to you?" I ask.

She presses pause and rolls over to look at me. "What's up?"

I lay out everything Ms. Coleson has asked her to do, careful to communicate to Imogene that she doesn't have to go through with any of it—it's entirely up to her.

"I'll do it," she says without thinking.

"You sure?" I pick up one of the sofa pillows, fluffing it before putting it back.

"Mom. If it means you might not go to prison, then yes. I'm the reason for all this. None of this would be happening if it wasn't for me."

"That's not true." I look at her with concern.

She is careful when making eye contact with me. "It is, and we both know it. You might have done it, but you did it for me. So, let me do this. Please."

"Okay. I will let Ms. Coleson know. Thank you."

I stare at my hands before lifting my head to Imogene, who has aborted the movie and is looking for something else to watch. She flicks through the options, her expression bored.

"I just want to keep you safe. It's my job," I say, hoping she'll understand why I have made the decisions I have. She stops scrolling and sits up, inching closer to me.

She moves so that her knees touch mine and leans in to take my hands in hers.

"Mom, all I've ever needed was for you to affirm me. To affirm doesn't mean to protect, and it definitely doesn't mean that you center your worry in my journey. I feel terrible that you might go to prison, but I feel worse for feeling any bad way about you because you have gone to such great lengths to affirm my gender. I needed that, but at the same time, I need you to affirm that I'm capable. Okay?"

"Okay," I whisper.

I stand and walk out of the living room. I don't know why I have this reaction, but my body shakes as I sob.

CHAPTER 44

WINNER, WINNER, TURKEY DINNER

Stacy

Beep. Beep. Beep. One by one, I scan cans of pumpkin puree, boxes of stuffing, and large, frozen turkeys that thud against the belt. The store is buzzing with the frantic energy of last-minute shoppers, everyone realizing that Thanksgiving is tomorrow. The line at my register stretches far enough to dissolve into a blur of impatient faces, and I can already feel a dull ache creeping into my hips from standing in one place for too long.

"Excuse me," says a voice. "I couldn't find rosemary in the produce section. Could there be some in the back?"

I glance up to see a woman in her fifties, her dark curly hair framing a pair of wire-frame glasses that make her eyes look twice their natural size. She has cut in front of other customers to ask this question.

"I'm not sure," I reply, trying to keep my tone polite as I scan items for a young mother wrangling three kids under five. "I can call someone in produce for you."

Before I can reach for the intercom, a small voice pipes up from in front of me. A little boy is holding a chocolate bar to his chest. "I want it!" the little boy whines.

"I told you no!" the mother snaps, her voice strained with exhaustion and impatience.

Another child, likely the second oldest, tugs at her sleeve. "I want one, too!"

The mother's shoulders slump, her resistance crumbling as she sighs. "Fine, we'll get one, but you need to share."

"No!" the older boy cries out. "I don't want to share!"

The mother's patience snaps. She snatches the chocolate from his hands and bends to his level. "Then you won't get any." Instantly, all three kids burst into tears. I feel a pang of sympathy for her.

Before I can say a word to reassure her, the rosemary-seeker huffs. "You know what? Forget it. I'll take my business to another store."

I take a deep breath and roll my eyes as subtly as possible. It's going to be a long day.

Beep. Beep. Beep. The lines snake out of the checkout lanes and into the narrow aisles meant for foot traffic, creating a maze of carts and people squeezing past each other. The sounds of babies crying, people muttering, intercom announcements, and the constant beeping all build upon each other until they are so loud my head throbs. For fifteen years, I handled the chaos of labor and delivery and faced high-stakes moments and impossible decisions, but this . . . this feels overwhelming.

An hour left, I tell myself, glancing at the clock. *Just sixty more minutes.*

Then I look up and see her. Jackie. I bite back an internal groan. Of all the days and people, it has to be Jackie. *Happy 40th birthday to me.*

I can't believe I didn't notice her until now, standing in my line. She stands with her shoulders back and has a smug expression, as if she smells something rotten. Of course, she had to choose my checkout line. I haven't seen her since my last shift at the hospital. I hope she isn't here to gloat.

I try to pretend as if I don't see her as I help the customers in front of her, but I have no choice but to face her when she approaches the payment stand.

"Did you find everything you were looking for?" I say in my best customer service voice. Maybe if I keep things professional and light, she will just check out and be on her way. But no luck.

"So, this is where you ended up. I'm surprised they let you work here. They weren't concerned that you might steal from the register?"

I'm thankful for the noise within the store because no one besides me heard what she said.

"I've never stolen anything from anyone," I reply flatly. I'm not about to let her get to me. I'm already facing the consequences of my decisions. I don't need her to rub salt in my wounds.

"Except Dr. Kilpatrick's credentials." Her lips stretch to the side as she states this.

I regret a lot of things, including using my friend to get Imogene the care I believe she deserves, but what I regret most right now is that I never told Jackie exactly what I think of her — she is a rigid bitch. I likely only have a few more months at this job, but I still need it. So, despite my impulses, I hold it together and keep my thoughts to myself.

I usually try to help customers bag their groceries as I scan, but I don't help Jackie. I instead stand and watch as she bags her items. It's not exactly vindication, but it's something.

I don't say another word until all her items are rung up.

"That will be one hundred and eight dollars and fifty-six cents."

She swipes her card, loads groceries into her cart, and leaves.

Garrett and I recently made the decision that he and Imogene will move to Colorado with his uncle, regardless of the outcome of my trial. It was the best decision we could make, given that Imogene needs gender-affirming care and our shitty financial situation.

Chances are, I won't be able to go with them. I'll be here. In the Florida state prison system. The thought is a dagger to my chest. I guess the only silver lining is that I will never, ever have to work with Jackie again.

Although I try not to let Jackie's appearance get under my skin, it has soured my mood. I was already tired and down about spending my last birthday before the trial managing anxious, hurried shoppers. Now, I'm feeling downright agitated. Keeping my irritation in check for the last hour of my shift is such a mental and emotional strain that by the time I clock out, I'm exhausted.

But when I get home, I don't have the luxury of rest. Tomorrow is Thanksgiving, and family holidays feel more precious than ever. I'm determined to make the most of it. I did the shopping earlier this week, but nothing's prepped. Tonight, will be all about brining the turkey, baking pies, and drying out slices of bread for homemade stuffing. And despite my exhaustion, I'm going to make myself enjoy every minute of it.

This year, though, there's a pang of sadness I can't shake. It's our first Thanksgiving without my father. In previous years, even when he was in the nursing home, we'd bring him home for the holidays. Grief blooms within me, but I try not to focus on it.

When I pull up to the house, I notice Garrett's truck in the driveway, and a quick look at my phone confirms he came home four hours early. Usually, he gets in a few hours after me. *Did he quit? Is he sick? Did he get fired?* I force myself to stop spiraling. Maybe his work just let the crew go early for the holiday.

But as soon as I walk through the door, a warm, unexpected aroma hits me—baked goods mingle with the tang of spices. I drop my purse and head toward the kitchen, where I find Garrett slicing oranges and adding them to a bucket of brine. In over sixteen years together, he's never helped with Thanksgiving dinner unless I directly asked.

I'm gobsmacked by the sight.

"Hey," I say, trying to hide my surprise. "What . . . what are you doing?"

"Oh, I'm glad you're home! Quick question—do you add anything to the pumpkin from the can, or do you just put it in the pie crust and bake it?" Garrett asks, eyebrows raised.

A laugh erupts from deep in my belly. "You have to mix it with the other ingredients for the pie filling," I tell him, still smiling. I don't know what is more unbelievable: him being here in the kitchen doing all of this, or him possibly thinking that puree pumpkin, with its earthy mild flavor, is the only ingredient in a pumpkin pie.

"Shit!" He groans and jerks his head slightly.

"Did you already make the pie?" I ask, trying not to laugh harder. This whole interaction is quite amusing.

"Yeah," he admits, slightly out of breath as he moves to the oven and opens it for me to see. Sure enough, he's just smoothed the contents of a can of pumpkin puree into the bottom of a graham cracker crust. Next to it is a pecan pie that looks pretty darn good, though.

"Why didn't you look up a recipe?"

"I didn't think I needed to! But I did look up a recipe for the brine and for the pecan pie. I just . . . thought the pumpkin pie would be easy."

I chuckle and shake my head. "We can salvage this. Hand me that pie." I grab my apron and step into the kitchen. He retrieves the pie pan from the oven and sets it on the counter. I scoop the pumpkin from the crust and into a mixing bowl.

"Sorry about that," Garrett says sheepishly, now chopping sage for the turkey brine.

I go to the fridge to grab some eggs, but as I open it, Garrett blurts out, "Wait, don't go in there!"

It's too late. My eyes land on a cake on the top shelf, frosted in white with the words "Happy 40th Stacy" sloppily scrawled in green icing. It's homemade. Garrett has bought cakes for me before but never made one himself.

The unexpected gesture swells inside me. He made me a cake. I turn to him, speechless.

"Imogene helped me. I had to redo the writing about five times. That's why it is a little messy," he says, wincing with embarrassment.

"Is this why you came home early?"

"Yeah. Happy birthday." He holds eye contact with me as if trying to read my mind. Though it only lasts a few seconds, the moment feels stretched. When he turns back to his brine, I let out a rush of air.

"Thank you," I whisper, but I'm uncertain if Garrett heard me because Imogene bounds into the kitchen. "Mom! Happy birthday!" She sprints around the island and hugs me.

"Thank you, sweetie. Thank you both." This time, I know Garrett hears me because he flicks his eyes up to mine and gives me a brief nod of acknowledgment before focusing on the task before him.

We spend the rest of the evening prepping for Thanksgiving, snacking on meat, cheese, and fruit for dinner as we work. Once we're finished, Garrett and Imogene dim the lights and sing "Happy Birthday" to me. The warmth of the moment lets me forget, if only briefly, about my run-in with Jackie, the trial, and their move to Colorado.

As we clean up, Imogene heads to her room, and Garrett washes dishes while I try to rearrange the fridge to fit all the food.

"Thank you again," I say quietly, glancing over at him. "That meant a lot to me."

He smiles. "No problem. I know it wasn't the fanciest birthday surprise, but with everything coming up, I thought it important to do something. Something that shows you how much I appreciate you."

His words catch me off guard.

"Appreciate me?" After all, I'm the one who threw our lives into chaos. We might be in a truce, but I still feel like I'm the one who ruined everything.

"Yes." He meets my gaze. "You've always worked so hard for our family, made sacrifices, and even if I don't or didn't agree with the ways you went about things, you did what you thought was best. I appreciate that."

I try to process his words. "But . . . I still don't get it. I've cost you everything. Because of what I did, you'll be a single parent. You had to give up your dream. I might've sacrificed my career for Imogene, but I took yours, too."

Garrett looks at me thoughtfully as he grabs a dish towel from the bar on the oven and dries his hands. "That wasn't my dream," he says after a pause. "I became a carpenter the day we met. Before that, I'd been unemployed because of the recession. I liked working with my hands, sure, but it was never a passion. It was just a way to make money."

I stare at him. "Wait, you weren't a carpenter until we met? What do you mean?"

He tells me about that day at the bar when he was offered a job as a carpenter's apprentice on the spot. Before that, he'd worked in sales and loved it because he enjoyed working with people, but he never quite made it back to that world. He'd hoped that opening his own business would bring back that connection, but it ended up being more than he could handle.

As he talks, we move to the stools at the kitchen island.

My brows pinch together. "You never told me any of this," I say.

"That's because when I told you I was a carpenter, you said it must be meant to be," he admits. "I didn't want you to reconsider that statement. I wanted it to be true. I wanted us to be meant to be."

I want to ask if that's still how he feels—if he still wants us to be "meant to be." But the thought of hoping, only to have it all slip away when the trial is over, makes me hesitant. I'd rather avoid heartache. So, instead, I just murmur, "Hmmm," letting the question remain unanswered.

CHAPTER 45

OPENING STATEMENTS

Garrett

"The defendant, Stacy Barnett, is charged with prescription fraud and child abuse and endangerment," the prosecution states bluntly.

Assistant District Attorney Mark Davis is a stocky man who only ellipses the bench by about a foot. His pants need tailoring, as they drag on the floor along the sides of his black dress shoes. He's the kind of man who has spent his whole life wishing he was tall, who believes that if God had given him eight more inches, he would be unstoppable. As a fairly tall man, I can confidently say the only real privilege of height is reaching the top shelf.

"The evidence will show that Mrs. Barnett committed a serious breach of medical ethics and law. A registered nurse, she used her professional position to fraudulently obtain prescription medication, specifically leuprolide, which is used as a hormone blocker. She did this under the guise of diagnosing herself with endometriosis."

Watching the opening statements is an out-of-body experience. In the months leading to today, my goal has only been to get us here. To sit tight, put my head down, and do what was needed to get my family through this. Now that we are here, it feels like I'm standing on the outside of an impenetrable glass building while my wife burns alive inside, and I want nothing more than to break through and save her, but I can't.

Davis strolls across the courtroom, pausing to make deliberate eye contact with the judge before continuing. He is going in for the kill.

"However, the gravity of her actions extends beyond this fraudulent activity. Mrs. Barnett administered this powerful hormone blocker to her minor child, who identifies as transgender. This act was conducted in direct violation of Florida law, which prohibits gender-affirming medical treatment for minors, and was done without legal authorization, proper medical oversight, or consent as required by the state."

Mr. Davis delivers this statement with a resolute tone, his piercing blue eyes scanning the courtroom as he speaks. The way he says "powerful hormone blocker" forces a scoff from me, but no one pays me any mind.

Since we began preparing for the trial, I've learned about the ins and outs of hormones and hormone therapy. I will likely be the one responsible for Imogene's care, and it was important to Stacy and Imogene that I educate myself. So, I did. Of all the methods of gender-affirming medical care, hormone blockers are among the least invasive, with minimal side effects and few long-term repercussions. But, of course, the prosecutor's job is to leave those facts out.

Mr. Davis walks back to his table, placing a hand on the top and leaning in, adopting a more conversational stance. "Prescription fraud and child abuse are serious offenses with significant implications for public health and safety. Mrs. Barnett's actions show a blatant disregard for medical regulations designed to protect patients and the integrity of the healthcare system. By using her professional status to circumvent these regulations, she has violated both the law, and the trust placed in her as a healthcare provider."

The sound of people talking fills the room as the courtroom door opens. I look behind me to see Ramon slip inside. My feelings about him are complicated.

From what Stacy has told me, he has kept his distance. At least, that's what I gather from the one time I asked Stacy about the status of their . . . friendship? I'd like to believe he's stayed away out of respect. But I also understand why he would choose to be here today. He was very much a part of Stacy and Imogene's journey from the beginning, and while it would be justified for me to tell him I don't want him here, it would also be a little selfish. And I'm done being selfish.

I've been selfish enough in the past. My selfishness was part of the reason Stacy made her decisions. She needed my help, but I would only do the things that felt easy. Today, the least I can do is let Ramon be here.

Focusing forward, Mr. Davis continues to deliver his opening statement. "We will present evidence showing that Mrs. Barnett knowingly and willfully engaged in these illegal activities. This includes testimony from medical experts about proper procedures for diagnosing and prescribing hormone treatments, as well as the risks and consequences of misuse. Additionally, we will provide documentation and witness testimony demonstrating the unauthorized nature of her actions."

Stacy sits beside her attorney, Ms. Coleson, straight and alert. I can only see the back of her head, and I wish I could read her mind right now. I've wanted to read her mind for some time. If only I could see into her head and know what she's thinking. Over the last several months, I have lived parallel to Stacy, but I want to be coincident with her, where our paths overlap rather than run beside each other.

It's true what they say: time does heal wounds. However, I'm not sure if I'm ready to admit this to her because I don't want to go back to the way our marriage was before, when we existed atop a bed of resentments. Sure, there is still hurt and anger at the circumstances of our life, but those resentments we held seem to not be as loud as they were before. We are no longer working against each other, but rather beside each other, and I don't want to mess that up.

There is a real possibility Stacy is going to prison, and I don't know what that means for the future of our marriage. Given the evidence in this case, Stacy's attorney's strategy is to appeal to the judge's sympathies rather than create reasonable doubt. She doesn't think she can secure a full acquittal for Stacy, but she believes she can persuade the judge to be lenient.

Stacy's only ask through all of this is that I get Imogene out of Florida as soon as possible. With our house currently under contract, we plan to go back to Colorado, but the long-term plan for Stacy feels quite uncertain.

"Your Honor, this case is not just about illegal prescriptions. It is about the abuse of professional power and the endangerment of a child's health. We seek a verdict that upholds the law, protects the integrity of the medical profession, and ensures justice for her child and the community."

Justice for our child. That's ridiculous. Justice for our child would have meant that she never had to go through any of this. When Stacy first approached me about hormone blockers, I thought it was a bad idea, but I also didn't spend a minute looking into it. My judgment was based on baseless assumptions.

Now that I know more, I realize that when Stacy came to me, I shouldn't have been so quick to shut her down. If I could go back in time and change one thing, it would be that. I would change the way I reacted when Stacy asked for my help.

"Thank you, Mr. Davis," the judge says. "Ms. Coleson?"

Stacy looks back at me, her lips pressed together in a thin line. Worry consumes her expression, and I try to give her a reassuring smile, but she has turned back around for Ms. Coleson's opening statement.

Ms. Coleson rises. She adjusts the neckline of her hot pink dress and smooths a stray blonde hair before stepping forward. Her pristine white pumps click against the floor, and the sound echoes in the courtroom chamber.

"Your Honor, today we stand before you to tell the story of Stacy Barnett, a devoted mother and dedicated nurse whose actions were driven by nothing more than love, desperation, and an overwhelming need to protect her child, Imogene."

With her head held high and her shoulders pushed back, Ms. Coleson puts off a quiet confidence. It's not cocky or conceded. No. Something else. It's knowingly adept. She knows she can win this, or at least she is damn good at pretending so. Her presence gives me a bit of hope.

"Stacy Barnett's entire life centers around caring for others. Her professional career as a nurse is a testament to her commitment to helping those in need. But beyond her professional duties, Stacy's primary focus has always been the well-being of her daughter, Imogene."

Ms. Coleson shakes her head and dips her chin, emphasizing her point.

"Imogene, a transgender minor, has faced significant challenges here in Florida. While laws should maintain order, protect rights and liberties, promote social welfare, and provide security, the law failed Stacy and Imogene, forcing Stacy to make difficult decisions for her daughter. The law effectively disenfranchised a young girl already enduring emotional, psychological, and social obstacles that many cannot begin to understand. As a mother, Stacy watched her child struggle and was determined to do everything in her power to provide Imogene with the care she needed."

I glance around the nearly empty courtroom, hoping to gauge the reaction of those present. Besides Ramon, a reporter and a few members of the public are scattered among the seats with impassive expressions. Their lack of reaction makes my palms sweat. Bryce and Flora will be here tomorrow, and Imogene is at school. We enrolled her in a different district after all that happened last year, and she seems to be doing better. I'm not sure she has made friends yet, but at least she has McKenzie after school and on the weekends.

"In her desperation to help her child, Stacy made decisions that, while legally questionable, were always intended to support Imogene. The prosecution will present these actions as criminal, but we must remember the context in which she made them. Stacy was not acting out of malice or self-interest, but out of a deep and abiding love for her daughter. She saw her daughter in pain, struggling with her identity, and she took steps she thought necessary to alleviate that suffering."

Stacy's shoulders relax as Ms. Coleson speaks. Her hands clench and unclench beside her, an attempt to control the tremors. Her hands only shake when she is under intense stress, and I've noticed the trembling has become more frequent since this all began. I want to go to her, to hold her hands in mine, to use my warmth and the pressure of my grip to steady her. I've had that urge for months, but I haven't acted on it because, frankly, I'm scared that she will hurt me again. Lie to me. Break my trust.

"Your Honor, we ask you to consider Stacy's intentions and the context of her actions. We ask you to see her not as a criminal but as a mother who, in her desperation, made choices she believed were in the best interest of her child. We will present evidence and testimony highlighting Stacy's unwavering commitment to Imogene, demonstrating that her love and necessity motivated her, not by a disregard for the law. We ask for your understanding and compassion as we tell Stacy's story."

After the opening statements, the prosecution calls their first witness: Linda, the HR Director at Sarasota Memorial Health. Linda is a petite woman with a round nose dusted with freckles, sitting above small, pink, heart-shaped lips. Her appearance is almost cherubic, but when she speaks, her tone is resolute and sharp.

As Mr. Davis sets the scene, asking her about her position and other introductory questions, Linda's demeanor remains steady. He leans forward and asks, "Can you describe the events that led to your meeting with Stacy Barnett?"

"Yes. We received an alert because a non-admitted patient record was accessed. Therefore, we conducted an investigation of our systems and discovered irregularities involving Mrs. Barnett. This led us to investigate further, where we found evidence suggesting she had accessed her own medical records and prescribed medication for herself using one of our provider's credentials."

"What specific evidence did you find that indicated Mrs. Barnett had committed prescription fraud?"

"We cross-referenced badge scans, camera footage, and electronic medical record logs."

"Did you meet with Stacy to ask her about her activity?"

"We did," she says.

"During your meeting with Mrs. Barnett, how did she respond to these allegations?"

"Initially, Stacy tried to deny the accusations, stating that she only assisted Dr. Kilpatrick with navigating the EMR. However, when confronted with the details, she admitted to her actions, citing her concern for her daughter, Imogene, as the reason behind her behavior."

After a series of additional questions addressing various aspects of the incident, Mark then asks, "In your professional opinion, how do Mrs. Barnett's actions impact the integrity of the hospital?"

"Stacy's actions severely undermine the trust placed in healthcare professionals. Using her position to commit fraud violated ethical standards. This behavior not only affects her credibility but also damages the hospital's reputation and the integrity of our healthcare system."

As Linda finishes her statement, her gaze shifts to Stacy. Though the movement is subtle, the intensity of her disapproval is evident. Stacy tenses under Linda's stare. Once again, I picture Stacy trapped inside a glass house, her fist pounding against the smooth, transparent walls. Fire licks the edges of the walls and crawls greedily across the floor, consuming everything in its path. I can't help. She locked herself inside. And I don't have the key.

"Did Mrs. Barnett have a history of misconduct or disciplinary issues at the hospital prior to this incident?"

"Yes." Linda straightens her spine, her expression suggesting a sense of vindication.

"Can you elaborate on that?" presses Mr. Davis.

"She has been written up for insubordination on several occasions. In fact, only days before she was suspended, there was a recommendation to write her up again for insubordination and disregard for patient safety."

Patient safety? That part surprises me. Stacy never mentioned being written up but given the state of our marriage in recent years, I'm not shocked that she didn't tell me, but I'm surprised that she would risk patient safety. Sitting here, I feel like I'm learning more about who she is today than I have in years.

"Thank you. No further questions."

Ms. Coleson switches places with Mr. Davis to question Linda.

"You mentioned that Mrs. Barnett admitted to her actions due to concern for her daughter. Can you describe her demeanor when she made this admission?"

"She was visibly emotional. She indicated she felt desperate and believed she had no other choice."

"Would you say that Mrs. Barnett's actions, while against policy, were motivated by her love and concern for her child?"

"Regardless of her intentions, her actions were still against the law."

"You also mentioned that Mrs. Barnett has a history of misconduct or disciplinary issues."

"Yes, that's right," Linda agrees.

"But isn't it true that Stacy was often written up for advocating for her patients? For example, her first written warning was due to insubordination after advocating for a female patient who was being discharged before she was medically ready, simply because she was an inmate?"

"Well, I'm not sure."

Ms. Coleson steps closer to Linda.

"And isn't it also true that Stacy's so-called disregard for patient safety stemmed from a disagreement with a doctor who insisted on a delivery position that led to complications? Finally, isn't it true that Stacy was disliked at the hospital because she was outspoken in her advocacy, a role she took seriously even when others did not?"

"I—I don't have the exact details of all those incidents," Linda responds, flustered.

"Thank you. No further questions."

It's now that I realize just how well I *do* know my wife. No, she never told me about the write-ups, but the context makes sense. Stacy is a pain in the ass. She is stubborn, opinionated, and relentless. She rarely backs down from a fight and would do anything to protect the people she cares about, including her patients. They're trying to paint her as reckless and negligent, but I know better. She's strong and passionate, and those qualities are part of the reason I fell in love with her.

The judge clears his throat. "We will now take a recess. Court will resume in one hour."

The gavel strikes, and the courtroom buzzes with muted conversation as the few people in the courtroom rise. Stacy turns to me. Her chest deflates as she lets out a large breath.

CHAPTER 46

MY GIRL

Stacy

Three days into the trial, the prosecution has finally exhausted their witnesses, including Mrs. Higgins, Jackie, and Lilly Dixon. Only Lilly stayed for the entire court proceedings after her testimony. She takes the seat next to Ramon, and I can't help but notice the parallel between them—two people who sacrificed their lives and careers for my daughter. If only they knew how much they have in common.

Now, it is time for the defense to present their case. Ms. Coleson puts me on the stand first. As I walk up, my fingers shake violently. Garrett, Ramon, Flora, and Bryce sit in the audience. My eyes scan their faces, but I don't linger long. I need to focus on my testimony.

I take the oath, but I'm not sure if any of the words that come out of my mouth are English. This all feels like some weird fever dream.

Ms. Coleson approaches to ask, "Mrs. Barnett, can you please state your name and occupation for the record?"

We go through the same routine introductions as with every other witness. Ms. Coleson then dives into the heart of the matter. "Can you explain why you prescribed leuprolide for yourself, and even more, administered it to your child?"

I take a deep breath, trying to steady my racing heart. "My daughter came out to me as trans just before Florida passed a law banning gender-affirming care for minors. Our family would have moved, but we couldn't—my dad was in a home here, my husband had built a business, and financially, moving just wasn't an option. I felt trapped, and my daughter was trapped."

"So, you committed prescription fraud because the law has removed your daughter's access to gender-affirming care?"

"Yes, care I believe is lifesaving. What parent wouldn't do everything in their power to save their child's life?"

"Can you describe your emotional and psychological state when you made these decisions?" Ms. Coleson asks, her voice gentle.

"I was terrified and overwhelmed," I admit, my voice breaking. "What no one seems to understand is the effects of puberty are nearly impossible to reverse. If I had let Imogene go through puberty—and being a passing trans woman was important to her—she would have needed numerous surgeries and invasive procedures to undo those changes. Some aspects would remain irreversible. Denying her access to hormone blockers is far more dangerous and expensive. I only wanted to give Imogene more time, allowing her to grow up and have autonomy over her body."

"Were your actions driven by any intent to commit fraud or cause harm?"

"No, never," I say firmly. "My actions were solely driven by love and a desire to do what was best for my child. I only wanted to help her and make sure she could live a happy and healthy life."

Ms. Coleson nods, encouraging me to continue. "What steps did you take to ensure the medication was administered safely?"

"I closely monitored Imogene for any side effects and took measures to mitigate any potential risks. I researched extensively to understand the correct dosage and administration. I might not be a doctor, but my medical knowledge is extensive. My primary concern was always her safety and well-being."

Ms. Coleson offers me a reassuring smile. "Thank you, Mrs. Barnett. No further questions."

The longer I sit on the stand, the easier it gets. My pulse slows and I'm better able to control the pitch of my voice, but that doesn't last long because when Ms. Coleson steps back, Mr. Davis strides forward. "Mrs. Barnett, do you understand the potential risks and dangers of administering hormone blockers? The side effects?"

"Yes, I understand the risks and side effects, which is why I monitored Imogene closely. Side effects for leuprolide are minimal."

Mark begins rattling off common side effects like he's reading a grocery list. "Common side effects include headaches, hot flashes, fatigue, mood changes, decreased bone density, stunted growth, impacts on blood

pressure and cholesterol, and even potential effects on future fertility."
He looks at me with narrowed eyes. "Doesn't sound minimal."

I feel my defenses rising, but I force myself to relax.

"To you it sounds scary, but most medications have side effects.
However, the benefit of taking medications usually outweighs the risk.
That is why we prescribe them."

Mark smirks. "Do you believe it's safe for someone like you, who is
not a doctor, to make these kinds of medical decisions?"

"I'm a nurse." Mr. Davis nods with a satisfied grin. He is so focused
on the child abuse charges that the prosecution has nearly abandoned
the prescription fraud.

"But you're not a doctor." He presses his lips together and nods, but
before I can respond, he adds, "'I will abstain from whatever is deleterious
and mischievous and will not take or knowingly administer any harmful
drug.'" He pauses before continuing, "Do you know what that's from?"

I swallow. "It is the Nightingale Pledge."

"Yes, and?" he asks smugly. I can feel my defenses rising, and I brace
myself for where he's about to steer this line of questioning.

"It is a statement of ethics and principles that nurses pledge to."

"You pledged to that, right, Mrs. Barnett?"

"I did, but—" I'm about to say that the drugs I administered weren't
harmful, but before I can finish my statement, Mr. Davis cuts me off.

"No further questions, Your Honor."

As I step down from the stand, my entire body is trembling. Ms.
Coleson said he would try to get a rise out of me. My nerves feel as if they
are attached to a jackhammer.

Ms. Coleson brings the psychiatrist Imogene has been working with
onto the stand next.

"Dr. Quade, could you please state your name and professional background for the record?"

"My name is Dr. Laura Quade, and I am a board-certified psychiatrist
with a specialization in adolescent mental health and transgender issues.
I have been practicing for over fifteen years."

"Dr. Quade, can you describe your involvement in this case?"

"I was hired by the defense to work with Imogene Barnett in the
months leading up to this trial. My role was to evaluate her mental health
and the impact of her past hormone therapy on her well-being."

"What methods did you use to evaluate Imogene?"

"I conducted a series of comprehensive evaluations, including clinical interviews, psychological assessments, and ongoing therapy sessions. These methods allowed me to understand Imogene's mental health and her overall well-being."

"Can you describe Imogene's mental health before she began hormone therapy?"

"Based on the information Imogene provided, before starting hormone therapy, Imogene exhibited signs of significant distress, including anxiety and depression. She struggled with her gender dysphoria, which affected her self-esteem and overall mental health."

"And how did her mental health change after beginning hormone therapy?"

"Although I didn't evaluate Imogene during the hormone therapy, she reported that during the time she was on the blockers, she experienced a notable decrease in anxiety about her gender and how her body would change through puberty. She wanted to eventually transition fully, but also understood that at her age, compromise is necessary."

"In your professional opinion, did the hormone blockers have a positive impact on Imogene's mental health?"

"Yes, absolutely. From my evaluations and her own accounts, the hormone blockers significantly improved Imogene's mental health during the time she was using them. They helped reduce her gender dysphoria and provided her with a sense of relief."

"Dr. Quade, can you speak to the importance of gender-affirming care for transgender adolescents?"

"Gender-affirming care can significantly reduce mental health issues, such as anxiety, depression, and suicidal ideation. Providing access to appropriate medical care and support is essential for their overall health and well-being."

"In your professional opinion, was Stacy Barnett's decision to administer hormone blockers to her child made with Imogene's best interests in mind?"

"Based on my evaluation, it is clear Stacy Barnett's decision was made out of love for her child. She sought to alleviate Imogene's distress and provide her with the support she needed. While her methods were not legally compliant, her intentions were focused on Imogene's best interests."

"Thank you, Dr. Quade. No further questions."

Mr. Davis stands to question Dr. Quade. She regards him with curiosity before his questions come.

"Dr. Quade, were you aware that the administration of hormone blockers to minors, especially without proper medical oversight, is illegal in Florida?"

Dr. Quade nods, maintaining a calm disposition. "Yes, I am aware of the legal restrictions in Florida."

"Given these legal restrictions, do you believe Mrs. Barnett's actions were appropriate?"

"While I understand the legal constraints, my evaluation is focused on the psychological and medical benefits to Imogene. Legally, Mrs. Barnett's actions were not compliant, but from a mental health perspective, the care provided had a positive impact on Imogene."

"Dr. Quade, do you think it is safe for a non-medical professional to administer hormone blockers without a doctor's supervision?"

"In general, it is always best for medical treatments to be administered under the supervision of a qualified healthcare provider." Dr. Quade's eyes flick up to the ceiling as she thinks. "However, in this specific case, the care was given with close attention to Imogene's well-being."

"No further questions, Your Honor." Mr. Davis sits and opens a file folder against his forearm before scribbling something inside.

Dr. Quade's testimony eases some of the tension in my shoulders. Although an expert witness guarantees nothing, we have successfully diverted the attention of the prosecution while also substantiated that my actions were not considered child abuse. A bit of hope swells in my chest.

Imogene is called to the stand next, and the hair on my arms rise along with my protective intuition. When she is seated, she looks directly at me. I wait for her to break eye contact, but she answers every question while holding my gaze. I breathe in deep and give her a gentle nod.

"Imogene, can you please state your name and age for the record?" Ms. Coleson asks.

"My name is Imogene Barnett, and I'm fifteen years old," she replies confidently.

"Imogene, can you describe your relationship with your mother, Stacy Barnett?"

Imogene nods. "My mom worries a lot. She's always fussing over me and asking me how I feel. She rarely leaves me alone. She won't even let me take Tylenol by myself, even though I'm fifteen and totally capable. Sometimes it's suffocating having a mom who loves you so much that she would do anything to make sure you live a long and happy life. But, at the same time, I'm so glad I have a mom who cares because many people don't. Mine just cares more than most and, even when that's annoying, it's also something I'm extremely grateful for."

My eyes sting with tears, but I continue to hold Imogene's gaze.

"Can you tell the court about your experience as a transgender teen and how it has affected you?"

"Being transgender is sometimes hard."

"Can you elaborate?"

"It's lonely. I often feel alienated, and sometimes I think other people would be happier if I just disappeared. If I could choose to feel differently, to feel connected with the gender I was assigned with at birth, I would, but I can't." Her voice wavers toward the middle of her statement, but she clears her throat, keeping her eyes on me.

"How did you feel when your mother administered hormone blockers to you?" Ms. Coleson asks.

"I felt relieved and hopeful."

"Did you understand the potential risks and benefits of taking hormone blockers?"

"Yes, my mom explained them to me. She told me about the benefits and about the risks. But we both felt the benefits were worth it."

"Can you describe how the hormone blockers have affected you?" Ms. Coleson continues.

"For a long time, I have had this constant feeling of impending doom about my body changing, whether I liked it or not. Knowing that made me super depressed. Being on hormone blockers made me feel like I had a little control over what happens to my body."

"How did you feel when you found out that your mother might face legal consequences for her actions?" Ms. Coleson asks, her voice softening.

"I felt scared but also like a terrible person. My mom has dedicated her whole life to making sure I'm okay. Everything she does is for me, and to think that caring for me is the reason she might go to prison . . . My mom isn't perfect. No parent is perfect, but she loves me and has only ever done what she believed was best." Her eyes turn glassy, and I swallow the lump in my throat.

"Imogene, is there anything you would like the court to understand about your mother's actions?"

Imogene looks at the judge, her eyes filled with determination. "I want the court to know that my mom loves me. She was just trying to help me and keep me safe. She didn't mean to break the law."

"Thank you, Imogene. I have no further questions," Ms. Coleson says, giving her a reassuring nod.

The prosecutor rises and approaches the stand for cross-examination. "Imogene, you mentioned your mother explained the risks and benefits of hormone blockers to you. Did she also explain that it was illegal for her to prescribe them to you?"

"She told me it was complicated and the laws in Florida had changed. But she said she didn't see any other way to help me," Imogene answers in a steady voice.

"Did you ever see a doctor or a mental health professional about your desire to transition and receive hormone therapy?" the prosecutor asks.

"No. Not for gender-affirming care."

"Imogene, do you understand that your mother's actions could have put you at risk given the lack of medical supervision?" the prosecutor presses.

Her jaw tenses and she takes her eyes off me to lock them onto Mr. Davis's face.

"She did not put me at risk. The state of Florida put me at risk. She only gave me back the autonomy you took from me."

The strength in her voice leaves no doubt that she means exactly what she says.

That's my girl.

CHAPTER 47

JUDGMENT DAY

Stacy

As we step outside the courthouse, I'm surrounded by everyone who has stayed to support me throughout the trial. It's such a contrast to the way things were before all this began, when I felt so isolated in shouldering impossible choices on my own. My burdens are no longer only mine. They are shared among many people who care, including Garrett.

Lilly and Ramon approach us at the same time. Lilly's enthusiasm takes me aback as she beams at Imogene. "Imogene! You did amazing up there. I barely recognized you!"

Imogene looks at her, puzzled. Barely recognized? Despite the months that have passed, Imogene hasn't changed all that much. She hasn't had access to hormone blockers, but puberty hasn't fully taken hold since her last injection. Sensing her confusion, Lilly laughs and waves her hand. "No, I just mean . . . you were so brave and sure of yourself. I was blown away."

"Oh. Thanks," Imogene says shyly, glancing between Garrett and I and Lilly as she processes the compliment.

Ramon nods. "She's right. You really did well. We were both impressed with your testimony."

At this, Imogene's eyes flick between Ramon and Garrett, gauging any tension. Garrett places a reassuring hand on her shoulder and pulls her back against his chest. "She did great," he says. Garrett's pride is evident in his expression, and Imogene's shoulders drop when she realizes no ill feelings are shared.

I notice the easy way Ramon and Lilly interact. They share a casual familiarity, but I thought they were strangers. "Wait, do you two know each other?" I ask.

"Not fully," Lilly replies, shrugging. "We just sat next to each other and, you know, shared commentary throughout the day." There's a slight grin on her face, and Ramon shrugs.

"Oh." I nod, but something in the way they interact catches my attention. They seem comfortable together.

Flora and Bryce turn to Ramon, and Flora nudges him playfully. "So, are we still on for dinner?" they ask, looking between him and Lilly with a smile.

"Uh, yeah," Ramon replies, then glances at Garrett, me, and Imogene. "You're welcome to come if you want."

Bryce, reading the situation, adds, "But no pressure. I thought you'd want some time together."

I nod. "Thank you. A quiet night with just the three of us is exactly what we need. Also, thank you for coming." We don't know how much longer we have, and if tonight is one of our last, I want it to be just us.

Ramon shrugs. "I came as much as I could, but I don't have any more personal days, so I probably won't be here for sentencing."

"That's okay," I tell him.

We all linger for a few minutes, chatting. Lilly looks at her watch, then glances at me. "I should get going, but I'm glad I could be here today. I'm hoping for the best."

Before she can turn to leave, Ramon steps in. He seems a little hesitant to push forward but does so anyway. "Why don't you come to dinner with us? And I can give you my number and you can keep me posted on deliberation."

"Really?" Her face lights up, glancing between him, Bryce, and Flora. "I'd love that." She smiles at Ramon, and there's a spark of something between them.

We all exchange hugs as the group readies to leave for dinner. Before Bryce hugs me, he says, "I talked to Steve today. He said he's driving down tomorrow morning with Opal."

"I don't know how long deliberation will take. It could be a week before we have a decision." I draw my brows together in concern.

"He doesn't care. He wants to be here for you, even if it takes a month."

I press my lips together and nod.

Then, Bryce grins and glances around conspiratorially before whispering, "But I might have also told them to come in full drag. I thought you would feel more supported that way." I chuckle and shake my head.

When we finally part ways with the group and are in the car to head home, Imogene asks, "So, what's next?"

I lift a shoulder. "We don't know yet. The judge is deliberating, but Ms. Coleson will call when he decides."

"Can I come with you? To court? I want to be there." We've made Imogene attend school every day of the trial except today because she was scheduled to testify.

I exchange a worried glance with Garrett. He doesn't interject, leaving the decision to me. I remember sitting in the cramped space between my mother's bed and the wall, cherishing every moment with her, knowing our time was limited. I missed school, time with friends, and typical teenage activities—but I wouldn't have traded any of it for that time with my mother. I take a deep breath and nod. "Yes, you can come. You don't have to go to school until they call. Even if it's a week, you can stay home until then."

At home, I can't help but feel a pang of sadness because our home will only be ours for a little while longer. Garrett has been busy fixing anything that could come up on an inspection, so power tools and buckets of paint sit in various corners. Now that we are under contract and no longer showing the house, I have packed what I can, and those boxes sit stacked on our living room floor. However, it's difficult to pack until we know what is going to happen. There's no point in Garrett and Imogene taking all my stuff to Colorado when I don't know when I'll be able to join them.

That night, we come together for what might be our last family dinner before my sentencing. The aroma of Garrett's chili and cornbread fills the air, a comforting reminder of normalcy. Garrett has been an unbelievable support. He went from needing a to-do list to taking action and anticipating our family needs. At the dinner table, we talk about mundane things—school, work, favorite memories—all the topics a normal family would discuss on a regular Thursday night. The laughter and chatter feel bittersweet.

After dinner, Imogene heads to her room to get ready for bed, and Garrett settles on the sofa, folding a basket full of his work clothes. There's a gravitational pull toward him that I can't shake. Usually, I force myself to sever the ties and walk away, but tonight, I allow gravity to guide me instead.

"Can we talk?"

"Sure. Do we have any more of those iron-on patches? I can't keep blowing out my crotch," he replies, not looking up from his task.

I stifle a laugh, swallowing it before sitting in front of him in one of our chairs. "I don't think so," I say.

"That's all right. I'll go to the store tomorrow," he says, still focused on his laundry.

"Garrett?" I say, trying to capture his attention.

"What's up?" He finally glances at me. This feels hard, but I push past it.

"I want to talk about our marriage. About us."

Garrett stops folding the gray cotton shirt in his hand and stares at it for a few moments before his eyes meet mine. He places the shirt back in the basket and rests his hands on his knees.

"I love—"

Garrett cuts me off, his words tumbling out as if he's held them back for too long. "I don't want a divorce."

"You don't?" I ask.

Garrett's eyes soften, and he shakes his head. "No. I'm honestly surprised that you still think I do. Haven't I shown that—"

"Yes, but . . . I don't know. I couldn't be certain where your head was at. This has all been a lot," I confess. "Part of me thought maybe separating was for the best. If I'm going to prison, what's the point? And even more, why would you want to stay married to me? I just wanted to let you know I love you, and regardless of what you want to do about our marriage, I understand."

Garrett stands and walks over to me, his eyes steady on my face. Once he is in front of where I sit, he grabs my hand and lifts me from my seat. My breath catches in my throat as I wait for his reaction.

"What I want is to be your husband."

I place a hand on his chest. "I'm probably going to prison, Garrett."

His green eyes search mine, and I remind myself to breathe. He places his hands on either side of my face and brings my lips to his. It feels like kissing him for the first time, and a dam made of uncertainty and heartbreak comes crashing down. Tears well and spill over, but we don't stop kissing, not even long enough to breathe. He steps closer to me, closing the gap that has grown between us over the years.

We had drifted so far apart that I didn't know if we would ever come back to each other, but now, in this moment, we feel just as close as we did the summer we met. As I kiss him, I can't help but think about how impractical it is to love him at a time like this, but I use the sensation of his mouth on mine to drown out the noise of worry.

I stop the kiss long enough to say, "Promise me that no matter what happens, you'll take care of Imogene. Please?"

He doesn't scold me for asking him to promise to do something he was already planning on doing. He allows me to worry and simply reassures me.

"I promise," he whispers against my lips.

The next morning, my hands tremble as I drag a comb through my hair. A door slams, and I jump out of my skin.

"Ahh!" I scream. A thud is followed by Garrett rushing into the bathroom.

"What? Are you okay?" He is out of breath.

I let out a shaky sigh and turn to Garrett. "I'm just a little on edge."

"Sorry, I was just carrying some boxes downstairs, and I shut the door too hard." I'm exhausted and stressed. With all my pent-up anxiety, I stayed up last night to pack anything I knew Garrett and Imogene would take with them. He leans in to kiss me, and I reciprocate, but my anxiety grows with every second in which there isn't a call. It's only 9:00 AM, and it could take days for the judge to decide. I don't know if I'll last days.

I lean into Garrett and take in his smell. For the last seven months, Garrett and I have lived as if we are strangers, cogs in a wheel, going through the motions of making things work well enough. We could have had this months ago if either of us had been ready, but we weren't, and now, we may not have this again for a very long time.

Around 1:00 PM, the phone finally rings. My heart leaps into my throat as I answer it. "Hello?"

"The judge is ready to announce the verdict and sentencing. Can you be here in an hour and a half?" Ms. Coleson's voice comes through the speaker.

"We'll be there."

The courtroom is charged with anticipation. I sit between Garrett and Imogene, gripping their hands. Ms. Coleson sits beside us. Dressed in full glam, Peach, Opal, Flora, and Illusion, wearing her magician's hat, are seated in the gallery.

The judge enters, and everyone stands. After a moment, he takes his seat and goes to speak, but then he notices the queens behind us. A confused expression flickers across his features before his face hardens, ready to deliver my sentence.

"Mrs. Barnett, this court has considered the evidence presented and the arguments made by both sides. It is evident that your actions, though illegal, were motivated by a desire to care for your child. Considering the newness of the laws surrounding gender-affirming care for minors, the particular circumstances of your case, and your lack of criminal history, I'm imposing a sentence of five years of probation. During this period, you will complete community service. Additionally, you are subject to a higher fine of five thousand dollars to account for the severity of your actions."

The room holds a collective breath as the judge finishes, and I can barely process the words. I was so certain I was going to prison that it takes me a full minute before I realize that I'm not. My knees buckle, and I sling an arm across my waist to steady myself.

My gaze pivots to Garrett and Imogene's faces, and their open mouths and wide eyes communicate their shared surprise. I look at the judge again and say without thinking, "Are you sure?"

He doesn't hear me, though, and I stand with my mouth open until Peach says behind me, "Hell yeah!"

I'm still in shock. Tears prick the corners of my eyes, and I breathe like I have just run a marathon. I'm not going to prison. I'm not going to prison!

My family and the queens come together, and I shift my gaze to each of their faces, so fucking thankful for all of them. I'm not going to prison. The realization drifts over me, and it takes a few minutes to collect myself, to feel steady enough to speak. But when I get to that point, I still have no way to adequately express the relief I feel.

Imogene and Garrett envelope me in a warm hug, and I find myself sobbing into Garrett's chest as Imogene clings to us both.

After several moments, he pulls away to examine my face. He sweeps tears from my cheeks and leans in to kiss me. "Today is a good day," he says to me.

As we leave the courthouse, I find Peach, who exited while I talked to Mrs. Coleson.

"Peach. You . . . I mean . . . thank you," I breathe out, speaking with as much sincerity as I can muster.

Peach smiles with pride. "We take care of our own."

That evening, we gathered for another family dinner, this time filled with laughter and lightness. The queens join us, and for the second time, we pull out the table leaf and play cribbage late into the night. Ms. Coleson said that I'll have to stay in Florida for the time being, but she will file a motion to request permission to relocate. Until then, we'll figure it out.

I realize that life has surprised me. Regardless of what is on the horizon, there is still love and joy to be had. And most importantly, although much of my life fell apart, I have people I can count on to get me through.

CHAPTER 48

THE STARS WE SHARE

Imogene

I sit cross-legged on my bed, surrounded by half-packed boxes and a growing sense of nostalgia. This house has been my home for as long as I can remember, and now we're leaving it behind. I try to focus on the positive, reminding myself that we're moving forward, but it's hard to shake the sadness.

McKenzie sits on the floor in front of me, a cardboard box in her hand. I throw stuffies at her, and she catches them, placing each one carefully into the box.

"She shoots, she scores!" I yell as I throw the last stuffy into the box.

"The crowd goes wild," McKenzie adds, and we both cup our hands around our mouths, imitating the sound of a cheering crowd.

Downstairs, Mom and Dad are moving furniture. Their voices rise as they argue. We pause to listen, shaking our heads.

"Some things never change."

I say this, but everything has changed. They are bickering, but it's more playful than anything else. Mom and Dad are the best they've ever been. I never noticed the divide between them because it was all I ever knew, but lately, they seem happy, and that makes me happy.

"If only we could choose the things that change," McKenzie replies as she lifts the box from her lap to grab the tape and a Sharpie from the top of my desk.

It feels unfair that I have to move just when McKenzie and I have found our way back to each other. After a long period of estrangement, we're finally in a good place.

"Do you think your mom will let you come visit me during breaks?" I ask.

"Maybe, but even if she doesn't, I'll make sure I visit after high school."

Although it's only like two and a half years away, after high school feels like a lifetime. The two years that McKenzie wasn't my best friend were the longest two years of my life. I worry that I'll fall back into a pit of isolation without her, but I'm trying to remain positive that this move will be good for me.

We continue packing in comfortable silence, punctuated by bursts of laughter as we reminisce about our childhood. A little while later, there's a knock at my door.

"We're ready downstairs if you are," Mom says, poking her head inside my room.

"We'll be down in a minute," I tell her.

Mom recently sat before the nursing board, and thankfully, they suspended her license for five years, the same length as her probation, rather than revoking it entirely. It's not ideal, but it's better than nothing. I wanted the nursing board to forgive Mom, but they didn't.

I told my therapist that I felt stuck between feelings of gratitude for all my mom has sacrificed and my lingering resentments. She said two things can be true at the same time: someone can sacrifice for us in a way that benefits us but is also self-serving. It finally made sense when I considered how I wanted Mom to keep her nursing license to soothe my feelings of responsibility. Yes, I wanted it for her, but I also wanted it for me.

Mom says I have nothing to feel guilty about. That although it sucks, maybe it's a good thing. You never know when life will surprise you. Just like going to therapy. I thought I would hate it and refused when Mom mentioned it years ago, but now, I'm surprised at how helpful it has been.

Downstairs, the kitchen island is covered with a dark blue tablecloth from the dollar store, glittery silver stars scattered across the top. A platter of star-shaped cookies sits next to a bowl of mini Milky Way bars Mom bought on clearance at work. Beside them is a jug of glittery blue juice marked "Galaxy Splash" and a tray of meats and cheeses.

Mom stands by the island, a proud smile on her face. "What do you think?" she asks.

McKenzie speaks up first. "It looks just like it used to!" The whole scene is a perfect replica of our last star party four years ago. To some, this modest spread might not be anything to brag about, but to me, it's perfect.

I stand before the island, scanning the contents before looking at Mom. "It's perfect. Thank you."

"Dad's already out back setting up the scope. Grab your snacks and meet us out there," she says with a smile before heading toward the back door.

Tomorrow, Dad and I will take a U-Haul to Colorado, and Mom will move into an apartment until she can join us. We don't know when that will be. It's crazy. As much as I wanted space from her, all I want now is for Mom to come with us.

McKenzie and I load our paper plates with snacks and fill plastic cups with the juice. We make our way outside, where it's pitch-black except for nearby streetlamps and porch lights. The surrounding light isn't ideal for planet and star-gazing but given it's our last night in the house I grew up in, I can't imagine being anywhere else.

We sit on blankets in the center of the yard, eating while I share space facts—some old ones that Dad, Mom, and McKenzie have all heard before and some new ones. They let me have my moment to shine.

Later, after Mom and Dad go inside, McKenzie and I lay on a blanket, staring at the stars. A gentle breeze sweeps through the yard, cradling the scent of salt and earth.

"I hate that you can't come with me," I say.

"Me too, but hey, no matter how far apart we are, we can always look up and see the same stars," she replies.

I groan.

"What? Was that too cheesy?" she asks, turning to look at me.

"No. It just isn't technically true. Like if I'm in New York and you're in Australia, we won't see the same stars because we'll be in different hemispheres."

McKenzie scoffs, rolling her eyes. "But you won't be in New York, and I won't be in Australia."

"True, but you said no matter how far apart we are."

"Imogene," she whines. "Seriously?"

"What you said was factually wrong!"

"Okay, well, what about when you're in Colorado and I'm here? Will we be looking at the same stars then?" she challenges, her eyebrows raised.

"Well, Colorado is at a higher latitude, so some stars that are close to the horizon in Florida will be higher in the sky in Colorado, but most stars will be visible in both states."

"So I was right?"

"You were right," I relent, giving up the fight.

"You're such a nerd," she says with a laugh, and I join in, finding comfort in her remark.

We fall into a comfortable silence, the night sky stretching endlessly above us.

In space, stars are born from chaos, their light reaching across the void to touch other realms. They exist within a collection, a family, a community, a constellation, and they have the privilege of belonging. I belong the way the stars do—to a family, some related, some found. But regardless, I belong.

GET EXCLUSIVE CONTENT FROM DESIREE MOORE BOOKS

I invite you to become a valued member of my VIP Readers Club. Join today to gain access to exclusive content, exciting updates on new books, and a **FREE Epilogue**. Dive back into the lives of Imogene, Stacy, and Garrett and witness their lives in Colorado.

To access the epilogue, simply sign up at my website.

Visit www.desireemoorebooks.com/readersclub to join.

ACKNOWLEDGMENTS

I want to express my deepest gratitude to the many people who made this book possible. To my family, thank you for your patience and understanding as I disappeared into my writing. Fred Longbine, Natalie Moore, and Rosslyn Moore, I couldn't do this without your love.

To my incredible street team, your support and dedication mean the world to me. A heartfelt thank you to the trans women and teens who generously shared their experiences with me. Your voices were critical in shaping this story, and I am deeply honored by your trust. To my sensitivity readers, your feedback and thoughtful care brought depth and authenticity to this book.

To the social workers, attorneys, nurses, and parents of LGBTQ teens who contributed their insights, your help brought this narrative to life in ways I never could have achieved alone.

A heartfelt thank you to Alex and Natalia Stylles-Knight, Anneliese Mulder, Ariel Blodgett, Basil Stuart, Becky Carp, Breeanna Rode, Brittni Mason, PrincESS of Genova, Brooke Begani, Christina Reyes, Danni-Cheree, Deb Stuart, DorieLou Strobel, Emily Monelle, Erin Summers, Heather Elmore, Hulkita, Jake Webb, Jazmin Bouchard, and Kelli Steele for your encouragement and support.

I am deeply grateful to Kelsey Maliszewski, Krystle Working Drury, LCSW, Lara Miller, Laura Louise Wheeler, Leasha Hayes, Lisa Kreinheder, Lyan Fahrenback, River Girl, Mey Valdivia Rude, Patsy Hickman, Regi Albaugh, Sandra Burtch, Shawna Lodge, Shellie Wilbur, Stephanie Russell, Stephanie Pietrick, Taylor Anne White, The Great and Powerful Linzy Taylor, Tom McDaniel, and Your Royal Highness, Amanda Hayes, the most lovely.

A special thanks to the team at Earley Editing for your soft hearts and sharp instincts. Your work made this story stronger.

And finally, this book is truly dedicated to Kayla Vos.

To my readers, thank you for believing in these stories and welcoming them into your hearts. Your support means everything.

www.ingramcontent.com/pod-product-compliance
Lightning Source LLC
Chambersburg PA
CBHW020139310726
48970CB00006B/1940